P9-CCP-570

Praise for **The Evolution of Love**

"Given our current seemingly endless string of natural disasters, this is a timely story and a compelling one. In the context of a twisting plot, in the company of appealing characters, Bledsoe asks us to think about the resilience of love and hate; what our responsibility to each other is; and who we really are, right down to our DNA. Highly recommended."

—Karen Joy Fowler, author of *We Are All Completely Beside Ourselves* and *The Jane Austen Book Club*

"A magnificent, searingly beautiful book, as insightful as it is compassionate. Bledsoe takes our hearts in her confident hands and leads us toward an evolution of more than just love."

—Elizabeth Percer, author of *All Stories are Love Stories*

"Lucy Jane Bledsoe's *The Evolution of Love* offers a terrifyingly detailed and believable vision of life in the Bay Area after a devastating earthquake. But more than that, she offers us a vision of what is possible when individuals, even in the most desperate circumstances, refuse to give up on love and hope. *The Evolution of Love* is the book we all need these days: a post-disaster page-turner that's also a blueprint for how we might live right now."

—Naomi J. Williams, author of *Landfalls*

"This fast-paced nail biter of a novel uses a disaster in the near future to explore a basic question: can love save us from ourselves? I read ravenously to find the answer. Lucy Jane Bledsoe is a brave and brainy writer, and *The Evolution of Love* is a rare mix of erudition, adventure, and hard-won wisdom."

—Summer Wood, author of *Raising Wrecker*

"Lucy Jane Bledsoe's writing leaps off the page with striking clarity. Her characters take you by the hand and lead you through their freshly broken lives, and with them you'll discover shelters of friendship and loyalty."

—Shanthi Sekaran, author of *Lucky Boy*

"In a lucid, urgent novel driven by timely concerns and authentic feeling, Bledsoe's characters reveal how our greatest hopes most often live in community."

—Edie Meidav, author of *Kingdom of the Young* and *Lola, California*

"As a child growing up in California I created a dystopian fantasy world fueled by the visions of Margaret Atwood, Aldous Huxley, and George Orwell. I worked hard to develop an internal GPS, which I was sure would come in useful once *The Tempest* was upon us and devised escape routes for every imaginable natural and man-made catastrophe. *EVOLUTION* was like reading from the pages of a book I lived, long ago. I was compelled to continue from the first pages, even when the going got tough and the realism felt a bit too real. I fell in love with and was frustrated by every flawed character, every new episode where every ounce of resilance was required. It is a gifted writer who can take me through a full range of human emotions and leave me wanting more. What happens next? I hope that Lucy Jane Bledsoe will make *EVOLUTION* just the beginning of a new beginning for our beleagured species."

—Del LaGrace Volcano, artist/activist/educator

Praise for A Thin Bright Line

"Gripping historical fiction about queer life at the height of the Cold War and the Civil Rights Movement."

—Alison Bechdel, author of *Fun Home*

"It triumphs as an intimate and humane evocation of day-to-day life under inhumane circumstances."

—*New York Times Book Review*

"A stirring and deeply felt story."

—*Kirkus Reviews*

"Empowering and bold....Bledsoe injects life and dimension through her often stunning dialogue. "

—*Publishers Weekly*

"Berkeley author Lucy Jane Bledsoe shows the sexy side of the 1950s in her new novel, *A Thin Bright Line*."

—*San Francisco Chronicle*

The Evolution of Love

a novel

ALSO BY LUCY JANE BLEDSOE

FICTION

A Thin Bright Line
The Big Bang Symphony: A Novel of Antarctica
Biting the Apple
This Wild Silence
Working Parts
Sweat: Stories and a Novella

NONFICTION

The Ice Cave: A Woman's Adventures
from the Mojave to the Antarctic

CHILDRENS

How to Survive in Antarctica
The Antarctic Scoop
Hoop Girlz
Cougar Canyon
Tracks in the Snow
The Big Bike Race

Lucy Jane Bledsoe

signature: Lucy Jane Bledsoe

The Evolution of Love

=== *a novel* ===

A VIREO BOOK | RARE BIRD BOOKS
LOS ANGELES, CALIF.

THIS IS A GENUINE VIREO BOOK

A Vireo Book | Rare Bird Books
453 South Spring Street, Suite 302
Los Angeles, CA 90013
rarebirdbooks.com

Copyright © 2018 by Lucy Jane Bledsoe

FIRST TRADE PAPERBACK ORIGINAL EDITION

All rights reserved, including the right to reproduce this book or portions
thereof in any form whatsoever, including but not limited to print, audio,
and electronic. For more information, address: A Vireo Book | Rare Bird
Books Subsidiary Rights Department, 453 South Spring Street, Suite 302,
Los Angeles, CA 90013.

Set in Warnock
Printed in the United States

10 9 8 7 6 5 4 3 2 1

Publisher's Cataloging-in-Publication data
Names: Bledsoe, Lucy Jane, author.
Title: The Evolution of love: a novel / Lucy Jane Bledsoe.
Description: Includes bibliographical references | First Trade Paperback
Original Edition | A Vireo Book | New York, NY; Los Angeles, CA:
Rare Bird Books, 2018.
Identifiers: ISBN 9781945572838
Subjects: LCSH Earthquakes—California—San Francisco—Fiction.
| Survival—Fiction. | Natural disasters—Fiction. | Sisters—Fiction. |
Homosexuality—Fiction. | Lesbians—Fiction. | BISAC FICTION / Disaster |
FICTION / General
Classification: LCC PS3552.L418 E96 2018 | DDC 813.54—dc23

"Genes hold culture on a leash."

—Edward O. Wilson, *On Human Nature*

"'Make love, not war' could be a bonobo slogan."

—Frans B. M. de Waal, *Peacemaking Among Primates*

PART ONE

1

LILY JUMPED DOWN INTO the earthy crevice that split the freeway. The dirt smelled metallic and organic, like a grave, and she quickly hoisted herself out the other side. She began walking west. All the refugees had walked in the opposite direction, leaving the region. She'd seen them on TV, the network reporters flying low in helicopters, filming the streams of people carrying children, pushing shopping carts, rolling suitcases, lugging pet carriers, and riding bicycles. Now, ten days later, the freeway was deserted.

She'd told herself, and her husband Tom, that she was coming to rescue Vicky. And she was. She would. She'd been rescuing her sister her entire life.

But she'd never done anything remotely this extreme. She knew the region had been evacuated yet somehow hadn't pictured everyone literally *gone*. She'd greatly underestimated what she'd need for food and water. The stark, devastated landscape heightened all her senses, as if her fear made the colors deeper, the smells headier, the sounds crisper. She couldn't give in to the terror; if she did, it might never end. She had no choice but to finish what she'd begun.

Lily checked her phone and confirmed the battery's death. She was severed from Tom, Nebraska, home. She was entirely alone on the wrecked highway, with big green hills to the east and a giant bay to the west. Heat shimmered off the pavement. The air sat perfectly still, the hot blue sky a weight. The sun arced toward the western horizon, as if rushing away from disaster.

Not her. She scuffed along toward the devastation.

For courage, she'd brought the entire packet of letters from Travis. Twenty years' worth, though they'd come infrequently enough, so the folder wasn't that bulky. She still remembered the way, as a thirteen-year-old girl, her fingers had trembled holding the light blue, tissuey loft of the airmail stationery, her eyes had vacuumed up the thin, black chicken scratch of his handwriting, and her heart had gulped down his stories about bonobos and life in the Congo. Just a pen pal, she'd never even met him, but there were times she had lived for his letters, for his belief in what was humanly possible. As she walked now, the sweat from her back soaked through the nylon of her backpack and into the manila folder.

Lily's pack also held a flashlight, toothbrush and paste, paper maps from AAA—on Tom's insistence, but she was thankful since her phone was already dead—one more sandwich, two empty water bottles, and a change of clothes. She had a credit card, although it'd probably be useless, and a wad of cash. Hopefully, as soon as she found Vicky, they could get out the same way she'd gotten in.

After flying to Sacramento, she'd paid a driver, who seemed too young to have a driver's license, let alone a car, to bring her as far into Oakland as he could. He'd honored their agreement, driving fast, swerving around the crashed cars still piled up on the freeway, having to stop when he reached the place where the pavement sheered apart. Without saying goodbye, he grabbed the promised cash, made a U-turn, and, tires screeching, fled back east.

Now as she walked, Lily heard helicopters droning in the distance and wondered if they were dropping food and supplies or just carrying more reporters, cameras perched on their shoulders. The freeway was littered with all the stuff that the evacuees had abandoned along the way: busted-open suitcases; a garbage bag full of stuffed animals; photo albums, the pages stomped upon and the pictures curling in the sun; an empty jewelry box; a life-size mannequin, left in a ditch; a full toolbox (through which Lily rifled, already acquiring a survivor's mentality); an empty trombone case; a smashed guitar; a rodent cage. Books, lots and lots of books, more books than Lily would have imagined. People had grabbed what they thought could save them, and then they'd cast off even those items.

Lily's feet hurt. Her adrenaline-induced verve waned. She began to realize that she wouldn't get to Vicky's house, wouldn't get anywhere at all, before dark. Trees lined the broken freeway. She saw nothing resembling shelter. She'd have to keep walking, in the dark, through the night.

A deep, satisfied snarling, soft and guttural, brought her terror home and right to the bone. The low primal sounds were so much more frightening than strident barking.

She saw the two dogs. Pit bulls. Both hind ends—one liver-colored, with a pale covering of bone-white fur, and the other a deep beige, glossier and skinnier—worked back and forth as they shifted their positions, trying to gain purchase, at the open driver's door of a crashed Miata.

The royal blue car had spun and hit a FedEx truck head-on. The impact must have been hard and at speed, throwing the driver into the windshield and killing him. He was slumped over the steering wheel, his head draped by the airbag, and the two pit bulls were gnawing him.

Lily vomited the tuna sandwiches she'd eaten earlier in the day. Her upchuck drew the attention of the dogs who pulled back from the dead body to look at her. The smell of vomit, much more enticing than a rotting corpse, lured them. Lily backed up slowly.

As the pit bulls lapped up her vomit, she climbed into the back of the FedEx truck and pulled the door shut. Pitch black inside, she stumbled over some boxes and fell onto her hands and knees. She stopped to listen for scrabbling at the door of the truck. Could they smell her remaining tuna sandwich? She crawled back toward the door and felt around for a latch. She found one, but it was too complicated to negotiate in the dark. She made sure the doors were securely pulled closed and then kicked boxes aside to make a space for herself. She lay on her back and closed her eyes.

Two days ago she was just Lily Jones, a tall thirty-three-year-old woman with a modest gardening business, living in the heart of the country in the small town where she'd grown up, strong-willed perhaps but not particularly daring, married to her childhood sweetheart. It was as if she'd jumped off a cliff. Though her spine pressed against the cold metal of the truck bed, the absence of light accentuated the feeling of free fall.

2

WHEN LILY SAW THE small crowd in the Trinity Church parking lot, she dropped back to hide behind the south-facing wall of the building. People! What a relief. The long trek into town had been eerie and desolate. She'd passed more corpses and bigger packs of pet dogs gone rogue. Trees lay like giant toothpicks across vast hollows where mudslides had carried away the saturated earth. At the bottoms of the slides, she'd traversed the expanses of mud, now hardened like concrete, with housing debris embedded like tumors. The untouched streets shocked, too, with curtains hanging in windows and birds singing merrily in the canopies of trees, worse in a way than the wrecked streets. The destruction seemed so random.

She'd seen a few people lurking along the sides of houses or peering out windows, but the few remaining inhabitants ducked out of sight the instant they saw her, as if there were a social protocol she didn't understand. A couple of National Guard soldiers told her about the meals program, and the sight of people gathered purposefully in the church parking lot, shouting and laughing, expectant, relieved her enormously. God, she was hungry.

She planned on picking out someone to ask for help: How did the food program work? Where were people sleeping? Did anyone know Vicky? But as she stepped out from behind the wall and drew closer, she couldn't choose. Despite the laughter, everyone looked grizzled and wan. Most were dirty. Who could blame them? They'd been living in the earthquake zone for eleven days now. Water was scarce and power was nonexistent.

Some people stared, but no one greeted her. Well, it wasn't a tea party. Of course people would be suspicious of newcomers. Suddenly she felt afraid, almost more afraid than she'd been of the dogs. Travis had once written that the best way to avoid being a victim was not to look like one, so she moved through the crowd with fake bravado, found herself at the foot of a short cement stairway, and climbed it. She heard a woman's voice behind her shout that it wasn't time for dinner yet, that no one was allowed to enter the hall early.

But now, standing on the small porch at the top of the stairs, she was practically on a stage in front of the crowd in the parking lot. If she turned to acknowledge the woman, if she walked back down the steps, they would know for sure that she was new. New and confused—and exhausted, thirsty, and hungry.

Lily pulled open the door and went on inside. The big community room reminded her of the one in Tom's family's church. Long folding tables, each spread with a plastic cloth, covered the beige linoleum floor. Folding chairs surrounded all the tables.

"Finally," said the only person in the room, a skinny woman with short hair so sparse that Lily could see her scalp. Her skin looked like that of a Bosc pear, a dull yellowish brown, badly in need of lotion. She might once have been beautiful with her defined jaw, high cheekbones, and sensual mouth. Intelligence, maybe too much intelligence, brightened her eyes, as if they could see right through Lily. She shouted, "Ron! She's here!"

A tall, muscular man wearing chinos and a sleeveless white undershirt came out of the kitchen. Tattoos covered his arms, the blue ink like a subtle tapestry on his dark skin. Cowry shells tipped his cornrows. He nodded.

"Ron will train you," she said to Lily and then shook her head with slow displeasure. "They said they'd give me someone five days ago. And this is what they send."

Ron raised both hands in the air in front of his chest and pushed down, the gesture people use to slow cars.

"I'm just saying, it's hard work. This skinny girl..." The woman shook her head again and headed for the kitchen, her gait bony and jerky like she was in pain, even though she didn't look much older than Lily.

"I'm no skinnier than you," Lily said to her back. Like rifling through the abandoned toolbox on the freeway, Lily was amazed to find herself deploying more survival tactics, in this case talking back to someone, speaking up for herself, as if her very life depended on it. Which it might.

The woman stopped, turned, huffed out a short laugh, and walked back.

Lily said, "I don't know who you're expecting, but—"

"Look, I shouldn't have said skinny. But you look like the sensitive type and I don't have time for that. I feed upward of two hundred people every day. Get here by four o'clock tomorrow. Earlier, if possible. Put this on." She pulled a white apron off a hook and took a paper shower cap and latex gloves out of a drawer. She tossed all of it on a counter next to Lily. "Start with the drink cups, like this." The woman dipped a ladle into a big metal vat of red drink and poured some into a paper cup. "Put them on the trays and stack the trays. Got it? I'll be opening the door in five minutes. They have to take the first tray. *The first tray.* Don't let anyone tell you they don't like the looks of that one or want a bigger serving, and they will tell you that and lots more. They take what they get and they move along. One milk and one chocolate pudding per person. That's it. No exceptions."

Lily couldn't stop herself. She picked up the Dixie cup of red drink and drained it. The woman and the man looked at each other. The man filled her cup and Lily drained it again. She knew she should tell them that she wasn't the person "they" were supposed to have sent five days ago. But she was too thirsty, and too hungry, to walk away from this vat of red drink and the basins of steaming hot food. She met eyes with the woman and nodded her agreement.

"Kalisha," the woman said. She pointed at the man. "Ron."

"I'm Lily Jones."

Kalisha looked her over and hitched away.

Lily went to work filling the rest of the Dixie cups and stacking the trays. The service area where she worked connected to the community room via a rectangular cutout. On Lily's side of the window was a propane-heated steam table. Covered stainless steel basins sat in hot water baths. Behind her was the kitchen, a big room with sinks, two refrigerators, an industrial-sized propane stove and oven, and a large work island. Propane cylinders covered much of the floor space.

"Excuse me?" she asked Ron, who was washing cooking pots at one of the sinks.

He glanced up.

She wanted to touch the labyrinthine images tattooed on his triceps, as if they were a kind of Braille message. Instead she touched her own scar, the one right under her chin. "Kalisha said you'd train me?"

Ron stepped around the propane cylinders and out to the service area. He lifted the cover off the first basin of food. The rich aroma of macaroni and cheese wafted into Lily's face. It was all she could do not to put her face in the glop and eat. The next basin held green beans and the third one a vegetarian dish of root vegetables and tofu with the sharp perfumed funk of cumin. Cartons of milk and plastic containers of chocolate pudding crowded the shelves below the steam table.

Ron pointed to the refrigerators behind him and then waved his arms in big Xs in front of his chest.

"No electricity?" Lily guessed.

He nodded and kicked one of the propane canisters. "D-d-de-de-l-l-l-l-l..." He couldn't get past the L, and Lily didn't know what he was trying to say. He returned to his sink and thrust his arms into the soapy water.

"Delivered today," Kalisha said, coming up behind her. "We've been cooking with fire in the parking lot until now. This is a major upgrade."

"You have water."

"We do. Lucky there. Our supply line never broke."

"How do you keep the milk cold?"

"We don't."

"Where do you get the food?"

"You don't need to know that. Just serve it."

The juice in all the cups on the top tier of trays sloshed hard. The flatware clattered in its tray. Propane cylinders toppled. The floor dropped and shook. A primitive sound leapt from Lily's belly and out her mouth.

"I don't even react anymore," Kalisha said. She paused and looked at Lily with something that might have been kindness. "Girl, you need to get a grip. That aftershock is nothing compared to the rabble I'm about to let in that door. You ready?"

3

As the clients crowded in, Ron showed Lily how to spoon food onto the plastic trays and line them up on the countertop just beyond the serving window. Lily dished out trays as fast as she could and made up answers to the diners' questions about the weather, the food, FEMA, and herself. She shoved forkfuls of beans and macaroni into her own mouth and no one batted an eyelash at her gluttony. Everyone was hungry. Sweat dampened the back of her T-shirt and her feet ached from walking all those miles, but a full belly calmed her. Kalisha thought she was too skinny, too sensitive, to handle this job and these homeless people, but she was wrong. Lily liked serving nourishing food to hungry people.

Kalisha shut the door promptly at five thirty, and by a quarter to six many of the clients had finished eating and were leaving. Lily found a wet sponge in the kitchen and headed out to the dining room. As she wiped down the tables, she asked everyone if they knew her sister, Vicky Jones. Most just shook their heads. Some said, "I'm sorry," with too much finality. By now, their faces told Lily, people have either turned up or they're dead.

But they didn't know her sister. Vicky found the exception to every single rule. It was her signature personality trait. Lily knew she was alive.

When she came to a young man, maybe twenty-five years old, holding an infant, she stopped to caress the rose-petal skin on the bottom of the baby's foot. "Where's his mom?"

The father looked up at Lily without expression. His white skin was too pale, his hair too limp, his eyes colorless and flat. "Support beam. Crushed her."

"Oh, God, I'm—" Lily turned fast, not wanting him to see her tears. She gathered up as many cartons of milk from the service area as she could carry and took them to the father. He scooped the cartons into his pack with a quick nod of thanks. Lily bent and kissed the little one on the head.

"Herbert," the man said. The idea of a baby named Herbert made Lily laugh, and the man laughed, too, probably not at his baby's name, just seizing any opportunity for levity.

When Lily finished with the tablecloths, she found a bucket and mop and washed the entire floor. She saw Kalisha glancing at her from time to time with a surprised expression on her face. Yep, skinny and sensitive, but with lots of initiative. When she finished the floor, she tossed her paper hat and latex gloves into the garbage can and peeled off her apron. As the white cloth cleared her head, she saw Kalisha slipping a plastic-wrapped sandwich into the left pocket of an old man's tweed jacket and an apple into the right one.

"You need to handwash that before you leave," Kalisha said to Lily, nodding at the bunched-up apron in her hands. Lily knew the type: she had to make a harsh remark to counter being caught doing a kindness. "By four o'clock tomorrow. Earlier is always better. We have two hundred people to feed."

As much as she wanted to keep pretending, Lily thought she had better tell the truth. "I'm not who you think I am. I mean, no one sent me here."

"What do you mean? Who are you?"

"I just came to eat. And you mistook me because I barged in early."

"Now what?" Kalisha said to the daft old man with bulging pockets.

"I'll fill in until whoever is supposed to be here comes. I mean, I'd like to. I can be here tomorrow at four." The church community room already felt like home base in this crazy geography.

Kalisha stared at her for a moment before saying, "Do I have a choice?"

"You always have a choice," the old man said in a thin, quavering voice.

Kalisha smiled at him.

"Maybe you could help me, too," Lily said. "I came here, from Nebraska, to look for my sister. Vicky Jones. Maybe she's been to the church? She looks like me, only sturdier. Short, thick hair, dishwater blonde. Her eyebrows are a few shades darker. Her skin is kind of a toasty almond color, like mine. Strong jaw. Great smile. Really beautiful smile." Lily paused. "Butch. She's kind of butch."

"I know Vicky," the old man said.

"You do?" Relief dropped Lily into one of the folding chairs.

"Sure," he said, as if the odd thing would be not knowing Vicky. Thick, coarse, and shaggy white hair covered his head. Fleshy lids draped over his pale blue, filmy eyes, but the clean-shaven skin on his cheeks was surprisingly smooth, pink, and mobile. He wore white sneakers, gray flannel trousers, a white button-down shirt, a brown tweed jacket, and a bright tie patterned with green and yellow Hawaiian orchids. He held a walking stick in each hand. "She lives next door to me."

"You live on Ridge Road?"

"Yes, ma'am. Next door to Vicky. She used to bring me food. Bad cook, but a delightful girl."

"Used to?"

"Everything's been a bit topsy-turvy since the earthquake."

Kalisha smiled again. "That's one way to put it."

"She might be staying at her girlfriend's house," he said.

"You know Sal?"

"Of course. The hyena lady!" The old man's watery eyes brightened with pleasure.

"Do you know where Sal lives?"

"No. I'm sorry, Vicky's sister."

"This is Lily," Kalisha said and then waved a hand at the old man. "Professor Vernadsky."

"Philosophy," he warbled proudly. "Fifty-four years at Berkeley."

As he started for the door, Kalisha went ahead to open it for him.

"Good night, Professor," she said and he waved one of his walking sticks at the now empty room.

Excited to have made contact with someone who knew her sister, Lily scrubbed her apron with soap in one of the kitchen sinks, then rinsed it as well as she could and hung it on a hook to dry. When she came back into the community room, she saw Kalisha sitting at a folding table, on the far side of the room, poring over a sheaf of papers.

"Bye! I'm leaving now." Lily waved. In one of his letters, Travis had explained that the gesture of waving had evolved from people showing they had no weapons in their hands. Lily raised her other hand, too, and waved both. Kalisha nodded.

Lily stepped out of the community room into a light too tender for the ruined urban landscape. What time had it gotten dark last night? How long did she have to figure out where she might sleep? She could never tell Tom that she'd slept in a crashed FedEx truck. Although the thought of his reaction almost made her smile.

At the bottom of the cement steps, a big girl stood with her legs slightly spread, as if guarding someone in a basketball game. The fat kid looked to be about sixteen years old. Maybe biracial, her skin was honey-colored, and acne covered her face. Her hair stuck out in five-inch-long unraveling braids. Rhinestone barrettes pinned down a couple of the loose braids, and several big loopy curls framed her scowling face. Lily remembered the girl coming through the line. She'd been alone and anxious. She'd asked for extra milk. A manufactured gardenia scent clouded the air around her.

"I saw you give that man all that milk," she said.

"He has an infant."

"I told you I wanted an extra milk. One extra."

Lily stepped around the overgrown child and started across the parking lot. She heard the community room door open and turned to see the girl disappear inside. Lily climbed back up the steps and reentered the community room in time to see the girl clump into the service area and grab four containers of chocolate pudding. She cradled her booty in folded arms, like it was a baby, and pushed past Lily and out the door.

As Kalisha shot after her, Lily waited inside. A moment later, Kalisha returned with the puddings. She dumped them onto the counter. "Did you tell Annie she could have these?"

"Of course not."

"You unlocked the door on your way out. You have to check the lock button every time."

"Okay."

"There's no room for error here."

"It was unlocked when I came in before dinner."

Kalisha gave her a strict teacher stare. "Because I was expecting someone. But really, I don't need to explain everything."

"Sorry."

"I'm trying to feed a couple hundred people a day, okay?"

"You've said."

Kalisha paused at Lily's sass. She cocked her head, as if about to mount an offensive, but then just sighed. "That oversize girl does not need extra chocolate pudding."

"I saw you give that old man an extra sandwich and apple."

"That's none of your business."

"The girl seems sad. She held those chocolate puddings like they were love."

"Chocolate pudding is nothing like love. Be on time tomorrow."

Lily left the church a second time, wishing she'd consulted her map inside the building, away from inquisitive eyes. She blinked hard at the dusk light, as if she could bring back the sun. The FedEx truck was beginning to feel like safety compared to her options for tonight. Vicky's street was two miles from here, up in the hills. She had tried to find it earlier in the afternoon but gotten hopelessly lost. By the time she had encountered the National Guard troops, thirst and hunger turned her around.

She sat on the top step of the church's stoop and pulled the Berkeley/Oakland map out of her backpack. Why hadn't she thought to ask Professor Vernadsky the route to Vicky's house? He'd said she *used to* bring him food. But that didn't necessarily mean anything; she probably knew he ate at the church. With Vicky, anything was possible. Lily bet she was ensconced in her house, keeping a low profile, figuring out how to thrive in the newly fractured city. That would be Vicky: turning catastrophe into opportunity. Lily closed her eyes and pictured her sister's ridiculously goofy smile. She would forgive Vicky whatever cockamamie excuses she gave for not getting in touch after the earthquake. She would listen, without an ounce of impatience or judgment, to Vicky's current exuberances. She badly wanted to try again, right now, to find her house. But the streets were a chaos of downed trees, telephone polls, and mudslides, and if she had been spectacularly unsuccessful navigating them in the daylight, doing so in the dark would be plain stupid.

She considered Tom's solution to her predicament. She found Joyce Renaldi's place on her map, and it was just a few blocks from Trinity Church. Why did going there feel like she'd been AWOL and was turning herself in?

As Lily got to her feet, an exaggerated throat-clearing drew her attention to the big girl sitting on the pavement with her shoulders against the exterior church wall, just below the cement steps. Her eyes were closed and her face was tipped to the sky, a pose of endurance. A scrawny blond boy sat beside her, twirling a coil of dirty hair. His pale skin was even more broken out than hers. He held an orange kitten against his chest. He squinted up at Lily and swatted the girl's thigh. "Annie."

"What?" she pretend-snarled. "What d'ya want?"

"Someone's here." He spoke barely louder than a whisper. Then he pulled up his knees, folded his arms across them, and hid his face. The orange kitten squeezed out of his lap and arched its back.

"Yeah, I know," Annie said without looking at Lily. She reached up and secured each of her two rhinestone barrettes.

Lily descended the steps and headed across the parking lot as if she hadn't seen or heard the two kids.

"Asshole." Annie spoke in a calm voice, as if merely saying, *Good day.*

Lily couldn't help turning around.

Annie elbowed her companion and said, "Sit up, Binky. Here's the bitch who wouldn't let me get your dinner."

Binky didn't raise his head, but he extended a hand to pet the kitten.

Annie said, "But you had no problem letting the white guy take extra."

"He had an infant."

"There was a Mexican chick with a baby. You didn't give her extra."

"Operative word: chick. She can nurse her baby. He can't."

"Yeah, well, I have Binky, and I can't nurse him, either. The pudding was for him."

"Binky is a grown boy. He can come to the church for dinner if he's hungry."

"Oh, right. Like he'd survive that zoo."

"What do you mean?"

She rolled her eyes like Lily was the densest person she'd ever met. The boy kept his face between his knees.

Annie said, "He's a fag. Obviously."

"I doubt the church discriminates."

"The church is a *building.* He gets the shit kicked out of him— by *people,* not buildings—like every week."

"I'm sorry."

"Sorry. She's sorry," Annie said to the top of the boy's head. "She's sorry."

Lily walked over and squatted a few feet away from the kids. "So he's safer out here by himself than inside with you?"

Annie looked at a spot of pavement off to the side and shook her head slowly, like she just couldn't believe Lily's obtuseness.

Then she snapped her gaze back and made challenging eye contact. "Binky doesn't like crowds."

Lily stood up. "Okay. So, you kids are staying in one of the shelters?"

"Now there's a brilliant idea. A) The shelters are like the most dangerous places. B) They separate dudes and chicks. C) If he goes into a men's shelter alone, he...well, use your imagination. Or maybe you really don't know. But trust me, this boy doesn't need to be in a shelter. He does need some chocolate pudding." Annie spoke of Binky as if he were her ward rather than her peer. She elbowed him again and said, "Get up."

Binky sprung to his feet and picked up the orange kitten. Maybe fourteen years old, each one of Binky's ribs showed through his tight white T-shirt. A length of rope held up his jeans. He wore brand-new Air Jordan high-tops, black with untied iridescent red laces. At first Lily thought the shoes had to be about three sizes too big, but then she noticed that the boy's hands were as big as his feet. In spite of his raw face, mismatched body parts, and overall dishevelment, a dancer's beauty graced his young body. He put the kitten on his shoulder and held out two hands to pull Annie up.

"Thanks, Bink," she said and smiled at her friend.

Lily walked away briskly, once again trying to air confidence.

"Where do you live?" Annie yelled to her back. Then, "Hey! I'm talking to you!" And finally, "Bitch!"

Lily walked downhill until she came to Martin Luther King Jr. Way, and then she turned right, passing the Big O Tire shop, which had all its windows busted out. After crossing University Avenue, she left the commercial district and entered a neighborhood, marveling at how spring already flourished out here, though it was only March. Beds of flowering impatiens glowed fuchsia and white and coral in the beginning-of-dusk light. Gangly magnolia trees dropped their floppy petals. At home, her clients called in the winter for the occasional pruning job, but most of her work came between May and September. In California, gardeners had work year round. Not that she was thinking of staying.

Lily tripped on something hard and black. At first she thought it was just another plastic bag of garbage in the street, but the rigid thing had fur, ears, and a tail. She kept moving, walking through the deepening shadows. She missed hearing the helicopters, the droning warp of their engines as they passed overhead, the sense of airborne authority. They made her feel as if someone, somewhere, had a handle on things. The pilots must have landed the choppers somewhere for the night. She pulled out her flashlight and tucked it into the front pocket of her jeans.

When she got to Joyce Renaldi's flat, the bottom half of a small Victorian, she stood on the sidewalk, dreading the next part. After she'd left for the airport, Tom had called Mrs. Renaldi, one of Lily's clients, and asked for Joyce's phone number. Then he'd called the Fair-Oaks-to-Berkeley transplant, asking if Lily might stay with her. It was so presumptuous of him. They hardly knew her. Joyce, a class behind them, had left Fair Oaks right after high school.

But where else could Lily go now? She supposed she could go to one of the shelters, but she didn't like the way Annie had spoken about them, and anyway, she didn't know where they were. It would be totally dark in a few minutes.

Stalling, Lily stroked the long spiked leaf of an iris. There were two tight helixes of deep purple buds shooting from the middle of the plant. Next to it were the dark green glossy leaves of a calla lily. Travis sometimes called her that and once asked if she'd been named for the creamy coil of a flower. She liked calla lilies very much. Elegance balanced their sturdiness.

The footsteps came quickly and from behind. By the time she realized they were uncomfortably close, it was too late. An arm tightened around her neck and closed off her breath. Lily made a sound that was a cross between a grunt and a gurgle. The assailant jammed his knee into her right buttock and someone else gasped.

Lily caught a whiff of gardenia.

"Come on," said a squeaky voice from a few feet away. "*Please.* Just come *on.*"

"She told on me to Kalisha. She gave those milks to that other guy."

Lily relaxed her body, tried to impart calm. The girl was surprisingly strong, and yet, for a moment, Lily felt as if Annie were holding rather than restraining her, a desperate clutch at an adult. The arm around her neck loosened enough for Lily to say, "Let go, Annie."

Annie stepped around to face Lily.

Binky was already running, a fast sprint, the loose red shoelaces flickering like hummingbird wings in the twilight. He disappeared around the corner.

"What do you think you're doing?" Lily asked her. "What do you want?"

"You've got a house." She jutted her chin toward Joyce's place.

"It's not mine."

"I'm hungry."

"Didn't you eat at the church?"

"All that food is shit. And Binky is really hungry."

"That food is not shit. It was delicious."

"Shit," she repeated, but quietly, her lower lip trembling.

"Where's your family?" Lily asked.

"That's none of your business."

"It sort of is. I mean, you're mugging me. Your family should be providing you with food and shelter."

It was the wrong thing to say. Obviously, her family *wasn't* providing her with food and shelter. Maybe they'd been killed in the earthquake. *Support beam, crushed her.*

"Binky and I are hungry. I need money."

"You're barking up the wrong tree. Good night, Annie." Lily stepped around her and walked up the three wooden steps to Joyce's porch. She didn't want to ring the bell until Annie had taken off, so she turned to check.

The girl hadn't moved. Lily snapped on her flashlight and shot the beam at Annie. Except for scrunching up her eyes, Annie didn't flinch. She just stood there with her arms hanging at her sides, hands curled into loose fists, messy braids shooting off her head like shouts.

She wore a long red T-shirt over purple leggings, topped by a too-big green army jacket. Her legs splayed out from the knees, her feet pointing in different directions.

Lily lowered the beam of light. "You better go find Binky," she said softly.

Annie gaped for another long moment, obviously wishing the incident had turned out differently. She said, "He doesn't do so well on his own."

"Go on, then." Lily watched the girl lumber slowly down the sidewalk, waiting until she was swallowed by the dark. Then she rang Joyce's doorbell.

4

A NNIE SAT ON THE curb and looked out into the black night. She should have at least taken the flashlight off that woman. Now even Binky was gone. She hated when he ran off like that—he was such a scaredy-cat. It took her forever to find him again, sometimes even a couple of days.

"Binky?" she stage-whispered. If she yelled, she could attract the attention of the wrong person, someone who would force her to go with them somewhere, since she was a minor, and that somewhere would be awful. Twice already adults had "found" her and tried to take her to the police. That was the good thing about the earthquake: turning someone in was much more problematic than it was under normal circumstances. Both times it had been easy to slip out of their grasp and get away.

Running away in the first place was the best thing she ever did in her life, a very smart move. Of course, there was the little complication of the worst disaster in the history of the universe, which happened just a few days after she arrived in Berkeley, but that kind of luck defined her life. It was exactly what she should have expected. So no biggie. Fine. An earthquake.

In any case, besides the general confusion providing good cover, the earthquake led her to Binky, and Binky was the best thing in her life. *Ever.* Past, present, future. The amazing part was that she'd told him everything, the true everything. It was like his skinny neediness, his desperate heart-on-his-sleeve way of going through life, forced Annie to be fully honest with him. A lie would snap him in half. He needed to hear pure truth. She thought maybe she was saving his life. She told him he was definitely saving hers, and she thought even that might be true. Together, they would make it. What "making it" meant, they didn't know, but they spent a lot of time considering the options. Binky wanted an island in the Pacific, a place that was always warm and where you could drink the milk out of coconuts. Usually Annie told him that's what they'd do, but if he was in a stronger mood, if he seemed relatively stable emotionally, then she told him *her* plan: to stay right here in Berkeley and open an animal shelter. They would save all the strays, and also rescue the animals that people abused. If they got enough land, they could take in the bigger ones, too, like circus animals who'd been forced to perform their entire lives. Binky sometimes liked that idea and said that staying in Berkeley would be a lot more practical. To be conciliatory in return, Annie said they'd get a vacation island and fly there whenever they wanted.

She was pretty certain he told her the truth about everything, too. Of course, she had no real way of knowing this. After all, she'd sworn to a million teachers, social workers, neighbors, and other kids that she was telling the absolute unadulterated truth when she'd been lying through her teeth. That test of looking someone in the eye while saying it? She passed every time. It was easy. Lying was the easiest thing in the world.

The scary part was how good it felt to tell the truth to Binky. She loved how he listened, batting his beautiful gray eyes at her, waving his faggy hands in the air at the exciting parts, even crying at the sad parts.

"Binky!" she called out again, this time using her whole voice, risking being heard. "Where are you?"

She hated his being gone. It felt beyond dismal. She wished she had something to eat. Sadness and hunger always felt exactly the same way, and she wanted to fill the hollow in her middle.

Annie pushed herself up from the curb and started walking. "Binky!" she called, now loud and repeatedly, as if he were a lost dog. "Binky!"

Cedar Rose Park, where they'd met the morning of the earthquake and where they still sometimes slept, was close by, so she went there first.

She heard the squeak of the swing set, the rub of the metal links connecting the chains to the frame, and as she drew closer, she saw a ghostly figure swinging in a short arc. Once she'd teasingly called him Caspar.

"I am not a ghost!" he had shrieked. "I am not a ghost!"

She'd said she was sorry. She would never call him that again. She made a point, after that, of telling him how beautiful she thought his paling-to-blue skin was, how she liked the way she could see his veins right on the surface, those baby blue rivers of blood. She'd trace them with her finger and smile at him.

Tonight, though, her fear of losing him, even for those few minutes, snapped her tenderness into kindling. "Why the fuck did you run away?" she called across the park.

Binky pushed off with his feet and swung higher. His right hand held the swing's chain and his left hand clutched the orange kitten on his lap.

"Come down off of there," Annie said, now standing by one of the swing set struts.

"You went too far this time," Binky said.

"Oh, and you have a better idea? We have to eat. We have to sleep. We need money."

"You attacked that lady."

"So what? She's prejudiced. She gave extra milks to some white dude and not to me."

"You *physically* attacked her."

"So what!" Annie lunged for the swing chain on its downstroke and grabbed hold. The swing wobbled violently and Binky yelped. Annie seized his forearm and pulled him off the black rubber seat. The orange kitten leapt onto the playground bark.

"Let go of me," Binky said, but his lithe body fell gently against hers. Annie wanted to kiss the side of his head, maybe his temple, but she didn't.

"Promise you won't do that again," he said.

"Do what?" There were a number of things he could be referring to.

"Jump someone."

"Okay, I promise."

"You said you've never lied to me and that you never would."

Annie felt trapped for a moment. But then she realized he was right. She should not be assaulting people, if for no other reason than it was bad for her and Binky. She could promise this and mean it. "I said I promise."

Binky scooped up the orange kitten who had been sitting on its behind, front paws neatly parallel, watching the argument.

"Let's walk," Binky said. They often walked all night. It was safer that way, keeping on their feet, staying awake when it was dark out. They could sleep later, when the sun came up.

So the two kids set out toward the hills, bumping elbows and hips, sniffling and clearing their throats, but otherwise simply walking.

5

JOYCE LOCKED THE DOOR behind them and walked to the kitchen at the back of the flat. She lit a camp stove and put on a pan of water. Lily remembered her as one of those smart, bossy, straight-A girls, the type who used jump ropes to play horse on the playground. She was small, compact, athletic, her frosted hair pulled back in a taut and stubby ponytail.

"You're lucky you found me here. I'm staying in San Francisco with Dennis. Why didn't you text?"

"My phone is dead."

"Call Tom. Let him know you're not." Joyce pushed her phone across the kitchen table.

"I'm sorry he pulled you into this. I'm sure you have enough on your plate."

"I really do. I have to be back in the city early tomorrow, which means I have to ride my bike in the dark to the ferry dock and catch the first one across. I only came over here to see if you'd arrived."

"I'm sorry. I'll be out of here in no time."

"He's worried. Call him." Joyce picked up her cup of tea, carried it into the bedroom, and shut the door.

"Lily!" Tom's voice sounded as if someone were strangling him, a cross between extreme relief and horrified disbelief.

"I made it. I'm at Joyce's."

"Vicky?"

"I'll go up to her house tomorrow."

"Sweetie." He hadn't called her that in a couple of years. The word sounded coolly medicinal now. She could taste what it was aiming at, how he was trying. "I'm worried about you."

"It shouldn't take long. I'll be back home in no time."

"Joyce told me that people are getting ugly. Attacking people who have stuff. Breaking into houses."

"I've seen just the opposite. I helped out in a free meals kitchen at Trinity Church this afternoon."

"She said that people are forming these things they're calling Clusters. They're starting to maraud. You're out there by yourself, completely clueless about how people are. You always have been." He paused and added, "I'm not being critical. That's, you know, who you are. But it only works in places like Fair Oaks."

"I haven't seen any 'marauding.'" What kind of word was that? "You know, people do sometimes work together. Help each other. Like the bonobos."

"Wow." Tom breathed the word hotly. "Okay. Fine."

She knew the *wow* wasn't about her defense of humanity.

"So that's what this is." He spoke slowly, accusingly.

Lily could feel the pause in their entire relationship, a quiet at the center of everything.

"I'm here to find Vicky. Who lives in the heart of a disaster zone. Who I haven't heard from since the earthquake."

"You said he was moving to Berkeley."

"And?"

"Just a coincidence."

Tom wasn't entirely wrong. She'd come here to find Vicky. But she might never have had the courage to come all the way to California, in the midst of a disaster, to look for Vicky if she hadn't been reading

Travis's letters all these years, learning that people can and do take great risks for those they love. His letters had felt like a giant precipice from which she viewed a brighter, more vibrant world. It was also true that his last letter told about his own crisis, and that he was going back to Berkeley. So yes, maybe it *was* a coincidence.

It was also possible that it wasn't.

She forced herself to speak calmly. "Travis was a homework assignment, in case you don't recall. And Vicky is my sister. My *sister*. We spend every Sunday with your entire extended family, every single Sunday, and I can't have a few days to look for Vicky who might be seriously hurt?"

Even conjuring the picture of an injured Vicky didn't change his course. "It's insane to be out there now. Please just come home."

"You're not going to help me with this, are you?"

"How *can* I help you? You went on your own." His voice cracked.

"I asked you to come with me. You wouldn't."

"Because it was a bad idea."

"I love you, Tom." She waited a beat for this to sink in. "And I'm sorry I had to do this. But I know Vicky is alive and I have to find her. I have to. I'll come home, I'll bring her home, as soon as I can."

"I don't like this. Any of it." His voice switched from emotion-laden cracking to petulance.

"I know you don't. I'll call you later, after I find a way to charge my phone."

He wouldn't say goodbye. She heard only heavy nose-breathing.

"Tom?"

More silence.

"Tom! What? What is it?"

"Nothing. Call me as soon as you find her."

Lily walked to the closed bedroom door, raised a fist, and knocked.

Joyce opened the door and held up a flat hand. "I need to get some sleep. So look. You can stay here for a few nights." She took the phone from Lily's hand. "You haven't asked me for advice. And I wasn't eavesdropping. But I couldn't exactly avoid hearing. Don't go back to

Trinity Church. I've heard things about that operation. Everything, everywhere, is sketchy now. My advice: check out Vicky's house, satisfy yourself that she's not there, get back to an airport, and fly home."

"She'll be there."

"A couple of nights."

"Thank you!" Lily said to the shutting bedroom door. "I appreciate you letting me stay here."

She lay down on the couch and pulled the sleeping bag Joyce had put out for her up to her chin. She would find Vicky in the morning. They would travel together back to Fair Oaks. Everything would be okay.

But she couldn't sleep. She kept hearing Tom's silences on the phone. For the past few months, he'd been an odd combination of extra attentive and extra distracted. She knew it was about the big fight they'd had, the biggest one of their entire relationship. The weather of that argument still clouded their every interaction. They couldn't seem to recover. She wished she knew how to get them past the stalemate.

How can you fight about babies? They'd married straight out of high school because of their eagerness to have a family. They'd picked out names. They'd talked about where they'd go on family vacations, how they'd dress and educate their children. But the children didn't happen. They'd done all the tests and found no detectable abnormalities. A rare few couples, the doctor had told them, just don't conceive.

Still, they had tried and tried, all the while agreeing against adoption.

Then Lily had changed her mind.

"Let's start thinking of alternatives," she'd said that night a few months ago.

"We're fine as we are. Sometimes you just have to accept circumstances. You're barren. Or whatever."

"What?"

"You know what I mean."

"Barren?" A word from a different century. It was almost as if he wanted to escalate a fight. "The doctor never said it was me."

"Okay. Fine. My point is, it's done."

"Nothing is 'done.' We're only thirty-three."

"Why can't we just move on?"

"Yes! Move on to other ideas. I've been thinking about adopting," Lily had said.

"We've talked about this."

"There are so many children who need homes."

"Out of the question."

"I like the idea."

"Think, Lil. Imagine the problems. Illnesses. Behavior issues. No. Absolutely not. I want my own children."

"They would be our *own* children. Ones we adopt."

"No."

"Can't we even talk about it? I thought we wanted a family."

"I want my own family."

His position infuriated her. It encapsulated everything that made him increasingly intolerable to her: his inability to see outside himself. It wasn't arrogance. It was a lack of imagination. He couldn't see beyond Fair Oaks. Or, apparently, even beyond his own DNA.

"I want children." All the heartbreak of the past years of trying had stuck in her throat. "Yours, mine, ours. I don't really care how we get them."

That was when he'd dropped what at the time seemed like a total non sequitur: "We're just really different people."

"That's brilliant. Yes, we're different people. You're a man and I'm a woman. I'm a gardener and you're a locksmith. Yes, we're *different*. And now we have a difference of opinion on adoption." She'd lost control of her decibels.

"I don't even know you anymore."

The statement had stunned her. For one thing, it was a lie. They'd been friends since they were eleven years old and married since they were eighteen. He knew her. "What are you saying?"

His face had briefly convulsed. She'd thought it was his sadness about children. He'd shook his head and forced himself to say, "I'm sorry."

Those two words, Lily had thought at the time, *they* were barren. Final. Empty. He hadn't looked at her as he'd said them. Both of them were afraid to broach the topic again in the weeks that followed.

She realized now, lying on Joyce's couch, that that argument had contributed to her coming to California. The idea of stepping outside her own biology, outside her own niche, excited Lily. Putting her life on the line to help someone she loved felt essential. The years were ticking by. She couldn't bear the thought that the only thing she'd ever contribute to humankind was planting a few ladies' gardens.

Lily's mouth felt mossy and she realized she hadn't brushed her teeth in about forty-eight hours. Joyce had water! She clicked on her flashlight and dug around in her pack for her toothbrush. She carried it to the kitchen and brushed her teeth for a long time. Then, as she tucked the toothbrush back into the pack, she saw her sweat-stained manila folder of letters from Travis. She pulled out his last one.

6

Dear Lily,

I'm posting this from Kinshasa. I've left the sanctuary. I'm staying in a hotel and will go to the airport in the morning. All is lost. All. Except for this shell of a body I inhabit. We humans are hardwired to survive. At any cost. So I'm leaving. My entire future is my betrayal. I'll return to Berkeley, the cushy university life. I'll fold the sanctuary and Oscar and Malcolm and Rosa and Coral, all of them, into my subconscious where no doubt they'll fester. But I'll survive. I'll be on that plane tomorrow morning.

I won't write you again. You were my hope. The holder of my message. Yeah, sure, some of the studies have been published and academia will mull the results. Others will do more research, if they can find any subjects to do it on.

The truth is, evolution will continue without you. Without me. Even without the bonobos. God knows thousands of species have gone extinct. And anyway, I've begun to believe that the best thing that could happen, certainly for the planet, but maybe even for humanity, is our extinction. Or near extinction, anyway. We've made a mess of this planet. Maybe recovery is only possible without us.

I want to tell you what happened, and I want to be truthful. Will you hold this last truth for me? There might come a day when I can face it, and myself, again. There might come a time when my failure could be used for some good. I can't imagine how. But I'm guessing you can imagine it. Please do. Not for me. For them.

Eight weeks ago, a wildlife trader had the gall to come right to the sanctuary gate. He had four bonobo babies with him. Four. He wanted 150,000 francs apiece, and he had a semiautomatic. His eyes were red and rheumy, and he was probably drunk. Yannick said call the police, and I started to do it, but Renée said no. The man had arrived in a Jeep. The police wouldn't get here in time to arrest him. Anyway, he said he would shoot all four bonobos if we called the police. I believed him. He lodged the gun against one of the juvenile's heads. With his other hand he gestured furiously for us to fork over the cash.

I don't know how it came to this. Maybe twenty years ago, yes. This kind of thing was standard. But Renée has worked tirelessly to build a relationship with the local officials, including the police, and pretty much single-handedly drove the wildlife market underground. It never went away, we knew that, but they didn't dare bring the bonobos to the open market anymore. It was a big win. It meant we could set up stings, and we did, successfully, many times, sending an undercover official to pick up a bonobo for sale and make the arrest. Maybe that was the problem: it'd happened too many times. This trader decided to change tactics. He was asking for so little money. In the past, traders had gotten much more for the babies.

Lily, I've written you the deepest truths I know. If people are hungry, they are desperate. They will eat even a creature that is damn near identical to their own species. I know that. I have learned not to judge. People are hungry. For food. For justice. And I am an outsider, a big blond healthy one. What right do I have to protect the resources of the Congo? Why should someone who has known only war and hunger listen to me when I try to tell them that bonobos might be our last chance out of human misery?

You also know that's what I believe. The bonobos are the key to our understanding of the possibility, the human possibility, for compassion and altruism. These cousins of ours exist only here in the Congo Basin and they're disappearing. The ugly truth is that I did feel like a hero. I believed so passionately, so desperately in these sweet creatures, our link to them, that I thought protecting them was the only worthy work on this planet. I believe that still. I do. And I have failed.

The four little ones with the trader were emaciated. Nearly hairless. Their ribs and elbows and knees stretching the skin. Yannick started to walk back up to the bungalows to get water and food for them, but the trader shouted for him to stay. Yannick shook his head with disgust. As usual, Renée focused on the bonobos. She sat down on the dusty road in front of our gate, her legs sprawled, and held out her arms. All four. All four, Lily, rushed to her. They threw their withered little arms around her neck and waist and thighs, anything they could grab onto, and just held on for dear life. She stroked their heads, cooed soothing words to them, let them nearly strangle her with their fear.

I was so relieved. She wouldn't let them down. Not Renée. She'd spent her whole life protecting their brothers and sisters and mothers and fathers. Renée would find a way.

I crouched and eased one away from her. The little girl threw her arms around my neck and held back her head to make eye contact. Such beautiful, grieving eyes. Her skin, though wrinkled from malnutrition, was nonetheless satiny. They were all too sad to even scream their anxiety.

We would bottle-feed them rich milk as we had so many others. I would peel mangoes and bananas for them. Yannick would treat their diseases. They would grow glossy coats and fatten up. Trust would be difficult for them—it always was for the orphans taken from the forest—and some would never learn it. But some would. Renée was a miracle worker.

She wiggled her face clear of baby bonobo arms. She looked up at the trader who now pointed his semiautomatic straight at her head. The foolish trader didn't know that she'd rather he shoot her than the bonobos.

She said, "We don't buy bonobos. They're protected. But we'll feed and nurture these four. Yannick is our vet and he'll make sure they get any medicines they need. Thank you for bringing them."

The man snorted. "Not possible," he said, of course in French. "I've traveled a long way with them. I had to feed them and give them places to sleep. I protected them from bad men who would steal and sell them. Rescuing them has been very expensive."

"No," Renée said, struggling to her feet and standing in front of the babies who still clung to her legs. "I'll ask you to please leave now."

He took three steps forward and held the gun to the head of the closest bonobo. His hands were shaking. I don't know from what. Fear? Alcohol? The ruins of his life? The ruins of his life. I saw then that he wanted the cash and if he didn't get it, he didn't really care what happened next. I knew he would pull that trigger, not once but four times.

I had 250,000 francs in my wallet. Renée knew this because she'd sent me the day before to fetch the money. We had a couple of builders coming to help us expand the nursery, and they wanted to be paid in cash. I made eye contact with Renée and placed my hand over the bulge of my wallet in my back pocket. She understood and held my eyes with her own. For too long. The trader saw.

I know that Renée wouldn't have initiated the transaction. Raised in the Congo, not a hundred miles from here, she'd staked her entire life, every penny she'd ever owned, the respect of her parents who thought she should go to medical or law school, on this sanctuary. Day in and day out, she'd used her local connections and her black skin—she wasn't just another do-gooder from the outside telling people what to do with their land and resources— to convince her fellow Congolese of the urgency in saving the bonobos. Her techniques have been brilliant and based on a degree of patience I will never possess. She has always said, "I will change one heart at a time."

I take full responsibility for what happened. I'm the one who touched my wallet. I asked the question. I allowed the possibility to be viewed by the trader.

But I'll never know why, after all these years of holding her ground against all forms of bribery and corruption and flat-out threats, Renée nodded at me. Did she nod at me? I thought she did. So I pulled the wallet from my pocket.

I handed the money to the man. He snatched it and jumped in his Jeep. The tires spat gravel and dust as he sped out of there, and we knew he'd be long gone before the police arrived, even if we called them.

Renée closed her eyes for a long cooling-off period as we listened to the Jeep skid away into the bush. When she opened them again, I saw her anger. She's been my boss for over twenty years, but I've never seen rage like that. She had always converted her rage into love. I don't know how a person does this. And I only know now why she finally failed, this time, at doing it. Renée saw further into the future than I did, she always could, and no amount of love was going to stop what I'd set in motion.

But at the time I thought she was just being human, giving in to righteous anger, and I was glad, I have to admit, to see her give in to it. Her control drives me nuts. Her ability to apply reason and rationality to emotional issues, to love, over and over and over again. I was glad to see her succumb to anger.

But she didn't succumb exactly. Of course not. She shook her head hard, just once, as if she could flick the anger into the forest, and then she turned to the terrified orphans who were now finally screaming their fear. I helped her calm them, and then we walked them up to the bungalows. One collapsed on the path, too weak to walk, and I had to pick her up.

Yannick walked up the trail behind us, and he said in a low voice to me, "You asshole. You idiot." I ignored him. We had saved four bonobos, and Renée had agreed on our course of action. Yannick and I have had our conflicts for years. This was no time to hash anything out. We had four babies who needed our immediate attention.

The weak one died that night. A second one died forty-eight hours later. The other two survived.

A week later, the trader was back. He had two more with him this time. I had no cash in my wallet and he shot them both in the heads. He flung the bodies in the back of his Jeep. He said he'd be back in two days time and we were to have cash on hand for the product he brought. He said a million francs a head wasn't the suggested price, it was the required one.

Yannick said the whole thing was my fault, that I'd always been a liability, that I couldn't be trusted to understand long-term strategy. He said they needed to cut me loose. I saw Renée consider this. She paused too long before she shook her head.

Renée went to town and planned with the police. They came out and set up an ambush. They waited for three weeks. The trader didn't come back. Maybe he'd paid the police off. Maybe he had spies watching from the forest. I don't know. But we eventually let down our guards. The police couldn't stay out at the sanctuary indefinitely and they left.

An emissary of the trader came on foot. He tried to bargain, tried to pretend he was on our side. He said he was helping save the bonobos and only needed funding for doing so. He said we could buy the last of the species from him or let the poachers finish the apes off.

With my 250,000 francs, I'd shot a hole straight through Renée's years of meticulous consistency. We had been winning the battle. The communities surrounding the sanctuary had come to understand the importance of protecting our sister species. The police were helping, for the most part, to catch and prosecute poachers and traders. There was still an underground market, people still ate bonobo steak, and foreigners still bought the animals for pets. But we'd slowed the leak. We were winning.

I had to try to correct my mistake. I started searching the forests for signs of poachers' camps. I walked to the village, too, and questioned everyone about illegal sales. When Renée found out about my activities, she asked me to stop. She said I was making things worse.

When some locals told me that for a fee they could tell me where the trader lived, I paid them. The man was arrested. I felt vindicated. Renée kissed me that night, on the cheek, and said, "Thank you." Looking back, I see the sadness in her eyes, the loss, the knowledge, and realize now that it was a kiss of forgiveness. Yannick, who lived in the village with his wife and children, who had walked to work and back every morning for nearly as many years as I had been at the sanctuary, quit.

A few nights later, at three in the morning, our chain-link fences were cut with wire cutters. Axes were used to break down the bungalow doors. That woke us, of course, the sound of splitting wood, and Renée and I raced down to the bonobos in time to witness the massacre. The masked men shot every last one in the head. A complete slaughter.

I wanted them to shoot me, too. I wrestled with one of the masked men, hoping he would. But they were smart. They knew leaving me and Renée to live was a better form of torture.

Love is slow work. It's meticulous work. It's holding out against evil.

I don't have it in me to love. I see that now.

Sincerely yours,

Travis

7

I N HIS FIRST LETTER, twenty years ago, Travis had explained all
about the bonobos. He'd written that hope for humanity was
dependent upon our understanding of this dwindling species.
Thrillingly, he'd told her that she, Lily Jones, had a role to play. It was
people like her—"an ordinary girl from Nebraska with no particular
passions"—who would change the world. Or not.

She'd read that letter maybe a hundred times. Her understanding
of his meaning, as well as her response to that meaning, kept changing
over the years. At first, at that age when she was just stepping beyond
girlhood, she felt seen. Growing up in Vicky's shadow, she'd never
considered the possibility that being ordinary could be a good thing.
Already five feet eight inches tall, gangly and gawky, wanting bright
blue rather than gray eyes, plump lips rather than thin ones, a pert
rather than Roman nose, the idea that she might have a role in world
transformation, that her very ordinariness could be useful, riveted her.
She wolfed down every word, phrase, sentence, paragraph of Travis's.
She wanted to hear more, much more.

Later, in her early twenties, she felt *not* seen. Yes, she was ordinary,
she embraced ordinary, married Tom for ordinary, and yet she did have

strong feelings. *Particular passions.* She wrote to Travis about them. She wanted him to know what she loved. Sometimes she resented the way he seemed to want to use her as a blank canvas for his ideas.

Then, a few years ago, she let go of worrying about how he saw her. What did it matter? He was a few thousand miles away. She loved his dedication to an ape in the Congo. She admired his gigantic life. Sure, he could be self-involved, but Travis was a window to the world beyond, and Lily had gazed and gazed and gazed.

How strange to think that he too might now be in Berkeley, California.

Of course, Tom had known about Travis from the very beginning. He'd also been in Mrs. Saunderson's eighth-grade Language Arts class when she'd made the assignment to find an interesting pen pal. Tom had written a few letters to a professional baseball player who'd never written back. He called Travis "the monkey guy," even though Lily had explained to him dozens of times that bonobos were apes, not monkeys.

But that was Tom. There was so much he didn't want to know. Lily didn't understand how he could be a good lover yet have no curiosity about what love *was*. When Lily asked him, he would say, "Love is what I feel for you." Or if she asked him why people fight, the question at the heart of Travis's research, Tom would shrug as if the answer were obvious and say, "People fight because they're confused about what they need."

Tom was always so clear and accurate. His opinions came across as airtight. Surely, though, there were deeper, more complex answers, too. Surely love is more than a marriage, more than a matrix of family holding a person in place. And fighting encompasses wars that sweep across entire nations, countless body bags and raw graves. Can we really attribute that to *confusion*?

"Your Hahvard man," Tom sometimes called Travis, pretending good-natured ribbing. He'd shake his head at the parts of Travis's letters that Lily read to him; as if Travis's research was some kind of self-indulgence, a grown man playing with pets; as if trying to understand our relationship to other species were a way to avoid getting down to real work.

On the morning of the earthquake, Lily was telling Tom about Travis's latest letter and the bonobo slaughter. She'd just said, "It's devastating. I can't bear it," and he'd looked at her for a long time. The handsome planes of his face twitched in sadness, so she knew he felt it, but what he'd said was, "How can something that happened on the other side of the world be devastating to *you*?"

She'd been about to explain—to try, anyway—when the doorbell rang. The lock shop's only employee, other than Tom and his dad, plunged through the back door. "Turn on the TV," Angelina said, nearly hyperventilating. "Vicky's in Berkeley, right?"

Lily pointed the remote and the TV blinked to life. Tom got Angelina a cup of coffee, adding sugar and lots of cream.

Thirty minutes earlier, at 5:26 a.m. Pacific time, a 7.4-magnitude earthquake, on the Hayward fault with an epicenter just south of Berkeley, rocked the Bay Area. A reporter cruised the city on a mountain bike, transmitting his breathy dispatches by satellite phone.

Most people had ridden the twenty-three seconds of ground shaking in their beds but now gathered in the streets in case their buildings failed. One woman claimed that the quake started with a series of vertical jolts and finished off with horizontal jerks that threw her off the mattress and onto the floor. Another informant actually laughed—maybe she didn't yet know the extent of the disaster— and said that the quake felt like riding a galloping horse.

"My goodness," Angelina offered and grasped the small gold cross that always hung between her large breasts. She made that annoying clucking sound in the back of her throat.

The networks reported that hundreds, and probably thousands, of chimneys had crumbled. Houses had slid off their foundations. Apartment and office buildings with weak ground-floor parking levels had sheered and buckled. Glass panels exploded shards of glass onto sidewalks. The landfill supporting the Oakland airport had turned to liquid and the runways twisted and broke. Due to several weeks of rain and the thoroughly saturated soil, sections of many streets and highways washed away with mudslides. Houses tumbled down hillsides on gushes of wet soil. The earth, for those few seconds, became as viscous as blood.

Lily punched and repunched Vicky's number, eventually screaming at the recording that said the system was overloaded.

"Towers are probably down," Tom said.

Angelina reached for the remote, held it out with a straight arm, and punched the button hard, as if she could change the course of the news by changing the channel.

"If anyone is fine out there, it's Vicky," Tom added.

As if he hadn't seen the collapsed buildings and hysterical grievers! The fact of the matter was he couldn't bear thinking of the tragedy, especially if it might be touching their lives. Lily knew it wasn't coldheartedness. Tom cared about Vicky. But any challenge to the status quo presented a wall.

"Besides," he carried on, "there's good news: they're saying there are hardly any fires due to all the wet weather. That's the worst danger in an earthquake."

"True," Angelina said.

Lily grabbed her jacket and pulled on rubber boots. She slammed the back door and tramped through the tangled garden out into the fallow field. She walked fast, kicking at the clumps of frozen weeds. The owner of the field had been trying for years to sell it. She'd tried to talk Tom into buying it; a few years of alfalfa would feed the soil back to life. This once had been prairie and she loved imagining the native grasses undulating in summer winds, the hot smell of green. Now the field was nothing but cold and dead. Lily grabbed a couple of frozen dirt clods and threw them as far as she could. Then she turned and looked at the house she and Tom lived in. It was the one he grew up in, the one his parents had before they built their new one. A hard gray sky framed the house, sealing it in place. Lily's heart beat too hard, too fast, and she threw more dirt clods trying to dispel the charge.

When she got back to the house, Tom and Angelina still sipped coffee and stared at the TV, as if binge-watching a thriller series. How could he seem so detached? The networks burst images of California like buckshot, anything the producers could get their hands on to go with the recorded voices. They interspersed these with cell phone videos showing survivors clutching their children, speaking in rapid, anxious voices, or keening as they pointed at rubble that trapped loved ones. Next came footage of the Bay Bridge snapping apart, as it had done in 1989, but with worse results. Three cars hurdled like toys off the roadway and into the bay. Lily could see the passengers, the earliest commuters, inside the cars.

A teary reporter announced that she'd just learned that the Transbay Tube, which ran underwater from Oakland to San Francisco, had broken free from its ground attachments due to liquefaction. There were thought to be two trains trapped in the tube. At first the tube slowly bobbed to the surface, leaving open the possibility that passengers could swim out the ends before drowning, but then it quickly filled with water and sank to the bottom of the bay. Over and over again, the networks showed the same woman's body floating near Oakland's shore as the rising sun turned the water a hard copper color. The skirt of her business suit billowed around her thighs and her dark hair veiled on the surface of the water.

By suppertime the networks showed people on the move, looking for clean water or family members. Refugees were leaving the region, walking in small groups, heading east and south and north to communities that were still intact and could offer shelter. Because of the damaged roads, no wheeled vehicles were able to get out or in, but helicopters had begun airlifting injured people and dropping supplies. The hospitals, running as well as they could on backup generators, were already overwhelmed to the point of treating people in the parking lots.

"I need to go out there," Lily said.

"Where?" Tom asked, as if the place, the actual geography, no longer existed. As if she were crazy.

"Berkeley. To see if Vicky is okay."

Tom looked at Lily in a way he hadn't looked at her in months, maybe even years. For a moment, he seemed to really want to see her.

And he did. He saw her concern for her sister, for sure, but Lily saw him see even more: the way her longing for her sister triggered everything else. Launched her. His brown eyes went opaque. He looked away. "Vicky will be fine. You know that."

Over and over again, they watched the woman's skirt billow on the coppery water of the San Francisco Bay. They watched the bridge buckle and entire hillsides slide. They listened to the people's screams.

8

Lily pretended to be asleep as Joyce wheeled her bicycle out of the flat. Then at dawn she washed her face, buried the key in her jeans pocket, and set out. The most direct route to Vicky's house crossed the university campus, but when she reached the northwestern entrance, she encountered strands of plastic police tape and large signs forbidding admittance. The signs were painted over with graffiti in three languages, and she decided that even if there were anyone on campus enforcing the closure, she could claim to have not been able to read the signs due to the vandalism. She stepped over the plastic tape and walked up the tree-lined creek.

The deserted campus, with its half-toppled buildings, looked sinister, as if all the ideas had been set loose and now swirled in the cold, bright air like ghosts, knowledge severed from people. Fissures had torn apart lawns and felled giant oaks. A buck, two does, and a spotted fawn grazed in front of the Biology building. She tried to distract herself from the spooky vacancy of the place by reading the names of the disciplines carved into the stone facades. Travis had taught here after finishing his degrees at Harvard and before going to the Congo. Which building would be his? She realized she didn't even know his department. Biology? Cultural Anthropology? Psychology? He'd never said.

"Halt!" The voice came from behind. Lily turned and saw the three National Guard troops, guns drawn, inching toward her as if she were a known terrorist. "On the ground! Now!"

She flattened her belly against a broken chunk of concrete, the edge shoving painfully against her ribs. Her mind went white blank, blotto. She didn't know if she could breathe. The voices seemed to come from down a long tunnel.

"It's just some girl."

"She's not supposed to be here."

"Put your gun away."

The last words nibbled into her blasted-out consciousness. Gun. Put it away. Yes.

As she slowly regained the ability to think, she remembered a trick Travis had told her about. He'd been trying to get back to the sanctuary and got stopped by a couple of guys in the Congolese National Army. He hadn't known what they wanted and hadn't wanted to find out. So he'd flashed his library card and said, "*New York Times.*" The guards had waved him through.

"*Omaha World-Herald!*" Lily shouted to the troops. She reached around to her pack, but one of the men shouted, "Don't move!" They didn't let her off the ground until they were ten feet away and then ordered her to get up very slowly.

"Keep quiet." The guard shook out a pair of handcuffs.

Another one looked at his watch. "You taking her in?" he asked. "'Cause it's almost our break time and I'm hungry."

"She doesn't exactly look dangerous," said the third.

"What kind of pussies are you?" asked the guy with the handcuffs. "We're supposed to—"

"I'm just looking for my sister," Lily said.

"I thought you said you were a reporter."

"I did. But...I meant to say I'm from a small town in Nebraska. I flew into the Sacramento airport day before yesterday. My sister lives on Ridge Road. I'm going there now. I'm sorry I trespassed on campus."

"You're not allowed up in the hills, either. Everyone's been evacuated."

Lily knew from what she'd seen on TV that in fact not everyone had left. Some had refused to leave their homes. That would be Vicky.

The chunk of cement beneath her sneakers jolted hard to the left. A breath of wind rustled through the live oaks, making the dry leaves clatter.

"Shit," said the hungry one, looking around quickly at the stone buildings, as if the aftershock might topple them. "Shit."

"I'm leaving," she told the troops, her stomach queasy from the aftershock. "I'm just going now."

The rumble of the day's first helicopters drowned out her last words. Two Black Hawks scudded overhead, their undersides dark and menacing, the blades slicing the sky. She and all three National Guard soldiers craned their necks to watch them fly over.

The guard with the handcuffs took hold of her elbow in his big hand and jerked her forward. She felt the fear in his grip.

"Where're you from?" she asked, stumbling along at his pace. She didn't expect him to answer. She just wanted to establish their mutual humanity. She was scared, too. Maybe he was also far from home.

"Arkansas."

She said, "Tornadoes."

"Yeah."

"You?" she asked the hungry one.

"San Diego."

"Wildfires."

The third one laughed. "North Dakota. Fucking blue balls."

When they reached the edge of campus, the man loosened his grip but didn't let her go. So she threw her other arm around his neck and hugged him.

"Stay safe," she said, as if she were the one tasked with guarding the public. Then she disengaged her elbow and walked away, heading down the hill, toward downtown. The men at her back remained completely silent. They let her go.

Once out of sight, Lily circled back and headed up the hill, staying clear of campus, taking any road that had a walkable surface. She scaled up-sided slabs of pavement and stepped over downed phone poles. She passed collapsed carports and crumbled chimneys. Because they'd evacuated the neighborhoods in the hills, and because the people who lived here were generally wealthier and therefore had places to go and the means to get there, these streets were even more deserted than the ones in the flatlands. An unnatural silence swarmed the abandoned homes. At least until the Black Hawks circled again. When they did, she hid under cars or behind piled rubble.

Following routes on her map was impossible. Entire streets were missing. Others were impassable. Time and again she got lost and had to turn back or look for alternative routes. The sun burned high in the sky, hot and brazen, when she saw a couple more National Guard soldiers. They were playing baseball on the brown grass of a park, using a two-by-four for a bat and dirt clods for balls, laughing each time one of the clods exploded. She kept a wide berth of the park and they never saw her.

Finally, after too many wrong turns, she reached the top of the ridge. She headed south along Grizzly Peak Boulevard until she saw the sign for Ridge Road. Vicky was two blocks away.

Lily had spent her childhood protecting her older sister. One summer evening, when the girls were ten and twelve years old, they were shooting baskets on the school playground. Vicky rattled on about the physics of a perfect shot, the math of the ball's arc. She had gotten too hot that morning and shaved off her hair. The bald-headedness had put her in a particularly happy mood. She'd said it made her feel free. Two boys who shot baskets at the other end of the outdoor court kept up a running commentary about Vicky's head. She flipped them off. One of the boys asked her to do that again. So she did, in that blind-to-consequences and good-natured way she had. The boy shoved her to the ground and cocked back a leg, getting ready to kick. Lily threw what was left of her warm Coke on the attacker, but he kicked Vicky anyway, so Lily hurled herself onto the boy's back and clamped her small hands around his neck, squeezing hard. As skinny as she was, with her legs wrapped around his torso, the bully had trouble loosening her hands. The tactic worked. After he managed to throw her, he and his friend ran, spitting and shouting. Lily liked to think she'd had one of those endorphins-drenched moments when people perform superhuman feats of strength to rescue loved ones.

By the time she got to high school, people started noticing Vicky's remarkable luck. Good stuff just happened for her, like the time she won a few thousand dollars at the dog races, or when she found Mr. Selby's gold watch and collected the finder's reward. Senior year she asked Brandie Gustafson to the prom, and Brandie said yes. Vicky liked to say, "It's all in the math," which maybe would have made sense except that she applied that even to Brandie. When Lily asked how she could use math to convince someone to be her date, her sister only wagged her eyebrows like Groucho Marx.

Lily and Tom were sophomores then, so they weren't allowed to go to the dance, but Lily made him bike out to the Marriott anyway. All evening they sat outside in the dark, cross-legged on the lawn, where they could see a lot of the dance through the floor-to-ceiling plate glass windows. Vicky prowled around the big room, drinking Cokes and talking to some of the other kids. She appeared to be laughing a lot. Once, near the end of the evening, she stepped outside, by herself, and looked up at the stars. She wore ill-fitting tux pants, too tight in the crotch, the suspenders entirely unnecessary. She hadn't ironed her white shirt and had the sleeves rolled up. She wore a rose-colored bow tie and no jacket. She wasn't smiling and her body slumped, as if she were beyond weary. Lily wished she'd just keep walking and go on home, but she turned around and went back to finish out the prom. Nothing happened that night, except that Brandie danced with a lot of boys but never with Vicky.

Vicky left Fair Oaks right after graduation, and most people predicted she'd be back by the end of the summer. Her luck wouldn't hold in the world at large. Her grades had been barely passing and she wore boys' clothes. People were kinder then, but they spoke of her as if she were prey. Only her math teacher knew that she could do large square roots in her head and explain the theoretical possibility of time travel. Only her family knew that she could take a computer apart and put it back together. The math teacher convinced her to be tested, but the school principal dismissed the results. He told the family that there was nothing even remotely useful about doing square roots in one's head, and he described her test scores as being some kind of fluke—or maybe a form of mental illness.

In the Bay Area, Vicky landed well-paid jobs in the electronics sector, where she could do just about anything as long as no one made her dress up or come to work at a certain time. She made a fortune designing a popular computer game called Ziggle, based on string theory, in which players could travel to and colonize not just other planets but other universes, and over the years she'd become a legend in Fair Oaks. Now even her former tormentors claimed a hand in nurturing her gift. People were always asking Lily if it was true that Vicky owned an Alfa Romeo and homes in both Aspen and Maui. Now folks said that Vicky had needed to leave Fair Oaks, that they had encouraged her to do so. California, they liked to say, was perfect for Vicky.

Lily ran down Ridge Road. She knew which house was Vicky's even before checking the street number. The place was sleek, a horizontal sprawl of three attached, module-like boxes. Someone, probably Vicky, had stripped the surrounding grounds of all landscaping and covered the area with gravel. A handsome array of solar panels covered the roof of the largest, middle module, tipped in orderly unison, looking like glassy ornaments. Even the colossal satellite dish on the garage fit the design of the house, an extravagant hat offsetting the elegant simplicity. The roof of the module closest to the street sloped up toward the west, allowing a big plane of windows to look out at the San Francisco Bay.

Of course the place looked untouched by the earthquake. Vicky's luck.

Lily walked up the flagstone pathway to the front door. Her sister was probably sitting at the kitchen table eating a sandwich.

Lily pressed the doorbell but didn't hear any dongs or chimes, and so she knocked, and then pounded. "Vicky?" she shouted. "Vicky!"

She walked around to the back of the house and tried the back door. Locked.

Professor Vernadsky hadn't seen her since the earthquake. Twelve days ago. What if a beam had fallen on her? Or a gas leak had poisoned her as she slept? Surely neighbors, ones more hardy than the old man, would have checked on everyone before fleeing from the area. Wouldn't they have?

Lily returned to the front, pried a loose flagstone out of the pathway, carried it back down the side of the house, hefted it over her head with the sharpest corner pointing forward, and heaved the rock into a window, shattering the glass. No alarm went off. It took several more bashings to make a big enough hole. She picked out the shards and climbed through.

Books covered the basement floor. There were no bookshelves, so they must have been stacked in towers around the perimeter of the room before the earthquake. She looked at a couple of spines and found what she expected—gaming theory and neutrinos, quarks and gluons, the origin of mass.

As Lily climbed the stairs to the first floor, she heard a series of faint thumps. Like footsteps. She stopped midway up the flight and listened. Would Vicky be hiding out in her own home? Afraid of marauders? Maybe no one answered doors. Maybe Lily was terrifying her sister right now, sending her scurrying into a hiding place.

Was that a door shutting?

When she reached the top of the stairs, Lily called out, "Vicky! It's me! Lily!"

All she wanted now was to see Vicky's smile. She'd ask for nothing more in life, she promised herself, if she could just see her sister's healthy zealous self. Vicky would probably scold her for coming all the way out here for "no good reason." Anyone else would be angry about the broken window, but Vicky would double over laughing at the image of her little sister heaving a flagstone through the window in her rescue mission.

"Vicky!" Lily shouted as loudly as she could. If Vicky had shut herself in a closet, who knew what she could hear. "It's ME! LILY!"

Lily walked into the open design of the top floor. A blond hardwood floor sat like a stage before two steps leading down into the white shag rug of the sunken living room. Floor-to-ceiling windows framed sunny views of Angel Island, Alcatraz, San Francisco, and the Golden Gate Bridge. Several large oil canvases, monochrome abstract pictures, had fallen off the walls. One frame had busted, crumpling the canvas. The massive, wall-mounted home theater screen, which had survived the quake, gleamed like a black mirror. The midcentury modern chair collection, nearly a dozen of them, was scattered randomly about the room.

The place had Vicky's name all over it, a kind of ostentatious ugliness, as if she'd aimed for lavishness but lost interest before finishing. Vicky always understood the ephemerality of her good fortune. That was the problem: she understood it too well. For Vicky, everything was fleeting, episodic, smoke and mirrors. At best, life was one good joke.

Lily called out her sister's name again as she stepped into the kitchen. Bits of quartz sparkled like tiny stars in the granite countertops. The stainless steel pulls, cold little bars that looked like miniature nuclear reactors, matched the appliances. The cabinets were a rich cherrywood. All of it was false evidence, like purposely placed decoys, planted to hide Vicky, the real Vicky. The Vicky who stood in her ill-fitting tux, looking up at the stars, slumped in sadness.

Lily pushed a hand through the pile of mail on the kitchen table, mostly unopened bills. One opened envelope was propped against the toaster. Lily pulled the sturdy sheet of stationery out of the envelope. Printed in purple ink across the top were the words, "From the Desk of Sal Wieczorek." Below, in an angry scrawl, was the message: "Fuck you. Don't call, come by, text, or email me again." The note was unsigned and there was no return address on the envelope.

Oh, Vicky. She'd no doubt done something worthy of the anger. Sal was the first woman she'd ever spoken of more than once or twice. About a year ago she'd called to say she'd fallen in love. Then she'd laughed and laughed, as if she'd said something as absurd as she'd become a vampire. Tom said Vicky had intimacy issues, which was probably true. Some people said she was autistic. Lily thought it was probably just a healthy dose of Attention Deficit Disorder. Whatever it was, she didn't stay focused on anything that wasn't science-related for more than a few weeks, including lovers. Sal was different. Lily heard about their nights playing Scrabble (shockingly domestic for Vicky), the vintage Harleys they bought together, the wine storage system they'd designed and were trying to patent, and Sal's hyenas. Sal sounded eccentric as hell, but who else would appreciate Lily's sister? Vicky said she laughed at all her jokes and that they had "cataclysmic" sex.

Many years ago, when Lily was fifteen years old and before she'd realized that her sister liked girls, she'd had the brilliant idea that Travis and Vicky should get together. The idea had been triggered by an unusually personal letter. Usually he wrote about the bonobos, but this time he told her about his breakup with a girlfriend.

Dear Lily,

How strange it is that my work explores questions of love and compassion, and yet I am not able to sustain a loving relationship. It rains today. The big glossy green leaves, rainforest fans, are dripping, dripping. My hair is soaked from walking for hours. I was looking for Candace and her baby Gillian. They're doing so well since they left the sanctuary. I love finding them nested high in a tree bed or loping along the floor of the forest, the baby's eyes wide with wonder, Candace watching out for danger. They know me. She smiles.

Right before we released them back into the wild, Yannick had to bring his own little baby to work one day. His wife had a doctor's appointment in Kinshasa. He was all out of sorts about this. I asked him why he didn't think it was his duty to help care for his young ones. He never appreciates my "Americanized" remarks. But when he carried his little Monique into the nursery, a look of delight crossed Candace's face. Her eyes just lit up. It was the most beautiful thing. Her baby Gillian was sitting on the ground a few feet away, gnawing on a mango pit, and Candace swept her up off the ground and carried her over to Yannick. She held Gillian up, under the armpits, for Yannick to see. Her delight was that they shared parenthood, that they both had beautiful daughters. Gruff Yannick couldn't resist Candace's charm and he laughed and laughed, and they both cuddled their baby girls, enchanted with love.

This is what I live for. I can't leave the sanctuary. I can't leave the bonobos. And I can't leave this dripping, wet, luscious forest. And yet.

Can I tell you everything? Do you mind?

Oh, yes, fifteen-year-old Lily practically panted as she read the letter. *Yes, tell me everything.*

Louise left me. The pain of that loss wracks through every joint in my body. And yet, I can't make myself do what she wants, which is go home. She doesn't want to live in the Congo and who the hell can blame her? I told her when I came here two years ago that I would stay just one year. After that I'd come home and we'd get married. But I didn't come home. I begged for another year.

Last month she flew here to get me. We had a great week together in Namibia, staying at some resort she'd found. Everything went great until, at the end of the week, she gave me a deadline. A short one. She said I had to be home by summer, by June to be exact. Or it was over.

I know she didn't mean to manipulate me with the cushy comfort of the resort, but it felt that way. I wish she'd told me her agenda upfront, so I could choose. She said she hadn't because if I'd said no—and here she paused in this heartbreaking way, the look in her eyes saying that she was pretty sure I would say no— then she wanted one last full memory with me. We would always have Namibia, she said, trying to be funny with the cliché.

The only thing I'm proud of is that I didn't ask for another year. I wanted to. I almost had to bite off my tongue to not say it. But the truth is, the poolside lounge chairs and fresh linens and fancy sauces over butterflied shrimp stirred an almost unbearable impatience in me. I can't stand resorts. I can't stand being idle. Most of all, I can't stand being away from the apes. I'd be sitting there listening to Louise tell me about one of her students, and I could think only of Rosa's leathery soft palms or Malcolm's earnest round stare. Their pink mouths wide open in their hoarse, breathy laughter. I had won their trust and to leave now would be to abandon much more than a few creatures. It would be to leave the last of a species, our hope for understanding why people fight and more importantly, how they cooperate. What it means to care for a community.

So Louise flew home. And I stay here in this crazed country where I have apes for love. I guess I'm crazy.

No, no, no, fifteen-year-old Lily hotly defended her pen pal as she inhaled the imagined scent of ape off the sheets of international airmail tissue and pictured perfectly the slow drifting Congo River. *You're not crazy. You're passionate. And right.*

Love, he wrote for the first time, Travis.

Lily touched that word, over and over again.

Still, she harbored no illusions. Lily knew that Travis was too old for her. Too smart. Too exotic. But, it dawned on her soon after receiving this letter, he would be perfect for Vicky, side by side with their brains and zeal. She carried the slim packet of letters, all the ones she'd received so far, to Vicky's bedroom and asked her to read them. She did. She read every last letter, in order, and Lily was gratified to have found something that intrigued her sister.

"This is very cool," she said to Lily when she finished. "Are you going to go visit him?"

Visit him? The thought had never occurred to Lily, but she pretended it had. "They'd never let me."

Vicky shrugged.

"But you'll be eighteen next year," Lily said. "*You* could go."

Vicky turned back to her laptop. "Why would *I* go?"

Lily knew her answers were ludicrous: because the Congo would suit you; because we have to do *something* with you; because she could imagine what might ignite between Travis and Vicky.

She'd already written to him about her sister. He was the one person she could tell Vicky stories to without feeling disloyal. She wrote a new letter then, searching for words to express condolence but hardly finding them—she was only fifteen—and so resorting to describing Vicky in much greater detail than ever before, stressing her good humor and extreme intelligence, hinting at her vulnerability, and insisting on her kindness.

Lily dropped the fantasy when later that year Vicky started carving girls' names into her bed frame, launched her blog for girl physicists, and wrote a Social Studies paper on Valerie Solanas's *SCUM Manifesto*. It wasn't the lesbian content, the principal told their parents, it was the threat of violence in Solanas's message. The parent/principal conference went nowhere. No one could accuse Vicky of behavior that even hinted at anything violent or threatening. In fact, this incident brought about Vicky's first experience of peer support. A small group of kids, the ones who ran the literary magazine, including editor Brandie Gustafson, organized a protest when Vicky got an F on the paper while Brett Wadsworth, who wrote his paper about the men who had murdered abortion providers, got an A. Vicky smiled and held her own council.

It became clear to Lily that Travis was not going to be the answer to the problem of Vicky. It also became clear that Vicky planned on solving the problem of herself on her own. Like that was going to work out any better than taking Brandie Gustafson to the prom. In fact, Lily hadn't had an opportunity to rescue Vicky since her failure to do so that prom night. Until now.

And this time was no dance.

"May I help you?"

Lily screamed and dropped to the kitchen floor, spinning around on her hands and knees to face the scratchy male voice.

"Sorry," said the freckled, sinewy man. "But who are you? What are you doing here?"

He stared down at her, the blade-like Adam's apple shifting up and down his throat, like he was nervous. Lily reached up and grabbed the edge of the kitchen table but she couldn't get to her feet. "What are *you* doing here?" she choked out.

"The bitch who lived here had some equipment that belongs to me."

Bitch? Lily rasped, "Where is she?"

"For real?"

Lily huffed to her feet. "*Where is she?*"

"She's gone."

"Gone *where*?"

He squinted and stepped toward Lily. "Look, I'm sorry if she was a friend of yours or something, but she's *gone* gone. As in, a lot of people didn't make it."

"No," Lily said, resisting the pull of an icy vacuum. "I don't believe that."

"To be honest, neither did I. At first. But I heard she bit the dust. And every time I come by to look for my stuff, she's not here. So."

"No."

The man cut his eyes to the side, scratched his neck, and started for the door.

"Wait!" Lily shouted not so much at him as at the cold, black hole sucking her into its vortex. "I need to see her. I need proof."

"Proof? Good luck with that. In any case, Vicky is kaput." He appeared to enjoy being the messenger of this news.

Lily couldn't stand another second in this awful man's presence. Kalisha would know where they took people. As if life were a board game and she needed only to get to that room, that clanging hothouse of humanity, to be safe, Lily turned and ran out of Vicky's house, down Ridge Road, and all the way to Trinity Church.

9

THE RISING SUN WAS a bright orange ball of jarring light and Kalisha liked it that way. Let it burn away the ache. Distract her from the void.

She sat on the cement stoop and watched daylight define Trinity Church's parking lot. The sheet of gray became cracks and weeds. A trapezoid of sunlight showcased the graffiti on an exterior wall of the church.

She knew that girl wouldn't be back. Tall and pale, like a eucalyptus tree, a strong gust of wind would blow her right over. The way her earnest gray eyes warped at the sight of the devastated clients. Sponging, mopping, asking everyone about her sister, she shot her wad of courage in one shift. Probably even felt righteous, like she'd contributed something. No, she wouldn't be back.

It hardly mattered. Without money, Kalisha couldn't keep the meals program going. She'd be out of food in two days. Her only option was Michael, and hard as she tried, she couldn't imagine her way to him.

She tossed the rest of her coffee out on the parking lot pavement and went inside to take a shower in the bathroom behind

Pastor Riley's office. After stripping, she stood looking at her skinny naked self in the mirror, unable not to care how Michael would see her. Well, shit, he knew what she looked like. No doubt he'd spied her on the street now and then, just as she'd spied him. Besides, he was married with children. It didn't matter that she wasn't beautiful anymore. After her shower, she put on a fresh shirt and pants and then took another look, squaring her shoulders at her image. "Hey, beautiful," he used to say when she answered the phone.

Instead of heading out the door, Kalisha scanned the bookshelf in Pastor Riley's office and plucked the copy of William James's *The Varieties of Religious Experience*. Two hours later, she was still reading, as if she could make up for lost physical beauty by tuning up her brain, as if Michael would quiz her on ethical and spiritual questions before writing a check.

For eight years, ever since she got out of prison, Kalisha had been avoiding actual contact with Michael. For each of those eight years, he'd sent whopping checks, once as big as thirty grand, usually more like ten or fifteen thousand, to the meals program. The checks came in December each year, his left-sloping handwriting as painfully dear to her as his face used to be. Every once in a long while, she'd see him on the street, but they didn't exactly haunt the same urban geographies. He dined at Chez Panisse, took hikes in Tilden, bought clothes on Fourth Street. She stayed close to downtown, the church, or other shabby public spaces used for NA meetings. If she did happen to see him, she detoured quickly, and they never spoke. She deposited the checks each December and used the money to buy food, utensils, a new stove.

It would have been easy to attribute the checks to his guilt, but she didn't let herself be that petty. He had loved her. He respected her journey, even though he hadn't been able to stay on it with her. And who could blame him?

Sometimes she did. They started it all together. She lost control. He didn't.

Michael and she were the only two black students in Cal's graduate program in Philosophy. They knew others expected them to hang out together, to have lots in common, and so they avoided each other at first. She thought he was a little pompous with his outsized Afro, high-water slacks, and persistent scowl, as if to make clear that he was always deep in thought. But she soon learned that he *was* always deep in thought. It took about two months for them to fall in love, and it was a love Kalisha had thought she'd never have—a man who respected her intelligence, who wanted to ask the biggest questions in the universe. Their most pressing practical problem was figuring out how they would find jobs at the same university because no one was going to hire two African-American philosophers in the same place.

In their second year, they dropped acid together. Most students of the mind do so at some point in their studies. It was fascinating to consider the frontiers of brain chemistry. And oh my, the universe they viewed. They believed they actually saw the colors and shapes of justice. Seeing that ideas could take on physical attributes moved both of them so deeply that they took a course in art history as a result.

Moving on to trying heroin—they always called it that back in the beginning, not dope, not smack; they were PhD candidates at a prestigious university—was not so common among their peers. It was a dangerous drug. She and Michael knew that. But it never, not once, occurred to her that there was something she couldn't do, that she would lose control. They experimented together twice. Making love while high was like swimming in the purest form of joy. Afterward, she experienced a quality of peace like none other.

Michael never used again. For him, the experience had been clinical research. He knew any further use could be deadly. Of course Kalisha knew that, too, yet she sought out and used the drug a couple more times without him finding out. It was impossible to hide the needle marks for long.

Kalisha used to be very angry at how quickly he jumped ship. He suggested she get help. He gave her the contacts for a couple of programs. Then he distanced himself from her in every imaginable way possible. He slammed the door shut hard.

By the time she was busted, she'd already dropped out of the graduate program. You couldn't exactly teach undergraduates, read hundreds of pages a week, and write a PhD thesis while high. She went to jail for two years. Of course any white girl in a PhD graduate program at the University of California would not have gone to prison, but her family in Chicago had no money to pay for lawyers, and anyway, she'd been too ashamed to ask them for help.

Her doctoral advisor, Professor Vernadsky, did everything he could. He made phone calls. He hired a lawyer. He testified on her behalf in court. It's possible that his involvement did more harm than good, given his eccentricity—and that was before the dementia— but Kalisha loved him for trying.

Professor Vernadsky wrote to her the entire time she was in prison, every single week. He wrote about what he was reading and how his philosophical views were changing. He'd quote Aristotle, the bits about the first condition for the highest form of love being that a person loves himself; how without an egoistic basis, a person can't extend sympathy and affection to others; how self-love is not about glorifying oneself or indulging pleasure; how it's about reflecting on what is noble and virtuous; how the reflective life is the highest form of self-love—and also the first step toward loving others. Professor Vernadsky managed to convince Kalisha that prison afforded her a small glimmer of opportunity because there she could reflect to her heart's content. His letters saved her life.

When she got out, Kalisha came back to Berkeley because she didn't know where else to go. Her grandmother had died, her father didn't want her in Chicago embarrassing him with her felony, and her mother reluctantly supported him. Professor Vernadsky, a longtime friend of Trinity Church's Pastor Riley, got her the job running the meals program. Living in the church hadn't been part of the deal, but getting an apartment in Berkeley as a felon was next to impossible, never mind making rent on her salary.

By then, Michael had earned his doctorate. She didn't know if he even tried to get a teaching job. He worked in insurance now and made lots of money. He was married with three kids and lived on La Loma Street. Just a few miles away. She could walk there now.

But even if he'd stayed after the earthquake—and he wouldn't have, no one with means had stayed—he'd need all his resources for his family. It was a stupid idea to walk to his house.

Kalisha sat reading in Pastor Riley's office until early afternoon when it was time to join Ron in the kitchen. Four o'clock came and went. The tall white girl was a no-show, as Kalisha knew she would be. At four thirty, she opened the door for the clients and served out the trays herself.

Someone always pounded on the door just after she locked up, and she never let them in. She knew some of the clients considered her hard-hearted, as if her strict adherence to rules were a sign of severe misanthropy. In truth, it was just the opposite. Keeping this program going kept her alive, kept lots of other people alive, too, and to do the job, she needed structure and boundaries. Maybe someone else could be looser, but she was the one running the meals program. Sometimes those rules and boundaries, that structure, felt like the only things holding her together.

So why she cracked open the door a quarter past six tonight, she didn't know. Maybe because she happened to be standing right there, next to the door, when the knocking occurred. Or maybe she sensed a significant presence. In fact, only Lily stood on the other side of the door, saliva frothing at the corners of her mouth and sweat running down her temples. Blood slathered her hands and a reddened cut messed up her left cheekbone.

"Please let me in."

"Food's already been put away."

"I didn't come for dinner."

"What happened to your face?"

"I tripped over a piece of rebar and fell onto another one. I'm so sorry I didn't get here on time tonight. I—"

"Excuse me?" A young dark-skinned man bounded up the cement stairs behind Lily.

"Closed," Kalisha told him. Then to Lily, "Listen, lady, I'm—"

"Lily. My name is Lily."

"Excuse me!" the young man called out again.

"We're *closed*," Kalisha told him.

"I'm looking for Kalisha Wilkerson."

"For what?"

"A delivery."

"A delivery of what?"

"I'm only supposed to speak to Kalisha Wilkerson. You're her, right?"

Kalisha nodded.

As the man handed her an envelope, a loud crash came from the community room, followed by shouting. Kalisha ran back inside as the two fighting men tumbled onto another folding table, knocking it down and scattering the diners. Plastic plates clattered to the floor. Four men helped Kalisha break up the fight and push the offenders out the door.

Lily used the distraction to slip inside. She put on latex gloves, wetted down a mop, and began wiping blood off the floor. Kalisha pretended not to notice. She dropped into a chair next to Professor Vernadsky, who smiled at her through peanut butter cookie crumbs. He said, "Whoops," presumably referring to the fight. When Lily finished mopping up the blood and rinsing out the mop, she sat down across from Kalisha and the professor.

"I'm sorry I was so late," Lily said.

"Two hours late is not late, it's a no-show."

"I went to my sister's house, and she wasn't there, and then I got completely lost on the way back down the hill."

Lily looked like she was in shock. She stumbled through her words and Kalisha guessed that the news wasn't good. Plus, she was a bloody mess from the rebar fall. "You need some Band-Aids."

"Where do they take bodies?" she asked.

Kalisha heard about newly confirmed deaths every single day. Survival meant not letting herself feel the emotional wreckage barreling through this room. Her job was to put food on the table. Keep people acting civilly. Occasionally dispense information.

"They don't. They bury them where they are."

Lily just stared, two vacant eyes.

Kalisha reached into her back pocket and retrieved the envelope. She looked at it for a long time, wondering who in the world it could be from. She didn't like mysteries. She tore open the seal. "Oh my god."

"What?" Professor Vernadsky asked.

Michael. As if she'd summoned him with her thoughts. She passed the check to the professor.

"Aristotle would be proud," he said tapping a finger on the dollar amount.

"A miracle," Kalisha said, her heart uncomfortably full. He still loved the part of her he could. It *was* a miracle.

"I doubt it," said the professor. "Just one good man doing right."

10

Rain fell all that night and continued to fall the next morning. Lily stood at the kitchen window of Joyce's flat and looked out at the downpour beating the weedy soil. Everything hurt. The trek yesterday from Vicky's house to the church had been hell. She'd staggered for what felt like hours from broken street to broken street, tears blinding her, as if the hilly neighborhoods were a maze designed to trap her in exhausted grief.

This morning, the word *gone* migrained through her skull. She needed to get to the word *body*. That was her next task, what she had to find. But her mind was a thicket; she couldn't see through the brambles.

Lily found a black plastic garbage bag under the kitchen sink and punched three holes in it, one for her head and two for her arms. She left Joyce's flat and slogged over to Kittredge Street where the public library was slated to reopen today. The crowd waiting for it was in high spirits. The wet survivors stomped their feet rhythmically, as if they were at a baseball game, and good-naturedly shouted for admittance. Street vendors spread cloths on the puddled sidewalk and laid out their wares, ignoring the sheeting rain and taking advantage of the gathered potential customers. One sold homegrown lettuces and zucchinis, another hand-dipped candles. One woman held a sign, the ink running, that claimed she could, for five dollars, find a missing person.

"How?" Lily asked her.

The woman tapped her temple and said, "Psychic."

Lily peeled off a five-dollar bill. She could just hear what Tom would say. But even in Nebraska, police departments used psychics. It wasn't that crazy, was it? The woman told Lily to concentrate as hard as she could, to imagine her sister in full detail. Lily squeezed her eyes shut and conjured Vicky's oblivious cheerfulness, deep intelligence, warm brown eyes, pelt of short, glossy hair, scattered presence.

After a few moments, the psychic started laughing.

"What? What are you laughing at?"

"What a goof!"

"Who?"

"Vicky! She's a real character, isn't she?" The psychic spoke with her eyes closed, her chin tipped up, and a beatific expression on her face.

"But where is she?"

"At home!" the woman cried out, and then chuckled again.

Lily felt an intense stab of anger. The woman preyed on grief-stricken survivors. She was worse than the marauders, in a way. At least the marauders acted out of animal honesty rather than calculated emotional exploitation.

She was about to tell the woman that she was a fraud, a scam artist, a swindler, when a spiky-haired librarian opened the front door and shouted, "We're open! Come on in!" A loud cheer went up and the crowd pushed into the library. Lily turned her back on the psychic and followed the stampeding library patrons in.

The elegance of the library interior was disconcerting. The massive slabs of marble and the dark oak molding harkened back to a time when opulence and books went together. The building had fared well in the quake, although lots of books had been thrown from the shelves. They lay splayed open and piled, in total disarray all over the floors, but still seemed to hum with hopeful knowledge. Volunteers had salvaged generators from abandoned schools and homes and installed them in the library to run computers and charging stations. Librarians had posted signs announcing meeting locations: Volunteer Road Repair in the Children's Room; Solar Panel Salvage and Installation in the Art & Music Room; Missing Persons Forum in the 600s, on the first floor. Librarians and volunteers shouted directions and library patrons clamored for help.

The line for the computers already stretched dozens of people long, so Lily found the phone books. Sal Wieczorek lived on Sea Breeze Court. Lily consulted her map; the address was most of the way back up the ridge. Yesterday Professor Vernadsky had shown her a direct route that used paths and avoided the National Guard posts. He'd marked it on her map with a canary yellow highlighter he carried in his shirt pocket, as if always on the ready to markup hefty philosophical tracts.

Clearly Vicky and Sal had been on pretty bad terms when the earthquake happened. But wouldn't she have looked for Vicky anyway? Wouldn't the earthquake have subverted her anger?

Lily slumped into a chair and stared at a wall. She didn't want to leave the warmth of the library. Anyway, she needed to call Tom and her phone was still dead.

The librarian whose job it was to guard the phone-charging station handed Lily a numbered tag matching the one she taped to Lily's phone. As Lily knelt down to plug her phone and charger into the last available outlet, a familiar voice said, "I want that phone. Give it here."

Lily stood and faced Annie. Binky hovered a few yards behind her, squirming uncomfortably at his friend's aggressiveness.

"Hi, Annie. How are you?"

The fat girl reached out and touched the scar under Lily's chin. "Someone try to slit your throat?" As she pulled her hand away, she left her middle finger extended.

"Come to the church for dinner tonight," Lily said.

She wandered into the reading room where volunteers were picking up books and reshelving them. Lily joined the effort, smoothing out bent pages, reading call numbers, and brushing off covers before setting them in their places. The spiky-haired librarian placed a boom box on one of the long tables and popped in a CD. Patti Smith's voice, like the soaring Art Deco windows, filled the room. Some volunteers danced the books to the shelves. Others read passages out loud, shouting to be heard over the music. It was pouring rain outside, but the library patrons were warm and drying out, happy to be working. Happy to be together. How Vicky would have loved these raucous strangers.

The phone-charging librarian fetched her after a while, when her phone was fully charged, so that the outlet could be used by someone else. Lily thanked her and, since she still had two hours before she was due at the church, got in line for the computers. That way she could save the charge on her phone; but more, she liked standing in the line, talking to other information-seekers, immersed in the warm, lively mayhem of the library.

First she wrote Vicky. It was macabre—and yet she couldn't not do it. As if cyberspace were some in-between place where the dead could still receive messages. "I love you," she wrote. "I hope you didn't suffer. I miss you. You're like a phantom limb: an intense presence and absence, simultaneously."

It did help, a little bit. Maybe that's what prayer was like. Speaking into the mystical void.

The fact of the matter was she had a friend, a real friend, nearby. She typed in Travis's email address. Even after the sanctuary got wired, he'd continued writing to her on paper and by hand. They'd only very occasionally emailed each other. Travis said he was a tactile person, that he needed pen and ink and paper, a physical connection to his friends. He proudly resisted technology, which struck her as unusual for a scientist, but then he had lived and worked in the Congo for so long. The bonobos, after all, did not have email, and his job, in a way, was to channel our intimate ancestors.

"I'm in Berkeley," she wrote. "I came to find Vicky. I've learned that she didn't survive the earthquake. I still need to find her—"

How do you type that word when it's your sister?

"—body. I serve dinner at Trinity Church on Bancroft Way every evening. I get there by four and leave about seven. If you're in Berkeley, please come by. I'd like to meet you in person! Your friend, Lily."

Tapping *Send* felt good. Urgently good. Her whole life Travis had been a private fable, a story attached to her by a filament of infrequent letters. Now she'd turned her entire life inside out. Her sister was gone, her husband hundreds of miles away, but Travis was right here. His message of hope pulsed neon. To think he was an actual person. One she could actually meet.

The church that evening smelled like wet dog, and the meals program clients weren't as cheerful as the library patrons. As she came through the service line, Annie gave Lily the finger again, and Lily gave Annie two cartons of milk. The girl's extended middle finger wilted and her hostile glare withered.

Lily dug out spoonfuls of hash and clanked the metal spoon on the plastic trays to release the food, over and over again, letting the rhythm of the movement hold her. She didn't need to tell any of the clients taking the trays that her sister was gone; everyone here hurt, too, had their own missing loved ones. Sharing that without having to talk about it, meeting other eyes soft with sadness, comforted Lily. At the end of her shift, Kalisha put a hand on her shoulder and squeezed gently, a thank you.

By seven o'clock, the rain had stopped. Lily climbed the hill as a full moon rose over the ridge. The air was cold, tangy, urgent.

Before the earthquake, Sea Breeze Court had been a short dead-end street. Now it was a dark hole. Sal Wieczorek's entire street had washed away in a mudslide. Roofs and stucco and window frames were crumpled along the route of the slide. Reminders of daily life—a mangled stand-up lamp, a toilet, a sodden bed—were stuck like fossils in the hardened mud. Lily picked her way across the slick surface. When she fell, she slid ten yards before hitting the trunk of a downed eucalyptus, leaving most of her body covered with earthy red slime. She lay in the mud and listened for a moan, a squeak, a breath. For anything human.

The moon glowed steady and cool.

It didn't look like anyone on Sea Breeze Court had survived. Lily couldn't bear the idea of her sister being buried in this rubble. But she wouldn't be, would she? She and Sal had quite clearly broken up.

She dug her phone out of her backpack and turned it on. She held it up to the moon, feeling like an early hominid asking for sanctions from the nature deities. Then she tried Vicky's number. She held the phone as far from her ear as possible and listened to the landscape, hoping to hear the ringtone—Space music? Wolf calls? Just beeps?—coming faintly from under the wreckage.

But nothing.

Just moonlight.

11

LILY LAY ON THE uncomfortable couch, her back aching, and stared at the framed print of Van Gogh's *Sunflowers*. Travis had seen real Van Gogh paintings in Paris. He'd written that the difference between looking at a Van Gogh print and looking at the original was as great as the difference between looking at a piece of chocolate and tasting it. Lily hoped so, because she just didn't see much in those creepy and slightly ridiculous sunflowers. Globs of yellow, blue, and brown paint. They looked as deranged as the painter seemed to have been. Who *can't* think about his ear when looking at one of his paintings?

The sunflowers trembled and the black plastic frame rattled against the wall. The entire couch shuddered. Another aftershock.

Lily stood and paced through the flat, stopping at the kitchen window. Moonlight washed the backyard in silvery light. Soggy blossoms covered the branches of the plum tree. Beyond the tree, tangles of wintering-over vegetables filled two raised beds. It would soon be time to begin spring cleanups in her clients' gardens.

"Let someone else do it," she said out loud. Then she looked over her shoulder, as if afraid someone had overheard her abandon.

Lily pulled her phone out of her pocket and tapped in Tom's number. She should have called him earlier in the day. He'd be asleep now. Maybe that's what she wanted: to catch him in an unalloyed state. She wanted the boy, the one who'd sledded with her when they were children, not the man who was so angry with her.

"Hey."

"Where are you?"

"Joyce's flat. There was another aftershock just now."

"You okay?"

Lily opened the back door and stepped out into the moonlight. She grabbed a handful of plum blossoms and squeezed. Rainwater ran down her forearm.

Tom waited.

"She's gone. She didn't make it."

It took Tom time to digest. Then all he could manage was, "No."

She understood. Vicky was a scream stuck in her throat. There were no words. And yet she had to find some. "It just doesn't seem possible."

"Yeah. I was sure she'd—"

"Well, she didn't."

"I'm so sorry."

"Yeah."

He listened to her tears for a moment and then said, "I'm buying you a plane ticket. SFO has reopened. You can take the ferry over."

"I have to find her."

"But you said..."

"Her...you know, remains."

"You can go back and do that in a few months. When things settle down."

"I need to find out what happened. I can't just leave her...her story...out here alone. I found where Sal lives."

"Who's Sal?"

"Vicky's girlfriend. I told you about her. She's the caretaker for some university researchers' hyenas."

When she'd first told him about Sal and her job, he'd laughed and laughed, and then said, "Only in Berkeley. If it's even true."

"Her entire street was demolished." Lily squeezed her eyes shut but couldn't block out the picture of Sea Breeze Court, the slick mud and random fragments of people's lives.

"I'm so sorry," he said again and then moved back into action mode. "I'll buy the ticket."

With her eyes still closed, Lily reached for her husband: his easy smile, the cowlick on the left side of his hairline, his loose gait. He'd been shortstop on the high school baseball team, and she'd loved the way his thighs looked in his uniform, especially when he squatted, dropping his mitt to the dust on the ground between his legs, scooping up a hard-hit ball. That image of him could still hold her, seemed symbolic of the straightforward way he approached life. His calm, low voice could ease any distressed old lady who'd locked her keys in the car. His big square hands could pick any lock. He was so good at problem solving. She'd once jokingly told him that he should run for president, and he'd laughed out loud, liking the compliment, apparently believing that he actually could handle the world's problems. And just like that, her admiration curdled. What she used to admire as his confidence she grew increasingly to think of as a kind of folk arrogance. He started so many sentences with, "It's simple. Those guys just need to..."

"I miss you," she said, and it wasn't a lie, just a very complicated truth. "Come home."

Lily wished she heard desire in those two words. For her. But she didn't. She heard only his aversion to the gaping unknown.

In the morning, Lily took a cold shower and set out. She needed to face the possibility that Vicky and Sal had somehow patched things up, that they were both on Sea Breeze Court the morning of the earthquake. But until she had definitive evidence of some kind, Lily wasn't giving up on finding her sister. Someone, somewhere, had to know something. Kalisha said they buried the bodies where they found them. She would look for a fresh grave in Vicky's backyard.

Maybe the psychic was right after all: maybe the "goof" was buried at home. By the time she reached the top of the ridge, the sun burned bright and warm. She turned onto Ridge Road.

A faint knocking sound grew louder the closer she got to Vicky's house. She soon realized that the sound was coming from inside the garage. Just as she arrived, the drumming stopped and the garage door began to lift open, a foot at a time. Lily backed up several steps before peering into the dark cavern, bracing herself for the creepy guy with the blade nose.

She saw the shiny chrome of a motorcycle leaning on its kickstand just inside the opening. Beyond, amid piles of outdoor equipment and household detritus, what appeared to be an upside-down double kayak lay across two sawhorses. A shadowy figure let go of the manual garage door opener, walked around to the backside of the kayak, and resumed beating the hull with his hands.

Was he living in Vicky's house? How'd he even get inside?

A voice bellowed out of the garage. "What the hell! No way!"

As he moved to the front of the cavern, and then out into the sunlight, Lily saw what she expected to see: freckled ropiness, a guitar pick Adam's apple, slit eyes, baby-fine hair. Her body stiffened in defense. She tried to find better words than, *Get out.*

But it wasn't him. There were no freckles, no prominent Adam's apple. This person was shorter, stockier, with clear skin and a thick head of short hair.

Lily's vision tunneled. Vertigo swept through her body, tingled, and then evaporated her head. She collapsed onto the driveway pavement.

"Whoa! *Hey!* What are you doing here? Are you okay? Lil? *Say* something!"

She pressed her palms into the gritty driveway pavement and struggled to stay conscious but barely succeeded. The vertigo dizzied her head and nausea swam out her limbs.

Vicky sat next to her, leaned against her. "Man, am I shocked to see *you.*"

"You..." Lily whinnied. "*You* shocked to see *me?*"

That feeling when you wake up from a nightmare and realize the horror wasn't real—that feeling, magnified by ten.

"Well, yeah. I mean, how did you even get here? Wait. You didn't come out here to look for me, did you?" Vicky snorted back a guffaw.

Lily managed to lift her head. Look at her sister. Who was suppressing *laughter.*

"You look bad," Vicky said. "Real bad. Let me get you a glass of water or something. Maybe a shot of vodka? Ha ha."

Lily reached up and touched her sister's face, half expecting her hand to go right through a ghost. Her voice was still a wheeze. "A man was here yesterday."

Vicky looked at her with astonishment, as if Lily's appearance was the bombshell. "Yesterday?"

"At your house."

"You were here yesterday?"

"He said you were gone."

"Yeah, I've been staying with Sal."

"What do you mean you've been staying with Sal? I went to her house. Or tried to. Her entire street is wiped out."

"She's staying out at the hyena compound, in the toolshed."

"I thought you two split up."

"How do you know about that?"

"I saw the note on your kitchen table."

"When were you in my kitchen?" Vicky looked flabbergasted.

"A man was here. He said you were dead."

"Oh. Paul. He still believes that shit?" A big grin.

"This is so not funny, Vicky."

Vicky blew a raspberry. "Whoa. Wow. No, I could see how it wouldn't be funny. To you." She snorted back another chortle. "No, I'm not laughing. I mean, I am. But you know me. It's what I do. I mean. Are you okay?"

What Lily wanted was to let the vertigo, nausea, iciness, and bone-weariness just take her. She wanted to lie back on this hard cement and pass out. Take a nap and wake up to sanity. How could she have forgotten how crazed conversations with her sister could be? And this one already promised to be a doozy. She forced herself to push aside the shock.

"Do you know this man?"

"Sure. He's my neighbor. He's Gloria's husband."

"Who's Gloria?"

"Paul's wife. My neighbor."

"What was he doing in your house?"

"That's a good question!"

"How did he get in?"

"Oh, he has a key."

"Why does he have a key?"

"Paul is head of the neighborhood association. You know the type, only place they have any power. Anyway, before the earthquake, he asked me to set up a Wi-Fi network for the street. So I did. That's how I got to know Gloria. I gave him a key so that if the network went down, and I wasn't home, he could come recycle the equipment."

"Why did he tell me you were dead?"

Vicky pointed at the camellia, blooming with deep red flowers, next to the open door of her garage. "Careful. Bees."

"I can tell when you're not telling me something."

"It's not worth telling. Gloria told him that. To protect me, so she says, though I think she was mainly protecting herself."

"I don't understand."

"Simply put, Paul is pissed off at me."

"Because you have his equipment?"

Vicky laughed. "No, I don't have his equipment." She used air quotes on the last word and ramped up her laughter. Then she faked a fresh realization. "Oh, his *electronic* equipment! Yeah, sure, I have it, but how can I give it back if I'm dead? Anyway, it's just one stupid router and one outdated laptop. I don't think he quite believes Gloria that I'm dead. He's using the equipment as an excuse to stake out my house. The good news is that I know for a fact he's making a trip to San Jose and won't be back until late tomorrow, at the earliest." Vicky grinned.

"He told me you were dead!"

"Yeah, I agree. That's intense. Uh, Lil? You really do need to be careful. The bees out here are feral. I'm just saying, because in California they're out year round, those that are left. We have wasps, too. The whole stinging gamut." She used her finger to pantomime a stinger and made a buzzing sound.

"Never mind about the bees!" But Lily did reach into her pack and feel around for her epinephrine auto-injector. She closed her fist around the plastic tube. "It's not just this Paul guy. Why haven't you called since the earthquake? I've been out of my mind with worry."

"God, I'm really sorry. I'm really, really sorry. I just figured you'd know I was okay. Besides, I lost my phone."

"You lose your phone about three times a year."

"So you should have known I was okay, that my phone was just lost. With the earthquake and everything shut down, I couldn't exactly replace it." Incredulously, Vicky's tone slid into defensiveness. As if Lily were the crazy one. "You came all the way out here to find me? Wow."

"You could have borrowed a phone to call your family."

"I'm sorry. I just didn't—I mean, it didn't occur to me— I'm really sorry."

"So you and Sal are back together?"

"No. We've just been having a little postapocalyptic fling. Kind of like breakup sex, only it's lasted for a couple weeks. She's really, really mad at me. Oh, shit. Hold on a minute. I have to finish this up before the glue dries."

Vicky rushed back into the garage where she bent to stir a wooden paddle in a metal can. She smeared some of the thick, black goo on the tops of two skateboards. Carefully grasping them by the edges, one in each hand, she pressed them against either side of the bow end of the kayak's hull.

"So anyway, besides playing dead for Paul, I've been sort of hiding from my landlord. He was sending me all these threatening messages, so I closed out my email account a couple of weeks ago."

"I thought you owned your house."

"I sold it last year. The buyers bought it as investment property and I'm renting from them. It's a good deal for them because I take care of the place. And yet they're still evicting me."

"They're evicting you?"

"They say I haven't paid rent in eight months."

"Have you?"

"I guess not. I was planning on moving out, as requested, but then the earthquake happened. Bonus days with Sal! I knew she'd be out at the hyena compound because she goes in to work at five in the morning. Meaning, she'd have been safely there when the earthquake hit. She was so glad to see me! She couldn't hide her relief that I hadn't gotten knocked unconscious, or worse, by a crashing bookshelf or something. In fact, she was so happy to see me that—"

"You don't have bookshelves."

"Smart, right? Anyway, she let me stay for a while. She has a generator and is pumping water from a stream. How could she turn me out? Then she did. I can't stay here. The Floreses gave me a deadline of midnight tomorrow. So I opened a new email account and put everything on Craigslist."

Lily could barely keep up. "Why'd you sell the house in the first place?"

"I needed the money." Vicky floated her hands off the two skateboards. "Excellent. We have adherence. Believe me, once dry, nothing can compromise the stick of this glue." She walked over to the Harley and touched the place where a burst of sunlight glinted off the chrome. "A guy's coming to see the bike in a minute. For a second, I thought you were him."

"You love that bike. You and Sal were going to ride across the country."

"I guess the earthquake put an end to that plan. She's a beaut, though, isn't she? Nineteen sixty-six Harley Electra-Glide with a shovelhead engine."

"The earthquake didn't put an end to that plan. Whatever you did to Sal put an end to it."

"She's crazy."

"You were just crowing about having bonus days with her."

"Disaster-induced happiness."

"You said you loved her."

"I do. I mean, I did. But I made a mistake."

"About loving her?"

"No. A behavioral mistake."

"Can't you fix it?"

"I guess you could say I made a series of mistakes. At a certain point the critical mass of mistakes makes them insurmountable."

Vicky sagged, a quick little emotional collapse, and then she rallied. "Check out my wheeled kayak! I'm making it land-worthy." She picked up two more skateboards from the floor of the garage, smeared the tops with the glue, and pressed them on either side of the stern hull of the kayak. This was twelve-year-old Vicky, the kid Lily grew up with in the heart of the country. You could never tell if she was a hundred paces ahead of everyone or a hundred paces behind.

One of the honeybees zipped over to Lily and buzzed around her head. Adrenaline propelled her to her feet. Anything with a stinger— yellow jackets, bumblebees, hornets—could kill her. She stepped into the garage and put her hand on the sleek white leather seat of the Harley. "What about your royalties from Ziggle?"

"A thousand new games have superseded that relic. But I'm working on a new one! It's called *Dark Matter*, and—"

"Do you have anything, any money, at all?"

"Stone-cold broke."

Lily knew the Alfa Romero and luxury homes were myths, but she'd believed her sister to be wealthy. "So, what are you going to do?"

"Do?" Her sister spoke as if getting evicted and being stone-cold broke weren't problems that needed to be addressed.

"You could come back to Nebraska with me."

Vicky looked at her for a long time, as if for once she were choosing her words carefully. "Wild horses couldn't drag me back there. You know that. Don't even try."

"How pissed off at you is this Paul guy?"

"Stop with the suspicious sister thing, okay? You came out here to rescue me but you're going to have to let go of that. I don't need rescuing."

"Oh, Vicky." Dumped by the love of her life. Broke. Homeless. Stalked by the head of the neighborhood association. But no problem. She had everything under control.

"Thank you, though," Vicky said. "Can I hug you?"

12

A TALL, SLIM MAN with a fresh haircut appeared at the top of the driveway, apparently traveling by foot. He wore a tight white T-shirt, an open, worn-out black leather jacket, skinny black jeans, and scuffed dress shoes.

"You the guy selling the Electra-Glide?"

"Yep." Vicky didn't bother correcting his gender assumption.

The man touched the headlight, and then glanced at Lily. "She's beautiful."

He had brown almond-shaped eyes with long lashes, a large forehead, and a cowboy nose. Two lines, long parentheses, enclosed his mouth, like his smile would be a secret. His pale white skin gleamed under the sheared sides of his short black hair, but a longer boyish lock flopped in front. A worn copy of Virginia Woolf's *Orlando* stuck out of his back pocket.

He ran two fingers around the circumference of the front hub, touched the chrome spokes. "I'd like to ride her," he said. "Before deciding."

"Sure," Vicky said.

"You should take a deposit," Lily advised.

"It's cool. Go for it."

Lily scowled at her. The man could just disappear with her motorcycle.

He pulled a wad of bills from his front pocket, peeled off several, and laid them on top of a pile of suitcases. "That's the full asking price. Looks like she's in great shape. I just want to ride her first."

"Absolutely." Vicky waved a hand at the cash as if it were inconsequential. "Take her for a spin."

"I'm Wesley, by the way."

"Vicky. This is my sister, Lily."

The man threw a leg over the bike and walked it out of the garage. He looked over his shoulder at Lily and said, "Come along?"

Vicky wore that prurient smile of hers. She wagged her eyebrows.

All at once, relief slammed into Lily. Vicky was alive. *Alive.* Ridiculous. In trouble. But alive.

So was Lily. Intensely, heartbreakingly alive. A sense of freedom, of wild possibility, rushed in where the vertigo had been just minutes ago.

Lily climbed on behind Wesley and grabbed two handfuls of his leather jacket. As if she were in one of Vicky's virtual gaming worlds where there were no real-life consequences of risky behavior. As if she regularly climbed on the backs of motorcycles with strange men. The copy of *Orlando* poked out of his back pocket, hitting her thigh, so she slid it out and tucked it inside the front of her own jeans. Just underneath the pungent smell of leather was a fresh scent, like green grass. Lily breathed it in, then felt embarrassed about her own smell. She'd showered this morning, but her clothes were pretty ripe. When she turned to wave goodbye to Vicky, her sister gave her a salacious wink. Lily gave her the finger.

Wesley lifted his feet and gave the bike gas. They motored down Ridge Road, turned left onto Grizzly Peak Boulevard, and headed for the top of the hill. He drove too fast for the broken road. Many of the rifts had been bridged with dirt and rocks and scrap lumber, but rather than inching over these sections, he gassed up the bike and bounced over the patches. He banked the Harley on the sharp turns, putting Lily at a forty-five-degree angle to the road. She could have dropped a hand and touched the pavement. She let go of his jacket and wrapped her arms all the way around his middle, pressed her cheek against the baby-soft leather.

As they crested the top of Grizzly Peak, she looked down on the glittering bay. She'd heard about the flotilla of sailboats occupied by a group of people who could simply sail away but chose to stay near home. She saw them now, the boats forming an armada, a tiny navy, the sails fluttering like handkerchiefs. Beyond the bay, the Golden Gate Bridge arched like an elegant collarbone, burnt-red against the blue sky, with the headlands on either side like soft green shoulders. To the north, Mount Tamalpais hulked black and sturdy. San Francisco's buildings stood tall and blocky, as if there'd been no earthquake at all.

The wind felt so good. The speed was intoxicating.

Alive. Vicky was alive. The relief kept coming in bigger and bigger waves, like tsunamis of joy.

She shouted, "Vicky is alive!"

Wesley looked over his shoulder and then accelerated, soaring down the backside of Grizzly Peak. Twice he leapt the Harley over crevices, like he was Evel Knievel. All her fears merged into thrill. She unlocked her hands and slipped them inside Wesley's unzipped jacket. His ribs felt prehistoric, his torso as skinny as grief. She slid one hand up his breastbone and held it, open-palmed, over the place of his heart. So bold. Like Travis's apes.

She laughed out loud, remembering an incident Travis had written to her about. A bonobo named Madonna got jealous when Travis had been playing with another one for too long. She ran over to him, locked her hairy legs around his middle, and smacked him on the lips. Before he knew it, Madonna had pushed her tongue in his mouth! "What a whiskery kiss," he'd written. "For the bonobos, sex is love. I think they're right."

Lily had looked up bonobo sexuality that evening and had been shocked to learn about their freewheeling ways. Not only did those apes have sex often and easily, not to mention with a variety of partners and in a multitude of styles, but scientists thought there was a correlation between their embrace of pleasure and their compassionate nature. Tom had been skeptical, but even he found the idea intriguing.

Well, Lily was a human being, not a bonobo, but apparently there wasn't a whole lot of difference between the two when it came down to the DNA, so she left her hands where they were and pressed her cheek against the soft leather on Wesley's back.

He took Fish Ranch Road to the freeway where the National Guard had a checkpoint. Two troops waved their arms in big X's over their heads, but Wesley didn't stop. He roared right by, flying along the deserted freeway, swerving around the shells of abandoned vehicles.

Then, suddenly, he braked hard and bucked the bike to a stop. Lily pulled away from his back and saw that they'd come to a fissure too big to jump. On the other side of the crevice were four crashed and spun cars. A head, a human head, appeared in the closest car's back window, like the ghost of a crash victim. Wesley cried out and then checked a sob in his throat, cutting it off, sounding as if he were gagging. His chest cavity inflated and deflated in big scared woofs.

Lily kept her arms around him and stared in horror. It wasn't a phantom. It was a living person. The head ducked back down, out of sight. He or she must have been living in the cavity of the car. Maybe there was a stream nearby. Lily pressed the side of her head against Wesley's back, needing the hard physicality, the vitality, of contact with his body, even if he was a complete stranger.

He walked the bike around 180 degrees, then sat still for a moment, looking out in the distance, his breath calming. On the way back, he drove slowly, though he still didn't stop at the National Guard checkpoint. When they reached the top of Grizzly Peak again, he pulled over.

Lily dismounted. Wesley climbed off, too, and put down the kickstand. They stood side by side looking out. So much air and sky, the bay a frothy slate green.

"Boy, that was spooky," he said. His voice was extra deep, almost comically so given his skinny nerdiness.

"I know." She wanted to step closer to see if she could get that grassy smell again.

"So you saw it, too? The head?"

"Yes."

"It's like...I don't know...the gap between alive and dead no longer exists. Here in the earthquake zone."

"I thought Vicky was dead until about an hour ago."

"I heard you shout her name."

"You just kind of take life for granted. And then, boom, you don't." Lily checked his face to see if he understood. "It changes everything."

Wesley nodded and scrunched up his face, suppressing tears. There was a little sunken place, over his solar plexus. Lily touched it. "You lost people."

"Yeah. Lots."

Lily had stopped saying the words *I'm sorry*. They were useless out here.

"My boss and my mom and my ex-wife. My sons lost their mom and grandma in one fell swoop. I'm buying the bike so I can go to see them."

"Where are they?"

"In Eugene. What about you?"

"I was at home in Nebraska. I came out here because I hadn't been able to contact my sister."

Wesley nodded. "I was driving my cab, taking a woman and her son to the airport. We were on an overpass that collapsed. How I survived, I don't know. I carried the kid all the way to the bookstore, my other job. Those first few days, I'd sit on the roof and watch the Black Hawks hover over victims. Men in fluorescent jackets being lowered in swinging cages. Plucking people from the piles."

"With the kid?"

"He died. I buried him behind the bookstore." His deep voice was clear, not gravelly, an echoing cave.

"Will you stay in Eugene?"

Wesley didn't answer for a long time. "Most people are desperate to leave here. I assumed I'd leave, too, as soon as I got the means.

But I don't know. I've been interviewing survivors, people who've stayed, by choice or otherwise, and posting their stories." He glanced at her. "My blog is called *The Earthquake Chronicles*. People need to tell their stories. To witness and be witnessed. It's something I can do."

His words made her think of the way she felt behind the steam table at Trinity Church, that acute sense of well-being as she handed out trays of hot food. To keep him talking, she asked, "Which job did you like best? Driving the cab or selling books?"

"The two jobs had a kind of symbiotic relationship. I mean, most of all, I love stories. Sometimes I think they might be the only thing that can save a culture. The way we talk about ourselves to each other. So I liked driving the cab because motion helps me think, especially in the middle of the night when the streets are so peaceful. That's when I'd get the best ideas for my novel. But then during the day I got to talk to people about books. I liked sussing out customers, figuring out what they wanted, even when they hadn't asked. Like, someone would come in for a Zagat guide and I'd convince them to leave with Alice Munro or Sherman Alexie.

"But Ramon was always pressuring me to drive more. He said he couldn't afford to leave a car with a driver who only used it part-time. Sometimes I had to take off in the middle of a shift at the bookstore to pick up a fare. Cynthia threatened to fire me about ten times.

"Geez," Wesley said. "I'm talking too much."

She didn't mean for her silence to be agreement. She was only thinking about stories saving culture and wondering if he knew about the bonobos. But he jumped back on the bike and started the engine, drowning out her eventual, "No, you aren't."

He didn't turn off the engine in Vicky's driveway, just shouted thanks, and waited for Lily to slide off. Then he opened the throttle and purred the bike down the street, his scuffed dress shoes resting on the foot pegs, his knees jutting out.

"Look at you," Vicky said. "All flushed."

13

OKAY, THIS ONE'S A 1929 Le Corbusier. Gorgeous, right? It looks like a woman lying down. A woman in cowhide. Go sit in the one hanging by the window. It's the Eero Aarnio Bubble Chair."

"What'd you do to chase her off?" Lily asked as she flopped onto the metallic silver cushion inside the clear orb. She pushed her feet against the carpet and swung herself.

"Those over there," Vicky pointed, "are my Eameses, including the Time-Life and four from the Evolutionary Aluminum Group. And, hey, look! The molded maple plywood Isamu Kenmochi!"

"You said you loved her."

"A Pierre Paulin back-to-back. And my Pierre Guariche La Vallee blanche daybed. All originals. All in pristine condition."

Lily swung herself higher in the bubble chair and said, "You always sabotage yourself."

No one knew her like Lily did. She supposed she could just fess up to the truth—which was that she hated this wrung-out feeling. No algorithm could address how much she liked Sal. It made her crazy, actually, thinking about the nutty mad fun they had. Sal's big-mouthed toothy laugh was her favorite thing in the world.

But that was the exact kind of thinking she needed to ditch. She needed to move on. Moving on was all about distraction. To stopgap the devastation and aloneness, she'd had to find a project, and she had, a brilliant one. Making the kayak land-worthy. Vicky couldn't wait to try out the new vehicle. But how would she propel it? Pushing sticks instead of paddles? If she hadn't just sold the motorcycle, she might have attached the motor to the wheeled kayak.

"I asked you a question."

Lily was here! How awesome was that? An even better distraction. Lily always calmed her. But this line of questioning needed to be aborted.

"I saw that look of abandoned thrill on your face," Vicky said.

"Now what are you talking about?"

"Lily Jones, the sensible one, joyriding with a complete stranger."

"He left you with a few hundred dollars. And he's reading Virginia Woolf. How dangerous can he be?"

"You kept his book. Guess he'll have to come back and get it."

"Don't change the subject. What'd you do to Sal?"

What a stroke of luck, the earthquake! The planet's crust shook hard, shuddering away the dreck, and left standing two women, on a hillside, all alone, their senses of humor and libidos intact. It was perfect. For a hot second, anyway.

But yesterday Sal couldn't have been clearer: the past two weeks were disaster-induced intimacy, nothing more. Her face all red the way it gets, she'd spelled it out: O-V-E-R. F-I-N-I-S-H-E-D. "I don't understand," Vicky had joked. "Could you just say what you mean?" No smile. Not even a swat of her hand to indicate the joke was really stupid. Sal just jammed her shovel into the dirt and continued turning over the soil in her vegetable patch.

Someone knocked on the front door and Lily leapt out of the bubble chair, as if she expected armed mobsters to bust in.

"Get a grip," Vicky said. "It's probably just the wine guy."

The big man was impeccably dressed in gray flannel pants and a pale green shirt. He held out a large, warm hand.

"So, you actually got a car up here?" Vicky asked him.

"I have a Subaru and there are doable routes, if you know where they are."

"Cool. Come on. I'll show you the wine."

"Exquisite," he said, hefting a bottle. "Wow. You have this? I didn't think there were any bottles left. Oh, and look at *this*."

A few minutes later he handed Vicky cash for the entire collection while Lily looked on with mute astonishment. When he went out the door to get his hand truck, Vicky said to her sister, "Craigslist is awesome. You can sell anything. And fast. Which is a good thing because I only have about ten percent charge left on my computer."

Would Sal let her come by, just to recharge her computer on the generator? Probably not.

"They're calling them Vultures," Lily said, that huffiness in her voice, signaling that she was about to explain something for Vicky's benefit. "People who buy up stuff from desperate people. At rock-bottom prices."

"Do I look desperate to you?" Vicky laughed at the look on Lily's face. "No, no, you're right. I sort of am, aren't I? I mean, I have to be out of the house by midnight tomorrow. And I need cash. So whatever the Vultures want to give me is very welcome."

"Sorry I'm late," said another man letting himself in the open front door. "Let me have a look at the chairs. I'll tell you right up front, people always think their knockoffs are originals." The slight but muscled man shifted across the room as if he were too caffeinated. He glanced at his watch.

"Originals," Lily said. "Every single one."

Ha! Lily was rallying! Vicky winked at her loyal sister.

The antiques dealer squatted before each chair, touching lightly, and began to almost vibrate with excitement, though he tried to conceal his avarice with a scowl. He commented on the small wine stain on the cream-colored upholstery of the Pierre Guariche. With its radiating stainless steel arms and legs cradling the daybed's seat, that piece was the most sensuous of the collection.

"I like the wine stain," Vicky said. "It's from a very silky Pinot I drank with Sal the night I taught her how to play chess. It adds intrigue, a touch of eroticism. Do you know—" Vicky continued, turning to Lily. "She actually beat me a couple of times. That woman's mind is whacked, but—" *Don't think about Sal.*

The dealer fingered the deep scratch in the Kenmochi. Vicky whispered to Lily that that had been made intentionally, with a car key, by a former girlfriend who stopped by unannounced and found Vicky with another woman. "*In flagrante delicto.*" She wagged her eyebrows. "Don't you think the arms on that chair, the way they curve wide, look like a woman's hips?"

"Hardly pristine condition, as you claimed in your ad," the man said, flicking his fingernail against the scratch.

Lily jumped in with, "Are you kidding? For chairs this old and beautiful? This is about as pristine as they come. The stain can be removed. The scratch is an easy repair."

The wine guy rolled three cases of wine by on his hand truck. He winked as he said, "These chairs are all midcentury originals, aren't they? Beautiful."

The antiques dealer did the watch trick again. "I've got to go." He waited for the wine dealer to get out the door with his load. "Look. You said you needed to be out by tomorrow."

"You put that on your Craigslist ad?" Lily nagged.

"I'm willing to help." The man pulled out his checkbook, scrawled a figure and his signature. He ripped off the check and handed it to Vicky. She glanced at the amount and tore it up.

"See?" she said to Lily. "I have things under control."

"It's a very generous offer," he said. "Take it or leave it."

"Cash only," Lily said.

"Hey," the wine dealer called from the front door. "I'm done. Come with me out to the car for a sec, will you?"

Lily followed Vicky out, as if she needed a bodyguard.

The long-limbed wine dealer climbed onto the Subaru's tailgate and swung up his legs, flipped over onto his hands and knees, and dug into one of the cases. "Ah. Yes. Here it is." Scooting back to sit on the tailgate, his legs dangling, he handed Vicky a musty bottle. "Stony

Brook Cab, 1984. Worth at least a hundred and drinking perfectly right now. Elegant." He kissed the bunched fingertips of one hand. "This is nirvana in a bottle."

"Hey, thanks!"

"Always give a little back," he said with another wink. "Wine is about so much more than business. It's poetry and friendship. It's art. History."

"See," Vicky said to Lily, right in front of the man. "Not everyone is a Vulture."

The antiques dealer stood in the front door and called out, "I'm very late for my next appointment. I'll make you one more offer, but it's my last." He flapped another check at Vicky.

"Just take it," Lily said. "We can cash it in—"

She caught herself, but Vicky knew she'd been about to say "in Nebraska." That wasn't going to happen. But checks could be cashed even here, if you knew where to go. Vicky took the check and walked back inside the house. She sat in the Kenmochi and caressed the curve of the wood, and then tore the check in half. "Nah."

"Vic." Lily actually snapped her fingers, as if bringing Vicky out of a hypnotic state. "You're moving. You have no way of taking these chairs with you."

"The wine guy got his Subaru up here."

"You don't have a Subaru. You don't even have a car."

"I'll go up five hundred," the Vulture said. "I know you're in a bind. But that's it. Don't play with me. I'll walk."

Vicky named a figure three times greater than the one he'd written on the check, mostly for Lily's benefit, to keep from getting scolded for not trying. But she didn't want to sell her chairs. They were so gorgeous and awesome and unique.

The man sniffed hard and left, tossing his card on the Le Corbusier.

"Where's that bottle? Let's celebrate."

"Celebrate what?"

"Life!" Vicky settled into one of the troughs of the Paulin back-to-back and used the corkscrew on her Swiss Army knife to pull out the cork.

"God, I'd love to get my hands on one of Paulin's tongue chairs. It'd be like resting in someone's mouth, your whole body held by her *tongue*."

"Do you know that bonobos tongue-kiss?"

"Ha! You still in touch with that ape researcher?" Vicky took a swig. "*Mm.* Good."

"Actually, he might be here. In Berkeley." Lily fell into the other trough of the back-to-back chair.

"No shit. Try this." Vicky handed the bottle over her head.

Lily took a swallow. "Piquant nose. Sexy legs."

Vicky hooted. "It's opening up nicely. Cherry musk. Hints of leather restraints. Silky panties finish."

Lily laughed. "You still haven't told me what happened with Sal."

"Tell me you weren't a bit besotted with that motorcycle fellow."

"What are you talking about?"

"The way you looked when you got off the bike."

"I'm married."

"What's that got to do with it?"

At least Lily laughed. But then she said, "You're coming back to Fair Oaks with me."

Just the sound of those two words, Fair Oaks, made Vicky shudder. "Are you in trouble or something? Lil, what's wrong?"

"No. *You're* in trouble. You're broke, remember? You're trapped in a disaster zone. Also homeless."

The words *trapped* and *disaster* gave Vicky a little frisson of pleasure. She chuckled.

"It's not funny."

"I'm not going anywhere."

"Where are you going to live?"

"I'll find an apartment."

"There *are* no apartments."

"Are you kidding? There're tons of apartments. The entire East Bay population has fled."

"Most of the city is still without power and water. There's hardly any food."

"Granted, it's all a little dicey. Nothing I can't ride out."

At first, when Sal still believed that Vicky could be reconditioned, she'd said, "Look. Natural selection rewards only those mutations that have highly favorable adaptive qualities, ones that enhance survival. Intelligence is definitely a positive trait. But not wildcard intelligence. Not random intelligence. A person needs a trajectory to go with her intelligence, a plan for it, ambition, and the ability to take steps toward a goal."

"I have goals," Vicky had said.

"Exactly. Goals. Plural. Like five million."

Vicky should have said, "*You're* my goal."

But Sal wouldn't have liked that, either. She wanted something romantic for herself. Goals when it came to house payments and jobs, yes, but complete and total abandonment of reason and success probabilities when it came to their relationship. Sal wanted fate and destiny. Sal was flat-out impossible.

"Victoria."

"Yes, Lillian?"

The sisters snorted short laughs. Then Lily went back to serious. "Maybe this one is something you *can't* ride out."

"I'm sorry. I really am. I should have called. I made you come all the way out here to find me. That's just plain fucked up. I'm sorry. But I'm not going back there. I'm staying here."

Lily heaved a big Lily sigh. Weight of the world.

"Okay," Vicky said. She figured she'd toss her sister a bone. "You're right about one thing."

"And that is?"

"Paul."

Lily twitched uncomfortably but waited for Vicky to elaborate.

"Which makes Sal right, too. I should have said those words to her: 'You're right.' Maybe I'd still have a place to live. Not to mention a girlfriend."

Okay, Vicky admitted to herself, she was in a little bit of trouble. Maybe Lily *could* help her. Just keep talking. Try to tell the story. The real story.

But that was the problem! How could anyone tell what was real?

"So she left you because of Paul?" Lily sounded incredulous.

"Partly. She has a list two pages long of why she left me. But he was definitely a deal-breaker."

"You're not...like...*involved* with him?"

"Oh gag. Hell no! Are you out of your mind? *No!*"

"So then what...?"

"She thought he was dangerous."

"Is he?"

"Please. The head of the neighborhood association?" Sometimes Vicky hated herself. Why did she fake bravado? With Lily, of all people.

"He was in your house."

Thank god Lily and Sal had never met. Vicky could just imagine how they'd enjoy ganging up on her. But she really did have this one under control: by the time he got back from San Jose, she'd be long gone.

Vicky shrugged, hoping to convey nonchalance to her sister.

Of course it didn't work. Lily was looking more alarmed by the second.

"Hello!" called a voice at the front door. "I've come to see about the bed and TV you're selling."

"Excellent," Vicky said, speaking both to the woman at the door and to the interruption of Lily's interrogation. She plunked the wine bottle onto the floor and launched herself out of the Paulin back-to-back chair. "Right this way!"

14

A FTER FINISHING AT THE church, Lily flew across campus on the bicycle Vicky had given her. Her black plastic garbage bag raincoat flapped in the wet breeze. Another fight in the Trinity Church community room, this one more like a brawl involving six men, had kept her late mopping up and discussing security measures with Kalisha and Ron. Meanwhile, it'd gotten dark and begun to rain again. She usually avoided the campus, which was still strictly off-limits to the public, but it was a much shorter route, especially on the bike. If she went fast, Arkansas, San Diego, and North Dakota might not even see her.

Despite the bloody fight, despite the lashing rain and deep darkness, Lily felt reckless and elated. The hundred-dollar Cabernet still trickled through her bloodstream, along with the endorphins from her motorcycle jaunt with the skinny man. Mainly this: *Vicky was alive.*

Nothing could take away the pure joy of that knowledge. Not even the sketchy circumstances of Vicky's situation. Maybe those circumstances even added to Lily's happiness. She wasn't crazy to have come. Vicky needed her.

She let herself in the door and careened happily into the front room, shouting, "Victoria! I'm home!"

The first thing she saw were the twitching flames of a dozen candles reflected in the floor-to-ceiling windows. Next she saw her sister sitting on the floor, back against one of those windows, elbows on her knees, holding a bottle of wine. Another woman, artificially blonde and plump, wearing a tight, lime-green cocktail dress, swung in the bubble chair. Matching lime-green heels rested on the carpet beneath her. Lily was pretty sure this wasn't Sal.

The woman startled out of the bubble chair, emitting a little cry of distress, hitched one of the heels onto her foot, and reached for the other. Her sudden movements caused the candle flames to shimmy, and one taper tipped over. Wax pooled onto the white shag carpet. Lily could hardly blame the woman for being alarmed. She probably looked crazy dressed in the black plastic garbage bag with holes cut out for her head and arms, wet hair plastered to her head, and snot running from her nose.

"Please meet my sister, Lillian." Vicky spoke in a smooth and suave voice that Lily wouldn't have recognized.

"Just Lily." She gave Vicky a stern glance and held out a damp hand. The woman placed a couple of shiny red claws against Lily's palm, withdrawing them quickly.

"I serve dinner at Trinity Church's free meals program," Lily said, as if that explained something. "There was a big fight tonight."

She shot Vicky another, less concealed look of pissed-off inquiry: *Who is this bimbo? And I thought you sold all the wine.*

"Gloria lives down the street," Vicky said, her eyes doing that evasive thing.

"Well, that's handy." Lily rustled down the hall to the bathroom. She peeled off the plastic bag and shook the rainwater into the bathtub.

Then, on second thought, she walked back down to the living room. She intended to remind Vicky of her impending homelessness and the need to deal with it. It was time for the floozy to go home.

Neither woman heard her reenter the big living room. They'd begun some lesbo scenario, which Lily really didn't want to see, so she skulked back to the bedroom. Her good mood fizzled. She was cold and tired. She really didn't need Vicky's shenanigans—

Wait. Gloria.

As in, Paul's wife, Gloria?

Lily lowered herself onto the bed and tried to wrap her mind around what she thought she'd just seen. It wasn't possible. Not even with Vicky.

Yet that was exactly what was happening: Vicky was kissing her neighbor Gloria, Paul's wife.

What was she supposed to do now? Some sort of intervention was in order. Wasn't it? She'd feel like someone's mom charging back into the living room and telling them to break it up. Vicky was two years older than she was, as in fully adult, a good thirty-five years old. Lily had no business telling her who she could and could not have sex with. Why oh why did Vicky love stirring hornets' nests?

She crawled under the covers of the king-size Tempur-Pedic, scooting to the far edge of the giant bed so that Vicky would have plenty of room, when she was finished with the floozy, to slide in on the side nearest the door. She pulled the covers over her head and let herself fall asleep.

Lily dreamed that she was in Vicky's red kayak on the San Francisco Bay. She paddled hard but wasn't strong enough to fight the outgoing tide. She got swept right through the Golden Gate, the water moving in violent rapids, shooting her out into the Pacific Ocean. She risked tipping the kayak by twisting her waist in the cockpit and looking back at the bridge, its red ribs arching across the gap. She turned forward again, looking west, in the direction of change and pioneering, and aimed for the horizon.

She didn't feel them fall onto the other side of the bed—just as the Tempur-Pedic company advertised—and she mistook their moans for her own dreaming lament. Only when the soft fabric, what she would later identify as Gloria's lime-green dress, landed on her head did consciousness begin to kindle.

Someone was panting her sister's name.

Lily's mind ignited. She lay in a state of paralyzed disbelief. This couldn't be happening.

It was.

Lily began to ease herself off her side of the mattress, thinking she'd roll under the bed. But that was a stupid solution. If Gloria spent the night, she'd be pinned there for hours. Lily had to pee, badly.

Someone kicked her. A moment of stillness, perhaps as the kicker briefly wondered what she'd kicked, was followed by the resumption of sexual quickening.

A hand flung across Lily's face, causing her to squawk.

Gloria vocalized next, hers a guttural, nearly prehistoric paroxysm of fright.

Vicky said, "What? *What?*" Then, "Oh, shit."

Lily bolted upright.

Gloria screamed a bloodcurdler. She shot off the bed and out the door.

"Your dress!" Lily shouted. She clicked on her flashlight and shone it at the naked woman lunging toward her. Gloria yanked the lime-green dress off the bed and, with it wadded in her hand, ran back out the bedroom door, her buttocks jiggling.

Vicky and Lily listened to Gloria's bare feet thump down the hall, make a couple of wrong turns—into the den, the bathroom—before she found her purse in the kitchen. The front door slammed.

"I hope she put the dress *on*," Lily said.

Vicky lay facedown on the bed and whimpered.

As Lily got up to go to the bathroom, the beam of her flashlight found, forsaken on the floor at the foot of the bed as if in a postmodern fairytale, one lime-green high heel.

"The bathroom stinks," she said coming back into the bedroom and sitting on her side of the bed. They'd been peeing down the bathtub drain, and Vicky had told her to just dig a hole in the backyard if she needed to shit.

"That's the Floreses' problem. We'll be out of here soon."

"*Why?*"

"I've explained all that to you. They're evicting—"

"No! Why that woman. Paul's *wife.*"

"She likes a little something on the side."

"And you're that little something."

Vicky smiled. "She's a poet. A damn good one, too. But you know the type. Everything is up for redefinition."

"Including her marriage."

"Including her marriage," Vicky answered solemnly, as if she were on a witness stand, talking about someone other than herself.

"Jesus. Do you not think or do you just get off on trouble?"

"Here we go."

"Where did you think I'd be? We sold the guest bed."

"I didn't invite her! She just showed up. In that dress! Paul's in San Jose for the night and she thought it was a good opportunity for a last little hurrah. Okay, you're right, I should have sent her right back home. But I figured, Sal's already dumped me. So."

Lily shined the flashlight on her sister's face. "Apparently you didn't send her packing even when Sal was in the picture."

"That was a mistake. I admit it. Gloria's very aggressive."

"It appears that her husband is pretty aggressive, too."

"True. He can be gnarly."

Vicky moved aside and then held up a hand in front of the flashlight beam to make beak shadows on the wall.

"You know, I've been thinking about the kayak," she said. "There's no way those glued skateboards are going to hold up under the duress of pavement friction."

"You said nothing would compromise the stick of that glue." Lily allowed herself to be drawn into the diversion, mostly so she could point out the inconsistency. But also because what could she possibly say now? What could she possibly do?

"I did say that. But it's not true. I have some giant bolts. I'm going to bolt the wheelbases of our in-line skates onto the kayak bottom. Then seal the bolts with that epoxy. The combination will work. Yeah, and the in-line skates will be more nimble, probably turn better than the skateboards."

"You have to be out of the house by midnight tomorrow."

"True."

"You don't have time to bolt in-line skates onto the kayak."

Vicky blew her signature raspberry. "That's a full twenty-four hours. Sal and I were going to use the in-line skates to get in shape. We tried once, for like ten minutes, but they hurt our feet. And the kayak hurt our backs. So it's perfect, put the two together and make something entirely new."

"How did Sal—and Paul, for that matter—find out about you and Gloria?"

"Oh, shit. You know what? I totally forgot to put the rest of the stuff in the garage on Craigslist! Posting the Harley was kind of emotional. I got derailed and just moved on to the house contents. Oh well. I don't need any of it. I'm going to live like a monk. How'd the bicycle work out? Take whatever else you want."

"Do me a favor?"

"Anything."

"Go apologize to Sal."

Vicky got out of bed and found the lime-green stiletto. She chucked it at Lily.

"Hey! That thing's lethal."

"I appreciate the relationship advice. But I'm just trying to put two and two together. Or maybe it's three and three. You take a rather arduous journey, by plane and crazy car and foot, to a region leveled by an earthquake. Who does that? That's one. The look on your face after your little romp with the Electra-Glide guy. What was his name? Doesn't matter. That's two. You did mention that your bonobo friend has also traveled from afar to arrive in Berkeley. *Three*. What's up with you and Tom?"

"Why are you changing the subject?" Lily asked.

"Why are *you* changing the subject?"

Lily couldn't help it; she grinned at her sister. Vicky clapped her hands and shouted, "Ah-ha! Got ya!"

15

As Lily carried her bike up the steps to Joyce's front porch, she realized that someone was coming up behind her. Annie didn't bother with the pretense of mugging her this time. She stood next to Lily, both of them dripping rainwater, waiting for her to finish unlocking the door.

"What's up?" Lily asked.

"I'm hungry."

"I didn't see you at dinner tonight."

"I missed it."

"That wasn't smart."

"Do you have anything here I could eat?"

Lily rolled the wet bike in after Annie and propped it against the wall, making a mental note to mop the drips off the hardwood floor. After tossing her soaked army jacket on the armchair, Annie touched everything, pulling out drawers, trying light switches and testing the TV remote, pressing the buttons in rapid succession, as if multiple clicks would make it work. She looked under the sleeping bag on the couch.

When her hand gripped the brass doorknob to Joyce's bedroom, Lily said, "Off-limits. Come on back to the kitchen. I'll make you some supper. Then you have to go."

Annie followed Lily into the kitchen where she finally stood still, watching. Lily had a hunk of cheese, a gooey bit of honeycomb, and a loaf of bread she'd bought from street vendors. The food was meant to be her morning meal for the week. She sliced the bread and cheese and laid it out on the table with the honeycomb and a knife.

Annie ate slowly, carefully, almost reverently. Lily didn't stop her from finishing the piece of cheese and every crumb of bread. She left a bit of honeycomb.

"Now you have to go."

Annie stood and stretched. "Why?"

"Because you can't be here."

Annie's back straightened and her eyes flat-lined. "I want some milk."

"I don't have any."

"Water."

After she drained one and then a second glass of water, Annie tore off a paper towel and wiped her mouth. She wadded the towel and handed it to Lily. She pulled up her purple leggings and tugged at her red T-shirt, arranging it around her chubby midsection. She popped her knuckles.

"Where are your parents?" Lily asked.

"Fighting terrorism."

"What do you mean?"

"Are you deaf or something?"

"It's time for you to go."

"Where am I supposed to sleep tonight?"

"I can't help you with that."

Annie walked to the window in the kitchen door and looked out. "I love plums."

"I'll bring you some when they're ripe. Come to the church tomorrow for your dinner. Time to go now."

Annie headed down the hall, and Lily thought she was leaving at last. Instead, she stopped in the living room, looked at the wadded sleeping bag, and scanned the floor, as if considering where she might sleep. Lily picked up the soggy green army jacket and held it out, but Annie folded her arms across her chest, hugging herself. Then, in three quick steps, she was back at Joyce's bedroom door. She flung it open and belly-flopped onto the bed, letting out a long groan that could have been pain, could have been pleasure. She lay motionless except for her right hand, which stroked the burgundy chenille throw.

"I can sleep here," she said in almost a whisper.

"You can leave now is what you can do. Come on, Annie. Get up."

She closed her eyes, her round body sinking deeply into the mattress. Lily wouldn't be able to physically move the girl off of Joyce's bed, even if she tried. She stared at the mess of adolescence, wondering what she was supposed to do. Were there any functioning agencies she could call? Would she call them, if there were?

"Annie. Please."

Keys clattered against the wood of the front door, and then the deadbolt scuffed along its little burrow. The door swung open; Joyce stepped over the threshold and paused. Her gaze went right to the puddle of rainwater on the hardwood floor under the bike. For an absurd moment, Lily mentally scrambled for a way to apologize for possible damage. But Joyce's gaze had already lasered across the living room and through the open bedroom door. Then, hushed and angry, "What's going on?"

Annie leapt off the bed, and Joyce shot into the kitchen, returning with a knife.

"Joyce! Hold up. This is Annie. I know her."

Joyce waved the knife at Annie. "Get out."

"You're overreacting." Lily reached for the knife but Joyce jerked it away. Strands of frosted hair fell across her eyes.

"She's just a girl who eats at Trinity Church. She followed me home and—"

"Home? You're a guest. And I told you to stay away from that church."

"Okay. Okay." Lily took Annie's elbow. "You have to go."

Annie did a good imitation of a gangster girl, but really, you only had to look a second longer to see that she was just a child. Her long eyelashes fluttered against sorrow, and the dimple at the side of her mouth twitched with fear. Lily could feel her trembling as she guided her toward the door. "I'll see you tomorrow, okay?"

Lily shut the door after Annie and noisily slid the deadbolt to reassure Joyce. She pressed her forehead against the door for a moment and then turned. "I'm sorry."

"She was on my bed."

"I know. I was trying to move her. She's just a hungry child."

"Hungry? Did you notice the size of that girl?"

"Please put down the knife."

Joyce sat on the couch and set the knife at her feet. She put her face in her hands. Then she lifted her head, clenched and unclenched her jaw. "I'm sorry. But *just* hungry? Do you know what hungry is driving people all over the East Bay to do? And *child*? Don't be so naïve. She's at least sixteen. She could have taken everything I own. It's not unheard of for sixteen to murder. Yes, don't look at me that way. Murder. For a sandwich, too. Maybe you haven't heard what's been going on." The veins in her throat strained against her white skin and her voice had climbed to a squeak. She stopped and inhaled more oxygen, then continued in a measured voice. "I'm sorry, but I need you to leave. I just can't take this risk anymore."

"Now? It's almost dark."

"You can stay tonight. But that's it."

"I found Vicky."

"Good. I'm glad to hear it. So now you can leave. Go home." She picked up the knife and waved it at the door, as if home were a few blocks away. "From what I hear, you have plenty to attend to there."

"What are you talking about?"

"Running away doesn't solve anything. Just go home."

Lily started shaking her head. The sensation was like an icy pinprick at the back of her skull, directly into her cerebellum. As if she hovered somewhere on the ceiling of the room, outside of herself, Lily watched the spot of cold colonize her brain, her chest, her bowels.

"I figured you knew," Joyce said with a trace of dread that didn't disguise the dose of smugness. "Fair Oaks is a small town. There're no secrets."

"Who *are* you?" Lily asked, suddenly outraged. Joyce, with her tight face, her assumptions and insinuations! She tossed the house key onto the floor and pushed her bike out the door. She pedaled off into the dusk light, riding hard, not stopping, except for the times she had to portage the bike over or around debris, until she arrived, hot and sweaty, on Ridge Road.

Vicky was supposed to have been out by midnight, but Lily hoped that she'd ignored that edict as she did most others. No one answered the door, and the broken basement window had been boarded up. Lily's key didn't work.

She sat on the front porch, under the eaves, and pulled out her phone. She looked at it for a long time, breathing deeply, taking in the astringent scent of the nearby junipers. Medicinal. Corrective.

"Did you get my message?" she asked when Tom answered. "I found Vicky!"

"Yeah. I got it. Thank god."

"I know. Thank god. I just feel so overwhelmed with..."

"With what?"

He had to ask? "Relief. Gratitude."

"Yeah. So she's fine?"

"It's...it's complicated."

"Complicated how?"

"She doesn't have anywhere to live. And she's broke." No need to go into the Gloria and Paul story. Nor her own. If he could see her now: getting ready to sleep outside in a black plastic garbage bag.

"So...what's your plan?"

"She won't come back to Fair Oaks with me."

"I guess that's her call."

"I can't just leave her out here homeless."

There was another one of those long silences that were becoming staples of their conversations. Then Tom said, "Why are we talking about Vicky?"

"Maybe because I came out here to find her?"

"I think we need to be honest with each other," Tom said.

"Okay. We always are."

"No. I don't think we have been. Not you. And not me."

Not him?

"We'll talk when I get home," Lily said.

"When is that going to be?"

Vicky was homeless. She was also in the crosshairs of Paul's fury. Lily couldn't leave her out here in that mess. But Tom had asked for honesty, and the truth was, she didn't want to leave. Not yet. The dilation of her world was thrilling, even as she sat in a garbage bag, homeless herself. She wanted at least a few more evenings in the noisy, hot, sweaty, clanging community room at Trinity Church where people shared vats of food and their wildest stories.

"I don't know," she admitted.

"I don't think you're coming back."

"I've only been gone seven days."

"I'm lonely. I've been lonely for years. You write these long letters to Travis. You take long walks out past the field. You're always looking outward."

"No. Tom. I just think—" But Lily couldn't finish that sentence; she had no idea what she thought about her marriage anymore. What she loved best about Tom was his steadfast truthfulness, his clear-sightedness, but she didn't want this truth-telling now.

He blurted, "I'm seeing Angelina."

For a hot moment, she thought he was joking. She really did. A cruel, angry joke. Angelina was a good five years older than Tom, spoke in aphorisms, did that clucking thing in the back of her throat, and passed all her vacation weeks at church camp. "You can't be serious."

Tom remained silent.

"*Angelina?*" They used to make fun of her duck walk. How, despite her churchy ways, she always wore V-neck sweaters that showcased her impressive bust, the little gold cross glinting in her cleavage.

"What am I supposed...?" he started and stopped.

"Fifteen fucking years."

"Come home, then."

So this was a threat?

"I need—" he started, the last word fraying.

"*What?*" Lily shouted. "What do you need, Tom?"

He couldn't answer the question, but she knew the answer. He didn't need her. He needed someone, apparently anyone, to stabilize his life. She clicked off her phone.

All night long, Lily lay under the juniper bushes in her plastic bag, her cheek pressed into the soil, shivering with cold and anger. Little bits of memory multiplied, brightened, came to life, breeding inside her like an algae bloom. The plates of cookies Angelina brought to the lock shop. The way Tom enthused about her honesty, her cheerfulness, her stalwartness. He'd said she was the perfect employee. Lily should have known, seen.

But *Angelina?* The name pooled like vomit in her stomach. The jarring dissonance between herself and that woman, who they were as people, was a cacophony of shock. He might as well have said he was seeing Mother Teresa.

"Come home, then," he'd said. And if she did, what exactly did he intend to do with Angelina? Shuttle her off to a permanent church retreat?

At the first gray light of dawn, Lily dragged herself out from under the juniper bushes, not wanting to be found by the Floreses—or worse, Paul—and rode her bicycle down to the library. She sat on the sidewalk in front, in her black plastic bag and damp clothing, surrounded by the drizzly morning fog, waiting for the doors to open.

Lily remembered standing on the sidewalk in front of the Fair Oaks library with her third-grade class. The teacher had asked what one building would be the most important to save if a town burned down. The children all wagged their hands, eager to answer that the building *right there*, in front of them, would be the most important. "That's right," the teacher had affirmed in her slow, edifying voice. "Why? Because the library contains all the wisdom people have amassed over the centuries, and we wouldn't have to start from square one again." Lily had been very impressed by the word *amassed*.

Now she wondered what exactly square one was. Drawing on cave walls? Wearing pelts? Gathering roots and berries, hunting gophers and bison? Had our cathedrals and skyscrapers, our fashion and multiple flavors of chocolate, moved us onto square two? With people on several continents ravaging one another, with couples the world over betraying one another, what good had all the wisdom amassed in the libraries done for humankind?

Did anyone even know what love was?

Tom used to say, "Love is what I feel for you."

As a child, Lily thought love was attacking her sister's attackers.

She'd told Kalisha that chocolate pudding might be love.

For Van Gogh, love was an ear.

Travis said sex is love. If that were true, then did Tom love Angelina?

When the library opened, Lily went directly to the encyclopedia and looked it up. The word love is derived from Germanic forms of the Sanskrit word *lubh*. The article went on to say that the word *lubh*, even back to its Sanskrit, has too wide a range of translations to be truly useful. The Greeks tried to solve this problem by having three terms: *eros, philia,* and *agape.*

These sounded to Lily like types of wine. Didn't the wine merchant say wine was love? Not exactly. He said it was poetry, friendship, art, and history. That's getting pretty close, isn't it? But that was the problem with the question, *What is love?* Close is easy. Lots of people get close. Getting it right, exactly right, is what no one has ever done before, not even Jesus or Buddha.

Lily knew she loved Tom. She knew he loved her. And yet their marriage seemed more like an institution than a feeling. What she wanted—what she needed—was the feeling.

16

THE GUY WHO'D BOUGHT the Harley Electra-Glide, Wesley, sat at one of the long oak tables in the far corner of the reading room, holding a book with both hands, as if it anchored him. He never looked up, no matter how much she stared. There was so much sadness in his spare camber, the slightly caved chest. His black hair looked fluffy with static electricity, as if just washed. It was calming to watch him across the room as she inched forward in the line for the computers.

Lily printed the email Tom had sent last week with the plane ticket confirmation code. "I forked out the dough for an open-ended ticket," he'd written. That must have killed him, paying extra. Seriously, what exactly was he going to do with Angelina if she used the ticket and came home? She folded the paper into a tiny square and pushed it deep into her front pocket.

Then she pulled off the garbage bag, although it was arguable whether her clothes were more presentable than the bag, and stuffed it into her backpack. She combed her fingers through her hair, which was decidedly not fluffy, though she'd washed it yesterday, albeit in cold water with bar soap.

Wesley didn't look up until she was standing right at his side.

"Hi. I'm Lily."

"Yeah, I remember. How're you doing?"

He had a brooding kind of smile. She fought an urge to tell him about Tom, managing, just barely, to curb herself. He had a heap of his own troubles. He didn't need to hear about hers.

"You haven't left for Eugene yet."

"I thought I'd wait for the rain to stop."

"I have your book." She dug *Orlando* out of her backpack.

"I wondered where I'd left it."

"My high school Language Arts teacher was so passionate about this book."

"How about you? Did you like it?"

"I loved it. The time-traveling androgynous character reminded me of Vicky."

Wesley laughed. "That's cool when an old book reminds you of something in your life now. I wouldn't say it's Woolf's most accomplished novel, but hands down it's her most daring one. I think it's brilliant." His deep voice kept being a surprise up against his skinny sadness.

"You said you were writing a novel. What's it about?"

"Oh. It's just a story I post serially."

"Funny or sad?"

"It's goofy. It's called *Wings on Fire*. Before the earthquake, I had three hundred twenty-four readers. But since I started *The Earthquake Chronicles*, my readership for both blogs has skyrocketed. The cross-pollination thing."

She liked the way he seemed both crushed and resilient. It felt like an honest combination. The need to tell about Tom was ballooning inside her.

"The bike is awesome," Wesley said. "Your sister took really good care of it."

"She's good with machines. Anything with working parts. Humans, not so much."

He laughed again. "So, are you heading home soon? Now that you've found her."

"I don't know. I have a job at Trinity Church. Serving dinner."

He nodded, maybe glanced at his book. Now was the time to say that it'd been nice to see him and walk away. Instead, she said, "My husband and I are breaking up."

Wesley looked startled. Of course he did. She made a face, which she hoped was wry, and turned to leave.

"Hold on a second." He stood, looking like a question mark with his long thin legs, jutting hipbones, and slight stoop in the shoulders. The fingertips of his right hand pressed the oak tabletop, as if he might topple without the support. "Are you okay?"

"Sorry. I don't even know you. Sharing that was inappropriate."

"I don't think appropriateness is a working concept anymore. Around here."

Lily laughed.

"Just survival."

"Just survival," she agreed and left, employing as decisive a gait as she could muster.

When, later that afternoon, she walked into the community room at the church, Kalisha did a double take and Ron asked, "Y-y-y-y-you ok-k-k-k-kay?"

"My husband is leaving me. He thinks I've left him."

"Th-th-that s-s-s-s-sucks." As he hugged her, the cowry shells on the tips of his cornrows tapped coolly against her face.

"Yeah. It does."

Later, after Kalisha locked the door, Lily cleaned up fast and then took a seat next to Professor Vernadsky, who was always the last to leave. He looked more dog-eared than usual today: his long hair wisped about his pink scalp like a cirrus cloud and his pale blue eyes were unfocused. He wore a bull's-eye tie-dye tie in concentric shades of electric blue and hot pink. He turned a damp gaze on her.

"I've been reading up on the meaning of love," she told him. She wouldn't mention that her source was the encyclopedia. "Tell me if I have this right. *Eros* is desire, but at least according to Plato, it transcends the particular. It's basically desiring or loving beauty itself."

"Well—"

She knew he'd try to equivocate. "Wait. Let me finish. *Philia* is more like friendship or family love, right? Whereas *agape* is like God's love for people and people's love for God. But it also includes loving all of humanity." Lily paused. "Like that's possible."

Professor Vernadsky folded his napkin and said, "The use of language to understand love presumes that love has a describable nature. So even before we can discuss the meaning of love, beguiling as that question is, we need to understand a few things about the philosophy of language, the relevance and appropriateness of meanings. In other words, the concept of love may be irreducible."

"That can't be right." She knew philosophy was all about chewy word arguments, but she thought it was also about believing there were answers. After a few decades at the university, he'd decided that the endeavor was pointless? Just like her marriage.

He tried to clarify his position by adding, "Love may well be an axiomatic, self-evident state of being that is corrupted by intellectual intrusion."

"Like a Kantian category?" She was pleased to have remembered this concept from her encyclopedia reading. Maybe this was why people studied hard subjects; engaging your brain distracted you from a broken heart.

"Try the Heisenberg Uncertainty Principle."

"That's physics."

"Philosophy has come to the end of its usefulness. It's been superseded by physics."

"But physics can't describe the exact nature of love!"

His eyes were the loveliest shade of pale blue, like lobelia blossoms. He blinked hard a few times and said, "Not yet."

Kalisha stopped by the table with his wrapped sandwich and a banana. She tucked them in the big outside pockets of his jacket.

"When you were at the university," Lily persisted with her inquiry, "did you know a professor named Travis Grayson? He was a bonobo researcher."

Kalisha hitched forward and her eyebrows shot up, as if *she* knew Travis Grayson. Likely she was just twitching with irritation at Lily's lollygagging, wanting her to get on with work.

"Bonobos!" The professor looked pleased. "The biological key to the question, 'What is love?'"

"Yes!" Lily said. "You know about them!"

"Fascinating creatures. Perhaps the genetic code to our salvation."

"That's what Travis says! Do you know him?"

"I've been retired for a long time. But I have a university directory at home. Come see me. We'll talk." Professor Vernadsky rose from his chair with a great deal of effort, and Lily handed him his walking sticks. He shuffled toward the door.

"Did you know Professor Vernadsky before the earthquake?" Lily asked Kalisha.

"I studied with him. He was my advisor."

"Really? You studied philosophy?" Lily instantly regretted showing her surprise.

Kalisha smirked briefly, but then jerked her head to the side, flicking away the insult and forgiving Lily her assumptions. "Yeah," she said. "He has a fair amount of dementia now, but he was a smart, smart man."

"So did you major in philosophy?"

"I was working on my doctorate." Kalisha spoke the words carefully, as if they were a lovely shell she held in cupped hands, close to her chest.

"Did you study love?"

She ran a work-weathered hand over her skull. And then, as if saying the word cost her something, "Epistemology."

"Um—?"

"Another time."

"Do you agree with Professor Vernadsky, that love can't be understood?"

"Yes."

"I think my husband and I are splitting up."

The planes of Kalisha's face softened and the dirty penny color of her eyes warmed, as if the copper had been polished. "Are you okay?"

"Everything is spinning."

Kalisha nodded and said, "Yes."

"It's like everything I thought I knew about my life may no longer be true."

"Let me know if you need anything."

"This." Lily swept her hand in the direction of the kitchen and community room. "I need this."

Kalisha smiled. Then she picked up the sponge and started wiping down tables Lily had already cleaned. Lily wrung out another sponge and helped redo them all.

17

KALISHA MADE HER WAY down the dark hallways of the church, carrying a lit candle. She didn't allow herself to go to the sanctuary often. She saved it for crucial moments, as if its potency would be drained if overused.

She stopped at the head of the aisle and held the candle up to the cross at the altar. "Hell of a mess you all have made," she said aloud, and then walked to the front pew where she took a seat.

Lily knew Travis Grayson. That surprised her. Maybe even alarmed her.

Had she joined his Cluster? What was this business about bonobos? She had a strong feeling she needed to figure out, understand, their connection. It frightened her, as if somewhere in the link between herself and Lily and Travis there was danger. But that was crazy thinking. Lily and Travis both had been so helpful.

She closed her eyes and held them tight. There was so much she wasn't afraid of: the instability of Earth's tectonic plates, falling ceilings and loosened gas pipes. She wasn't even afraid of hunger. But the unknown. Unanswered questions. The unrelenting need to feel more intensely. These terrified her.

She ran her fingers along the scar-covered veins on the insides of her elbows. The scars always reminded her of God, how He—She, It, whatever—came to her when she was using. The clarity, the beauty of the universe, of her own soul. But of course that God happened to be dope. And if a skinny white boy (maybe black, according to Michael) who lived two thousand years ago couldn't do anything about the pain and suffering on earth today, neither could heroin.

But no, see, that was the problem. That was the greatest temptation of all. Dope was the conduit, the path, but it did lead to God. She believed that. It allowed her to see and feel Him—Her, It, whatever. If Jesus had known about brain chemistry, what would he have done with the information? Probably mainlined. Who didn't want to experience God?

Kalisha had been clean for ten years, but the desire, the chemical love, could still come on with a vicious intensity whenever she felt a void.

And how wide the void had yawned during those first days after the earthquake. She'd sat on her stoop every morning and watched the flow of people moving like rivers to the bay where rescue boats hauled them off. She could have gone. But where? She pictured high school gymnasiums full of people on cots, covered by gray army blankets, waiting for transportation to welcoming relatives in other parts of the state, or other states altogether. She pictured herself lying on one of the cots, under one of the blankets, with nowhere to go.

On the third morning, as she sat in the sun, the flow of people thinning, a man strode across the church parking lot, headed for her stoop. A floppy midsize mutt, ancient-looking with his gray muzzle and bloodshot eyes, tried to keep up. Both the dog and the man were limping. The man, a few years older than she was, had shaggy blond hair and wore dirty jeans and a ripped red flannel shirt. Maybe he was handsome—she wouldn't know, she'd never been attracted to white guys. But he had a zealous energy that unnerved her.

The scars on the insides of her arms and on her groin started singing. Maybe he had a couple of bags in his back pocket. Dealers had a way of knowing where their clients were, and also when they were ripe. Ten years was nothing, nothing at all. She thought she could hear the plastic slipping against the denim of his jeans pocket.

Her will drained from her like blood from a wound. She did try to plug the hole. She summoned a mental picture of the community room full of diners. But the picture only reminded her that she could no longer feed them. She thought of Michael: the roundness of his cheeks and belly; his expressive hands with the oddly short fingers; the way he talked faster when ideas excited him; the bit of gray she'd recently glimpsed in his hair; his ever-present scowl. He tried so hard. At everything.

None of that stopped the flashback, the sweet spiritual syrup opening her horizons, turning all of existence into an eternal blue sky. She'd sell anything for it.

The blond guy stopped in front of her. The old mutt flopped at his feet, as if weary from a very long journey.

"Yes," she said before he even asked a question.

"Are you Kalisha Wilkerson?"

She nodded, wondering but not surprised that he knew her name. Knowing you, all about you, kept them safer. You were revealed, findable, theirs.

"Travis Grayson." He tapped his chest and smiled. "Look, I understand you have a soup kitchen."

"It's a free meals program."

"Right. I've got food. I can help."

"You've got food?"

"Yeah, a lot."

"How'd you get it?"

"Does it matter?"

"You Robin Hood or something?"

He grinned, pleased with the comparison. "I can go with that. Anyway, do you want the food?"

"I don't have power for my kitchen."

The man glanced around the empty parking lot. "There's no reason we can't build you a wood-burning oven out here. There's wood all over town. My Cluster will supply it."

"Your Cluster?" It was the first time she'd heard the term.

Later that very morning, Travis Grayson returned with a crew of young people. They scavenged stones, mixed cement, and built a large oven right in the middle of the parking lot. They gathered wood, split it into oven-sized pieces, and piled it against the wall of the church. At noon, a black Chevy Blazer backed into the parking lot and the young people unloaded a crazy assemblage of food.

Ron balked at the idea of cooking outside in a stone oven, but somehow they managed to serve a potato, black-eyed pea, and ham stew at four thirty.

For three days, Travis and his crew delivered truckloads of food and firewood. Kalisha's flock dined al fresco every evening, eating the concoctions made from the ingredients at hand, including an apple crumble, zucchini-carrot salad, *carne asada* tacos, and many less-exciting dishes. The Trinity Church parking lot was a maelstrom of fire, food, laughter, and lots of tears, too. Kalisha had to consider God. He, She, It, whatever, had sent Travis. How else could she explain the miracle?

Then, on the fourth day, Travis didn't come. Nor did he come the next day or the one after that. Kalisha had no idea if he'd run out of stores to loot or if he'd finally gone back to a swanky home in some place like Sausalito.

But she was grateful. He'd gotten her back on her feet and, more importantly, the meals program up and running again. Lots of people hadn't left the East Bay, and they were the ones who needed food most of all.

Kalisha got up from the church pew and carried her lit candle to the altar. She found the box of candles inside the cavity of the pulpit and took out two. She shoved them into the candleholders on the side table near the crashed picture of Jesus. She lit one for Travis. She lit another one for Michael. Then she backed up and looked at her flickering thank yous.

"But who is Lily?" she asked.

18

L ILY SPENT THE NEXT three days in the library, standing in line for the computers and then using her turns to read Wesley's blogs.

The Earthquake Chronicles were surprisingly funny. She knew some of the people he'd written about because they ate at the church, and she liked how he found the humor and heart in even the most desperate characters and events. Some of his subjects might not like what he'd written, though, which probably explained why he himself didn't eat at the church. She read all the way through the blog, finishing with his first entries, the ones about himself.

"Slow down," his fare had told him as his taxicab slid onto the freeway overpass, just moments before the earthquake. He glanced in the rearview mirror. At first he saw only the glaring headlights of the truck behind him, but then he saw that the young woman was holding her little boy's hand. The child looked about ten years old, the same age Wesley's boys had been when Carolyn left him for Hank.

The truck's headlights flooded the cab's interior, and then the truck itself plowed into Wesley's rear bumper, crumpling the trunk of the car. The overpass collapsed and the cab plunged to the roadway below, landing upright on a giant slab of the overpass cement. Huge chunks of concrete pounded down around the cab, and a light blue mini landed on Wesley's hood. He sat still while clouds of debris rained down.

Later he would not be able to say how much time had passed before he came out of shock. Seconds? Minutes? It could even have been more than an hour. His consciousness came in slowly, like lights blinking on one at a time in a cityscape. He punched away the airbag, and then touched himself, first his legs, and then his arms and chest. When he touched his forehead, his hand came away bloody. He had no idea how badly he was injured. He closed his eyes and slept.

A man tugged open the driver door and asked Wesley if he was okay.

It took him a long time to remember where he was and why. The man waited patiently for him to say, "I think so."

"How about your passengers?"

Wesley found that his legs worked. He climbed out of his cab and looked, with the stranger, into the window of the backseat. The boy's head was covered in blood, but his eyes were open! The door was jammed shut, but the man had a tire iron, and they managed to pry it open. Wesley knelt down and took the boy's hands. The child was so still, he couldn't tell if he was dead or alive.

As he gently lifted him out of the backseat, the boy moaned. The other man crawled in for the boy's mother and then crawled out again without her. He shook his head at Wesley.

"Can you take the child?" the man asked. "I'll move on to the next car."

Wesley wanted to ask, take the child where? But of course there was no answer to that question, and so, with the boy draped across his arms and held against his chest, Wesley started walking. Blood from his own head wound dripped onto the boy's jacket. Getting away from the freeway exchange was like traversing a small mountain range. He had to take long detours around crevasses and duck under giant spears of rebar. There were other survivors, some stumbling away from the devastation, others helping excavate the trapped and wounded. With the young boy in his arms, no one stopped Wesley, and at last he made it beyond the worst of the overpass rubble.

He had no idea where to go, so he walked toward the bookstore, even though it was a few miles away. He spoke softly to the boy, telling him he would be okay and that they'd get somewhere warm and safe. Twice the boy said, "Mama."

Then, after about an hour of walking, the boy went limp. Wesley put him down and held a finger against his jugular. "Hey!" he said. "Hey. Kid. Come on." But the boy was gone.

Wesley couldn't just leave him beside the road, so he picked him up again, cradling him, and walked. The glass door of the bookstore was shattered, but he used his key anyway. Wesley kicked a space clear of books and laid the dead boy on the hardwood floor.

The next morning he buried him in the small plot of dirt behind the bookstore. Later that same day, he also buried his mother and Carolyn in their respective backyards. He hadn't been able to find his ex-wife's husband, Hank.

In the post he'd written about buying the Harley, Wesley called Lily "the motorcycle girl." "I can hardly remember what she looked like," he wrote, "but she had an unedited presence, as if there were none of the usual veils between her and the rest of the world."

Lily had never read about herself in the third person before. The words jarred her. Were they true? Perhaps they had been on that day: she'd just found Vicky, alive.

Every day Lily looked for Wesley in the library, but she never saw him again. When a new post appeared in *The Earthquake Chronicles*, she learned that he'd taken his trip to Oregon. After visiting his two sons in Eugene, he rode the Harley down the coast on Highway 101, going nowhere at all, doubling back to ride the most beautiful sections two or three times. At night, he camped on the beaches, cold and windy, wrapped in gray fog. He lay in driftwood shelters listening to the sound of the surf. Sometimes the clouds parted and he stared into the black star-studded sky. He wrote that the salty air, sloshing sea, and starlight were intensely beautiful, as if his losses dialed up his ability to feel, hear, and see. A broken heart, he wrote, is the same thing as an open heart, by definition.

At night, after serving dinner at the church, Lily slept in a motel room at the intersection of Cedar Street and San Pablo Avenue. The owner only took cash, so it wasn't a long-term solution. But at least for a few nights she had a roof, a door that locked, and plumbing that worked.

On her fourth morning in the motel, the ring on her phone trembled through her dreams and she awoke with a gasp. It was her slippery sister. She fell back on the motel bed and closed her eyes. "Where have you been?"

"Didn't you get my emails?"

"You know I got them. I answered them. But you haven't told me where you are."

"My email could be hacked. I don't like sharing sensitive info online."

"Like where you live?" Even as Lily scoffed the question, she thought of shifty Paul. Waiting for Vicky in her own house.

"No lectures today. Guess what! I've got an awesome studio apartment. Right by the Oakland airport. Cool, huh? Excellent access."

"Access to what? The airport is closed."

"Yeah, but when it does open, I'll be able to walk to the terminal."

"I thought you lost your phone."

"I found it!" Vicky crowed. "Guess where."

Lily let her spine sink into the mattress, corralled patience. "Where?"

"You have to guess."

"In one of the in-line skates."

"Ha! Good guess. But no. It was under the cushion of the bubble chair!"

"Okay."

"And, even better, I was able to pay my bill. They were going to disconnect in one day. My usual good luck."

"I've been worried about you."

"No need. It's awesome out here. A lot of Oakland is still without power, but since the Air Force is working from the airport, we're up and running. All kinds of amenities."

"Who's 'we'?"

"I'm working for the Hegenberger Cluster. I love this neighborhood. It's awesome."

"You've joined a Cluster?"

"I don't know about 'joined.' I'm helping them rig solar and build a few computers. This is anarchy at its best. People figuring out our needs and taking care of them. I'm off the grid, baby."

"With the Air Force next door? You're not exactly on your own."

"And guess what. This will make you happy."

Vicky wouldn't go on until Lily said, "What?"

"I have all the chairs. They're safe and sound, right here with me."

"How'd you do that?"

"With a great deal of difficulty. I hired a couple of guys who had not only a truck but one with gas in the tank. You can imagine what I had to pay them. Anyway, mission accomplished."

"Okay."

"Yep. Everything is turning up roses."

"Okay."

"You sound kind of sad." It wasn't the sort of observation Vicky usually made.

"I'm fine." She had no idea how to tell Vicky about Tom.

"Hey. Another plus about my new digs. Miles away from Gloria." Vicky waited for Lily to say something. "I thought you'd approve. She has no idea where I am."

"It would be smart to keep it that way." She could just see Vicky texting Gloria in one of her irrationally buoyant moments.

"You still at Joyce's place?"

Lily cleared her throat instead of answering. It was stupid to be prideful. But she didn't really want to admit that in fact she was now the homeless one.

"You can stay with me, you know. Come on out. My place is kind of tiny. But you're totally welcome. You know that."

"Just be safe," Lily said.

"This isn't Kansas anymore, Dorothy."

"No, it's not."

"Call me!" Vicky's optimism, as usual, was sincere.

19

LILY CHECKED OUT OF the motel. She couldn't squander the rest of her cash on the room. She'd heard there was an intermittently functioning ATM in downtown Berkeley. She'd also heard that the armed guards the bank had hired were as likely to take your cash as anyone. In any case, the money in their checking account wouldn't cover many more nights in a motel and it wasn't hers alone to spend. Withdrawing her half of their savings made a statement she wasn't ready to make.

She shoved her remaining cash in her bra, stuffed her belongings into her backpack, and rode her bicycle up the hill. When she reached the house on Ridge Road, she tried the garage door, but it was locked. There was a window to the garage, but it was too high to reach and awkwardly placed above the stairs leading down to the front porch. She unearthed another flagstone, a small one this time, and shoved it in the front of her jeans. Then she climbed up on the stairway's railing, her fingers clutching the windowsill. In order to bash in the window with the rock, she'd have to let go with one hand. She looked down at her feet, tentatively braced on the thin metal railing, and carefully reached for the flagstone tucked in her jeans. She began to totter and had to use both hands to grasp the sill again. She considered using her skull to knock a hole in the glass, but that was a pretty stupid idea. She'd just have to will good balance. Again she reached for the flagstone, lifted it to the glass, and bashed. The window shattered. She managed four more bashes before she fell, landing hard on her hip. She climbed back up on the railing and this time smashed out the entire window. It took her nearly half an hour to pick out the small crags of glass in the sill. She emptied her backpack and laid it across the bottom of the window to protect herself from any remaining shards, then hefted herself up and into the garage.

From inside, it was easy to manually open the garage door.

Lily tried to make quick decisions. She grabbed the tent and a sleeping bag. Then, against all reason, she hoisted the red plastic double kayak by its bow handle and wheeled it out of the garage. She put the tent and sleeping bag in the front cockpit and shoved the paddle alongside the gear, securing one end under the bow and laying the shaft alongside the seats.

After shutting the garage door, Lily started down Ridge Road pushing her bicycle in one hand and pulling the kayak with the other. Lake Anza, an artificial lake made by damming Wildcat Canyon Creek, was just a quarter mile away. A boat belonged to water. She'd take the kayak there. She stopped next door and hid her bicycle in the brambles in front of Professor Vernadsky's house. He hadn't been at the church the last couple of nights. She would check on him after she stashed the kayak.

At the bottom of Ridge Road, Lily crossed Wildcat Canyon Road and began the gentle descent of Central Park Drive toward the lake. Vicky had done an excellent job converting the kayak; the wheels turned with silent ease.

Lily's mind, on the other hand, was not working so well. She was having trouble assembling her thoughts, focusing on a plan. She inventoried her possessions: bicycle, tent, sleeping bag, maps, flashlight, toothbrush, phone, packet of letters from a bonobo researcher. Some cash. A wheeled kayak. She remembered reading somewhere that homelessness triggered mental illness in a shockingly short period of time.

There was, of course, the plane ticket. It would deliver her to a wrecked marriage and a handful of winter gardens, covered with snow, waiting for her labor.

These past three days as she read in the library, served dinners in the church, and slept in the motel, she'd been waiting for Tom to call back. She'd fully expected him to. But he hadn't. He meant it. He meant Angelina.

Lily straddled the rear cockpit of the kayak and lowered her behind onto the seat, hooking her knees over the lip so that she could use her feet as brakes. She held the paddle aloft and began to ride the kayak down the hill. She rolled slowly, gliding along the woodsy road into the regional park, disappearing herself into the vessel's sensuality, with its pointed ends and swelled middle, the way it slipped through the air.

The ride reminded her of sledding that first time with Tom. They were eleven years old, and she a good foot taller. She'd pulled the sled to the top of the hill on the Knickerbocker place, where they all sledded in the winter, and she called his name, as if she were choosing him for a team. They joked about that years later, the way she'd said, "Hey, you, Tommy. Come here," and he did. She pointed at the sled and he climbed on, placing his feet on the steering bar, taking hold of the rope. "Lie down," she told him. So he did that, too, swinging his legs around and pressing his belly against the wooden sled slats. It was Lily's father's old Fearless Flyer, nearly an antique, and she'd inherited his pride in it. She climbed on Tommy's back, the length of her against him. She put her head to the side of his, her face in his neck, and breathed in what was still a little boy smell, sugary cereal and milk and a sweet kind of sweat. "Go," she said. He gripped the steering bar and pushed off with a foot. They flew, the iced air sheering her face, his buttocks under her pelvis, her budding breasts sore as they pressed against his back. She could feel him steer with his whole body, using lean and their combined weight. She closed her eyes, sank more deeply into him, and felt that first inkling of eroticism. The speed and his nearness lodged in her throat, and she cried out with joy, wanting the ride to never, never ever, end. When it finally did, when they sailed onto the flats of the Knickerbocker farm, neither of them dragged their feet to slow the sled. They let the momentum take them as far as it would, and even after they came to a complete stop, she lay on top of Tommy for a few more seconds before rolling off. You would think they could have laughed then, but the moment was too potent, too loaded with the future, and Lily jumped up purposefully and strode away. They didn't touch again for three years.

The kayak picked up speed, careening down the hill, and Lily didn't know if she could control it. She tried to drag her feet, but she was going too fast and contact with the road wrenched her ankles. She knew she'd ruin the plastic paddle if she tried to slow her ride by jamming it against the pavement. So she gave up and flew down the hill in her crazy vessel, hoping there were no earthquake-severed sections of the road. The oak, pine, and redwood trees blurred on either side of her. When she came to a moderate turn, she used lean and her body weight, just as Tommy had, and the wheels on the bottom of the kayak responded beautifully, taking her along the curve of the road. Down they went, as if the kayak had a mind of its own, as if it were determined to reach water.

She approached a four-way stop at the bottom of the hill, with the lake off to the right, but she couldn't turn that sharply. Nor could she stop. So she sailed right on through the stop sign and coasted up the short incline, finally rolling to a stop. She climbed out on shaky legs and looked around.

She was alone in the trees, under the cold, blue sky.

She could have called Tom back herself. But she hadn't. Instead, she was choosing homelessness over the American Dream. Now she just had to find out why.

Lily wheeled the boat around and pulled it the rest of the way down the hill to Lake Anza. She was surprised to find the place deserted. Maybe it was just another myth that a community of earthquake refugees—the Lake Anza Cluster, people at the church called them—lived near its shores. The pale green water lay flat and opaque, bringing to mind the expression, "a body of water." There appeared to be nothing here, no ducks or snakes or even insects, nothing at all. Silence thickened the air.

She pulled the kayak across the top of the spillway, which shouldn't have held up in the earthquake but had. Big gray boulders butted up against the far shore, and a stand of tall reeds flanked the edges of the rocks. Overhead, the leafy eucalyptus branches shivered in a sudden breeze. The water rippled like a traveling message.

She stopped for a moment and listened, hoping for clarity or direction. Nothing.

When she reached the other side of the lake, she dragged the boat into the woods, forcing her way through the undergrowth. Then she flipped it over, sat on the hull, and wiped the sweat from her face with the bottom of her T-shirt. She had no imaginable use for a boat. Yet her urge to hoard had begun to feel primal.

Taking the tent and sleeping bag with her, Lily pushed her way back out of the brush and continued walking along the path that circled the lake, trying to be practical, considering her camping options. When she heard a splash behind her, she turned to see a long-haired little boy, no more than eight years old. He crouched at the water's edge, wearing only a T-shirt, sloshing what looked like a pair of pants in the lake. He smiled at her, and then stood suddenly, his little penis bobbing. He held up the dripping jeans. "I peed them," he said. He folded the jeans in half, wrung them as hard as his twig arms would allow, and then tossed them over his shoulder. He sat on a rock, pulled on and tied a pair of dirty sneakers. "Bye!" he called. The naked little boy scampered up the steep bank, heading straight into the park wilderness.

Lily thought about following him, but she wasn't ready to join a Cluster, to live with strangers. Lake Anza was too obvious a camping spot.

She carried the tent and sleeping bag back up to Ridge Road and stopped in front of Professor Vernadsky's house. The gate had rusted off its hinges and the rotting boards lay against towering blackberry brambles. She pushed through the small opening in the stickers and dropped her gear on the professor's front patio.

The earthquake had toppled his chimney and shifted a portion of the house off its footing, opening up a jagged crack in the siding big enough for a small body to slide through, but the house clearly had been disintegrating, returning to a state of nature, for years, since long before the earthquake. The paint was all but gone, dry rot marbled the siding, trees grew up through cracks in the patio, and thick moss covered the roof.

His walking sticks lay in front of the door, one crossed over the other, and the door was ajar. Lily knocked, and when there was no answer, she knocked harder. She called out his name. That didn't rouse him, either, so she gently pushed open the door.

A terrible stench filled the air. With its long south-facing windows, the house was a giant solarium. One of the windows had busted out altogether, and a small greenway grew in from the backyard, grasses and strawberry plants and even bright orange nasturtiums. Termites nibbled away at the rotting wooden floor. The professor sat, with his back to Lily, on what was left of the couch. Wads of its stuffing spilled out of the fabric, and mice were busy burrowing into the homes they'd made there. A blue jay roosted on top of his head, pecking its beak at his white hair, like a little passerine hairdresser.

"Professor," Lily said, approaching slowly so as to not scare him. "Professor Vernadsky, it's me, Lily."

The blue jay flew across the room, perching on a lamp, but the professor still didn't turn around, so she inched closer and put a hand on the back of his shoulder. Using her hand as a pivot, she circled around to the front of him.

His eyes, his beautiful lobelia-blue eyes, were already gone. Lily dry retched so hard it felt as if her stomach might heave out her mouth.

She didn't trust herself on the bicycle, so she left it along with her tent and sleeping bag, hidden in the professor's blackberry brambles, and ran down the hill to the church.

She poured drinks and set out trays. She served hamburgers, tater tots, bean casserole, and carrots. She even smiled at the clients, chatted with regulars, commented on how Herbert had more color in his cheeks, and snuck him extra milk.

The horror of what she'd seen held her up like a broomstick holds up a scarecrow, a rod through her center. She was glad for all the diners, their living vibrancy, even for Annie. At least the ill-tempered girl was still safe.

"Give me the vegan option," she told Lily.

"You're not vegan."

"I said give me vegan."

"You drink milk and ate my cheese. That's not vegan."

"I'm not through with you," Annie said, grabbing a burgerless tray.

"Keep moving," Lily said. "There's a line behind you."

"Just wait to see who knows how to use a knife, bitch."

Joyce had been the one wielding a knife, not Lily, and she almost made that correction but caught herself in time. "Move along."

Annie pulled the tray close to her face and sniffed. Lily expected her to wrinkle her nose, fake a gag, comment on the bean odor, maybe even drop the whole mess to the floor, but she breathed in slowly and quietly, as if the casserole reminded her of something she loved. "Give me one for Benjamin."

"Benjamin?"

"Binky."

They did keep to-go boxes for special situations, like the guy who had a bedridden wife. Lily scooped a large serving of bean casserole into one of these, closed the lid, and gave it to Annie. The girl hesitated, as if about to accidentally say thank you, but instead said, "Milk, too."

Lily handed her two milks.

An hour later, she wiped down the tables and mopped the floor. Then she interrupted Kalisha, who was dressing down Ron for cooking too many hamburgers.

20

THE NEWS KNOCKED KALISHA down. She landed in a chair. Knowing it was coming had not prepared her. She looked around her dining room, trying to stabilize herself by taking inventory: chairs, tables, four walls, floor, and ceiling. This sanctuary of need and nourishment was a direct result of his kindness to her.

"Let's go now," she said to Lily.

"Go where?"

"To bury him."

Lily shook her head.

"If we don't, who will?"

"We should call the authorities."

"You're kidding, right? I don't know who cleans up your shit, but—"

"Nobody cleans up my shit."

"The 'authorities' are a fiction. At least for people like me and Professor Vernadsky."

"Hey. L-l-l-l-l-l—" Ron tried to articulate. He finally got out, "Lily's not the enemy. Not even close."

His stuttering gave Kalisha time to breathe, and the moment softened. "I know," she said. "But that doesn't change the fact that he has to be buried."

"Y-y-y-y-you need some r-r-r-rest," Ron told her, clearly glad to have the subject changed from his mistake with the hamburger meat. "B-b-b-b-bury h-h-h-him t-t-t-t-to-m-m-m-m-morrow."

"Professor Vernadsky was good to me." Kalisha threw off her apron. "We'll go now."

"It'll be dark soon," Lily said.

"We've got time."

They walked up the hill in silence, Lily sagging in reluctance and Kalisha staving off memories, unsuccessfully. She hadn't been to the professor's home since she dropped out of the doctorate program. Back then, on Sunday afternoons, he always had his small cadre of graduate students over for wine and cheese. His wife, a small, wise woman with a deeply ironic sense of humor and a fondness for martinis, was still alive then. Kalisha and Michael had loved everything about her, including how she spotted instantly the pretentious students and ignored them wholly, even though she was the hostess at these gatherings. The professor himself was always too immersed in his world of ideas to notice, or care about, the social jostling among his students, but his wife did. Mrs. Vernadsky had stared at Kalisha that first year with transparent admiration. She and Michael wanted a house just like theirs, lively with comfy sofas and good food and lots of talk, red-tailed hawks swooping by the big windows.

"Sweet Jesus," Kalisha said once they reached the front porch, shocked by the degree of dilapidation.

"You should see the inside."

"I'll go on in. That looks like a gardening shed. Why don't you see if you can find a shovel?"

Kalisha put her palm against the door, but she couldn't make herself push it open. Instead, she waited while Lily pawed through the tools and then emerged with a rusty shovel. She stood on the patio, holding the long-handled tool as grimly as the man holds the pitchfork in *American Gothic*.

"We may as well dig the grave before going in," Kalisha said, trying to hold onto a slim thread of sense. She wished her anger would come back, anything at all that might fortify her. "Backyard?"

Lily nodded and followed her down the side path. Kalisha stopped halfway, turned, and took Lily's hand. "I'm glad you're with me. Thank you for coming."

They picked a place under a lemon tree. Lily started digging, but Kalisha took the shovel after just a couple of minutes. It felt better to be doing physical labor. She struck the soil over and over again with the tip of the blade and tossed the clods every which way. After a while, Lily eased the shovel out of Kalisha's hands and took a long turn. She also seemed eager to sweat, to punish her muscles, and they nearly fought over who got to dig the most. By the time they finished making a big enough hole, night had fallen. Lily clicked on her flashlight and shined it into the grave.

Kalisha leaned on the wooden shaft of the shovel. "Wheelbarrow?"

They found an ancient rusted metal one in the garden shed and by tipping it on its side were able to get it through the front door. They both took off their T-shirts and tied them over their noses and mouths. Lily stood the flashlight on its end on the coffee table, and it cast a ghoulish cone of light.

Kalisha couldn't look at him, not yet. The room, even in its wild state, flooded her with memories: wine and cheese; Aristotle and Diderot; the belief, no, the *conviction*, that life could be understood, that meaning could be excavated from the ruins of human endeavor, language, and history. Here, in this room that was in the process of returning to Rousseau's paradisial nature, they had talked and talked, and laughed and laughed. Most of all, they had believed in their own powers.

How utterly Kalisha had failed. The worst memory of her entire life was of the day Mrs. Vernadsky came to see her in prison. Her gray hair in that messy pixie cut, the penetrating gray eyes, the full mouth that loved to smirk, all transformed into a tableau of confusion. Kalisha saw how she struggled for compassion but felt something more like outrage. She shifted in her chair on the other side of the table as if she could hardly sit still with her disappointment. She did extend her hands toward Kalisha, but they were closed together, a knot of fingers. For her, even more than for her husband, the waste of a mind was the greatest failing. Kalisha wished with all her heart that she had refused to see her.

"Please don't come again," she said at the end of the short visit, and she didn't.

Now Kalisha was making the final visit, and strangely, the salon of ideas turned wildly verdant soothed her. We all come to the same end.

Maybe nature *was* paradise.

Maybe the mess she'd made of her life wasn't such a mess after all. Michael, who'd also inhabited this room, young and earnest with his too-big hair and too-short pants, had thought she'd accomplished something. He'd said so with his checks. That's all Kalisha had ever wanted—to do something half-worthy.

She walked around to the other side of the coffee table and looked at the professor. She felt a flood of love for the old man, and for his wife, too. Death is a kind of forgiveness, and this one saddened Kalisha but also released her.

"Let's get you buried," she told the corpse.

Kalisha shoved her hands under his butt, and Lily lifted from under his armpits, and they managed to jimmy the rigid old man into the wheelbarrow.

Unfortunately, they hadn't thought about getting the load back out the front door. They ended up having to dump him onto the floor, his body frozen in the sitting position, and then sidle the empty wheelbarrow through the opening. Kalisha dragged the body by the legs, while Lily protected his head with her hands, out to the porch. They tipped the wheelbarrow onto its side, lugged him in, and then righted the load. The body shifted to the bottom. By now they were handling him as if he were a bag of cement, but even so, Kalisha was glad to be doing it. Handling death is a lot easier than ignoring it.

Lily lifted her T-shirt mask so that she could carry the flashlight in her mouth. They bounced him down the stairs at the side of the house and then tilted the wheelbarrow at the edge of the fresh grave. No wonder there was a whole industry surrounding death. Making it look graceful was a lot of work. They didn't even try.

Together they tugged the professor into the pit. Then Kalisha crouched on the edge, her elbows on her extended knees, and looked at her philosophy teacher. When she accidentally fell back on her butt, she and Lily both laughed. The flashlight shot out of Lily's mouth and into the grave. "Shit!" she cried, and then they laughed harder.

"Oh!" Lily cried, uneasy about laughing. "Sorry! Sorry!"

"It's okay," Kalisha said, and somehow it *was* okay. The laughing didn't feel disrespectful. It felt just the opposite, like a form of deep appreciation.

"Love is love," Lily agreed. "Irreducible."

Then Lily lay on her belly and reached down to retrieve the flashlight, snatching it quickly, as if afraid that she might be sucked into the hole with Professor Vernadsky. She scrambled to her feet, and they both stood, looking down, two women in their bras, T-shirts tied around their faces like bandits, staring at the body they'd just dumped in a grave. Neither of them wanted to shovel the dirt back over him.

Lily used the side of her foot and kicked in a few clods. Kalisha didn't join her until Lily had pushed in an entire layer of soil. Then she picked up the shovel and, taking turns, they got him buried.

Kalisha stood up straight, on the side of the fresh mound, with her hands behind her back. Vernadsky hadn't believed in God, but she prayed anyway. Then, out loud, in a firm and steady voice, "Thank you, Professor Vernadsky."

Lily said, "I *lubh* you."

21

LILY BOUGHT ANOTHER NIGHT in the motel, and then in the morning pedaled up Grizzly Peak Boulevard with her tent and sleeping bag strapped onto her handlebars. She could go stay with Vicky, but that was nearly twenty miles away. She'd have to give up her job at the church, and Lily wasn't willing to do that. She guessed that Sal would not be interested in meeting her, but it occurred to Lily that maybe there was a good camping place near the hyena compound. People stayed away from that area because it was rumored that some of the hyenas had escaped after the earthquake. It might be perfect: close enough to the church and away from the dangers of the city.

As Lily neared the turnoff for the fire trail that led out to the hyena compound, she heard a motorcycle gaining on her from behind. It passed, a burst of sunlight glinting off the chrome, and she recognized the lank curve of his body. Wesley leaned into the bend in the road and disappeared around the corner. A quick memory of her ride with him, that dilated joy, shimmered inside her.

So he was back from Oregon.

Besides *The Earthquake Chronicles,* she'd read all the installments of *Wings on Fire.* Wesley had invented a newly evolved hominid species that could fly. These humanlike creatures not only had wings, some freak genetic mutation gave them spectacular endurance. His protagonist, Suzette, could fly from the Amazon River to New York with as few as three resting stops. In one episode, Suzette alighted next to a gargoyle on the north tower of Chartres Cathedral and held very still, poised with her wings folded, to see if the tourists would notice her. She flew off at dusk, her wings black expanses against a violet sky, and found a quiet place in Paris for dinner where she humored herself by ordering Crêpes Suzette. Later, on a mountain in Uganda, she perched in a tree and tried to speak with a silverback gorilla, who grunted at her but of course didn't speak any of the eight languages Suzette knew. She wanted to hug him, to console him, because she knew his country was war-torn and his habitat ravaged, but the silverback would not acknowledge her beyond the grunts. This broke Suzette's heart, but at the same time, she understood, and so she flew on. In another installment, she got caught in a hurricane in the Caribbean. Wesley spent too many paragraphs describing her screaming battles against the blasting winds, the ripping of her wings, and her terrible fear. But Lily loved the part, after the storm had ended, where she floated on her back in the warm Caribbean water, her battered wings spread to their fullest, and rested.

Wesley thought stories could save people. Maybe. Stories and food.

Lily needed Kalisha's bracing realism. Ron's stuttering compassion. She needed all the clients who came for dinner every afternoon: the teenage boy who always held up his thumb, forefinger, and baby finger to sign "I love you"; the elderly woman who sang her a few lines of a different song everyday; the painfully shy man whose greeting warmed up incrementally week by week but who still couldn't manage eye contact; and, of course, Herbert and his dad.

Standing at the steam table and serving up plates of hot food in Trinity Church felt the opposite of being homeless. She hadn't felt this awake in years. If Wesley could choose to stay here in the heart of disaster to tell survivors' stories, couldn't she stay to serve them dinner?

Lily turned off the paved road and onto the fire trail that began at the university's Space Sciences Laboratory. The lab looked like a prison the way the building had been secured with giant sheets of plywood and endless strands of barbed wire fencing, though she saw no guards. No one stopped her from heading out the fire trail. She wended through a mile of university-owned wilderness: eucalyptus and bay laurel trees, with an occasional Monterey pine. A long chain-link fence, topped with more strands of barbed wire, followed the trail on the left-hand side. The fence belonged to the Berkeley Field Station for the Study of Behavior, Ecology, and Reproduction, where Sal worked. Or used to work, before the earthquake.

Lily's bicycle bounced along the dirt and rock road, jarring her hands and arms and loosening the bundle tied to her handlebars. About a mile out, she saw the toolshed, a small rustic building situated behind the fence and a good distance up the hill. So that's where Vicky had her bonus days with Sal. Today she saw no sign of Sal, nor any other people. Lily continued on another half-mile, until she came to a faint trail leading down to the right. She took this and soon entered open chaparral. She braked and stood with a foot on either side of her bicycle, perched on the top of a small knoll, looking out on a sweeping view of the entire Bay Area.

Home, she thought. Her life was in as much shambles as the cities in the earthquake zone below, and yet she felt a little buzz of hope. She dropped her bike and unfurled her tent.

PART TWO

22

LILY STEPPED OUT OF the Trinity Church community room into a purple twilight. She paused at the top of the steps and breathed in the damp air. She thought she could smell the bay, just there, on the edge of the city. Or, actually, in the center of many cities, connected to the ocean and other continents by that delicate red bridge. Of course, it wasn't delicate at all. It had survived the earthquake. But from her tent, perched high on the hillside, the Golden Gate Bridge looked like a piece of jewelry strung across the throat of the Bay Area.

The community room had been especially stuffy tonight—they were feeding a record number of people, the big room jammed with chairs and voices—and she'd needed a quick breath of fresh air after finishing the cleanup. She was about to go back inside to retrieve her bicycle when she saw the man emerge from the shadows on the other side of the parking lot. He strode toward her, slowing when he noticed her standing on the stoop watching him approach. Thirty yards away, he lifted a hand and called out, "I'm looking for Lily Jones. I think she works here."

Lily wished she could pretend, for just a minute, that she wasn't Lily Jones. She wished she could observe him from a distance, how he walked, talked, gestured, smiled.

The man now standing before her was shorter, and handsomer, than Lily expected him to be. His smile was complicated, an expression of will mixed with dread, a here-for-better-or-worse smile. She couldn't see the color of his eyes in the dusk light, but his teeth were perfect, bright white and straight. His longish blond hair made him look younger than his forty-four years.

"Lily?" he asked.

She nodded, too overwhelmed to speak.

"Travis Grayson."

He held out a hand and she managed to shake it.

"Look at you," he said, emotion thickening his voice.

Lily glanced down at her chest and the tops of her thighs, foolishly following his directions.

"Lily Jones," he said. "A real person."

It'd been nearly two weeks since she'd written to him. She'd figured that either he'd never gotten to Berkeley or he'd meant what he said about not contacting her again.

"Of course you're real," he carried on. "I mean, I don't know, I just didn't expect…"

"Wow," Lily finally said.

"Yeah. Wow."

There was something alarming about him, both fervent and vulnerable, as if he'd just stepped across a railroad track moments before a train whooshed through. She reached out a hand but didn't touch him. "Are you okay?"

"Yeah. Yes. I'm good. I'm sorry I didn't come sooner. It's been crazy. I'm sorry about Vicky."

"Oh! I found her! She's fine. Totally alive." Lily tried to laugh. "Although I almost lost her again. It's all so complicated here."

Travis was saying, "Oh, good. Good. Good," all while she bumbled her explanation of Vicky. Then, "It is. Yes, it is. Complicated." His smile. His eyes. Just a man. If he'd wanted her to be the holder of ordinary, she'd wanted him to be the holder of extraordinary. The one who would tell her about the possibility for human salvation. Not just a guy with a hundred-watt smile and devastated eyes. She almost wished he hadn't come.

"Are you sure you're okay?" she asked.

"I'm so glad you found your sister."

"She's living out by the Oakland airport now."

"The Hegenberger Cluster?"

"You know them?"

"Come on. Let's get a cup of tea. There's a lot to talk about."

"Tea? Where?"

"I know a place."

Leaving her bicycle inside, Lily cantered down the steps. How so very strange to be walking alongside Travis Grayson! All these years he'd been airmail tissue and lofty ideas, and now so quickly he was reduced to a limping gait and a hyper smile.

A few blocks away, he used a key to open the front door to a Craftsman bungalow. Lit candles stood on all the ledges and the wooden paneling glowed warm reddish brown. A few young people sat on the floor of the front room, dipping pieces of bread into a central pot.

"Hey," Travis said to the young people.

"Hey," they all said back.

"You hungry?" he asked Lily.

She hesitated, stalled by a mix of confusion and curiosity. "I just ate."

Travis picked up one of the three camp stoves sitting on the floor next to the built-in bookshelves. He grabbed a lit candle, too. "Let's go upstairs."

"Whose house is this?" Lily asked, her hand sliding along the polished wooden banister as they climbed to the second floor.

"Dunno. We've been using it for a while now, but we probably need to move on soon. It's best to not get too attached to any shelters. You never know when you're going to get busted. Moving often is the best way to stay safe." He motioned for her to step into one of the bedrooms.

"Who's 'we'?"

"I'm with the San Pablo Reservoir Cluster. Here, hold the candle for me." He crouched to fiddle with the stove. "We have a couple of houses down here in the flatlands that we use for various purposes. Like, new members stay here until we accept them as permanent residents."

"Permanent residents?"

"Up at the reservoir. We vet people before accepting them."

A blue flame hissed to life on the camp stove. He told her to hold on a second and went downstairs to get a pan of water and some tea. When he returned, he handed her a book of matches. "Light the others?"

There were six fat candles sitting on the dresser. Her hands shook as she held the match flame to the wicks. For so many years, Travis Grayson had been her Land of Oz, a brightly colored place beyond her reach. And now here she was, in his presence, in his niche, as if they were two inhabitants of a new ecosystem. He shut the bedroom door, and they sat cross-legged on the floor in front of the stove, their campfire. The shadows and light shimmied on the walls.

Travis stared at her for a long time, then slowly shook his head. "I had no idea you..."

"What." She bit off the question inflection, not sure she wanted to hear what he'd had no idea about.

"You're just beautiful, that's all. I didn't know."

He lowered his eyes, as if to show he didn't mean anything other than an observation. But the kindness of his comment blew right into the vacuum sucked out by her loneliness, hunger, and exhaustion. She wanted to move over next to him, lean against him, fall asleep with him. All at once she was glad he was just a man, human, contained by skin and bones like everyone else. Still, she stayed where she was: the hiss of the stove, the closed door, the trembling candlelight all made Lily feel as if she were dreaming, nothing she could trust.

"You first," he said. "Tell me everything. How did you get here?"

She told him everything: the flight to Sacramento, the car ride to the edge of Oakland, the hike along the freeway, the pit bulls and corpse in the Miata, the night in the FedEx truck, thinking Vicky was dead and then finding her, being harangued by Annie, and her eviction from Joyce's flat. She told him about finding and burying Professor Vernadsky's body. She couldn't stop talking once she started. He laughed out loud at her description of Angelina.

Until she said, "He's leaving me for her."

"No," he said, sobering up quickly. "That's not possible."

She tried to swallow down the hard knot in her throat.

"You've been so solidly married. He was your childhood sweetheart. Like, the boy next door."

She nodded.

"So...why?"

Because of you, she wanted to say. But no, not Travis Grayson, the flesh-and-blood man sitting here now. Tom was jealous of him, true, but that was wrong. It had never been the man himself. And yet, Travis had been smack in the center of that biggest fight of all, the one about Tom's DNA and Lily's world of children who needed love. His letters, the bonobos, had shown her a way forward.

"You don't have to answer that," Travis said.

"I'm not sure I can."

"How'd you get this scar?"

His fingers on her chin felt too potent. She took a sip of the mint tea. "When I was eight, I tripped on a hose at a gas station. I fell face-first onto a broken bottle."

"Ouch."

"It was a long time ago."

Lily glanced at the warm, clean bed. Was it his? His glance followed hers. Then he asked, "Where are you living?"

People didn't ask that question. She had, a few times in the beginning, and noticed how people scowled slightly, as if she'd been rude. Now she understood. She'd been in her camp for five nights and hadn't told anyone where she was sleeping, not even Vicky.

But this was Travis Grayson. If anyone could understand her plan, it would be him. First, she'd find a way to reunite Vicky and Sal. That would take routing Vicky out of East Oakland. It would take finding a way to make Sal acknowledge Lily. All that had to happen before she could engineer their reconciliation. Kalisha might want to join them, and maybe even Ron and his girlfriend. Vicky said there was a stream near Sal's toolshed, although Lily hadn't yet found it. She'd been hauling water from the church to her campsite. They could build another couple of shelters. None of it would be permanent, but they'd be stronger together. Maybe Wesley the motorcycle guy would want to join them. She'd even thought of a name: the Hyena Cluster.

She sipped her tea and carefully chose her words. "I love my job at the church. I want to keep feeding people. So—"

He nodded hard, admiringly. "You'd fit in our Cluster really well. You're exactly the kind of person we need. Letting that hungry girl into the flat was the right thing to do. People shouldn't lock up resources they aren't using. In our Cluster, we share everything."

Lily touched the bulge at her breast, her thin packet of money. Travis mistook the gesture, thought she was touching her heart.

"Yeah," he said. "It's devastating what's happening."

"I'm sorry. About the sanctuary. About the bonobos."

"That's the past. I'm exactly where I want to be."

"Your turn," she said, "to tell me everything." She thought he'd start where everyone started, with the earthquake.

But he didn't. "You probably gathered from my letters that I was in love with Renée."

Actually, Lily hadn't gathered that.

"She wasn't in love with me. She never had been. But years ago we had a little thing. It ended. I knew it was over. It's not like I didn't give up hope. I did give it up. But I stayed and stayed and stayed anyway."

"You stayed for the bonobos."

"Yeah," he said. "Yeah, that's true. But I never had the kind of flawless dedication Renée had. No one could possibly match her devotion to them. Yannick hated me for wanting her. He saw it every day and scorned me. Renée saw it, too, but for her, desire is just part of the human condition. It didn't bother her that I loved her. If she could use my love for her to benefit the bonobos, she would. She did."

The flash of bitterness, maybe even anger, surprised Lily. She drank more minty tea and rallied to his side. "Why did Yannick care if you loved Renée?"

"He thought it was vulgar, an American wanting a Congolese woman. He had very strict standards of marriage and family. She was royalty to him and I was common, a nobody. He thought that I thought I was important because of my nationality. He believed that the only reason I stayed at the sanctuary all those years was because of her."

"He knew about your research!"

Travis shrugged. "He always thought I'd fail. When I did, he saw me as a virus that had been infecting them for years. He and Renée had a shouting match about me, in front of me, and her defense weakened. I saw it weaken. I saw her give up on me."

"No one cared about the bonobos more than you."

He gave her a crooked smile. "Maybe. But it's true that I caused the end of the sanctuary."

Lily shook her head. "No. No, you didn't."

"So here I am. Getting on with my life."

"Back to your teaching job, when the university opens again."

"Actually, I feel really lucky to have landed here now. Yannick is right, in a way. I need to take care of the mess in my own backyard. Where I can be more effective. There is so much work to do."

"Travis?" She touched his hand, as if gently waking him from a nightmare. "Where were you for the earthquake?"

His right eye twitched and he reached up a knuckled fist to rub it. "A dog and a baby," he said. "They got me through."

"What do you mean?" She resisted the urge to touch him again, but wished there were a way to calm him.

He sat up straighter and squared his shoulders. "First order of business is getting control of the region. The troops need to go. They've killed at least a hundred innocent people, calling them looters or squatters. FEMA still hasn't sent the promised trailers. And really, trailers? I mean, is that the best they can do? The feds have always hated California and they always will. We're on our own, that's a fact. But that's also a good thing. I *want* them to leave us alone."

"You've never before sounded cynical like this."

"I'm not cynical. I'm the opposite of cynical. I'm practical. Above all else, I'm practical. I want people to have food and shelter. Washington is filled with cowards, and so is Sacramento. This is an opportunity for true rule by the people, for the people. An opportunity for us to take care of ourselves. And the exciting part is that we're doing it."

"That's what Vicky says."

"So she's with the Hegenberger Cluster?"

Lily nodded.

"Where exactly is she living?"

Lily hesitated only for a moment. "She's on Eighty-First Avenue. She's doing electronics for them."

"Ah!" Travis's eyes brightened. They were green, she decided. "Yeah! See? It's like that. People have what we need to take care of ourselves, if only the authorities didn't interfere. We have the complete toolkit to make food, to make clean energy. All the tech is there. What's not there is the political will. The collapse of the infrastructure means we don't have to fight against the machine anymore. We're on our own. We're organizing to make it work."

"Things are getting better, though," Lily said. "Power is back in some places. Lots of people have water now."

"Sure, the wealthier neighborhoods are doing okay. But it's mainly poor people, people who were living in multifamily buildings, who lost their homes. Those structures are not being rebuilt."

Lily knew this was true. The number of clients at the Trinity Church free meals program had increased, not decreased.

"What's worse, the government is targeting those of us who are trying to make it work for ourselves. Increasingly, refugees are having to hide. They've sent in troops to actually close down a few of the camps. It's becoming illegal to try to live."

"You haven't had any of your tea. Are you sure you're okay?"

"Ah," he said and blew out a long breath. He looked at the darkest corner of the room. "Yeah. Pretty much."

He seemed stunned. But who wasn't? She felt off-kilter, too.

"It's you," he said shaking his head in slow disbelief. "I can't believe you're sitting here with me. My Nebraska girl. I told you everything, didn't I?"

"Probably because you thought you'd never meet me in person."

"Yeah, actually. I think that is probably what I assumed. And now here you are. A real person, after all."

Lily laughed. "I think I'm real. A bit hard to know for sure lately."

He touched her scar again. This time she let her chin sink into his hand. Why not? His warm palm. The ancient light of six fat candles. The clean, cushioned bed. The man to whom, for twenty years, she'd written her most deeply felt sentences. Those words, candles, sheets, and hands spun a silky web.

"Tell me," she whispered. "Where were you for the earthquake?"

Travis shook his blond mane and then got to his feet, pacing to the dark window. "People don't get what's happening. They're getting crushed by the system every day. The earthquake is one giant metaphor. One giant wakeup call."

He wasn't going to answer her questions. Not now, anyway. The withholding felt like bait and she rose to her feet, too, joining him at the window. She put a hand on the small of his back. The fabric of his worn T-shirt was soft, and she lifted the hem of the shirt. The muscles on his back spasmed, as if her touch hurt him.

"You seem sad," she said, purposely using a much softer word than the one she meant.

He nodded but looked away.

She was scaring herself. Touching Travis felt like another survival behavior, like hoarding tools, like eating found fruit rinds, like sleeping on hillsides. She was still married. She wasn't a bonobo. There were rules in place, and yet she felt as if there were no gravity in this dark room, as if she were in suspension, and all that mattered were touch and hunger. And truly: Why not?

As she stepped around to face him, he looked surprised. She tried to see the surprise as warning but only wanted to soothe his devastation. *Her* devastation. She traced his collarbone, ran her fingers down his ribs, held him at the hips, began to pull him toward her. Until she felt the edge of a hard object in his pocket.

"What's this?"

Travis withdrew the gun and tried to hand it to her.

"Why?" she asked, stepping away. "What are you doing with this?"

"You're so innocent," he said softly. "You really don't get what's going on here, do you?"

Lily searched his face for meaning. In the candlelight, she couldn't see much more than small caves of shadow and the glistening white of his eyes. "I need to go," she said, backing up slowly, afraid to leave, afraid of stepping into the abyss of loneliness just outside that door, but even more afraid of the gun.

23

L ILY FLED THE CANDLELIT bedroom and the Craftsman bungalow, but she couldn't get free of that whirlpool of feeling. His intensity, his listening, his convictions; it was as if Travis and Tom were two different countries. Was that the choice? Frightening zeal or bland disconnection?

She wanted her own country.

Lily hiked up the hill, not paying attention, forgetting to walk with intention and confidence, trying to fathom why Travis would have a handgun, an object that negated everything she thought he stood for.

She needed to get back on track with her plan. The loneliness had gouged her out, left her empty and vulnerable. She'd been alone on her hillside for five nights, the solitude interrupted only by the few hours in the church and a couple of phone calls with Vicky. The loss of Tom was a tide sucking her out to sea. She needed to act rationally. Take steps. She would make Sal acknowledge her and convince Vicky to move back to Berkeley. Tomorrow she'd talk to Kalisha about her plan.

The band of ferals circled Lily near La Loma Park, the place where the two National Guard soldiers, Eduardo and William, were usually stationed. She'd been sneaking the guards snacks from the church and sometimes sat in the park with them exchanging news. Both were from Texas. Tonight they were nowhere to be seen. The kids corralled her, the way humpback whales do prey, moving her toward the jungle gym. They pushed her against the bars of the structure. Some of the ferals couldn't have been older than six, but there were at least seven of them, and they stuffed their hands in her pockets, yanked off her sneakers, reached into her bra where they found the last of her cash.

The children didn't even frighten her, not now after that womb of candlelight with an armed man at its center. Not now with her husband leaving her, or her leaving her husband, and her life a gaping maw before her. A bunch of hungry children. That at least was something she understood.

"I'd like to keep my sneakers," she said. But they walked off with them anyway, shouting at one another, beginning to brawl over who got the cash. Then one little boy, inexplicably, snatched one sneaker from each of two other ferals, retraced his steps, and hurled them at her. Maybe she looked like his mother.

Lily sat on the ground and tied on her shoes. Luckily she'd left her bicycle at the church, though it made for a long walk out to her campsite. When she got to Grizzly Peak Boulevard, she took a right, passed the turnoff for Ridge Road, and continued on to the fire trail. She walked out through the forest of eucalyptus and bay laurels and stopped at the place where in daylight she could see the toolshed on the hillside high above the trail. Sal did a good job of making herself scarce. Every time she passed, Lily looked for signs of life: movement, drying clothing, an open door. Twice she'd stood here at the fence and shouted Sal's name, but she'd never gotten a response. The place looked uninhabited, and maybe it was—maybe Sal had moved on. Lily hoped not. Despite everything that had happened between them, she was pretty sure that Sal was the key to Vicky. And Lily needed Vicky.

When she got to her camp, Lily sat on the big stone in front of her tent and looked out into the night, like some kind of twenty-first-century pioneer. Parts of the cities below were lit, but there were whole pockets of darkness. The bay was a giant black amoeba, a harbor of exceptional proportions. The Hayward fault, the one that had slipped so dramatically twenty-seven days ago, ran under the northern end of the bay. The mayor of Fair Oaks, a not particularly compassionate woman, had actually joked, one morning in the café a few days after the quake, about how it was too bad the entire state hadn't snapped off from the rest of the continent. It was true what Travis said about some people not liking California. The place was uncommon with its crashing coastline and too-warm winters, with its tendency to reject the status quo and its arrogance about doing so.

Her own arrogance had drawn her out here to California. A belief that she could save someone. A desire to be a part of something bigger than marriage and work. Those letters from Travis had started coming when she was thirteen years old, a little girl, and she'd devoured his outsized hope. The letters had kept coming, too, for years and years, like some parallel stream to her real life, one in which she was still thirteen and could dream massive dreams. How foolish she had been. How foolish she still was: she'd just tried to kiss Travis Grayson!

Who was just a man. A man with a gun. Another man with a gun.

And yet. She'd read all the science backing up his letters, the books by Frans de Waal and the hard-to-find articles by Adrienne L. Zihlman. The thrilling truths Travis was uncovering about the bonobos were true. Maybe he himself didn't matter at all. What mattered was the research that confirmed her belief in human goodness. How could that be foolish?

Lily retrieved the manila folder from her tent and clicked on her flashlight. She knew exactly which letter she wanted to reread. He'd written it many years ago.

Dear Lily,

I wonder why I stay. The stomach ailments. The wars. The wrenching grief each time we can't save a bonobo. But I have a theory. I need to see it tested. And this is the only place where that can happen.

The question is this: Can humans ever live together in peace? It hasn't happened yet. For centuries, despots have ransacked as much of the planet as they can. It goes on and on and on. The only thing that changes is the skill with which these madmen plunder. They keep developing technologies that allow them to take more resources and more lives. Leaving people with less and less.

Okay, that's the historical model. But history is only a few thousand years old. What if we used a biological model instead?

Consider evolution. Organisms with successful traits reproduce more. They pass along the successful traits. Over time, a larger and larger percentage of the population has these traits. Right?

What if compassion and altruism turn out, over time, to be successful traits? They do in fact exist as traits, whether successful or not, right now. People cooperate all the time. Even the everyday activity of driving on freeways takes an extraordinary amount of cooperation. Of course there are exceptions, but the vast majority drive in the correct lanes, use turn signals, follow the rules that we've all agreed upon.

Bonobos are great at compassion and altruism. They give a helping hand to sick members of their communities. They share food. They share lovers! I've told you all the stories. And here's a fact that no one disputes: we've descended from them as closely as we've descended from the more conflict-driven chimpanzees.

What if these inherited traits of love are the ones that drive our evolution? What if, in the long, long run, the warlike people tear each other to pieces and are less successful at reproduction? And the people who have learned to cooperate and make peace are in fact more successful at carrying on? Evolution is a slow but mighty creep toward survival. It's in our genes. It can take thousands and thousands of years. This is not something we would be able to detect in history. Probably not in our lifetimes. But I need to know it's possible, and these creatures, my sweet bonobos, give that to me. That's why I stay. For the hope. For the reminder that I possess genes that are nudging me in the right direction.

The evolution of love. It's possible, Calla Lily. It is.

Love,

Travis

24

VICKY COULDN'T BELIEVE HER good fortune. Starting from scratch was like designing a virtual world for a computer game. Even better, the tools and resources available to her were not the usual ones. She got to play with a whole new set of challenges.

The neighborhood around the Oakland airport had been built on landfill. During the earthquake, the ground rolled and boiled like wet mud. Actually, it *became* wet mud. Navigating the now buckled streets was difficult. There were known routes for getting just about everywhere, and these were always congested, even though, of the diminished population left after the earthquake, an even smaller number had cars. Gas had to be bought on the outside, and at exorbitant prices, but some people did buy it. As much as she hated exercise, buying another bicycle—she'd given her old one to Lily—had been a good idea; she could pedal roads that weren't passable by car.

Some of the buildings in Vicky's new neighborhood had withstood the liquefaction, but most had at least popped out their windows, and others lay in ruins. Even so, the neighborhood had an odd tidiness. The streets and sidewalks had been picked clean. People scavenged every scrap of metal, every loose chunk of asphalt, every last piece of glass. Even the makeshift homes, car bodies, and foundation chunk huts had swept entryways and airtight cooking chimneys.

Vicky lived in a small stucco building that used to house four apartments but was now half rubble. The flight of stairs to the second floor was in one piece, free-floating, flanked on either side by caved-in walls and jagged arms of rebar. As she climbed, she could look right down into the bottom two apartments. People had cleared out the central spaces but could do nothing about the giant holes overhead. Both rain and sun soaked what was left of the rooms. Vicky inhabited the only intact apartment in the building, a small second-story studio. She had a door with a lock, four walls, and a ceiling.

At the sound of a forceful and sustained knock on her exterior door, Vicky held very still. She did not answer. You just never knew what people wanted, and friendly visitors would call out with a voice greeting, so you knew who it was and what they wanted. So far, she'd allowed no one in her studio. Most people were amazingly cool, but she had a lot of valuable equipment in here, not to mention the chairs. Caution wasn't exactly her forte, but she was trying to heed her sister's most recent warning. "Just be safe," Lily had said. Vicky had cracked a joke, of course, but Lily was right. Anyway, she was having way too much fun to spoil it by letting some asshole steal her computers and chairs.

The pounding on her door intensified.

Who could it be? Vicky wished the pull of curiosity weren't so great in her makeup. Was inquisitiveness a genetic trait? She'd have Lily ask her bonobo researcher.

Oh, what the hell. The guy wouldn't let up and she *was* curious to find out who was so interested in gaining access to her apartment. She could handle whatever. So she called out, "Who is it?"

"Me!"

Vicky pulled open the door to find Lily, gripping her bicycle, on the free-floating precipice that was her entryway.

"Lily! Welcome! Hi!" She grabbed her sister's arm and pulled her in, then shut and locked the door. "Why didn't you say it was you? Welcome to my humble abode!" Lily looked quizzically dubious, so Vicky launched right into a tour of her one room, pointing out the high points and improvements.

The walls were cracked, but she'd stuffed the bigger cavities with newspaper. The lone window had busted out, but she'd put up plastic sheeting with duct tape. The Time-Life chair fronted a plywood-and-cinder-block desk, and the clear plastic Bubble chair lolled up against a corner of the room. The other chairs were shoved and stacked against the wall opposite the window. Vicky opened the only interior door and showed her the cramped toilet and shower stall.

"Here, let me open the window for some fresh air." Vicky ripped down the top half of the plastic sheeting and showed Lily how she'd super-glued large jagged pieces of broken glass all around the window's exterior frame to discourage intruders.

"Even the electric works," she bragged, pointing out a long outlet strip plugged into the wall.

Lily gestured at the husks and innards of several computers strewn about the studio. "What's all this stuff?"

"I'm working," she stage-whispered. "Have to be a little circumspect, though. I don't really want the world to know I have all these electronics in here. Clients would kill me if I lost their data. I tell them I have a shop. Ha ha. I hire people to do the pickup and delivery. Makes it look like I got a whole sophisticated operation."

"Right," Lily said and almost rolled her eyes.

"Anyway, my price is right. And people know I'm good. I'm back in the black. Making good money. How're things at Joyce's? Have you talked to Tom?"

"I'm glad you're okay."

"Are *you*?"

"Travis came by the church."

"Hot diggity! The bonobo!"

"He's actually a man, not a bonobo."

She enjoyed how Lily flushed red, the way her voice deepened and quavered. Vicky imitated her. "He's a *maaan*."

"Stop it."

"You slept with him!"

Lily huffed in annoyance.

"Hot diggity! How was he?"

"I didn't sleep with him. I'm still married, you know."

"Still?"

"Tom's seeing Angelina. Remember her?"

"What?"

"You heard me."

"I don't believe it."

Shit, was Lily about to cry?

"He's always so über-virtuous. I'm just kind of shocked."

"Well, that's something. Shocking you."

"Who's Angelina?"

"Five years older than me. Last name Hudson."

"I think I remember her. She was a senior when I was a freshman. Tits so big she sort of waddles when she walks?"

"Uh huh. Makes a weird clucking sound in the back of her throat."

"Yes! God, I remember that! What do you mean, 'seeing'?"

Lily made an exasperated face. She'd managed to suppress the tears, anyway. Maybe Vicky should hug her?

"So that's why you came out to California."

"No! It didn't start until—" Vicky saw Lily realize that she had no idea when it had started. "I came out here to see if you were okay."

"And yet, here he is. The bonobo researcher. And now you're single!"

"Vicky, it doesn't feel that good. Being single. Breaking up with Tom."

"Speaking of sex," Vicky said. She tapped a metal box sprouting colorful plastic-sheathed wires. "I met someone. I'm doing this job for a 'restaurant'"—Vicky used her fingers to make air quotes—"that opened near here. More like a glorified food cart. Gotta admire folks working with what we got. Anyway, they have awesome food. Big hunks of meat and roasted everything. I think they're shooting urban deer! People do have to eat. It's just the next step after the street markets. Gives new meaning to the term 'free enterprise.'"

Lily shook her head, looking very censorial.

"Faith, sister. Hang in. We're going to be in Fat City again real soon."

"Don't you miss Sal?"

Now this really *was* irritating. Her married-for-decades sister could almost fuck some dude who studies apes in the Congo, but she was supposed to miss a woman she'd been with for not quite two years and with whom, by the way, she'd broken up.

"So I was about to tell you about this babe. She's the owner of this new 'restaurant.'" Vicky let out a low huff. "I'd say Sicilian or something. Her, not the food. Big mane of black hair with red highlights. Dark skin with lots of soft dark hairs on her forearms. Faint little mustache. *And—*" She used her hands to shape a full figure, followed by a whistle. "Then this husky voice that just begs for—"

"Shut *up*, Vicky."

"What?"

"You told me that Sal likes you for who you really are. You had a real relationship. Whoever this 'babe' is, you don't even know her. Get real here. We're in the middle of a crisis. It's time to know who your family is, who your friends are. Your real ones."

Vicky stood very still in the middle of her assemblage of computer parts and plastic sheeting, duct tape and antique chairs, watching Lily talk, waiting her out. Her words were a squall that would pass.

"Sal *liked* you."

"You're *not* okay about the Tom thing, are you?"

Lily paced to the door, as if she were about to leave, but then turned quickly. "'The Tom thing'? He's been my husband for fifteen years."

Vicky wagged her head, trying hard to be a helpful listener. She'd much rather do that than endure lectures about Sal.

Lily dug in. "Look. We need a concrete plan. It doesn't help to live in a fantasy world. I know you're brilliant. I know you can debug or program anything. But brilliance isn't enough anymore. This is the age of survival."

Vicky snickered.

"Okay, fine," Lily said, grabbing the stem of her bicycle.

"No, no, no! Don't go! I'm sorry. I've just never seen you like this. It was the 'age of survival' part."

"What's so funny about that?"

"Nothing really. I—" She got interrupted by an airplane sheering the sound waves. An Air Force fighter plane filled the view from the window, soaring skyward. When the quiet resumed, Vicky started to finish her thought, but another flying object, a yellow jacket, zipped right into the open half of the window.

"Shit." Lily patted her pockets. "I left my epinephrine in the tent."

"Tent?"

The wasp flew directly across the room and landed on Lily's cheek.

"Don't move," Vicky said. As the yellow jacket crawled up Lily's cheekbone toward her eye, it was as if Vicky could feel its tiny legs tickling her own face.

Vicky lunged, her hand performing a cross between a caress and a punch, abrupt and snappy, and scooped the yellow jacket off Lily's cheek. She carried it in her closed hands to the window and freed the little stinging terrorist. She taped the plastic sheeting back over the window.

"Thank you," Lily said quietly.

"You're welcome," Vicky said.

"I have to get to the church and it's a long ride back across Oakland and Berkeley."

"Okay. Thank you for visiting."

"I wanted to make sure you're okay."

"I'm dandy."

"I want you to apologize to Sal and move back to Berkeley."

So Lily had an agenda. Vicky could see it in the way she held her mouth, twisted off to the side. Sal. Berkeley. Leading to what? Lily thought she was being shrewd, introducing a few key starter steps.

Clearly Lily had forgotten about the sticky issue of Gloria. Not to mention her spouse and head of the neighborhood association, that snake Paul. Moving to Berkeley would be like jumping into a live-action computer game; every physical move she made would have to be calculated to keep from getting in either of their paths.

Hey, that was kind of a good idea! She could design Gloria as a playboy bunny, big hair and tits, and Paul as a writhing serpent. Vicky tried to kill the smile tugging at her mouth.

"I mean it," Lily said, all parental. "You know I'm right."

"My house has been repossessed." Vicky was proud of having thought of a practical answer.

"I know. We'd need to find another place to live."

Acquiescing would probably be the easiest route through this little bog. "Okay."

"Weak response. We'll talk about this more later. I'm going to be late."

"Okay. Call me." Vicky held an imaginary phone to her face.

The second Lily left, Vicky, deflated, got downright sad. She walked around her studio, touching her computer parts and chairs, trying to regain her sense of adventure.

It was Sal. Why did Lily keep insisting on bringing her up, as if Vicky had some sort of choice in the matter?

Wait. Maybe Lily was right. Maybe she did have a choice.

Maybe love could be like a computer game, too. Maybe there was a formula. Or a set of defining criteria. You figure them out, and you win.

Vicky sat down at one of her computers and brought up a spreadsheet. No, that was too confining. She could design a game, but that would take weeks.

See, that was the problem with love. It slipped out of all the ordinary parameters. It refused to be programmed. She usually told herself that love wasn't real. It was just a biological reaction to some human needs. Whatever.

But maybe she was wrong. Maybe it was real. A thing in the room. A thing in her body, even. Was it possible that love truly existed, maybe more than any other thing? But how could something that couldn't be measured be real?

Here was a new idea: maybe love couldn't be measured or quantified, but it could succeed if you followed certain regulations.

Hadn't Sal been telling her that all along? Vicky opened a simple word processing program and tapped out a list. "Communication. Kindness. Honesty." And seriously, the main thing girls wanted—who didn't know this?—was to be the only one. Maybe it was a stupid rule. But it did have a simple correlating behavior. She picked up her phone and sent a text canceling her date with the Sicilian babe. She might lose the restaurant account, too—and how rational was that?—but the risk was exciting. If love was a game, another kind of challenge, maybe she could handle being in it.

It wasn't until Vicky emerged from this intriguing train of thought that she remembered the word "tent." She ran out the door and looked in every direction, but Lily was long gone.

25

L ILY AWOKE AT DAYBREAK, as she did every morning, to birdsong. Most of the voices twittered and chirped, with some doing entire melodic riffs, but there was one strange whooping bird that she always heard. Its voice started low, climbing smoothly to a crescendo. It sounded nothing at all like any bird in Nebraska.

She climbed out of her tent into a blue day caressed by a soft breeze. Coyote brush—scrappy chest-high plants, small but sturdy, with fibrous branches and deep green leaves—covered the hillside. Soon they would bloom, bringing bees. The air had a pungent herbal scent, a mix of snake and rabbit and sage and grass, bay leaves and dust.

Lily secured her camp, which meant zipping up her tent, and rode her bicycle up to the main fire trail. When she got to the place where a locked chain-link gate interrupted the fence, she braked and stood straddling the bike. Just up the hill she could see the toolshed.

"Hey!" she shouted. "Sal! Are you up there?"

She listened to a long interlude of pattering leaves and the cawing of a crow.

"I'm safe! Friendly!"

Lily dropped her bike and began climbing the chain-link gate. Pushing her sneaker toes through the metal diamonds was easy, but the wire dug painfully into her hands. As she grasped the top tube and tried to figure out a way to throw her leg up and over, a deep voice boomed, "Who are you?"

Lily startled so hard she fell off the fence.

A woman stepped out from behind the shed. She held a garden hoe over her head and her heavy breasts bounced angrily as she lunged down the hill. Lily was glad the chain-link fence separated them because it looked as if the woman would not hesitate to hack her to pieces with that hoe.

"I see you riding by every day," she bellowed. "You're not allowed out here. It's university property."

Sal looked like a cover girl gone off the rails, like her beauty had been lobotomized, sexy with one big shock treatment. She had flashing bright brown eyes; long, thick, and tangled auburn hair; generous breasts and hips stuffed a little too tightly into her clothes. Her hands were rough and cracked, and she had two deep scowl lines between her eyes, evidently from a lifetime, about forty years, of bucking expectations.

"I'm Vicky's sister!"

"Really?" She'd reached the other side of the fence but hadn't lowered the hoe. "Where is she?"

"She found a place in East Oakland, by the airport."

Sal tossed the hoe aside. She sorted through a bunch of keys on the ring attached to her belt loop and then moved her hip toward the lock on the fence gate so she could unlock it. She held the gate open while Lily entered and then locked it up again.

Sal took big steps and moved quickly, despite her size, up the hill. The shed sat in a grove of eucalyptus trees, their smooth skins in shades of cream and taupe and tan, peeling in papery strips. Lily's feet rustled through the cast-off bark and she stopped to pick up a strip the color of smoke. Someone in another century would have written a letter on the smooth interior of the bark. She tucked the piece inside her backpack, taking care to not crack it.

Sal barged in the door of the shed. Tools and equipment filled the place. A pile of blankets took up one corner, presumably Sal's bed, and another corner, closed off with half walls, housed a toilet and sink. The biggest object in the room was Sal's 1966 Harley Electra-Glide, the one that matched Vicky's, now Wesley's. It stood rather gloriously next to the back wall, braced by its kickstand.

Sal lit a Coleman stove and put on a pan of water. She opened a plastic bag and withdrew a hunk of bread, which she plunked on the table along with a knife and a jar of jam. She took a seat on a plastic crate and gestured toward the one folding chair. Neither had spoken a word since those at the gate. Sal sat with her knees apart, her hands grasped and hanging between her thighs, her mouth held tightly closed around her teeth. Lily didn't take the chair. Instead she wandered over to the dry-erase board and pretended to be interested in the purple and green and red data, obviously weeks old and half rubbed off. Across the tops were names. Of the hyenas? Below the names, in columns, were numbers. Pounds of food consumed? Numbers of hours slept? Times they'd bitten their keeper?

In the 1980s, a couple of university researchers brought twenty hyena infants from Kenya to live in the Berkeley Field Station for the Study of Behavior, Ecology, and Reproduction. They had been surprisingly successful in that last purpose, having reproduced themselves into a clan of over fifty individuals. Not too long ago, the researchers gave away many to zoos around the world. There were, at the time of the earthquake, twenty-two left in the compound. The animals weren't exactly a secret, but the scientists tried as much as possible to keep them under wraps. The public wasn't keen on the idea of the colony living in their midst. What if they got out?

"Where are the hyenas?"

"They've been relocated."

Lily sat on the chair and helped herself to a slice of bread, spooning on a liberal portion of jam. Sal poured the boiling water into two mugs and dropped a handful of leaves into each.

"I heard that there was a mudslide breach in the fences. That some of them are roaming free."

"Nope. They're all safe in Arizona. During the firestorm of ninety-one, they tranquilized everyone and loaded them into station wagons, drove them down to campus where they were kept in classrooms until the fire danger passed. But this time, with the earthquake, the roads were impassable, and so we had to helicopter them out."

Sal finished her first slice of bread and jam and prepared another one, licking all ten of her fingers after screwing the lid back on the jam jar. She narrowed her eyes at Lily. "They're probably the most underappreciated, least understood mammals on earth. They're actually very sweet. They used to nuzzle me every morning after breakfast."

Lily knew this. Vicky's eyes had shone with pride when she'd described Sal's prowess with the beasts. She also knew that with their powerful teeth and jaws and industrial-strength digestive tracts, spotted hyenas could polish off an entire zebra—including every last piece of hide and bone—in a few minutes.

"Still," Lily said. "You don't really want a bunch of hyenas at large in Berkeley."

"I told you: they've been airlifted out."

"I guess that'd be a priority."

"So you came out from Nebraska."

"I hadn't heard from Vicky and I was worried about her."

"She was staying here with me."

"I saw the note you wrote her. The fuck-you-don't-ever-contact-me-again one."

Sal smiled, or maybe just bared her teeth.

"What'd she do?"

"She slept with some bimbo poet. A neighbor."

"She only did it because she's terrified of intimacy."

"Thanks, Freud. That's really helpful."

"So why'd you let her stay here with you?"

Sal shrugged. "She didn't have anywhere to stay. And, well, you know Vicky. I wasn't going to leave her on the street. She'd get eaten alive. I have water and a generator. She rigged some solar for me." Sal swished her tea and studied the leaves; she couldn't suppress her smile and then a lubricious chuckle. "Truth be told, it was exciting. Kind of postapocalyptic, you know? We actually had a really nice time. For me, it was bittersweet, knowing we were through, but having this reprieve on the hillside, in the woods, away from everything, our own little shelter..." She shrugged again, the smile fading. "It was like an anti-honeymoon. A celebration of the ending."

"That doesn't make any sense."

"It did to me."

"You still love her. That's why you let her stay."

"Possibly. But then she revealed a bit more about her tawdry doings. Apparently the bimbo told her husband that Vicky had died in the earthquake. So Vicky was essentially hiding out here, i.e., using me."

"She was really happy to be with you. It wasn't just that she was hiding out."

"Arguable. But the last thing I need is some jealous husband finding my refuge."

"He still thinks she's dead."

Sal shrugged. "Not my problem anymore."

Lily knew that Vicky loved Sal. That she hadn't been simply hiding. But this was a new kink in Lily's scheme: with Vicky at the hyena compound, Sal felt like a target. Before they could all live out here together, the threat of Paul would have to be removed.

"The truth is," Lily said, "Vicky does love you."

Sal waved a hand through the air in front of her face as if clearing away a bad smell.

"I grew up with Vicky. I know how impossible she is. And I don't use that word lightly. But." Lily knew this was going to sound trite at best. "She has such a big heart. She really does."

"Right. I know that. It's big enough to include several women."

Several? Lily had imagined just the one transgression. But of course, besides Gloria in the lime high heels, there was now some Sicilian babe with the mustache. "She's just scared shitless. That's something people don't know about Vicky."

"And I'm supposed to wait...for what?"

"Maybe she'll grow up."

Sal blew her nose. "I'll put our names on the retirement home waiting list. I'll look forward to some rousing games of shuffleboard."

Lily laughed.

"Anyway, it's my own damn fault. I knew Vicky was trouble from the moment I met her."

"Vicky is gold," Lily said. "She just needs a little taming. Or maybe just training."

That gave Sal pause. She appeared to be considering the possibility, the viability, of taming or training Vicky. But then she said, "Gold is a metal. It can't be tamed or trained."

Lily pressed on. "The other thing about Vicky is that she never lies. She loves you. That's a fact."

Sal bit a nail and looked to the far corner of the room. "Enough about that little shit. Come outside. I'll show you my garden."

Sal had leveled and cultivated a rich bed of soil behind the shed. She'd planted neat rows of ragged greens, including chard, squash, green beans, and lettuce. "I foraged the plants from abandoned gardens. Most were volunteers."

"You have traps, too," Lily said, pointing to one of three.

"Oh, yeah," she said dismissively. A breeze blew through the tall eucalyptuses. The leaves shuddered with a passing secret.

"Are you, like, eating rabbit?"

Sal squatted by a corner of the garden plot. "I don't get enough sun here. I'll be lucky if anything grows at all, but I have to try."

"You have the Harley. Why don't you leave?"

Still resting on her haunches, Sal didn't answer that question, either. Instead, she asked, "Why are you camping on my hillside?"

Her hillside? It was a fitting claim, actually. Sal looked like a woman who'd lost herself to the wild, as if ancient strands of survivalist genes were knotted up in her DNA. She wasn't leaving because she wanted to reinvent agriculture and trap game. In another few years, she might be making moonshine, too. *Her* hillside.

26

Dear Lily,

There is so much I want to say to you.

It was such a shock to meet you in person. I've always known you were the real deal, the most genuine person I've ever "met." I used to like to think of you as my epistolary soul mate. Maybe I just didn't expect our connection to hold up in real life. Or I was afraid that it wouldn't.

The first thing I want to say is that I'm sorry about the gun. I wish I'd put it in a dresser drawer before you had to discover it in my pocket.

But maybe I can explain. About it, and everything else.

The morning of the earthquake, I was lying awake in my own bed, wondering why I'd left Melissa's. I'd stayed until almost two in the morning. It was unkind to have gotten up then and come back to my own apartment. There were only those few hours left of the night, and I couldn't sleep anyway. We could have had coffee together. What would that have cost me?

I'd only been back in the country a couple of weeks. I'd found the apartment, right by campus, and there she was: Melissa, in her Indian print skirts and white peasant blouses, those little red

Moroccan slippers with tiny mirrors stitched all over them, her extra-long hair and quiet voice. She was very upfront in saying she didn't want a relationship, and that suited me fine. I couldn't bear to want more.

So there I was, lying in my own bed, feeling guilty and worried, until finally I fell asleep.

Gunshots woke me. A fast sweat drenched my entire body. I threw off the covers, tried to remember which Kinshasa hotel I was sleeping in. The soldiers were right outside my room, smashing things, blowing things up. The walls were slamming and the floor was cracking. My head ached with confusion. I didn't know where I was. Maybe still at the sanctuary? I ran to the window, thinking I had to get to the bonobos.

No. The apes were already gone.

I was in Berkeley, California. But a war in Berkeley? How could that be?

The floor beneath my bare feet plunged, tearing the floorboards from the walls and knocking me to my hands and knees. So many screams, in a dozen different tones, put me back in the bush, the apes and birds vocalizing their terror at a predator in their midst.

I tied on my shoes, ran across the buckled floor, and tried to open my door, but it was jammed shut. When I kicked it out, I found nothing but a hole in the stairwell. I ran back to the window, looked out, and saw that the ground was much closer than it used to be. The parking level below my apartment had given way. I jumped.

A sharp pain shot from my foot up my leg, and I sat on the pavement, thinking, earthquake. This was an earthquake.

Another part of the apartment building gave way and the entire structure sank several more feet. I tried to get up but couldn't put weight on my sprained ankle, so I used my arms to push and scooted backward on my butt, away from the tumbling building, until everything stilled.

"Carlos!" a voice screamed, and I looked up to see a woman leaning from the window of the top floor. She lifted a baby out the opening and held it over the space between her arms and the pavement below.

"Si, si, si!" shouted the man who must have been Carlos, and the woman dropped her baby, the air billowing its diaper, head fuzz standing on end, a wail opening its mouth. The head jerked back as the baby landed in Carlos's arms.

I swear, Lily, I felt something like an electric jolt to my heart. The man had done it. Carlos had caught the baby. I feel like he saved my life, too. Seeing that baby safe in Carlos's arms. It was possible: falling and being caught. Several minutes later I witnessed the mother somehow emerging from the wreckage to be reunited with her baby and Carlos.

I finally stood up. I could walk on my ankle, though it hurt like hell. I found Melissa. Her legs and feet, including the little red Moroccan slippers with the tiny mirrors stitched all over them, were sticking out of the rubble. Her elderly dog Jagger sat by her legs, growling when I tried to take the slippers. So I sat down next to both of them and waited. Even though it was stupid to stay so close to the unstable building. How could I leave her? Jagger whined and panted. I pet him and told him, "Easy, boy."

I have no idea how much time passed. Maybe only minutes. Maybe hours. My mind kept slipping back to the Congo, with all the shouting and swarms of people, and the air so thick with panic you could chew it. I pet Jagger and tried not to look at Melissa's legs and feet. Somehow, even with all that chaos flowing all around me, an important realization came to me: this was a disaster in which I had no hand. More, this was my opportunity for redemption.

I got up and made a crutch out of a board. That old dog decided to trust me. He got up, too, and shambled right alongside me as I walked away from the wrecked apartment building. You should have seen him. He had big dopey eyes, a gray muzzle, and one misshapen front leg, the result of having a car door shut on it when he was a puppy. We had matching limps.

That night we slept in the wooded area on the western edge of campus. The next day we hobbled around Berkeley gathering food from grocery stores. When I met someone I thought I could trust, I told them my plan. Soon there were four of us and I'd found a classroom on campus with a broken window, and that's where we stockpiled the provisions.

It was so easy in the beginning. The National Guard hadn't yet arrived. Everyone was focused on getting out or finding loved ones. You just walked in, smashing a door or window if necessary, and took what you needed. A few of the property owners tried to put guards in place, but most of these gatekeepers abandoned their posts within a few hours. No one wanted to stick around.

Most survivors took just enough food for their own use, but we hauled garbage bags full of cans, jars, apples, oranges, hams, and beans back to the classroom on campus. When we weren't harvesting, we distributed, pushing loaded shopping carts, stopping when we found people, and offering up the food. We also built shelters using whatever we could find in the earthquake wreckage—wood, chunks of cement, sheet rock, plastic tarps. Sometimes we simply left these shelters for homeless families to find, and sometimes we steered folks to them. Doing the construction was fun, and people were grateful. On the third day, I found an abandoned black Chevy Blazer, and Vinh hotwired it. This allowed us to travel farther afield and collect even more food. I loved it when we got to broken places in the road and all four of us—in the early days it was just me, Vinh, Janis, and Josh—would build road patches to help travelers.

All the while, I felt like I'd finally begun doing what I am meant to do. This, I thought, is what life should be. We weren't the only ones helping, either. All around the city, people's bonobo natures were manifesting themselves. I hadn't felt this happy since my first year at the sanctuary.

Of course, there were exceptions to the decency of most people. Josh had a gun, and I was glad he did. It made us feel safe camping next to the creek on campus. Looking back now, those first days after the earthquake seem so innocent, so easy and energizing. We made shelters for stranded families and then brought them food. I could have done that forever.

But when the National Guard arrived, they cleared campus. We had to decamp. By then, we had twenty-four members and we needed a better site anyway. We moved to the western shore of San Pablo Reservoir. That was an exciting day. I'd anticipated the move, so we'd already liberated a number of tents and sleeping bags from REI. Our little tent city went up in just over an hour. We dragged four picnic tables into the meadow.

I climbed up top of one of the picnic tables and asked everyone to gather. It was a glorious moment, a bit of shy sunlight resting against the bare skin on my arms, the damp air freshening everything. I waited for everyone to quiet, letting the moment intensify, a nice long silence to ground our new community.

I told them how proud I was of everyone. We had plenty of food and two vehicles. We'd found another black Chevy Blazer. It was like having a fleet! I told them my dream of creating a sanctuary for people. A place where we, and eventually others, could be safe. How this was our chance to build a new society from the ground up. I said that I'd start working on everyone's assignments, based on their skills, but that for now everyone should take the afternoon off. A few of the men stripped off their shirts and pants, hooted like chimpanzees, and made running dives into the water.

It was a perfect moment, Lily.

Then it got ruined.

"Hey, man." It was the kid, Josh.

"What's up, Josh?"

"I need to talk to you."

"I have a minute or two. What's on your mind?"

"I don't know how to say this."

"You can say anything to me."

"I gotta go. I mean leave the Cluster."

I don't know why. But I had an urge to punch him. The kid had been with me from the beginning, when it was just me, him, Vinh, and Janis. He'd been part of the core. How could he be thinking of leaving? Still, this impulse to hit the kid was out of place. I tried to calm myself by reaching down and petting Jagger.

Josh kept talking, all nervous and twitchy. "I mean, I'm really grateful for everything you've taught me. All your experiences in the Congo, building shit from scratch, just using the junk at hand to make shelters. I mean, it's, like, the coolest experience of my life, but…"

"But you wanted summer camp, not a paradigm shift."

"No. No, I do want a paradigm shift. I totally get everything you've told us about the bonobos, how kindness and cooperation are just as much a part of our ancestral baggage as, you know, violence and everything. I just need to… Yeah, I guess I want to see, like, my parents. They're worried about me."

Thankfully my anger drained away right then. There would always be deserters. Cowards. Josh would be replaced by a dozen others.

"Do what you need to do." I even felt affectionate toward him, the poor sop.

"I'm sorry, man. I mean…"

"Josh, this isn't about me. I got a whole army here. It's about you. You need to do the right thing for yourself, and I can't tell you what that is."

The kid looked down at his sneakers. We both knew that the right thing, the ethical decision, was to stay and help the people of Berkeley and Oakland build a new society from the muck of the earthquake. Nothing could be clearer. But fear was fear, and the boy clearly wanted his mama.

"Go," I said. "Thank you for your service."

"I need my gun."

"What?"

"My gun. You borrowed it. Remember? The first night."

"You're too young to carry a gun." I got up from the picnic table and started to walk away.

"That gun belongs to my dad. I can't give it to you. I need to take it back home."

Maybe you think I should have given him the gun. But it's crazy out here and he's just a kid. Besides, I had to protect the needs of the Cluster.

Which is what I told him. "I'm sorry. The Cluster needs the gun a lot more than your daddy does."

"What? What are you talking about? Just give me the gun and I'll leave."

I felt bad for the kid. I really did. But that didn't change what was right. I stripped off my clothes and dived into the reservoir where a few of the guys were splashing and yelping. I kicked hard, swimming past the roughhousers. It felt good, the cold shock of the water. Josh would never find the gun. I'd hidden it well. And what I'd said was true. Josh might get grounded, or have to endure his father shouting at him, but that gun would be serving a much greater good here. I swam all the way to the other side of the reservoir, glad to test my strength and endurance, and then swam back. By then, Josh was gone. But so was my elation at establishing the new encampment.

I wished Josh hadn't mentioned the bonobos. What we were doing had everything to do with them, their utter sweetness, and yet their memory sometimes brings up my worst feelings. I want so badly to put all that, the agony of the night of the slaughter, behind me. I want to do good, enough good to make up for my culpability. But sometimes the pull of anger is like a tide. I can actually feel it buckling the backs of my knees.

I took Jagger into one of the tents and had a nap. Jagger always calmed me. He liked to sleep spooned against me. I've never had a dog before and I was blindsided by my affection for him. What a comfort that old dog was to me.

The thing is, the kid's defection was a wakeup call. Others were grumbling. I knew we needed to strengthen our numbers. So the next day I started actively recruiting. We certainly have solid credentials: plenty of food and water, a safe encampment, the two SUVs. It feels funny sometimes, trying to convince other people about the rightness of my vision, but as long as I'm feeding people, sheltering them, I feel happy.

Two mornings ago, I woke up to find Jagger gone. This in itself was not unusual. I always left the tent flap unzipped so Jagger could go out to do his business. But when he didn't return shortly, I went looking. An hour later I found him lying next to the shore of the reservoir, a good distance away from the encampment. He was dead.

It was just like the earthquake. I lost track of where I was again. Total emotional entropy. Everything harsh and metallic. I heard the barbed wire being snipped by the murderers. I heard the screams of the bonobos and saw the fury of Yannick. I felt that same iciness in my bowels that I'd felt when Renée told me to leave. It all came back to me, the hell of my hotel room in Kinshasa waiting for a plane out, my belief in our ancestral potential for compassion destroyed.

You would think I could look after a dog.

But that's the thing. I had taken care of Jagger. I'd seen to his every need. Someone else was responsible for this death.

At breakfast I appointed an Inner Council, my three most trustworthy men and of course myself, and called an immediate meeting. This new development disgruntled some Cluster members. They'd accepted my informal leadership—after all, I'd organized the Cluster—but they whined about making the leadership more official.

We met at the picnic table farthest from the tents and I told the Inner Council that their first task was to find out what killed Jagger. Only one of the men balked, and I dismissed him then and there. If he didn't understand the importance of protocol and detail, how the death of a dog could be the beginning of rot at the heart of the community, then I didn't need the man.

Don't judge me, Lily. Communities can unravel so quickly. I needed to act swiftly because I felt that things were deteriorating. As it turns out, I was right.

A few hours later, my two Inner Council members reported to me that Jagger had gotten into some spoiled meat that someone left in an open garbage bin.

"Find out who did it," I said, and a few minutes later, they delivered the name of a woman who'd been a particularly vocal member of the community, often disagreeing with me. I went directly and told her to leave the encampment. When she feigned shock and asked what she'd done, I told her she was careless and a danger to the community. I couldn't even say Jagger's name for fear of breaking down. When she said, "Fuck you," I realized she'd done it on purpose, killed my dog because of her envy.

I walked for hours that afternoon, feeling devastated over the loss of Jagger. As always, the thought of you loomed over me like an angel, my only solace. Inane, I know, using the word angel. It's the opposite of everything I believe in. That's part of why I hadn't come to find you sooner. I enjoy my secret little fantasy of your innocence, our outside-of-real-life correspondence. Not only did I not want to find out that you were just another flawed human being, I didn't want you to see me this broken. That afternoon, walking along the shore of San Pablo Reservoir, I realized it was now or never. I'd take the risk.

So I went right away, that day Jagger died, and there you were, on the porch of Trinity Church's meals program room. Exactly where you said you'd be. Artless, candid, beautiful. I had no idea I'd feel so much.

I hope you will forgive me for taking so long. For the gun. For not being as forthcoming about my story as you've been. For everything.

Love,

Travis

27

I'M PREGNANT," ANNIE TOLD Lily.

Lily fumbled the spoonful of succotash she'd just scooped up. She set down the serving spoon and wiped up the spilled glop. Then she faced Annie, visibly upset and having no idea what to say. "Have you seen a doctor?"

Annie broke out in a big grin, that single dimple piercing the spot next to her mouth, and then shouted, "Ha! You're so stupid. As if."

The day before, Annie had asked Lily for $2,000, and the day before that she'd said she'd joined the Army. Lily had known to ignore those comments. She did in fact feel stupid now for having believed the girl's claim of pregnancy.

Annie took a tray of succotash and cocked a finger at Lily. "I know where you're staying, bitch. I'm watching you."

"I moved."

"Yeah. I know that, too."

"Here's a milk for Binky."

"What I want is your bike, white girl."

"You know, I'm really tired today, Annie. Would you please cut the crap and move on?"

The next day, Annie came in with three long plum branches, small deep red leaves replacing the few remaining wilted blossoms. "The plums will be ripe soon. I can't wait." She reached the bouquet through the serving window and tapped Lily on the head, as if it were a wand.

"Where'd you get those?"

"Where do you think?"

Lily had tried to help her. She'd done nothing to harm her. True, Annie had been treated like an infestation in Joyce's apartment, and it had been Lily who'd taken her by the elbow and led her out the door, but it hadn't been Lily's fault. Annie's point with the plum branches was that she had returned to Joyce's flat, may well have broken into it, might even be staying there. She wanted Lily to know.

After dinner, Lily went to the library. She charged her phone. She shared news with other regulars. The whole while she thought about Annie lounging on Joyce's big queen-size bed. She knew she ought to leave it alone. She owed Joyce nothing. She owed Annie even less. But when she left the library, well after dark, she found herself riding to Joyce's flat. She found the windows all boarded up. Maybe Annie had just been goading her, yet again.

Lily stowed the bicycle and walked down the side path as quietly as she could, feeling her way along the house and fence with her hands. Every time her feet cracked a stick or crunched some dry leaves, she froze, as if she were sneaking up on a crime scene. She ought to leave this alone, but something stronger than curiosity drew her forward. Once in the backyard, she checked the back door and found no signs of a forced entry.

Lily sat on the back stoop and let her eyes adjust to the silvery starlight. The dandelions under the plum tree were all beaten down, and Lily imagined Annie and Binky stomping around, stretching their arms up to break off the red-leafed branches. Beyond the plum tree were the two big raised beds where Joyce used to grow vegetables. A couple of volunteer tomato plants, already bearing small green globes, twined through arching rosemary and bolting thyme. What a wild place, this state of California, where fruits and herbs grew in April.

Lily took one last deep breath of the garden air and rose to her feet. She was about to leave when she noticed a dark heap at the far end of the yard, up against the back fence.

She stepped around the raised beds, moving as silently as possible, and stopped just three feet away. The thin, ashen-skinned boy lay on his side with the rotund, golden-skinned girl spooning him from behind, her arm wrapped around his waist. He clutched her hand in both of his. Binky and Annie slept soundly, their sides rising and falling. They didn't have a blanket or sleeping bag, just each other's warmth.

Retracing her footsteps, Lily slunk back down along the side of the house and fetched her bicycle. She rode up the hill in the dark, shouldering her bike up the series of connected paths that Professor Vernadsky had told her about, and then climbed back on to ride out the fire trail. She considered stopping again at Sal's fence, demanding admittance. But she didn't. Sal relished her independence, her solitude, her traps and vegetable sprouts. She didn't want Lily's company. Lily rode on to her own camp.

That night, she lay awake for a long time. She listened to the rooting, right outside her tent, of some small animal digging into safety. She listened to the call-and-response of two great-horned owls, friends or maybe even lovers, in the canopy of nearby trees. She felt so alone. Even Annie had Binky.

28

LILY SCRUBBED HER SHIRT and jeans in the Trinity Church community room's bathroom sink. The powdered soap chapped her hands and was hard to rinse out—she always found clumps of it dried on her clothes—but it was better than nothing. She tried to stick to a washing routine; her clothes once a week and her own body at least every other evening. Even so, some serious slippage had occurred in the last few days, as if she'd just crossed over the line from civilized to savage.

She put on her one other shirt and the pair of shorts she'd found in the library free box and packed her wet clothes in her backpack. She'd hang them to dry on the coyote brush near her tent. Then she scoured her face red and washed her hair. Rinsing with the cold water took forever. As she stood with her head under the faucet, she wondered why she had to keep deciding, over and over again, to not answer Travis's letter.

It was the obvious right choice. Yet that last part, about his not wanting to find out that she was just another flawed human being, about his being broken, resonated so perfectly with her own feelings. She wanted to address his sorrows. As if the slaughter of the bonobos wasn't enough, there was the death of his ex-lover, Melissa. And now the dog. She'd never not answered his letters.

He'd had a man deliver this one, handing it to her through the service window a couple of days ago. The handwriting alone unsettled her. It made her feel thirteen years old, connected to a longing that was both old and young, sweet and bitter. But she *wasn't* thirteen. Furthermore, she didn't have a messenger. Was he even checking email? She didn't have a phone number for him. Anyway, email or texts seemed cold next to the ink and paper of his handwritten letter. She'd have to go to the reservoir herself, and that felt like a commitment of some kind. One she wasn't ready to make. She had a plan and her sanity depended upon sticking to it.

Lily examined herself in the cracked mirror. Her grubby clothes hung loose and big. Her eyes looked as though they'd sunk farther back into her skull. Her wet hair straggled down to her shoulders. She'd lost at least ten pounds since she came to California. A fresh desperation zinged her pupils, even she could see it, and sharing that, merging her desperation with his, would undo her. She knew it would. She needed to reach for strength.

Lily swung on her backpack. She called a thank you to Kalisha— no one else was allowed to use the church bathroom and Lily was grateful for the privilege—as she walked through the now empty community room.

"Are you okay?" Kalisha asked, as if she could see what Lily had seen in the mirror.

"I'm dandy!" Lily called out, using Vicky's word.

"Take care of yourself," Kalisha said.

"I will."

Kalisha leveled a look at her, like she wasn't convinced.

Lily stepped outside thinking she might go to the library again. She liked joining the evening crowd who gathered to tell stories or just read communally. As the door clunked shut behind her, she heard a gentle, "Hey."

Travis stood with his shoulders and the sole of one sneaker propped against the pale pink exterior wall of the church, hands in his front pockets. He wore stone-colored khaki shorts with a cobalt blue T-shirt. A soft blond fur covered his legs. A fresh haircut, the thick blondness sheered short, made him look defenseless.

He pushed off the wall and came toward her. Instead of feeling alarmed, she felt relieved. She didn't have to decide: here he was.

"I'm so sorry about Jagger."

"So you read my letter?"

"Yes." Did he think she wouldn't?

"I hope it wasn't too intense."

"It was pretty intense."

He smiled then, his ultra-white teeth so bright. "Sorry."

"It's okay."

"I hope so. I've missed you. Already."

How could he miss her? They'd only met once. She tried to find the appropriate apprehension in her feelings, but all she felt was a pleasurable collapse of will. They had been friends for a couple of decades. Maybe she could help him. Anyway, Wesley had said appropriateness was no longer a working concept.

Lily fell in step beside him, pushing her bicycle. When they reached the park in front of the crumbled Berkeley City Hall, they waded right into the weeds. With the warm weather of spring, the grasses had shot sky-high, and all kinds of wildflowers, yellow dandelions and orange poppies and blue forget-me-nots, had taken up residence. Travis plopped down in the tall urban growth and crossed his legs. Lily laid her bicycle on its side and parted a place in the vegetation for herself. They had a little fort, the grasses and weeds higher than their heads. Lily sat with her legs crossed like Travis's, their knees just touching. He reached out and tucked her hair behind each ear. His hands shook.

"Come live with the San Pablo Reservoir Cluster," he said. "Plenty of food and good water. I want you with us. Your gardening skills would be excellent to have. We're already planting."

Her gardening skills? She felt slightly offended but also reassured. Falsely reassured: she knew this was more than just a business proposition, but it was lovely to rest against the pretense.

"Whenever you're ready," he said, "but the sooner the better. You know how dangerous it's becoming. From all directions—pissed off citizens and the police and military. You need to think about who you're going to ally yourself with."

"Travis?" Lily took his still-trembling hands, feeling the way his need sandpapered against the fear. It'd only been a few months since his bonobos were slaughtered, since he'd lived in the bush, where warfare and disease were daily threats, with a man who hated him and a woman who didn't love him enough. "You're not in the Congo anymore."

He withdrew his hands. "There's a rally tomorrow. Come with me." He began to carry on, all over again, about FEMA, the National Guard, how survivors had been abandoned by their own government.

"Travis!" She nearly had to shout. "Look at me."

He seemed unable to focus, his green eyes jumping from a bunch of orange poppies beyond her shoulder, to the path of the Black Hawk flying overhead, to his own sneaker. The startled look in his eyes and the shaking in his hands reminded her of the Gulf War vet whom Tom and his dad had hired. The guy flinched at the sound of the key cutter, and his mind sometimes ground to a halt in the middle of writing up an order. He'd just stand there with the pen in his hand, not moving, not even hearing what the customer was saying. Tom and his dad tried to live with these symptoms, but when he lost his temper at a woman who had her child on a harness leash, shouting obscenities at her right in the shop, they had to let him go.

Why shouldn't she soothe Travis? They were both adults. Both single. He wasn't the mythic correspondent of her youth. She wasn't the starry-eyed innocent of her youth, either. They were two heartbroken human beings who needed comfort.

She rose to her knees and pulled his head against her chest. He turned his face in and wrapped his arms around her. She thought of his first letter, how she'd held it with both hands, the thrill of seeing beyond Fair Oaks; of the first time he used the word "love"; of his belief in the possibility of love; and of his dedication to an ape in the Congo. Travis, her wild card.

Why not? Had she anything at all to lose?

They tumbled back into the tall grasses, kissing, unbuttoning, and unzipping. The weeds and dirt clods scratched her backside and she didn't care. His face smashed into the dirt next to her neck, and her legs gripped his thighs. The lovemaking was unwieldy, crazy, warmed by the sun, and anointed by the ripe green smell of the grasses. They talked between rounds, about ordinary things like what they liked to eat and how they'd been sleeping, as if making love to the person who'd been your pen pal, from the other side of the earth, for twenty years, was the most normal thing in the world.

"Like the bonobos," Lily said after a while, and Travis reared back. His surprise pleased her. When he then laughed, she realized it was the first time she'd heard him laugh, fully, from deep within. She let her gaze span the sky as she listened to his genuine chesty joy. Why not like the bonobos? We *are* bonobos, for all intents and purposes. Except for some apparently interfering genes that block our ease with pleasure. Everything is about sex for that crazy ape. They have sex while they're eating, while they're grooming, while they're playing. They don't set it aside as something to do in private, separate from the rest of life. They have sex in public, if they want to. Males with males, females with females, all kinds of positions, too. They squeal and bare their teeth in pleasure. What's more, they don't just selfishly satisfy themselves. They hold eye contact while mating, monitor their partners' responses, adjust their attentions accordingly. No shame, no modesty, no inhibitions.

Lily was glad she'd reminded him, because clearly Travis was losing his way. She wanted to return him to his own grand vision.

"My favorite studies," she said, and he propped himself up on an elbow, looking downright amazed at how closely she'd followed his work. His eyes were agates, golden clear and smoky cloudy both. Lily spoke calmly, pretended she didn't notice his curious alarm. "Are the ones about oxytocin, how a synthesis of the hormone is released in male brains after sex. When scientists inject it into male rats, their aggressive behavior nosedives. So there's a correlation between sexually uninhibited societies and peaceful societies. Bonobos are compassionate and altruistic precisely *because* they celebrate sexuality."

She couldn't believe she'd just said those two words, "celebrate sexuality," out loud. She laughed, willing him to return to his laughter, but he sat up and folded his arms over his knees. As she started to reach for him, she heard a buzz and then saw the bee alighting on the purple blossom of a lupine. She dove for her backpack and dug around for the epinephrine.

"What?" He rose up on his knees. "What's wrong?"

"Nothing," she said once she'd fisted the medicine and the bee had flown away. "Just that I'm allergic."

"Move out to the reservoir," he said. "I can keep you safe."

"I want so much more than safety."

Travis nodded. "Come to the march tomorrow. We can talk about it more then."

"Look," she said, lying back again and pointing her nose toward the sky. "So much blue."

But just then a chopper ripped open the blue, the noise of its engine a prolonged psychic aftershock.

29

Lily locked her bike to a metal pole and found Travis where he said he'd be, waiting for her on the corner of Fourteenth and Washington in downtown Oakland. His smile was guarded—did he regret the day before?—and his hands curled into loose fists. She hugged him hello. "Don't worry," she said. "Everything's fine."

They milled, side by side, through the gathering crowd. Travis knew a lot of people. He shook their hands and bumped their shoulders, his energy amping up with every passing minute. By the time the march began at noon, he twitched with excitement.

As they headed down Broadway, Travis bounced along by her side, as if there were springs in the balls of his feet. People shouted, called out insults about the president and the governor, sometimes chanting in unison. Travis's voice deepened as he hollered along with them, and soon he was hoarse.

The crowd thickened. With people pressing so close, Lily could almost walk with her eyes closed and let the jostling guide her. She took Travis's arm, afraid that she might lose him in the crush.

Someone screamed. It was a shriek, intentional and prolonged, like a warning. The group picked up its pace. The voices grew louder, one massive conversation barreling down Broadway. The crowd tightened, then began running. She grabbed the tail of Travis's shirt, trying to keep up, but his entire body seemed to uncoil, spring forward in the mob, and she lost him. She tried to make her way over to the sidewalk, but it was like wading against an undertow. She gave up and let the surge carry her forward.

She heard a dull crunch, like the sound of a car being driven into a wall, followed by shattering glass, the flying shards tinkling like chimes as they landed on car hoods. A woman's voice rang out, "Stop it! Stop now!" A long pause followed, as if everyone stopped to listen and consider, and then a roar of voices crescendoed all at once.

Lily chanted, too. The crowd was running again, and she felt supported by the press of bodies, by the charging throng, like they were the cells of one moving beast. It felt good, even joyful, to demand their inalienable rights for food and water and shelter. She felt filled with purpose, and she thought: *For this I left Tom and Fair Oaks, to be a part of something bigger, much bigger.* Her heart pounded with the running and adrenaline, and she even liked the flying arms and legs, the collisions between bodies. *Humanity,* she thought, as if she were part of a tribe raiding another village. For a moment, it felt like truth.

The storefront window next to her exploded. Glass daggers flew past her face and lodged in her hair. The crowd surged backward, and she got pushed aside and then knocked down, one hand sinking into glass. Another woman, trying to escape, tripped on her leg and fell across her, the weight of the woman's body forcing Lily's face to the pavement. She yelled Travis's name.

Lily tried to get up as the crowd dispersed, people running in all directions. Not fifteen yards away, she spotted Travis, hefting a green garbage bin. The top of the bin flapped open, and banana peels and coffee grounds and onion skins tumbled onto his shoulders and head. Oblivious to the rot raining down on him, Travis charged forward with the bin, leading with the smaller bottom end, and smashed it through the window of a sandwich shop. Lily was amazed that he had that much strength.

Then she saw: it wasn't strength. Rage uncoiled in his arms and legs as he heaved the bin again, this time hurling it through the hole he'd made in the window, letting it drop like a bomb inside the shop, spilling the rest of its garbage. Lily couldn't move. She froze in place on her hands and knees, caught between her memory of his sunny smile and this display of fury. The window he'd smashed hadn't belonged to a corporate bank or even a giant retail chain. That window was the sole source of light in a tiny lunch shop that sold premade sandwiches and boxed salads, probably owned by one family. The window had survived the earthquake, only to be destroyed by Travis.

"Travis!" she yelled, hoping to bring him out of the spell and also needing help herself.

A siren seared the already heated air. He didn't hear her. She yelled his name again as she got to her feet and picked the glass off her clothes. A warm, sticky ooze of blood bathed her entire hand. The siren snaked closer. Travis was gone. A swarm of people who'd been running toward Telegraph Avenue moved back toward her. She saw why. A riot squad rounded the corner, marching forward in their knee-high shiny boots and helmets, carrying batons and bulletproof shields.

A few men stayed to throw random street debris at the police, and one guy charged them with no weapon at all, as if he could take on the fully geared-up police with his fists. Lily ran with the remaining crowd. Splinter groups took rights and lefts, and she went alone down an alley, cursing herself as she did for how easily she could be trapped there. But near the end of the alley, she realized that no one had pursued her, and if she simply stopped running, there would be no reason for anyone to chase her. She hadn't done anything wrong, other than sleep with a man who smashed the windows of innocent peoples' shops.

Lily leaned her back against the stone wall of the building and slid down until she was sitting. Her hand throbbed with pain and thirst parched her throat. She was losing a lot of blood. Bile rose in her esophagus as she examined her hand and found the piece of glass in the pad at the base of her palm. Another inch and it would have been her wrist. The shard was slippery with blood and it took four tries before she was able to pull it out. It hurt like hell. She took off her T-shirt and used her teeth to tear a hole in the fabric. Then she ripped out a strip of the jersey and bound her hand as tightly as possible, hoping the wrap would staunch the flow of blood. She pulled the neck opening of the T-shirt back over her head and adjusted it so that at least most of her bra was covered by the remaining shirt. She rested her head back against the stone wall, the scenario of Travis heaving the garbage bin through the window replaying over and over in her mind.

Lily dug out her phone and called Tom.

His "hello," both syllables extended, a big friendly welcome to the caller, sounded exactly like his dad's, probably like his granddad's, too. She could just see him, maybe on his rubber kneepads before a lockset on a door, grasping his tools in one hand as he fished the phone out of his pocket with the other, not bothering to look at who was calling.

"Hi, Tommy." Why did she use his childhood name? "It's me." Then, absurdly, she added, "Lily."

They hadn't spoken since he'd confessed about Angelina. His two-week silence since then told her everything she needed to know. God, she was sick of cowards. When he finally spoke, iron gates bracketed his greeting. "What's up?"

"I'm in downtown Oakland at a demonstration for victims of the earthquake." How badly, even now, she wanted him to hear, to understand. "It was wild. Some demonstrators got out of hand, started breaking windows."

He took a breath, and in that breath she heard his entire opinion of the big-city stupidity. As she waited for him to say something, she counted the pulses of pain in her palm.

"It's dinnertime here."

That's right: it was Sunday. Was he sitting at the table, surrounded by his siblings and their spouses and children? She wanted to ask him to tell his mom hi for her, but his mom was probably less interested in hearing from her than he was. She wondered if he *had* checked who was calling but answered anyway, pretending not to know.

"I didn't get arrested. Or hurt." She looked at the blood soaking through the strip of T-shirt wrapped around her hand.

"Well, I assumed that."

"I won't hold you up."

"We're getting ready to sit down. Maybe I can call you later."

"You could have come with me, Tom."

She tried to picture him at her side now: holding a hand-painted sign that said, *Water is a human right*; or sleeping next to her in the tent on the hillside; or mopping the floor at Trinity Church. But she couldn't place him outside of Fair Oaks. He'd only been as far west as Laramie and as far east as Des Moines, and he claimed to be fully satisfied with his range. "Why would you ever go anywhere else?" he'd say when neighbors or friends went on vacations.

"I didn't ask for anything outrageous," she continued. "I asked you to consider adoption. I asked you to be patient while I looked for my missing sister. You wouldn't do either."

She heard his footsteps, and then a door shutting. She pictured him in the den of his parents' house, letting himself down in his dad's big brown leather chair. He said, "I know."

"But you're not sorry."

"You were going to go out there, whether I came or not. By the time you decided, I was superfluous to you and your plans."

"That's not true."

"How do you think it makes me look? Sitting here in Fair Oaks while my wife mucks around in a disaster zone on her own?"

"How you *look*?"

"You didn't care what I thought. You found a way out and you took it. At least be honest about that."

The wild joy of her motorcycle ride with Wesley, those feelings of liberated abandon, popped spontaneously into her thoughts. Followed by the rather more recent memory of sex with Travis in the weeds. "Okay," she said. "But I don't think it's quite that simple. But okay."

"Look." He coughed and she heard a thump, as if he'd banged his fist on the leathery arm of the chair. "You're going to hear this sooner or later, better sooner. Angelina is expecting."

She had about five seconds of amusement. What a ludicrous term. Expecting *what?* A package? A high return on an investment? To enjoy the summer? Who used that archaic half sentence anymore?

And then her five seconds ended. The truth body-slammed her. He had found someone who could conceive his child. Deliver his DNA.

Lily clicked off her phone and screamed. She got up and stumbled over to a pile of bricks, picked one up in her good hand, and hurled it at the alley wall a couple feet in front of her. It bounced back and hit her in the shin.

Her hand hurt like hell. Her husband was having a baby—was *expecting*—with another woman. Travis was a maniac. She was homeless. Lily sat in the dark alley and cried herself empty.

Then, when there was no other possible course of action, she got to her feet and walked to the corner of Fourteenth and Washington where she'd locked her bike. It was still there. She touched the top tube in gratitude, her vehicle of salvation, pretty much all she had left.

Riding one-handed was tricky, but she made it to the church parking lot. As she carried her bike up the stairs to the door of the community room, she started to black out and had to sit down, dropping the bike. She heard it clatter down the short flight of cement stairs.

Kalisha and Ron carried her inside. They washed her wound and dressed it with antibiotic ointment, gauze, and adhesive tape. They gave her a fresh T-shirt. After a couple of glasses of water and a plate of Ron's corned beef hash, Kalisha handed her some latex gloves and suggested she get to work.

"Sh-sh-sh-sh-shit, g-g-g-g-girl," Ron said.

Kalisha gave him her deadpan look. "What, you want to drop grapes in her mouth while she reclines on the duvet and recovers? People gotta eat."

As the clients crowded in the door at four thirty, the room filled with the smells of unwashed bodies, but also of trees and sunshine.

Flatware clanked on the plastic trays and the rubber feet on chairs scudded across the linoleum. Lily dug into the vat of Ron's corned beef hash and dumped the servings onto the plastic trays, followed by watery splats of peas. To each tray she added a chocolate chip cookie, and then clunked it onto the shelf beyond the serving window. Blood seeped through the gauze and pooled under the latex glove, and some of the clients eyed her hand with distaste, but no one turned away the tray of food. She missed the professor.

Riding uphill with her sliced hand was impossible, so Lily walked the bicycle, hoping she wouldn't run into the ferals. She did. As the wild children approached, their hair matted and their hands mud-crusted, she unwrapped the gauze from her hand. Fresh blood spurted out of her wound and she shouted, "HIV positive! Come and get it."

The oldest one backed up, and the mid-aged ones followed. The littlest one, no older than six, kept coming for her bike. The child's eyes were zombie blank, hungry blank, and she almost handed him the bike. But of course she couldn't do that, and even if she did, the older kids would take it from him. She was forced to kick him away. It was the first time she'd purposely hurt someone physically, and his sobs of pain nearly broke her heart. But, holding her bloody hand in the air as a threat, she walked away with her bicycle.

Lily arrived at her campsite as the orange light of sunset washed over the bay and cities. She held some bay laurel leaves tight against her wound to stop the bleeding. Then she squeezed antibiotic ointment from the tube Kalisha and Ron had given her onto the deep cut and wrapped it with fresh gauze and tape.

Lily was glad for the physical pain in her hand, so acute and focused, the way it kept her cued up to life, her literal life, her biological existence. If it became infected, she could lose her hand. Her arm. Die. She needed the pain.

Tom, on the other hand, was multiplying his life. Having a baby. With Angelina. Who was a good five years older than she was, nearly beyond her childbearing years, and yet she was indeed bearing a child. The betrayal reached all the way back to that first sled ride, as if all along he'd been cuing up *his* life, his DNA, his chance at immortality. A baby to carry on his genes.

Lily held her hand in the air to ease the throbbing and checked her phone with the other one. The battery was almost dead.

"Hey," she said when Vicky answered. "I don't have much juice on the phone."

"I've been trying to call you!"

"I know. Sorry."

"You'll never guess who visited me."

"Sal?" Lily hoped.

"Nope. Try again."

Vicky's ridiculous cheerfulness was a balm. So Lily put off her own news and played along. "The Sicilian babe."

"Ha! Nope. You get one more try."

"Bill Gates, offering you a job."

"Close, but it's even better."

Vicky always landed on her feet. What a charade Lily had constructed for herself all these decades, pretending that Vicky was the vulnerable one. "I give up."

"Travis! Your bonobo guy!"

It seemed to get dark all at once. The bay was a silky silver now, and the cities were twitching pockets of light. Lily couldn't even speak.

"He's totally cool," Vicky said. "I can see why you've been hepped up all these years."

He'd said nothing about this today at the march or yesterday in the field in front of City Hall. Why hadn't he told her?

"I'm confused," Lily stuttered. "Why did he visit you? How did he know how to find you?"

"He said *you* told him where I am."

That was true. She had, that first night in the Craftsman bungalow, in the candlelit bedroom.

"He asked me to help him set up an electronics hub for his Cluster. We're going totally off the grid. Starting a community that's completely self-sufficient. I'm the electronics czar. Ha!"

A cool burning, like dry ice, filled her belly.

"I haven't been this excited about a project in years. I've never had this kind of freedom before. My whole life I've been hooking up other people's electronic dreams. Working for the suits. Following their shortsighted, profit-driven, dim ideas. We're going to blast open the whole idea of access for all. Besides, the timing is perfect. I had to leave my apartment on Eighty-First."

"What do you mean, you had to leave your apartment? Why?"

"I'm totally psyched."

"Are you telling me you're joining the San Pablo Reservoir Cluster?"

Lily took the long silence to mean that Vicky was considering her choices, that she heard the caution in Lily's voice, but after the quick high-pitched beeps, Lily realized that her phone battery had died.

Foolishly, she persisted in shouting, "Vicky? Vicky!"

30

THE MORNING DAWNED HOT and dry, and Lily heard a single buzzing. The coyote brush, which honeybees love, already had tight little buds. At least one bee had arrived early, hoping to work its way into the nascent blossoms.

Sting me, Lily thought. She bent at the waist, bringing her face just inches from the bee, and had a good look. It was a rich golden color, with black stripes, its head and thorax fuzzy. Even the segmented black legs had a golden fringe of fuzz. It had black alien eyes, translucent fairy wings, and the potent little stinger shooting out its hind end.

As a child, she'd hated bees. They interfered with the carefreeness of summer, and she associated them with two trips to the emergency room. Tom had often teased her about becoming a gardener. To him, it was pure idiocy. Why would you choose to put yourself in harm's way?

She'd tried to tell him how becoming a gardener was her way of befriending her earliest demons. And in the process, she learned that in fact the bees were her tiny coworkers. They pollinated the flowers she nurtured. And now these pollinating colleagues of hers were mysteriously dying off. After all these years of thinking they might kill her, it turned out that her own species was killing them. Maybe she put herself in harm's way to mend broken alliances.

Lily grabbed her bicycle and took off, flying all the way down the hill to San Pablo Reservoir, which lay east of the cities, on the other side of the Berkeley Hills, between the Sobrante and San Pablo Ridges. The dam on the north end impounded San Pablo Creek, making a lake nearly three miles long and half a mile wide. The surrounding hills were cut by perpendicular canyons, running down to the edge of the reservoir, creating long, narrow inlets, lots of nooks and crannies where an encampment could hide.

Lily searched for Travis's Cluster, riding slowly back and forth on San Pablo Dam Road. She could use the fingers of her injured hand to lightly hold onto one side of the handlebars and to help steer, but it hurt. She stopped often to rest and also to search the wooded shoreline for flashes of color, any evidence of a camp. When she reached the end of the reservoir, she turned around and tried again, this time taking spur roads down to the water. The third turnoff led to a paved parking lot. The only vehicles in the big parking lot were two black Chevy Blazers, parked side by side, facing the reservoir.

A burly guy with a bulbous nose and black beard manned what used to be the fee kiosk. He shot out of the little booth, holding up a hand to stop her, as if she were barreling through in a Hummer rather than tottering along one-handed on a bicycle.

"Name your business," he said after she'd put both feet on the ground. He stood with his arms out to the sides, like there were invisible cushions between them and his body.

"I'm looking for Travis Grayson."

"And you are?"

"Lily Jones. He invited me."

The man went back inside the kiosk and activated an old-fashioned walkie-talkie. "Dirty blonde here to see you. Tall. Skinny. A Lily Jones." He listened for a moment, and then, "Yeah, okay, sorry. I didn't know." Another listen and then, "Gotcha. Over and out." To Lily he said, "He'll be here in a moment, Miss Jones."

She rolled her eyes, unable to contain her impatience. "My name is Lily."

A few minutes later, Travis emerged from the woods and jogged across the parking lot. "Lily! Hey! I'm so glad you've come."

"Who's the thug?"

"Necessary precaution. Whoa. What happened to your hand?"

"Can we go somewhere to talk?"

"Are you okay?"

"I lost you yesterday."

"Yeah, sorry about that. I looked for you. I didn't know where you'd gone."

"To Trinity Church, as usual."

"I couldn't get over to Berkeley. We had a lot of fallout from the march. We had to meet."

"Where can we talk?"

Travis took her bicycle and handed it over to the guard. Then he held her shoulders tightly and said, "You don't look so good."

"Vicky said you went out to her apartment on Eighty-First. She said she's working for you."

"Yeah! Vicky is amazing. I mean, you've told me about her for years, but wow, she's brilliant. Funny, too. Come on. I'll take you out to the encampment and get you set up. Privacy isn't exactly one of the privileges we're offering, at least not yet, but I do have an empty tent at the moment, and I'm going to give it to you."

He took her elbow and began leading her across the parking lot. Lily looked over her shoulder at her bicycle, not liking to let it out of her sight. Without it, she would never make it back to Trinity Church. But she was hungry and the sun was hot. She barely had the strength to disengage her elbow from his grip. They took a path to the shore of the reservoir. The heat jiggled the air sitting on the lake. It'd been days since she'd had a full-body wash and she longed to dive in. A flock of Canadian geese honked overhead, flying in a ragged V-shape formation.

They walked along the beach to a grove of pines, at the back of an inlet, and there was the encampment, set back from the water and tucked deeply into the woods. A rainbow of tarps were strung between the trunks of the trees. Under the tarps was an assortment of tables loaded with plastic basins, cookware, and lanterns. One table was loaded with fresh produce: a mound of carrots, strewn apples, a pile of onions, and more heads of cabbage than she could count.

Tents of all sizes and shapes sprawled behind the tarps and tables. The morning sun poured its light onto the camp, making it look bright and cheerful despite the absence of people.

"Hungry?" Travis asked. "Sit."

Lily dropped into a camp chair facing the water and resisted the urge to tell Travis about Angelina's pregnancy. That wasn't why she was here.

He handed her a plate bedecked with a fat steak, avocado, and tomato sandwich. The pile of delectables was like a religious visitation. She thought she saw a glow around the entire sandwich. Lily hadn't had a tomato slice or avocado wedge in weeks. Eating it probably meant that she was agreeing to something, but she didn't care. She lifted the sandwich to her mouth and didn't set it down until she'd polished off every morsel. She ate one of the apples, too, and drank the cups of fresh water Travis handed her.

"Where is everyone?"

"Deployed for the day."

"Where's Vicky?"

"I'll explain all that later."

"It's weird you didn't tell me that you've been in touch with my sister."

"I know. Sorry about that. But for now we need to be a bit circumspect about our projects. I can only share details with the leadership of the Cluster."

"And Vicky is now part of that leadership?"

Travis squatted a few feet in front of Lily's chair. The sun backlit his body, leaving his face in shadow. He pulled at a tuft of grass. A light breeze came up, and the reservoir lapped behind him.

"I need answers," Lily said. "I need to see Vicky. Where is she?"

"It's a little complicated. There're a lot of shifting alliances right now. I don't need the world knowing where she is."

"I'm not the world. I'm her sister."

"No, I get that. That's why I'm telling you."

"Kind of late, though. You didn't tell me any of this yesterday."

"The march took priority."

"Why'd you break that window?"

"People need water, food, and shelter. No one will listen if we say 'please' and wait patiently."

"But what about your life work? With the bonobos. Their peacefulness. I thought that was the whole point..." Lily wanted to say, "of you."

"Listen. The earthquake destroyed the economy. It turns out that that could be a good thing. We can redefine the whole concept of meeting people's needs. It's going to be a lot of work, but we need to be ready."

"For what?"

"For the struggle."

"You're sounding kind of extreme. I mean, what about our bonobo nature?"

"I wish there was time. I wish we could wait for evolution to ferret out these madmen who run our governments. But it's too late for that. I need something faster than evolution. We have to act now. People are hungry."

"But the bonobos!"

"We're humans, not bonobos, and the human belief system is driven by ignorance and fear. Yes, you're right, we do have compassion and altruism in our makeup as well, but we won't live long enough as a species for those qualities to come to the fore. We'll never get there. At least not in my lifetime."

"But that window you smashed. It didn't belong to the government."

"Yeah, I know. You're right. I got carried away. But does it really matter? Now. In this moment on earth. We're pretty much doomed. It's going to be all over soon enough. We need to position ourselves to be ready for it when it comes."

"'It' being the apocalypse," Lily said dryly.

Travis shrugged. He stood and walked to the edge of the reservoir, looked north, the sun now lighting his blond hair and pink face. "I hear the sarcasm in your voice. You think I've crossed some line. But you know, I think the apocalypse—any apocalypse—might just be the best thing for the planet. There'll be scars, but a few species will survive. Then evolution can head down an entirely different path without us. It might be nice."

"You're not taking into account all the suffering that will occur as we go down."

"The suffering is already happening. People are dying worldwide from poverty and drought. From the toxins we're pouring into the air and water. Not to mention the endless wars. This already *is* the apocalypse—the slow, painful version. If something comes along to take us all out a little quicker, I'm all for it."

Another flock of geese flew overhead, these in a crazy S formation, as if they too had lost their way.

He wasn't telling her where Vicky was. She had to decide which course of action would get her to her sister sooner: set out looking on her own or keep engaging with him. Hundreds of square miles of wilderness surrounded the reservoir. Vicky could be anywhere. Worse than the vast geography, Travis's imagination was as prodigious as Vicky's. God knew what the two of them could cook up together. She had to keep his trust.

Lily set her empty plate on the ground and got up. "Can we walk awhile?"

They followed the shoreline without talking. Lily listened to the rippling of the water, the flapping of bird wings, the soft hush of wind. She tried to figure out the best way to get the information she needed from Travis.

When they reached another inlet, he said, "Want to swim?"

More than anything, she wanted to swim. She stripped off her clothes and piled them on a forked willow branch. She also peeled the bandage off the base of her palm. The bleeding had stopped and, thanks to Kalisha's antibiotic ointment, the cut didn't look infected.

She splashed into the reservoir. The pleasure of the cool water sluicing over her entire body, rinsing her hot skin, overwhelmed all her senses, wiped out the possibility of thought. Lily dove under, stretching her arms out in front, the backs of her hands together, and then stroked outward with cupped palms. The nerve endings in her wound zinged with pain, but she continued swimming underwater for another few yards until she needed to breathe. She surfaced into the sunlight and flipped onto her back. Her breasts floated and her toes broke the glossy skin of the lake. She could hear Travis splashing toward her, so she righted herself, dogpaddling as he approached. She let him wrap his arms and legs around her. They both sunk, bubbling underwater, going deeper. It was as if he were taking her down with him, their own apocalyptic duet, and it felt sweet, for a moment, as if she wanted that, too. His skin was slick and smooth.

Then, she wanted to breathe. She pushed him away, panicked that he would not release her, but he did, and she shot to the surface. He followed a moment later, and before he could grab her again, she swam to shore.

He had almost outwitted her, figured out a way—with the food and the swim—to derail her. She didn't really think he was that cunning. But then she wouldn't have thought she was this cunning, either. A person's degree of cunning may be determined by the level of the stakes.

She sat on a patch of bright green grass to dry in the sun. Travis sat next to her. She ought to put on her clothes. The water droplets, warm sun, and spring grasses all felt so primal, prehistoric. So before Tom.

She found herself saying, "Tom and I have been best friends since we were children."

"I know."

"The word 'betrayal' feels inadequate."

"You've left him, too."

"That's true. I have."

"You and me," he said.

His response shouldn't have shocked her, but it did. He'd ridden her words, her truthful disclosure, to his own end. She began shaking her head, searching for a temperate way to say no. He leaned over and kissed her.

"What's wrong?" he asked, pulling away quickly.

"I need you as a friend."

"What do you mean?" He looked as if she'd slapped him.

"We shouldn't have. The other day."

"Bullshit. I love you."

"Oh. No. No, Travis. I don't think—"

"You don't think what?"

He leapt to his feet and walked to the water's edge. He scooped a handful of mud and returned, crouching before her. He used two fingers to paint a streak down the middle of her face. He dabbed mud on each of her cheeks as well.

"What are you doing?"

He smiled at his work. "You're looking a bit savage."

"Where's Vicky?" she asked. "Just tell me."

He painted circles around her breasts. She was afraid to bat away his hands.

"I need to see my sister." It was stupid to have let her phone die.

"First tell me you love me." Then he laughed, as if he were joking, and sat beside her. He dabbed himself with mud as he spoke. "Okay. There's a small rogue Cluster that's been living just up the hill, at Lake Anza. They're totally disorganized, barely squeaking by. The people are hungry, some quite ill. I wanted to do something for them. They have something I need: a location where we can set up our tech center. Reception down here in the canyon is for shit. So I'm organizing Lake Anza as an electronics hub. Vicky's setting it up for us. She's rigging solar panels, engineering internet capability, everything. I've deployed a team of builders to put together a secure bunker for the equipment and they're almost finished."

"She's there now?"

"Let's go get you set up in your tent. Then I'll take you over there."

Lily jumped up and dove back into the reservoir. She washed her face, arms, legs, and also between her legs. She swished her wounded hand back and forth vigorously. She floated on her back and scrubbed her scalp. Then she swam to shore and dressed. Travis sat quietly, nakedly, arms crossed on his raised knees, watching her.

"There's no hurry," he said. "Look. I'm sorry I pressured you. I'm just worn a little thin right now."

She stood in front of the mud-painted man. "I know where Lake Anza is. I can go on my own."

"No problem. Dinner is at six. We can do your tent then."

Lily stared at Travis for a long moment. She wanted, more than anything, to shout, *No*. He would not see her later. She did not love him. She was no longer thirteen years old, nor fifteen years old, nor even twenty-two years old. She was thirty-three years old and her husband was leaving her for a woman with whom he was having a baby. She needed her sister.

But she was afraid to say no, even to make sudden movements, afraid what she might trigger. Instead she backed away and forced herself to say, "Great. Good. I'll see you then." She touched her fingers to her lips—oh, she'd never been this calculating, this disingenuous—and blew a kiss his way.

Lily found her bicycle still propped against the guard's kiosk. She pedaled off fast, under the blazing midafternoon sun, before the guard or Travis could detain her. She rode back along the reservoir and then up Wildcat Canyon Road until she came to the turnoff. She soared down the same hill she'd ridden in the wheeled kayak.

Lake Anza looked just as deserted as it had a couple of weeks ago. She walked along the spillway and then hid her bicycle next to the kayak, still nestled deep in the undergrowth on the far side of the lake. She climbed the embankment where she'd seen the little long-haired boy go, following a faint path up into the woods.

Lily found the camp in a small clearing about two hundred yards from the lake. Three women tended a fire burning inside a ring of rocks. They'd placed a storm grate across the rocks, and several steaks sizzled on the hot metal. The women fanned the smoke to diffuse it before it reached the sky. Two men worked at a rustic table made of rough-hewn planks, one slicing apples into wedges, the other chopping onions, cabbages, and carrots. Lily recognized the makings of their meal: these were the same foods at Travis's camp. Five children raced around the trampled grasses, chasing each other and swatting the ground with willow whips, behaving exactly like children except for the absence of squealing and laughter. The hot midday air held everything—people, food, vegetation—in a tense stasis.

Two of the women gasped at the sight of the stranger. The man chopping onions swung around with the knife in his hand. They all looked haunted, hungry, and ill.

"I'm looking for my sister Vicky."

"Your sister?" one of the women said.

"I heard she's working here."

The men shared glances. One shrugged angrily and turned back to his apple slicing. The other said to the women, "We need to leave. Now."

All three women looked at the children who'd stopped their play and stood in a huddle, the oldest one standing behind the others, her arms draped around as many little bodies as she could fit in her embrace. Lily read the whole situation: the children were hungry; Travis provided steaks and vegetables; the mothers wanted to stay.

Then Lily saw the giant live oak tree, with its curling dark branches and full canopy of green leaves, growing just beyond the far side of the clearing. Vicky's bubble chair hung from a horizontal limb. The clear globe of plastic with the silver cushion inside, the original Eero Aarnio, swayed back and forth.

Lily raised her voice. "Where's Vicky?"

"Not so loud," the apple man said. "You have to leave. This is a private camp."

"She's my sister. I need to find her."

"She's not here."

"We got to get out of here," the onion man said to the rest of the group. "We have no idea what we've gotten into. We don't know who these people are. Winnie? Darlene? I'm serious. Let's take the kids and go."

"And go where?" one of the women said in a flat voice.

"Bring me a plate," said another mother. "These steaks are ready."

It was already four thirty by the time Lily got to town, but she went to the library instead of the church. She needed to charge her phone and locate Vicky. Kalisha would have to manage without her today.

After plugging in her phone, Lily went directly to the reference desk.

"Travis Grayson," she told the same librarian who'd opened the library doors for the first time after the earthquake. "He's with the university, but I don't know which department. He's been studying bonobos in the Congo for a couple of decades. I need anything you can find."

The young, spiky-haired information specialist nodded briskly, delighted by the fresh challenge, and announced her search attempts as she went. She started by checking university directories, both current and archival.

"Nothing!" she said loudly. "But that means little. Especially if he's been out of the country for so long. Hold on here. We'll find Travis Grayson!" she ballyhooed, as if research were a bucking horse and she the rider. "It's remarkable," she said, eyes riveted on her computer screen and fingers rat-tat-tatting away on the keyboard, "what a deep Google search can find. The key is to not give up after a couple of screens."

It's not as if Lily had never Googled him before. But he was in the freaking Congo, she'd told herself when nothing came up. People there didn't tweet their every bowel movement like they did here.

After ten minutes, Lily wanted the librarian to stop looking. She'd changed her mind about not showing up for work. The community room at Trinity would be full by now, and everyone would be eating. Kalisha would be angry. Or maybe even worried. She needed to get over to the church and apologize.

"No, no, no. I'm not busy." The reference warrior waved at the empty space behind Lily, indicating the lack of a line, and then attacked the keyboard anew, her eyelids flicking through webpages. "I just want to look at a few other sources. You said he teaches at UC, but so far he's definitely not turning up in any professorial way in the last ten years."

"He's been in the Congo," Lily said impatiently, as if it were the librarian's fault that Travis was unfindable. She imagined Tom shaking his head slowly, looking at her with pleasurable sympathy. Firmly, trying to close the case, Lily said, "Thank you. You've been really helpful."

It was too late to go to the church. Anyway, she needed to let her phone finish charging so she could call Vicky. She'd apologize to Kalisha and Ron tomorrow. She got in line for the computers. When her turn came up, she opened the website for the bonobo sanctuary. She'd looked here many times over the years. It was a minimal site, but Renée occasionally put up pictures of the apes, and every once in a while she posted news. Lily found a brief write-up about the raid, and though Renée provided few details, the general outline followed Travis's account, so far as she could tell using her high school French.

Lily clicked the contact link at the bottom of the site and wrote in English: "I'm considering hiring Travis Grayson. I understand he worked as a researcher at the sanctuary. Would you recommend him?"

She looked up at the institutional clock on the library wall with its stark white face and practical black hands. Kalisha would be wiping down tables by now.

A small aftershock shuddered through the building, rattling the windows and tables. Everyone looked up from their books and computers. A few stood, preparing to leave, but it was nothing—just a quick shake.

Lily clicked through her old emails, reading the ones from Tom, including the one with the plane ticket information. Angelina must have gotten pregnant before Lily left Fair Oaks. If she'd stayed, would Tom ever have told her? Would Angelina ever have told *him*? Maybe she would have quietly moved to another town, far from Fair Oaks, to raise their child. Well, that was no longer necessary, although surely a woman like Angelina would insist on marriage.

This last thought almost made her sorry for Tom. A sitting duck, he could be counted on to do the right thing.

But no. Here was the most painful part of the whole deal: his tone of voice. She'd heard sadness, definitely, and anger. But she'd also detected an unmistakable substratum of happiness. He wanted Angelina. He wanted the baby.

Not the sharpest knife in the drawer, he'd said when he first hired her. But he had never wanted sharp. He'd wanted a big pillow he could sink into, a place to bury his eyes and ears, blunt any pain life might bring. The thought of him smiling at her was unbearable. The thought of her gigundous and soon-to-be-lactating breasts made her sick.

Lily thought of Van Gogh cutting off his ear and sending it to his ex. It didn't seem crazy. It seemed like a reasonable response.

She was about to close out her email program when a new message blinked in.

Renée Ojukwu wrote just two sentences: "Travis Grayson worked as a groundskeeper at the sanctuary for twenty-one years. He is no longer with us."

It took five or six reads before she could comprehend the words on the screen. She rubbed her eyes, even tapped the monitor, as if the missing parts of Renée's message would blink into place. Ridiculously, briefly, she wondered whether the words "groundskeeper" and "researcher" were interchangeable in the Congo.

Lily shouldered her backpack, yanked her phone from the power strip, and stepped out into the evening light. She sat on the sidewalk pavement in front of the library, beside her locked bicycle. Her whole world pixilated, broke up into shattered pieces, and then tried to come back into focus, tried to find a new whole. But it wouldn't come together. She pressed her palms against the warm concrete and leaned her head back against the spokes of her bike. Rock and metal, this was all she had now.

Travis had lied about who he was for twenty years. Vicky had joined his anarchic Cluster. Tom was having a baby with a stupid woman five years his senior.

She might have sat there for the rest of the night, stunned by the betrayals, if it weren't for the spiky-haired librarian who bounded out the library door, crying, "Oh, thank god, you're still here! I found him!"

The woman crouched down in front of Lily waving a piece of paper. "Total fluke that I found this," she said. "It's from an article in a Kinshasa newspaper that someone translated and quoted on her blog. Listen." She read a short description of the raid at the sanctuary, and then held up her forefinger for the crucial line. "'Neither sanctuary director Renée Ojukwu'—I have no idea how to say that name. Anyway, 'Neither sanctuary director Renée Ojukwu, nor groundskeeper Travis Grayson, the only two people present at the time of the raid, would comment on the attack.'"

Lily looked at the crouching librarian's face, glowing with excitement about her gold nugget of information. Then she looked over her own shoulder at the towering green stucco building, which contained all the wisdom people had amassed over the centuries so we wouldn't have to start again from square one. This woman, this excited librarian squatted before her, spent her days searching for facts in that building. The contrast, between her tenacious dedication to truth and Travis's lifetime of deception, made Lily want to laugh out loud. Or spit. Or scream. She stood up.

"You okay?" the librarian asked.

"I'm not sure."

"This has to be him," she said cautiously, sensing more to the story than she knew but unable to let go of celebrating her research coup. "How many Travis Graysons work with bonobos in the Congo?"

"That's totally him," Lily said. "It's incredible that you found this. Thank you so much."

"Sure. No problem. But, I mean, it doesn't really say where he is now. So, it's pretty incomplete."

"Actually," Lily said. "It's exactly what I needed to know. Entirely and completely."

The librarian's face slackened into cautious pleasure. "Well, take care. You know where the shelters are, right?"

She assumed Lily was homeless. But of course she *was* homeless. There was no reason she shouldn't also look it.

"Thank you," Lily said again and rolled her bike into the street.

31

LILY CALLED VICKY FROM her hillside camp just as the first stars began showing in the sky. She did her best to disguise her own distress. "It's me. Where are you?"

"Travis told me you came by!"

"I don't want you working with him." She realized she was holding her breath and let it out.

"Excuse me? He's been like your best thing for your entire life."

"He isn't a university professor. He lied. He's a little nuts."

"Who isn't? Anyway, what we're doing is really cool."

"What you're doing is called being homeless." Lily picked up a small stone and held it tight in her fist.

"Look, Lil, maybe you need to go home to Tom. Maybe you need to just do that."

"I told you he's with Angelina now."

"Like that's going to last. Everyone makes mistakes. Forgive him. Get over it. Go home. You need each other. You were practically *born* married."

"They're having a baby." Lily threw the stone as far as she could. She heard a soft *puh* sound when it landed.

"What?"

"He's happy about it. They really are together."

Vicky was quiet for a moment and then, "So. You're with Travis. So."

"I'm not with Travis."

"That's weird. He said you were."

"Please listen to me. He's going off some deep end."

"We all are," Vicky said cheerfully.

"No, we're not. I came out here to help you and—"

"I'm not stupid, and I don't need help."

The last thing Lily wanted was a fight with Vicky. "I never said you were stupid. You're the smartest person I know. But I've been learning a lot more about Travis. He means well. I think. But he's very skilled at roping people into his...his delusions."

"You think I don't know how to read people. That I let people take advantage of me."

"You do."

"And you?"

Touché. How desperate he must have been, defrauding a little girl, needing a stranger's admiration so badly he built a fictional life. Maybe he actually believed he *was* a primate researcher and a university professor.

"I think you should go home," Vicky said again. "Things will snap into place once you get there."

That was such a Vicky thing to say: *things will snap into place.*

"No." Lily looked out into the darkening expanse. Tom wanted the deep code in his own cells. Travis wanted someone to calm his desperation. "I'm not going back there. And I'm not with Travis." She paused, trying to figure out how to articulate what she did want, her idea about the Hyena Cluster.

"Okay. Well, cool. We agree about Nebraska, anyway. But don't try to talk me out of this. I want to see if we can live off the grid, create our own network that responds directly to people's needs. It's an extraordinary opportunity. To build from scratch the perfect communications hub. I'm having a blast!"

"Please be careful," Lily whispered.

"For crying out loud! I'm having fun!"

"I love you," Lily said. "I just want to say that."

32

WALKING DOWN TELEGRAPH AVENUE had been Annie's idea. She liked to steel her nerves. Sharpen her senses. Brave the worst.

"I'd rather go over to the swings," Binky said, reaching up to pet the head of the big orange kitten who rode on his shoulders.

"We always go there."

"It's fun."

"I want some gum," she said, determined to stay their course.

"We don't even have any money," Binky pouted, but he continued with her up Dwight Way.

As they approached Telegraph Avenue, Annie's skin prickled. There was a table set up at the intersection, run by some interfaith group who attempted to address youth needs. They called out as you went by, asking if you were hungry or wanted help getting home. Annie felt sorry for them. They were clueless. The kids who hung out on Telegraph Avenue maybe were hungry and maybe wanted to go home, but Annie doubted it. They were entrepreneurs. On this street you could buy anything. If you wanted something they didn't have on hand, they could get it within twenty-four hours. Mostly, though, they had weed, dope, and meth.

Annie and Binky turned left, ignoring the inquiries from the interfaith table, and started down Telegraph Avenue. It was stupid to have come here. Annie was scared. She was even breathing hard, and how fucked up was that? But the thing was, once they got to the end of the street, made it to the university, and turned left onto Bancroft, they'd be almost free. A few more blocks after that, and they'd be pretty much safe again. Or a hell of a lot safer, anyway. In the meantime, they'd be mentally tougher. Maybe they'd make a second go of it, right after.

"Have you ever had a mango?" Binky asked.

"Duh," Annie said, but she hadn't.

"It's like a peach, only sweeter and more perfumy."

He always did this—talk about their island when he was nervous. It annoyed her the way he sometimes seemed to actually think it was real.

"Papayas are creamy. You can squeeze lime on them and they're, like, better than soda."

"Lots of things are better than soda."

"Okay, better than donuts. I'm just saying, on the island we can be really healthy. We'll sit in the wet sand, and it'll be balmy, because it's the tropics, and the frothy, warm waves will wash up over our legs."

"We can't go to a tropical island." There, she'd said it. Binky looked like she'd slapped him. She didn't want to be mean, but sometimes you had to face the facts.

"Come on, Annie. You know we will. You have to believe in your dreams."

"You sound like a Hallmark card." It was something her grandma once had said to her.

Binky stopped right there in the street and with the kitten still draped across his shoulders, front and back paws hanging on either side of his neck, he put his arms around her. He acted as if she were the one who needed looking after. She wanted to push him away but couldn't. Why would so skinny a boy want to hug her? She left her face in the crook of his neck, her cheek against the orange fur, and breathed deeply. She loved his sweet smell, like vanilla soft serve. "You probably still believe in Santa Claus," she said.

"No Santa? What do you mean?" Binky asked, pulling away from her, his eyes wide with mock shock. He laughed and put his arm through hers. "It's creepy here. Let's go faster."

"I want gum."

"Okay," Binky said. "Then we'll go."

They walked another block, and had just one more to go, when Binky said, "I know that kid."

Two older boys, one white and one black, walked toward them. The black kid stared hard. He clearly recognized Binky, too, but Annie didn't like the quality of his recognition.

"Don't, Binky," she said, but it was already too late.

"Hey," he was calling out. "You got any gum?"

"Not them," Annie said. "Let's turn down Channing."

"No, it's cool. He and I—"

"Faggot," the boy said.

"*Me* a faggot?" Binky said, his eyes blinking rapidly. He never talked back to people who hassled them. Why now? "You're the faggot. I should know."

"Fucking A, Bink." She pulled his arm and looked back, trying to see the interfaith table, which was a good three blocks behind them.

"What?" Never had that one word sounded so hostile. "Say that again." The two boys stood before them now, hatred fizzing off their skin.

"We just want some gum," Annie said, as if the derailed request could be put back on the tracks. "I got a dollar."

"Shut up, fatso."

The white boy twisted her arm behind her back and reached into her pockets to get the dollar. "You don't have no dollar, pig girl."

"Leave her alone!" Binky shrieked.

"Leave her alone!" the kid mocked his shriek.

The first kick came from the black kid, straight to the groin. Binky screamed as he went down. He tossed the orange kitten to the side and cried, "Run, kitty!" The orange kitten shot down the street. The two boys forced laughter and shouted, "Run, kitty!" over and over again in falsettos.

The white boy kicked Binky in the head. Way too hard.

Annie yelled for help, but then, as their kicking became frenzied, she stopped because it seemed as if her voice triggered their mania. She whispered, "Please please please please mama mama mama," and felt every blow as if it landed on her own body.

They stood panting, looking down at Binky lying in a bath of blood. The white boy cracked his knuckles and huffed big gusts of air out his flared nostrils, his eyes rolling. The black boy spread his feet apart, forcing himself to keep looking at Binky splayed on the sidewalk, and she saw tears in his eyes. He spit to the side, as if to dispel them.

"You'd just bounce, lard bucket," the white boy said to Annie, and they walked away, the black boy veering away from his companion.

Annie knelt down next to Binky. "Get up. We gotta get out of here. Come on. *Hurry.*"

Binky lay on the pavement, his face in his own blood, his right knee cocked up and his left leg out straight. Both hands lay palms down above his head. His eyes were closed, his long lashes dark against his lavender eyelids.

"I said get the fuck up, Benjamin. *Now.*"

No one used Telegraph Avenue anymore except for the ferals, and now, after the beating, even they kept their distance, turning down side streets the second they caught sight of Binky on the ground. In the far distance, Annie could see the people working the interfaith table shuffling through their flyers, heads down. They were worthless.

"Okay," she said and sat down with her back against the bricks of the storefront. "You can rest a minute, Binky. Then we'll go. We'll get those cuts taken care of. Then we're heading straight for the island. Don't you think? I'm sick of this dump. I'll get us plane tickets. Don't worry, I'll finesse it. Shit, if I need to suck a few dicks, I'll do it. I know, I know, you said never again. But for our island? I will. Once we're there, we'll be home free. Coconut milk and mangoes. Warm ocean saltwater on our wounds. We'll make us a house out of driftwood, right? Right, Binky?

"Okay, Binky. Get up. Get the fuck up now. They're coming back. They'll fucking kill you this time. It's *them*, Bink. Get the fuck up."

Annie stood up, grabbed Binky's hands, and dragged him down the sidewalk. It wasn't too hard, him being so skinny, but she wasn't fast enough. The two boys strode toward her with their wrecked faces.

She didn't mean to let go of Binky. She didn't mean to leave him. She didn't mean to run.

When she got to the church, she shoved past the line of people moving slowly in the door. Kalisha, rather than Lily, stood behind the service window serving up the trays, angrily splatting food onto the plastic. Annie leaned over a filled tray, her big fat hideous stomach smashing the food, and yelled, "Where's Lily? Where the fuck is Lily?"

33

LILY STOOD IN THE church parking lot, holding her bicycle, trying to formulate the words for an apology to Kalisha about yesterday's no-show. Leniency wasn't Kalisha's strong suit. Lily would be direct, just say she was sorry and that it wouldn't happen again.

As she lifted her bicycle to carry it up the steps to the community room door, Annie catapulted across the pavement, wild-eyed, her hair a mess of unkempt curls and her leggings shredded. The big girl grabbed Lily's arm so abruptly, she pulled her and the bicycle to the ground.

Annie dropped to her knees, still clutching Lily. "Where have you *been?* I've been *looking* and *looking* for you!"

Lily pried Annie's hands off of her. The girl fell back on her butt, knees out and feet together, her legs making an O. She sobbed big wracking sobs.

"Annie, *what?*"

"Binky's dead."

"What do you mean, dead?" Like there were gradations.

"We just wanted some gum and they said faggot and then Binky who never ever talks back to anyone said you're the faggot and there were other people right there but no one stopped them they just kicked him and kicked him and he was screaming help and I couldn't help I tried but all I could do was hit their backs and I think he was dead like in seconds the guys didn't even run away they just walked and Binky's there on the pavement all broken blood everywhere and he's broken and dead and I don't know what to do I don't know what—"

"Annie." Lily squatted and touched her foot. "Where did this happen?"

"Telegraph Avenue!"

"When?"

"Yesterday, yesterday, yesterday, you weren't here why not we just wanted gum and they killed him." Her wailing grew louder and the few early arrivals in the parking lot backed away.

Lily looked over her shoulder at the door to the community room. Kalisha was already mad at her. She could be a tiny bit late today. She'd apologize for everything later this afternoon.

"I bet he's okay," Lily said. "Come on. Get up. We'll find him." She tried pulling Annie to her feet, but the girl was crying too hard to move, so Lily put her hands under Annie's armpits and lugged until she stood. "Show me where."

The blood had soaked into the sidewalk pavement and dried in the shape of an amoeba. "See, he's moved on," Lily said. "We'll find him and get him help. Where do you two go when you need somewhere safe? I bet he's gone there."

Annie pointed to a loose pile of clothing in a nearby doorway, like the bones and pelt left by a coyote. Even the black Air Jordans with the shimmering red laces were there, next to the briefs, jeans, and T-shirt, serving as a warning, a reminder. No one would abandon a fine pair of sneakers. The attackers had to be somewhere nearby, watching.

Lily glanced around, knowing that she looked exactly like a victim. She was skinny and confused, accompanied by a grief-stricken teenage girl. At any moment, they would pluck her bike from her hands, knock her down, take her pack, too.

"Let's go," she said, but the look on Annie's face stopped her cold. The girl's eyes were huge, but unseeing, and her mouth bunched up, as if it were filled with venom. It was hatred. Pure icy hatred.

In that moment, Lily saw how wrath gets handed off, how cruelty passes from the torturer to the victim, how it's impossible for it to be otherwise. The grief is too great to assimilate and it curdles into instant hatred.

Annie was too young to absorb that much poison.

So Lily walked over to the pile of clothes in the doorway and picked up the sneakers.

"What are you doing?" Annie hissed.

Lily hoped that maybe Annie had to spit out the wad of venom to speak at all. She tied the laces together and draped the sneakers around her neck. "You have to have something to hold onto Binky."

Here they came, two big boys, maybe seventeen years old, a team of killers. "What you doing, bitch?"

Lily heard Annie's hard, terrified breathing. She knew she stood to lose everything, certainly her bike and probably her life. She didn't bother trying to summon courage. She couldn't possibly look intimidating to the boys. Instead, she drew the deepest breath she could draw and looked the white boy in the eye. She said, "He was my son."

The boy took a step back, and then another. Lily saw a void behind him, a big swallowing hole, a motherlove of his own, one that either existed and caused him pain or did not exist and still caused him pain. A great swallowing filled his eyes, even as he tried to hold steady.

Lily shifted her stare to the black boy. He spit to the side. More venom released, maybe.

"Annie," she said, without unlocking her eyes from the boy's. "Do you want anything else here?"

Annie couldn't speak, and so with the leather shoes resting against her breasts, Lily grasped the handlebars of the bicycle with one hand and linked her other arm through Annie's, and they walked away, her ears straining to hear what the boys were doing behind them. After a few blocks, at Dwight Way, Lily turned and looked. They were alone.

"You two doing okay?" a volunteer at the interfaith table called out. Lily considered hopping on the bicycle and fleeing. She could leave Annie with these church people. There was still time to apologize to Kalisha. Just the thought gave her a dizzying rush. She needed to choose safety.

Annie disengaged her arm from Lily's and turned left, heading up Dwight Way. *Good,* Lily thought. She would watch the child cross the street and then be on her way.

When there were ten yards separating them, Annie turned and waited, her eyes fixed on Lily. The sight of those chubby legs splayed at the knees, the dimples on either side of her mouth, the crazy hair, the trusting expectation, all tugged hard at a place under Lily's sternum. She remembered the mugging that had felt more like a hug than an assault. *Why me?* Lily wanted to know and walked forward to close the gap.

A couple of blocks east, Annie turned into a dead-end alley. Lily stood at the mouth of the alley watching as the girl hoisted herself up on the metal rungs of a dumpster and peered inside. A moment later she fell to the ground, hitting her hip hard and dry heaving.

Lily knew without looking. She also knew that she couldn't let Annie experience this alone. She leaned the bike against the alley wall, stepped around Annie, and climbed up to have a look.

Binky lay in the dumpster, stripped naked and pale, amidst the garbage. His face was bashed in and his bones were broken. Flies touched down and flitted off his body. Annie had known to look in the dumpster, which meant she'd seen other bodies disposed of here.

"Come on," Lily said, coaxing Annie up off the dirty ground. She led her out of the alley. When they got to People's Park, Lily made her sit on a bench. She pulled the flip-flops off the girl's feet and pushed on the Air Jordans. They were big, but Lily tied the red laces tight. She explained that they were going to her camp and that it was a long walk, uphill. Lily had no idea what she'd do with the girl in her camp, but at least she could sleep, and they'd both be safe.

They stopped often to rest but finally arrived at dusk. Lily unzipped the tent and helped Annie into the sleeping bag. The girl rolled onto her side and clutched her arms against her chest, the same way she'd slept in Joyce's overgrown backyard, under the stars, only then she'd had Binky pressed against her, their unspeakable tenderness.

"Get some sleep," Lily said and started to pull out of the tent. But Annie twisted around and clamped her arms around Lily's middle. She tucked her head into Lily's neck and held her so tight they both had trouble breathing.

Lily reached behind and grabbed both of Annie's wrists, loosening her grip. She folded the girl's arms in front of her chest. "Get some sleep."

Lily backed away on her hands and knees. She zipped up the tent and sat outside on her rock, looking down at the cities and up at the big moon rising above the eucalyptus trees behind her.

She'd never felt this empty in her life. As if every effort she'd ever made had failed spectacularly. Vicky was building an imaginary empire with Travis. Tom was already cooing over his and Angelina's embryo. Binky's pale, thin body lay dead in a dumpster. She'd even failed Kalisha by not showing up two days in a row.

Everything she'd ever believed in was wrong. Bad people do win. The bonobos were going extinct for a reason. A tiny population was left in the Congo, and soon they too would be gone.

Lily slid off the rock and stretched out on her back in the dirt, looking up at the nothing of space. Vicky didn't think it was nothing. Lily wished her sister were here to tell her stories about the constellations. She wished she remembered the stories Vicky had once told her; maybe Annie would like to hear them, too. When she woke up a few hours later, at the start of dawn, she rolled over on her side to check the tent. The door flap was open. Annie was gone. So was her bicycle.

PART THREE

34

L ILY WALKED SLOWLY DOWN the hill to the library. She had no
husband, no money, no bicycle, and apparently no sister, either.
Vicky didn't answer her phone this morning, though Lily had tried
calling, over and over again, until her phone charge fizzled out.

She definitely no longer had a job. She'd missed two afternoons
at the church, been a complete deadbeat no-show. She supposed
Kalisha couldn't turn her away as a client, so at least she'd have dinner
tonight—if she dared show her face.

Lily entered the library reluctantly, as if she didn't deserve to be
there either, but soon couldn't resist its spell. The marble stone flooring
cooled the air. The big oak tables and straight-back chairs suggested
the possibility of solutions. The walls of books gave the place such
authority: all the wisdom amassed over the centuries, according to her
third-grade teacher. Lily thought she had perhaps arrived at square
one. Was that so bad?

She gave her phone to the librarian supervising the charging
stations, signed the new release form, and got in line for the
computers. A clown entertained a group of children in the corner,

and Lily watched the show, dismayed by how little it took to cheer her up, until she reached the front of the computer line.

"Dear Wesley," she wrote. Her fingers flew as she spared no detail. Why should she? She had nothing but time and stories. When her fifteen minutes were up, she hit *Send* and then got back in line.

Forty-five minutes later, she sat down at another station, reopened her email program, and was astonished to find a response.

Dear Lily,

Thank you for writing. I like the way you talked about your friend Kalisha and burying the philosophy professor under the lemon tree, how eventually he'll be nutrients for the fruit. I also like what you said about history being shortsighted, how the cycles of biology are a better way of viewing our relationship to earth. Or even to the universe.

I write novels. Only I can't, haven't ever, finished one. I'm afraid of where every story goes. I don't want to be caught in that cycle of painful fate. It seems like the only real truths are painful. All the stories that end well, end too soft. Your narrative was about a dead man and a grave. But the lemons…the body. I don't know. I liked it. It wasn't soft. It moved into the future. Biology: a different kind of fate, maybe?

Gratefully,

Wesley

⊞ ⊞ ⊞

Dear Wesley,

That's the whole thing about evolution. It's the most exciting narrative of all because it's about change over time. Real change. Change that sticks. Change that improves the odds for the changed. Change that increases the intricacy of our dependence on one another. There are billions of examples. Like how people need bees to pollinate our crops. That lemon tree, it needs Professor Vernadsky's body.

Travis may be crazy. Or ruined. Or just plain sad. But he didn't lie about the bonobos. I've read books and articles. What Travis told me about our link to them, and their capacity for love and compassion, is all true.

The thing is, when people think of evolution, they think of creatures battling it out for survival. That's not what Darwin meant by "survival of the fittest." What if natural selection favors altruism? What if love improves our chances for survival? Maybe love and survival are the same thing!

I don't know what love is. I don't think anyone does. But maybe our human descendants will evolve there, to an understanding of love.

Lily

Her time was up, and her phone wasn't fully charged, but she unplugged it anyway and dropped onto the floor in a corner of the reading room where she checked, every five seconds, for a reply from Wesley. She didn't have to wait long.

# # #

Dear Lily,

Are you in Berkeley?

Wesley

# # #

Dear Wesley,

Yes. I can't seem to leave. I've been reading your blog posts. You went back to Oregon?

Lily

# # #

Dear Lily,

I did, but I'm on my way back down again. I can't seem to stay away. I love the vibrancy of the community that remains in the East Bay.

Wesley

# # #

Lily thought of the way, during the motorcycle ride, she'd held her hand over his heart, as bold as a bonobo. She wrote,

I'd like to see you. Meet me tomorrow at the library? After my shift at 7:30? I mean, if you want. I'll be there, in any case. I'm off to the church now.

Lily got to her feet and shoved her phone in her backpack. She felt like she knew Wesley from reading all of *The Earthquake Chronicles* and *Wings on Fire*. But that didn't mean that he knew her. Or even that she really knew him. He'd either come tomorrow or he wouldn't. She slung on her backpack and set out for the church.

It was a hot afternoon. A layer of heat shimmered above the pavement. An eerie silence squeezed the air. Weeds grew in the church parking lot cracks, as always, but they looked more aggressive, as if they were now the primary occupants. The sun shone starkly against the pale pink building. Fresh tags, angry hieroglyphics, were splashed in red paint across the lower parts of the walls.

Where were all the early arrivals? The folks who gathered in the parking lot to shoot the breeze before dinner?

Lily ran up the cement steps to the community room door. A scrawled sign read: *Meals Program Closed.* The door was locked.

35

MOMENTS AFTER RON LEFT for the evening, someone pounded on the community room door. Kalisha thought, *Lily!* She'd been worried all afternoon. Lily hadn't missed a dinner in three weeks. So Kalisha opened the door, and two white men, one burly with a black beard and the other pale and freckled, pushed in. Just beyond, in the parking lot and pulled up to the stoop, were two black Chevy Blazers.

The men ignored her completely as they shook open plastic trash bags and began filling them with food from the pantry. Kalisha sat down on a folding chair in the community room and watched. Even if she had any fight left in her, she knew it would be useless against these two goons. When they'd taken all the food out to the trucks, they loaded up utensils from the kitchen. They walked back and forth, carrying armloads and bagfuls of whatever wasn't nailed down. They even took a dozen folding chairs. In less than thirty minutes, they'd gutted the free meals program, her heart, her life. Each of the men got behind the wheel of a Blazer, started the engine, and drove away.

Kalisha didn't hesitate. She didn't think. She didn't consider. She didn't even lock the door to the church behind her. It was getting dark, but there were always vendors on Telegraph Avenue. She walked quickly and arrived in a few minutes.

There they were, the dealers, so obvious with their hands in their pockets, their smirks, their confident gaits. Her desire skyrocketed. A searing need. God in a needle. Nothing could be simpler. It felt like a script that had been written for her and her alone.

Kalisha had seen these fellows and experienced these feelings hundreds of times. But tonight was different. Tonight, side by side with the hunger, she felt an urge to laugh. It was a bitter laugh, for sure, but laughter nonetheless. These hustlers looked ridiculous: stripped, raw, savage.

Young ferals sprawled in the entryways of the closed storefronts. She looked closely at their faces, wondering if any were her clients, but none were, these lowlifes who couldn't be bothered even with nutrition and certainly not with the community associated with people coming together for meals.

How dare they. The dealers. To these children. To her.

And yet a physical stasis held Kalisha at Telegraph Avenue and Dwight Way. The crosshatch of feelings bound her as tightly as a set of ropes.

"Candles?" said a voice behind her.

She turned and saw a woman with long, ratty Shakespearean hair and dressed in layers of shirts, gym shorts over warm-up pants, and a moth-eaten cape. She was folding up a card table and at her feet sat a cardboard box.

"Whatchya looking for?" she asked.

"Candles," Kalisha said, wondering if she'd really heard that word.

"How many you need?"

Then the biggest joke of all occurred to Kalisha. She hadn't any money!

"Another time, maybe," she said.

"Look." The woman opened her box and held up a couple of the hand-dipped candles. "I have all the colors. Most are rainbow. The colors change as you burn them."

"They're beautiful."

The woman bent and gathered a big handful, the hard wax cylinders making a pleasant clunking sound as she bundled them. She held them out to Kalisha.

"I'm sorry. I don't have any cash at the moment."

"But now you have some candles." The woman shook her full and extended hands, meaning, *go on, take them*.

Kalisha did, her own hands covering the candlemaker's hands for a second as they made the exchange.

"The box is too heavy to carry when it's full, anyway," the woman said. "You're doing me a favor." Then she interwove the cardboard flaps on the box top, balanced the load on one hip, and hefted the folded card table in her opposite hand. "Good night."

Kalisha spent that evening reading in Pastor Riley's office. She read bits from all kinds of authors: St. Augustine, Mircea Eliade, Paul Tillich, St. Teresa of Avila, Alan Watts, and William James. Even Aristotle. It felt good to tackle those mountains, revisit her favorite ideas, hold and arrange the shots at truth. She wasn't denying what she'd experienced today—Lily was a no-show and at least one of those trucks belonged to Travis Grayson—but she wanted to fill her mind with as much faith, grace, and wisdom as she could before drawing conclusions.

The next morning she went to her regular NA meeting, but she didn't tell the group that the free meals program had been raided, nor about her trip up to Telegraph Avenue. She didn't want their murmurs of understanding. What she wanted was a way around her suspicions. But she had a logical mind and she couldn't stop herself from trying to fit the pieces together. She hated the picture coming into view: Lily knew Travis Grayson; she didn't show up yesterday afternoon; but Travis's black Chevy Blazer did.

After the meeting, that man Carter asked if he could walk her home. They'd talked a few times, standing on the sidewalk out in front of the senior center where the meetings were held, and she liked him. Maybe a lot, she wasn't sure. He was a slight man, with nice eyes, skin several shades darker than hers, and gray hair, though he wasn't old.

He was a sculptor and a carpenter, bright and kind, but he'd only been clean for two years, and she didn't trust the strength of his abstinence. Also, he was soupy; his tendency to quote proverbs annoyed her. She needed someone with a bit of razor in his spleen, a man who knew words to be tools.

Besides, she couldn't tell him that she lived in a church.

Before walking away, she heard herself say maybe another time, leave a door open, and she almost turned around to say, actually, no never. She would have, if she could have thought of a way to say that without sounding completely heartless.

She wasn't heartless. But the raid of the free meals program had left a void. A massive one. She needed to be very, very careful about what she let tumble in.

That afternoon she put up a sign telling the clients that the meals program was closed. At four o'clock, she pulled a table over to the wall by the door and stood on it to look out the high window. She could see the entire parking lot, the steps, and the stoop. She watched for Lily. Any moment she expected to see the tall, skinny, crazy white girl come running up, sweaty and maybe bloody again, who knew what she got herself into when not at the church. She'd pound on the door. Explain where she'd been. Kalisha would act angry. She longed for that relief.

But Lily didn't come, for a second day in a row.

Late that night, Kalisha sat cross-legged in front of the altar, watching the last of her Shakespearean candles burn. They were nubs by now, each surrounded by a pool of multihued wax. When she'd lit them the night before, she'd designated one for Michael, one for Professor Vernadsky, one for Lily, two for Ron and his girlfriend, the remaining three for her grandma and two estranged parents, but by now she thought of them as a single glow of forgiveness.

When you've lost everything, that's really all there is to grasp.

In the last of the candlelight, she considered her foolish and devastating mistake with heroin, her betrayal of Michael, her high-stakes treachery with her own life, and laughed out loud at the big joke: she'd survived it all. All that was left was forgiving herself.

36

L ILY WANDERED AROUND BERKELEY for a couple of hours, dirty and hungry and bleary-eyed, asking people if they knew why the meals program was closed today. No one knew; or if they did, they weren't saying.

Reckless with despair, she even walked down the full length of Telegraph Avenue looking for Annie. She entertained fantasies of strangling the two boys who'd killed Binky. She had nothing to lose anymore, other than her life, and this afternoon, that didn't seem all that valuable.

If she were thinking clearly, she would have known that the closure of the meals program had nothing to do with her not showing up two days in a row. Surely Kalisha could have done the extra work herself. Or someone else could have served the trays. It wasn't rocket science. But all her thoughts landed in the dump heap of blame; she'd failed the one and only place where she thought she was making a difference.

Eventually Lily walked up the hill and over to Professor Vernadsky's house, next door to Vicky's old place. She went down the side path to the backyard. She crouched on the edge of the professor's grave, a mound of crumbled soil. She thought of how she and Kalisha had sweat and cried and laughed together. She wondered if she'd ever see her friend again. The sign only said, "Meals program closed." Maybe it'd reopen tomorrow, but there'd been a finality in the handwriting, a fury.

An hour later, Lily stepped out of the eucalyptus and bay laurel forest and onto her knoll. It hadn't rained in three weeks, and the bone-dry dirt clods crunched under her feet as she descended the slope to her campsite. White fuzzy flowers, like shredded cotton balls, covered the coyote brush. A hot wind blew across the hillside, quivering the blue taffeta of the tent and sweeping away any bees.

The air inside the tent was sweltering, so she lay outside on the ground, the hot wind drying her sweat. She watched the dimming sky, breathed in the scent of the scrub brush. Why was she so stubborn? Why hadn't she been able to hold still, stay in Fair Oaks, accept a comfortable life? She'd broken her own heart by insisting on having wings.

Ha! As Vicky would say. Wings like Suzette. What a crazy imagination that guy Wesley had. And what losses, his mother and ex-wife. A broken heart, he'd written, is the same thing as an open heart, by definition.

Sometime during the night, in her sleep, she rolled onto her front, her left cheek pressing into the dry soil. She mistook the first vibrations for some kind of dream epiphany, an orgasm of the psyche. But it was the ground beneath her that shook. The earth itself rolled, bucked. She could feel its heat, rhythm, fluidity, as if the planet and she were making love, her skin and belly pressed against the earth's undulations.

Lily sat up and looked around. A big orange moon was making its slow lob across the sky. The wind had died and the air was perfectly still. Nothing else seemed changed, at least not up here. Exhausted, Lily lay back down and returned to sleep.

The whooping birds woke her a while later. They were going crazy with their barking and yapping and howling. She imagined them cowering in confusion for that hour after the earthquake, then letting loose their fear and angst.

They weren't birds, of course. She knew that.

The cities looked nervous and murky, but a strange rusty light tinged the western sky. She counted three plumes of smoke, thin and tentative, twisting upward. She thought she saw fire north of Berkeley.

Lily retrieved her jug from the tent and drained the remaining water.

Flames exploded over Richmond, the entire skyline blazing red. Four ear-splitting blasts shot through the airwaves. The Chevron oil refinery was on fire.

Lily turned in circles, as if there were somewhere to go, until she became dizzy and had to stand still, watching the fires scorch high in the sky. Here, a thousand feet above the igniting city, she might be safe. The first siren pierced the orange dawn.

Lily sat and drew her knees against her chest. As day broke, more and more pillars of smoke rose, creating another kind of darkness. More sirens tore through the streets. More explosions, in other parts of the urban landscape, burst their hot blue-and-yellow flames. Thick black smoke billowed over all of Richmond.

Then the wind picked up again. For now just a warm breath, but if it strengthened, the city fires could blow right up the hillsides where the dry vegetation would feed the flames much more readily than the buildings below.

Lily had to find Vicky. Quickly. They'd have to go east, over the hills. She had to make good decisions. Should she take the tent?

The sound of bicycle tires skidding down the trail toward her campsite startled Lily to her feet. She glanced around, looking for a weapon. She grabbed a large rock and held it over her shoulder, poised for heaving.

Riding toward her was a fat boy with black curls cropped close to his head. He wore tan madras shorts and no shirt, his stomach and breasts jiggling as he bounced down the trail. He had a small nylon knapsack on his back. On his feet were the black Air Jordans with sparkly red shoelaces. He tossed the bicycle to the ground, and Lily thought he would tackle her, but he stopped short, ten feet away, his face anguished with the effort to not cry.

"Annie," she whispered.

The child bent over, putting her hands on her knees to catch her breath. Then she did start crying, her back heaving. When she straightened up again, a red mess of acne flaming her face, she shouted, "I didn't steal your bike!"

"I thought you had."

"Hello? It's right there!" Annie swung an arm in the direction of the dropped bicycle. "I wasn't going to just leave Binky in the filth. There're flowers all over up here. I picked a huge clump, all the colors, white and blue and pink and yellow, and I took the bike so I could go fast and get to him before daylight. I sprinkled them on top of him." Choking sobs jammed up her voice again. She took big shivering breaths. "I thought I'd be back before you even knew I was gone but then I got lost trying to find you. And then I did. Find you. Not you, the tent. Yesterday. But you weren't here. So I went to the church. And it was closed. Now there's been another earthquake!"

Her hair was more hacked than cut, but very short. The tan madras shorts were boys' shorts.

"Don't fucking look at me like that."

Lily looked away.

"Besides, we needed food," Annie said. She slung the knapsack to the ground and opened the drawstring. She pulled out a bottle of water and handed it to Lily, and then set half a loaf of bread and a jar of peanut butter on the ground. "So you should probably thank me."

Lily drank. When she tried to hand the bottle back, Annie wouldn't take it. "I have oranges, too. And cookies."

"Thank you."

"You're welcome."

Lily ate two sandwiches, an orange, and half a dozen cookies. Annie watched her eat, her long lashes blinking back more tears.

"I have to go get my sister," Lily said. "And you need to go home."

"I'm staying with you." The salty streaks of sweat dried on her soft chest and stomach.

"Where are your parents?"

"Dead. *Duh.*"

"Do you have a guardian?"

"Grandma said they deserved it for being stupid enough to join the Army. Now she's saddled with me."

"Grandma sounds like a gem."

"I'm on my own."

"You're only, what, sixteen or seventeen years old?"

"Thirteen." And then, "I said don't look at me like that."

"I'm just surprised. I thought you were a lot older. And I don't understand the haircut and shorts."

"Are you completely stupid?"

"No, not completely."

"Maybe you didn't see Binky in the dumpster."

Lily lay back in the dirt, looked up at the smoky sky and listened to the shushing sound of the wind, as if it were advising calm. Thirteen, not sixteen. Indefinite gender. Hostile and vulnerable. When someone in the city far below began screaming, Lily sat back up and said, "I did see him, Annie. Tell you what we're going to do now."

Annie nodded hard. She might as well have saluted, so attentively did she wait for the plan.

"My sister is at Lake Anza. I think. I hope. We're going to go get her. Then we're getting out of here."

"You and me together."

"I have a plane ticket for Omaha, Nebraska. Maybe I can get Tom to send another couple." She couldn't imagine showing up in Fair Oaks with this kid. If anyone had any better ideas along the way, she would be happy to entertain them. For now, this was the best plan she could fathom.

Someone whooped. This was followed by a bark-roar that morphed into a low wail, rising to a high grunt.

Annie scrambled to her feet. "The wolf!"

"It's not a wolf."

"Yes, it *is*. I saw a wolf here yesterday!"

Lily stopped herself from scanning the surrounding chaparral. "No, you didn't. There aren't any wolves in Berkeley."

"I did. Black nose, scruffy coat—"

"No, Annie."

"Yes."

"Come on. Grab the bike. Let's go."

"Then what was it?"

"Pack up the food."

When they reached the turnoff to Sal's shed, Lily told Annie to wait. She ran up to the locked chain-link gate and weaved her fingers in the metal diamonds as she shouted, "Sal!"

Sal stepped right out of the shed, as if she'd been waiting.

"Come on," Lily called up. "It's time to leave."

Sal clumped down to the fence but didn't unlock the gate. Strands of her thick auburn hair stuck to her damp face. Her mouth hung open and she breathed irregularly, like an animal in fear. She didn't speak.

"Open the gate," Lily said and gently rattled the chain links.

"I'm staying."

"The city is on fire. It's bad. The sooner we leave the better. It's only going to get harder."

Sal shook her head.

"We're going to pick up Vicky. Come with us. Give her another chance."

Sal's tawny eyes flickered, but then she flipped her hair off the back of her neck. "She's thirty-five years old. I'm almost forty. Radical personality change is unlikely."

"Maybe. But a small shift in the right direction could help a lot, right?"

"I'm quite happy on my own."

"It's already a hot day. If this wind picks up, the fires could sweep right up the hill. You won't survive. Neither will they."

"They?"

"I know why you're here. Some of the hyenas are at large. I hear them whooping in the mornings. You have to let them go."

"The hyenas were airlifted out."

"Except for how many?"

Sal looked up into the canopy of a live oak. She shook her head. "How many?"

"Just two."

Lily looked around quickly, half expecting to see a couple of glistening snouts, four round fuzzy ears, four onyx eyes opaque with distrust, snarling black lips pulled back over inky gums and bone-crushing teeth. She jumped when Annie, who'd joined her at the fence, grabbed a handful of her T-shirt.

"I told you so," Annie said. "You wouldn't believe *me*."

"They're not wolves." The last thing Lily needed at the moment was to be arguing with a thirteen-year-old. "Please just keep quiet, okay?"

"Same dif. Wolves, hyenas."

"You've been trying to trap them," Lily said to Sal.

"No. They're way too smart for that."

"Right. There's nothing you can do for them. So come on with me."

"Us," Annie said.

"It's my job to protect them. I was trapping rabbit to feed them."

"Was?"

"I rarely see them anymore. They're probably feeding on deer."

"So they don't need you."

Sal crossed her arms. "I love them."

Lily couldn't quite believe she was having an extended conversation about the safety of a couple of hyenas when her own life was at risk. "If the fire sweeps up here, they'll die and so will you."

"I can't leave them."

"They'll be fine."

"It's a male and a female."

"So?"

"If they have pups, the entire course of evolution on the North American continent could be radically changed. For starters, they'd wipe out the deer in probably one generation."

Annie gasped.

"You can't control everything," Lily said. "In fact, you can't control anything. The hyenas were on this continent before us. So maybe they're back. They have as much of a right to make a living as we do. Come on, Annie." Lily turned her back on Sal.

"Shouldn't she be coming with us?" Annie said pointing at Sal.

"Yes, she should be. But she's a stubborn cow."

"Lily!" Sal shouted once she and Annie were back down on the fire trail.

Lily turned and looked up at the wild woman gripping the chain-link fence.

"Tell Vicky I love her." An unmistakable husk of desire wrapped her voice.

Lily waved a dismissing hand but knew she'd deliver the message. If ever she got a chance.

37

VICKY HAD A PREMONITION. It came to her as a quick mental burst. The sensation unnerved her. At first she was interested only in the experience itself. What did it mean to feel strongly that something was about to happen? How was she supposed to read it? Was she supposed to just ride out the thing that was about to happen? Or should she try to take some sort of action?

Whatever it was, it was undeniable. Something bad was about to happen, and it was going to be her fault. Only what? She needed to think.

Yes, she'd better try to take action.

So Vicky left the electronics bunker, hidden in the trees on the hillside above Lake Anza, and walked down to the camp. The kids sat at the picnic table eating sandwiches, and the adults pored over maps that Vicky had hand-drawn from electronic images. She climbed into the Eero Aarnio Bubble Chair, hanging from the live oak, and pushed off with her feet to swing and think.

The day was terribly hot, and the inside of the bubble was like an oven, so she leaned forward, out the opening of the chair, letting her face feel the rush of air as she swung. Maybe later she'd have a swim in the lake.

She'd made a mistake. She could admit that now. Travis was, as Lily had said, outside acceptable levels of mental health.

But so what? She'd moved on from his plans to her own. The folks here at Lake Anza wanted to leave, and she was helping them put together an exit plan. She'd spent the last few days in the electronics bunker trying to strengthen the computers' connection to the satellites. They worked only intermittently, but when they did, she researched resources for stranded earthquake victims, finding transportation and emergency housing, like way stations on the Underground Railroad, for their journey out. It had been slow and laborious, but she'd put together safe passage for her charges.

Other than that, she'd tried to improve the camp ambiance with humor. No one much laughed at her jokes, which made her miss Sal, acutely.

Still, her timing had been excellent. The new earthquake this morning jolted—ha, ha—everyone into action. The three remaining families were packing up their belongings and they'd soon be on their way. Then Vicky could figure out what to do with herself.

Two men stepped into the camp clearing. She recognized them both. One was Travis's guard, the guy who looked like Pluto. The other, unfortunately, was Paul.

So here was the bad thing.

At least she'd been right! Vicky loved being right.

But now she needed to decide, quite quickly, on a course of action.

She launched herself out of the bubble chair and flew a good ten feet, landing in front of the fire pit. She wrenched her ankle and startled the two men. Paul gaped. And Vicky made the mistake of laughing.

38

ANNIE NEEDED TO PROTECT Lily. She was too skinny. Her complexion was so pale, with a hint of a rash, and her hair hung limp and lifeless. Besides, she didn't even know what to be afraid of. She just *did* things.

Choose love over fear, Binky liked to say. Stupid, stupid, stupid.

Lily could get herself killed.

Not on Annie's watch.

Binky had been killed because Annie was a big fat sissy. Stupid, stupid, stupid. Thinking she could wear girls' clothes. No more. She was going to be a man. Grandma had been right about that much. If nothing else, Annie needed to be a man so she could protect Lily.

Annie walked on the street side, keeping herself between the occasional cars and Lily. Sometimes she held out her hand, signaling to the drivers that they should give them more space on the side of the road.

"Did you get enough to eat?" Annie asked.

Lily gave her that surprised look she had, kind of permanently baffled, but Annie knew it wasn't real. Lily sometimes acted confused when she actually wasn't, even if she thought she was. Binky would have called that circular thinking. Whatever.

"I have more peanut butter and bread."

"Thanks. I'm good for now."

She'd liked watching Lily eat the sandwiches, orange, and cookies. The food that she, Annie, had provided. Maybe at the lake she could catch some fish and they could cook it over a campfire. Soon the fruit would start ripening, too: blackberries and plums.

They arrived at the lake a little before eight o'clock that morning. Annie had heard about Lake Anza, but she'd never been here before. The place looked haunted, all quiet and deserted, the water reflecting the flat, gray sky. You could smell smoke from the burning cities.

"What's that?" Annie asked, pointing at a large clear globe—it looked like a deep-sea capsule—bobbing against the reeds on the far side of the lake.

Lily took off, running the length of the spillway. She waded into the lake without even taking off her sneakers. She parted the reeds to get to the floating plastic bubble, grabbed hold of an edge of the opening, and dragged it out of the water. Annie jogged, pushing the bicycle, to catch up. She found Lily trying to tip the bubble so that the water would drain out. Inside was a soaking wet metallic silver cushion, blackened by a bunch of cigarette burns. Lily let go of the bubble and ran up the hill, water squishing out of her sneakers.

When Annie arrived at the clearing, breathing hard from pushing the bicycle up the hill, she found Lily crouched next to someone lying on the ground. A man and a woman stood next to a gnarly picnic table.

"Come on, Winnie," the man said. "We can leave now."

"Who did this?" Lily yelled.

Annie set down the bike and came closer. Was this Vicky? A deep gash on her cheek gushed blood. Her eyes were swollen shut and one arm was bent all crazy, like it was broken. Annie watched her chest and saw movement, breath.

"Take this," the woman said, handing Lily a bloody rag. "I've been applying pressure. That's all I know to do."

"I asked who did this!"

Annie put a hand on Lily's shoulder. She gripped hard, fighting back that feeling that her head was going to explode. She wanted to kill the person who did this.

The man took Winnie's arm and began pulling her away from the camp.

"Wait!" Lily yelled at the couple's retreating backs.

The woman turned, but the man kept walking.

"You have to tell me what happened."

The man whirled around angrily. "We have to go. We've done all we can for your sister."

"They wanted the key to the electronics bunker," Winnie said in a pain-dulled voice. "Vicky told them no."

"Travis?"

"He wasn't here. But he calls the shots."

"He doesn't believe in violence." As if saying the words would make them true.

"You're delusional," the man said to Lily. He checked the position of the sun, then took Winnie's arm again. "Let's go."

"Help me move her down to the lake before you go."

"You can't move her. She's broken."

"It's the last thing I'll ask of you."

"What are you going to—?" The man looked aghast, glancing at Vicky and then at the lake water, as if Lily planned on drowning her sister, as Annie's grandma had done to that litter of kittens.

"Please just help me."

Winnie put a hand on the man's forearm. "A few more minutes isn't going to change anything. Vicky did all that work to help us. We have her maps. The places to stay once we get east of the hills."

"Please," Lily said.

"Those thugs will be back any minute." The man spoke impatiently.

"I'm going to cradle her shoulders in my hands and let her head rest on my forearms," Lily said. "Annie, you get her legs. You two get on either side and try to support her back and butt. We're carrying her to the beginning of the spillway."

Everyone grunted, swore, sweat, and stumbled. Vicky cried out once, then lost consciousness again. They had to put her down twice. But they did it. They reached the end of the lake and set Vicky down next to the soggy bubble chair.

Lily handed Annie the bloody rag, and she knew just what to do. She rinsed it out in the lake and then held it against Vicky's gash, applying gentle pressure. Lily took a blue button-down shirt from her backpack and used it to loosely tie Vicky's broken arm against her body.

Then Lily pushed into the undergrowth next to the trail. Annie figured she had to pee, but a moment later she emerged dragging a kayak. Annie had heard how native people sometimes put elders in canoes and floated them out to their deaths.

"What are you staring at?" Annie asked the couple who still stood on the spillway, watching. "I thought you were leaving."

"Since you're still here," Lily said, "help me lift her in."

As Lily worked her sister's legs into the front cockpit, and the others supported her upper body, Vicky howled with pain. Which meant she was still alive.

"Comfy?" Lily asked, shifting her sister's body into as upright a position as possible on the plastic seat. Her neck cocked at a bad angle, but there was nothing they could do about that. Lily lodged the paddle in the back cockpit. Annie rinsed the cloth again.

"So," Lily said to the man and woman. "You're coming with us?"

"No!" They walked backward a few steps, eyes wild.

"The city is on fire," Lily told them. "You'll do best by walking east from here."

The man took Winnie's hand, and they hoofed their way across the spillway.

Lily brushed Vicky's bangs off her forehead. "I'm going to get you out of here." Vicky's lips twitched. It might have been a smile.

"Hey, guess what," Lily said. "I just saw Sal. She says to tell you she loves you."

It *was* a smile. Her mouth wrenched apart. Her swollen eyes blinked.

Annie filled both of their water bottles, Lily lifted the stern handle, and they trekked along the spillway and across the Lake Anza parking lot. As they began climbing the hill up to Wildcat Canyon Road, Annie asked, "What if the thugs come back?"

Lily didn't answer.

"I wish I had a gun."

"No, you don't."

"I would kill them."

"No one is coming back."

"They will. They always do."

Lily set down the kayak and shook the ache out of her pulling arm.

Annie waited, straddling the bike. She pushed the soles of both Air Jordans hard onto the pavement, trying to tamp down that feeling of wanting to stab someone. Sometimes the only thing she could see, as if it were imprinted on her pupils, was the picture of Binky's naked body in the dumpster.

Lily looked out at the lake. "You know what, Annie?"

She shook her head. Binky said revenge was useless, a dead end.

"You're only thirteen years old and you already know a lot about who you want to be. You stand by your friends to the end. You left a home that didn't fit. You walk for miles to get where you want to get. You're fierce."

"No, I'm not."

"And you know what those thugs have?"

"I'm not fierce."

"They have a whole lot of fear. They don't know what they want. They only have fake fierceness."

"They kill people."

Lily cocked her head one way and then another, as if killing people was neither here nor there. "So maybe they'll come kill us today. We don't know, do we? But there are a few things we do know. I got my sister here and she's still breathing. We have your strong legs on a bicycle. We have a rolling kayak, and let me tell you, that's pretty unique. We have your fierceness and my naïveté."

"What's naïveté?"

"A fresh path through known territory."

"Right," Annie said. "We have each other, too."

Lily paused. "Yep. We do."

39

THE FIRS LINING THE road, their evergreen color and peppery scent, lifted Lily's spirits. Smoke blanched the sky, as if the entire world were about to be sucked upward, but at least for this one moment, on this wooded road leading up from the lake, Vicky was alive and they had a way forward. Maybe courage was nothing more than one foot in front of another.

Her arms throbbed from hauling the boat. They stopped often so she could right Vicky's body or drip water into her mouth. At one stop, Annie peeled an orange and squeezed juice onto Vicky's tongue. At last they reached the end of Wildcat Canyon Road and the top of Spruce Street. The route slid downhill from there, all the way to the bay. They sat on a curb to rest and Lily made peanut butter sandwiches, spreading with her finger. They filled their water bottles from someone's functional lawn spigot. Vicky hadn't been conscious since they'd started rolling, but part of Lily was glad for that. The pain would be more than anyone should endure.

"I can help pull her," Annie said again.

Lily considered the offer, but Annie looked worn out, and they had a long way yet to go. "You stay on the bike. From here, gravity will do most of the work. I'll just need to control the speed and direction of the kayak."

"Who's Travis?" Annie asked as they set off again.

"A man who's lost his way."

"Did he tell those guys to beat up Vicky?"

"I don't think so."

"Are you delusional?"

"No."

"A woman who's lost her way?"

Lily laughed. "I don't think I'm lost. Not yet, anyway."

"You're not."

Annie's confidence in her was disarming.

"You know exactly where you're going," Annie said.

That wasn't true, obviously, but she didn't need to contradict the kid.

As they dropped in elevation, the smoke thickened. Soon Lily's eyes burned and tears streamed down all their faces, even Vicky's. They encountered more and more people, all of whom headed in the opposite direction, up the hill, mostly on foot but a few crawling along in cars, and so, although they got a lot of strange looks, they didn't run into any obstacles. No one cared to get ahead of anyone advancing toward the fires and rubble of the wrecked city. At least five people told them that the hospital had closed down again, and that the Red Cross station had just one doctor and dozens of patients waiting. One man said he had room for another passenger in his car. Lily urged Annie to go, but she refused. She might have given him Vicky, but Lily knew her sister wouldn't be a priority for the people in that car. They might leave her beside the road if she got in the way of their needs.

Once they reached the flatter part of the city, none of the outdoor spigots worked. More water mains must have ruptured. Lily rationed her sips from the water bottle. The pain and exhaustion—in her feet, eyes, arms, throat—numbed everything. She just wanted to sit down and quit. Her plan was pure lunacy, and there were lots of missing pieces to it. Meanwhile, the girl who loved to complain about everything, from the amount of salt in a casserole to the color of paint on the community room walls, coasted along stoically. Lily guessed that adversity was Annie's natural medium.

Halfway down Cedar Street, the smoke became so thick she couldn't see more than a few feet ahead of her. A block later, they came to an invisible wall of heat. It felt as if, should they take another step forward, their eyebrows and lashes would singe right off their faces. A hot waft of air pushed a hole through the smoke and they caught a brief glimpse of the fire, a two-story home engulfed in flames fifty feet high. Annie and Lily turned left, onto a side street heading south, and continued in that direction until the heat lessened and they could turn west again. Lily kept trying the taps of people's outdoor spigots, but none worked. With the water mains out, the fire department would need to rely on much slower backup systems that siphoned water from the bay. She heard, but couldn't see, helicopters.

Late in the morning, having dodged two more house fires, and with Lily limping, they crossed over Frontage Road and arrived at the edge of the bay. The salty water lay motionless in its basin. The tall grasses stood hearty in the caked shoreline mud. There was no wind.

Lily half expected the water to be hot, like the air, and felt a surge of pleasure at the icy splash on her face. She rinsed out her bloody T-shirt and carried it, dripping with cold saltwater, to wash Vicky's wound. Her moan was the most welcome sound she'd ever heard. Still alive.

The bay was balefully quiet. Even the community living on the flotilla of sailboats had vanished. Would there be a rescue effort this time? No one knew for sure how many people remained in the East Bay. And anyway, maybe today's shaker only ranked as an aftershock. For the original one, a month ago, hundreds of people had walked down to the water's edge, some jumping in and swimming to the fleets of volunteers who patrolled the coast looking for stranded people. If any vessels searched the shorelines this morning, Lily couldn't see them. Surely the San Francisco ferry fleet would be dispatched soon.

But Lily hadn't come this far to sit and wait. She strained her eyes to look southwest through the smoky air, then she looked back over her shoulder at her unconscious sister. She had a kayak, she had a plane ticket, and the airport lurked just over there, across that big body of water. Lily knew her idea was preposterous. But what was the alternative? The trick was to act rather than think.

Lily walked back through the tall grasses to where her companions waited. She put a hand on the top of Annie's curly head. "Listen to me."

"I'll help."

"This bicycle is your safety. You can ride away from a fire faster than you can walk or run. Whatever you do, don't lose the bicycle."

"I'm coming with you."

"I'll be back," Lily said, not breaking eye contact, wondering how she could possibly make such a promise. Then she said the words. "I promise."

Annie wiped the sweat off her face with the back of her arm. The nylon knapsack stuck to her shirtless back and perspiration soaked her madras shorts.

"You know where the library is, right?"

"But I'm coming with you."

"I'm taking Vicky across the bay. To the airport."

Her big eyes widened with an intense emotion Lily couldn't read: Fear? Anger? Admiration? Lily wanted to scream with the pressure of it. She hadn't asked for this child's tenacious hold on her.

"It's her only chance," Lily said.

Now Annie narrowed her eyes and screwed up her mouth.

"Right here, by the water, might be the safest place for now." Lily glanced behind Annie, up at the city, unsure.

"I can't swim," Annie said.

"It's okay. The water is too cold, anyway. But you could stand in it, up to your knees or something, if you had to, right?"

Lily waited, but Annie didn't acknowledge the question.

"I don't know how long this will take me. I also don't know if I can get back to this exact spot on the shore. You need to go where it's safe, and you're going to have to make that judgment. Okay? You have the bike. Whatever you do, don't lose it. Go anywhere you need to go to be safe." Lily gripped her soft shoulders too forcefully. "But look at me, Annie! Listen. If you can, meet me at the downtown library this evening at seven thirty."

Lily's stomach wrenched at the sight of the girl's trust. She'd done nothing to deserve it. Furthermore, she had no idea if she'd survive the paddle, or if she'd ever make it back to this side of the bay. She knew that if she did in fact get to San Francisco, she should stay there and save herself. She should have made the girl get in the car with that family who offered to take her.

Annie sloughed off her knapsack and dug inside. She held out the last orange. Lily hesitated, but took it. Then she swung off her own pack. She found a pen and the crumbled piece of eucalyptus bark in an inside pocket. She wrote "I love you" on the intact portion of the bark and stuffed it back in the pack, not knowing who the recipient of the message was supposed to be but needing to say it to someone. Lily then shoved her driver's license and the folded sheet of paper with the flight confirmation code in her bra. She tossed the orange and her water bottle in the kayak. She handed the pack to Annie. "Keep this for me."

Annie clutched the pack to her chest.

"Don't lose the bike," Lily said sternly, like some suburban mother on the back porch as her child headed out to play.

She lugged the kayak, with the dead weight of Vicky inside, through the grasses and over the humped dry mud. The weeds wrapped around the in-line skate wheels, preventing them from rolling and making this last pull grueling. As Lily yanked the boat, hauling it one jerky foot at a time, Vicky yelped in pain. *Good*, Lily thought, *good.*

At last the stern end of the kayak slipped into the water. Lily pushed the rest of the boat in while keeping hold of the bow handle. "Okay," she said out loud. "Okay." Keeping her hands on the boat's deck, she waded out to the rear cockpit. Her feet sank up to her ankles in the mud and for a moment she thought she might not make it into the boat. She'd slowly sink into the bay, sucked to her death by mud, while her sister drifted under the hot sun, baking to death.

Lily threw her body across the deck of the kayak and kicked backward with her left foot. It popped out of the mud. She did the same with her right foot. The boat tipped onto its side as she slid her first leg into the cockpit, nearly capsizing, but she shifted her weight and angled in the other leg. She wrangled the paddle out of the cockpit and gripped the shaft in both hands, holding it aloft. She let herself float for a moment, catching her breath. A kayak, she remembered Vicky saying, is the perfect aquatic machine. It was true. The way the cold saltwater cradled the sleek vessel, accepting its weight, relieved her tremendously. The pointed ends and slender body would slice right through the bay. Lily took a deep breath and sank a blade into the water. The boat slid forward. She managed a stroke on the other side, and then again on the right, until she achieved a rhythmic paddling.

Before pivoting in the seat to look behind herself, Lily waited until she thought she wouldn't be able to see her anymore through the smoke, but she could see her. Annie sat on the bicycle, faced forward, eyes trained on Lily as she slipped away.

Lily passed under the Bay Bridge, riding a powerful incoming tide. Seawater gushed in the Golden Gate, squeezing through that small opening with such force that once it got released into the bay, it flooded to the north and south ends. She needed only guide the boat's bow toward South San Francisco and the tide would sweep her, with Vicky flopped in the forward cockpit, to the airport.

She ought to have been very afraid. Instead, a humming boldness buoyed her. Her arms no longer hurt. She felt downright strong. She paddled with the current and talked to Vicky. She talked nonstop, hoping her voice would keep her sister's brain firing. She told her all the stories in Wesley's two blogs. She told her about Binky in the dumpster. She told her about Sal's remaining two hyenas and the possibility of their changing the entire course of evolution on the North American continent. She told Vicky that human evolution was about choice, selection, and how Vicky needed to select Sal, even if they couldn't change anything whatsoever in the course of evolution, on this continent or on any other one.

When the sun hovered directly overhead, Lily saw a small armada of rescue boats enter the bay through the Golden Gate. There was no way she could paddle back, against the current, toward them. She half-heartedly waved her paddle in the air, but they were a good five miles off and no doubt searching the eastern shoreline, not the middle of the bay where she whizzed along with her drooped human load. She needed to stay focused on her plan. If they spied her and had the means to take Vicky to a hospital, that would be good. But she had no flares or any other way of getting their attention.

So Lily kept paddling and kept talking.

"I suppose," she said after she'd exhausted every other topic she could think of, "we need to talk about Travis."

She let a few moments of silence pass, as if she were listening to Vicky's response.

"Yes," she said, as if there had been one. "I can't deny that he sustained me for many years. Just letters. Thin pieces of paper with words on them. I let his stories nourish me. Ha!" Lily laughed hoarsely, inhaling the smoky white air. "That reminds me of something Wesley wrote. You don't know Wesley. *I* don't know Wesley. But that's never stopped me, has it? Wesley said that he likes stories—he used the word "narratives"—that move into the future. Maybe he's talking about momentum. I got some of that going now, don't I?"

Lily reached the paddle forward and tried to tap her sister's shoulder, but the weight of the blade on the end of the shaft slipped and she bonked Vicky on the head.

"Oh, shit. I'm sorry! Are you okay?"

She was gratified by a moan.

"Anyway," Lily gulped forward. She talked about Louise, Travis's girlfriend, going to the Congo to bring him home, and her ultimatum in Namibia; about his being in love with Renée; Yannick's distrust; and the last bonobo trader. She moved on to how he came to Berkeley to take cover, and to *recover,* and how the apartment building collapsed on his lover with the mirrored Moroccan slippers. Lily took extra care with the narratives about her own relationship to Travis. She skipped nothing: the candlelit Craftsman bungalow, sex in the tall grasses, the muddy banks of the San Pablo reservoir.

"I'm almost glad he lied about being a university researcher. Because the story of the bonobos is my favorite story of all, the most truthful, the most hopeful. I'm glad to unlink Travis Grayson from them. They're mine now. Separate from him. My own. He lied about himself but he hadn't lied about the apes.

"I guess I'll never know if he told those men to hurt you. But I don't think so. Not directly. He wouldn't have. What I do know, though, is that at some point he started to hate. Hatred is the most contagious substance on earth. And yeah, Vicky, it *is* a substance. I saw it knotted in his muscled back as he heaved that garbage bin through an innocent shop owner's window. It had begun to flow like a stream of venom in his voice. A person can be the source of violence without ever bloodying his own hands."

Vicky sagged in the front cockpit of the kayak like a giant rag doll. Talking and paddling were the only things Lily could think to do, so she kept them up steadily, even as her tongue became a dry stump of wood.

It must have been about two in the afternoon—the hazy sun tilted west—when she saw the runways extending straight to the edge of the bay. She drew on reserves of physical and mental strength she didn't know she possessed to paddle the kayak the last mile, pulling right up to the jagged rocks protecting that stretch of the shore.

She found nowhere to land the boat. That was the point of the border of giant rocks, of course—to keep terrorists, interlopers, and criminals out. Lily paddled a hundred yards in each direction, looking for an opening, maybe a place where the earthquake and aftershocks had shaken some of the boulders out of place, making a tiny harbor.

She found only deep water sloshing against impossibly sharp rocks.

The smoke-choked sunlight sat heavy on the bay. Vicky began moaning, a nonstop symphony of low, guttural vocalizations.

"*Now* you want to talk," Lily said.

A seagull landed on one of the nearby black boulders, lifted its tail feathers, and squirted out a stream of white shit. Lightened, it bent its scaly stalks of legs and pushed off, wings out, and sailed away. Lily thought of Wesley's character Suzette. Wings would come in handy.

Vicky's garble began to sound like words.

There. A flattish rock. Don't think, act. It had gotten her this far.

Lily pulled herself out of the cockpit and slid into the deadly cold water. She worked her way around to the bow of the boat and took hold of the handle. By then they'd drifted several yards away from the flattish rock. She held onto the boat and tried to kick, but the cold already had numbed her legs. The chill reached for her core, pulled hard on her torso, and she struggled to keep her chin up above the waterline.

"Yeah," Vicky said. Distinctly, she made that affirmative sound, kind of shouting it as if Lily had just sung a particularly good riff.

She ordered her brain to order her legs to kick, her one arm to stroke. It was like writing a command in longhand and sending a runner to deliver it. She could see that her arm splashed through the water. Her legs must have been kicking, too, because she moved toward the flattish rock, although from here, at the surface of the water, it didn't look flat at all. Still holding the kayak handle with her left hand, Lily threw her right arm over the hump of the rock and pulled herself up onto it, the crags tearing the bare flesh of her arm and ripping through her T-shirt, cutting into her belly. She flipped over, onto her butt, pulled the kayak alongside her rock, and leaned forward. She could touch Vicky's face. She slapped it.

"Come on." Another slap.

"Yeah," Vicky said again. And maybe, "Where are we?"

"Your legs are fine. You have to use them now."

Vicky's eyes opened, rolled back, and then closed again. Lily kept talking. She used Sal's name, conjured her bright hair and toothy smile, her shout-laugh and bawdy sense of humor, her deep affection for one of the planet's most vicious animals, not to mention for Vicky herself, and her high-stakes play with the biosphere. Lily may have gotten a smile somewhere in that story, so she upped the ante, appealing to her sister's well-developed prurient side, trying to conjure a verbal display of all the women she hadn't yet experienced but could if she only got herself out of that kayak. She talked about all the good wines Vicky had yet to drink, the electronic opportunities as yet unexplored. Lily sat on that painfully bumpy rock for over an hour trying to talk her sister into consciousness. Vicky, with her broken arm and ribs and smashed face, had to not just get out of the kayak—she had to climb up these rocks to the runway.

Lily would never know if her words made any difference. Maybe some dream of Vicky's own, some life narrative, some hormone surge that makes people do extraordinary things, kicked in. In the late afternoon, Vicky supported her broken ribcage against the lip of the cockpit and started to pull out her legs. Lily sat on the rock, leaned forward and wrapped her arms under Vicky's armpits and pulled. Vicky passed in and out of consciousness. When out, Lily had to hold her, in whatever position, and wait in the barbecue heat of smoke and sun, until she came to again. But each time Vicky did, she kicked her legs and moaned with pain as Lily pulled whatever part she could pull.

Then—and later, Lily wouldn't be able to recount how exactly— Vicky was draped on the rock. Gulls circled overhead, like she was some fish carcass they were eager to sample. The kayak had gotten away, but thanks to slack tide, it lulled against the rocks just a couple of yards down. Lily left Vicky on the rock and climbed over the boulders to fetch it. She pulled the boat up out the bay and left it cradled between two rocks.

As she returned to Vicky, she heard the high whine of a plane engine. She couldn't see anything from her vantage on the rocky shore barrier until it was nearly upon them, hurdling down the runway, gathering speed, headed straight their way. The underside of the long fuselage, the jet engines like bulging triceps on the bottoms of the wings, soared just a few yards over their heads. Four sets of black wheels sucked up into the plane's interior. Slowly the aerial scream faded.

The moment of pure terror ended, but Lily thought she might have permanently lost her hearing. She sat touching her parts—her heart hadn't ruptured, no skin had been sliced away, and she could in fact still hear—until she realized that Vicky was on the move. The fright must have discharged a massive dose of adrenaline, because Vicky began using her legs and one good arm like a crab, scrabbling herself across the boulders, making almost better time than Lily who followed with four good limbs.

They made the runway. Vicky lurched to her feet, eyes opening and shutting. Lily took her sister's good arm and wrapped it around her own neck. She grabbed the back of Vicky's jeans, like a mother cat with a kitten, and began to haul her along.

This is the moment Lily would remember best: her limping, saltwater sundried on her skin and, for all she knew, bits of seaweed in her hair; Vicky ambulating, eyes rolling; both of them advancing across the tarmac. For those few moments, the entire world seemed to hold still.

The calm, if you could call it that, was soon disturbed by the sound of another engine, this time that of an SUV. It roared down the runway as if the plan was to simply mow them down. Lily and Vicky both dropped onto the tarmac, all the way down on their stomachs, animals in submission.

The SUV stopped a few feet in front of them and two men jumped out of the truck and drew guns. Both were white, young, and quite ready to shoot.

Slowly, the absurdity of the threat dawned on the two guards. They weren't facing machine-gun-toting operatives spouting angry rhetoric or shouting demands. Instead, they had two unarmed women on their stomachs, whimpering. One was sunburnt, skinny, in a bloody and shredded T-shirt, visibly wasted. The other was barely conscious and broken in several places. The men lowered their guns.

The curly-headed one kept his face hard and expressionless, but Lily saw a bit of concern soften the face of the towheaded one.

"How the hell?" the latter asked.

"I paddled our kayak." Lily reached into the neck of her T-shirt and they both raised their guns again. Curly-head spread his legs and held his gun with both hands. Lily pulled the soaked folded sheet of paper and driver's license out of her bra.

"San Francisco/Omaha. A fully paid open ticket for my sister, Lily Jones. She has a broken arm and some broken ribs. A bad cut on her face. I need to put her on a plane."

Towhead glanced at his colleague, who scowled and said, "You can't do that."

"Do what?" Lily asked.

The man waved his gun, pointing behind her, over her head. He didn't know what she'd done. But she did. She'd survived an earthquake, paddled across the bay with an unconscious body in a double kayak, scaled the rock barrier herself, and somehow motivated her sister to do the same. She had to seize the uncanny moment, this window of humanity, before procedures and rules slammed into place.

"The East Bay is on fire," she said. "The water mains are out. I have a plane ticket, all paid for. All I want is to put my sister on a plane."

"Can she walk?" Towhead asked.

"Yes. She can walk. Get up, Vicky."

"You said 'Lily,'" Curly-head said.

"Get up, Lily," Lily said.

Towhead came over to help Lily lift her.

"What are you doing?" Curly-head asked his partner. "We can't do this."

Lily refrained from asking him what he thought the alternative was. Shoot them dead and throw them to the gulls?

She and Towhead fitted Vicky into the back of the SUV. She gave him the wet piece of paper with the confirmation code and her driver's license.

"We have to arrest her. But at least she'll get her arm set and her face stitched."

"Thank you," Lily said.

Curly-head reached for Lily's arm, and she shook him off.

"You're under arrest."

"I'm leaving now." She walked backward. "There's no real point in arresting me. I'm leaving. I'm unarmed. I'm no threat to anybody. I probably haven't even broken any law. Besides, I'm guessing you have your hands full with a whole lot of more important stuff."

"Stop," he said. "You can't just walk onto the tarmac of an international airport."

"I'm leaving," Lily said again. She'd backed up enough so that the lowering sun shined right in her face. She couldn't see the two security guards at all, just a bright yellow burst of light. She could only imagine what she looked like to them. Her thin hair was plastered to her head. The white serrated scar on her chin would be exaggerated by the surrounding sunburn. Her T-shirt and pants hung loosely, blotched with watery bloodstains. Skinny and ragged. Not even a little bit fierce. A woman stripped down to biology. Just another animal trying to survive.

And they were just men. They ate, shat, and made love. They didn't have a single reason in the world to shoot or detain her. Lily turned her back and ran. She pounded across the tarmac, the smoky air burning her lungs, her ankles shrieking with pain, her stomach hollow with hunger. She leapt over the shore rocks and shoved the kayak into the water. She splashed after it, dunking all the way under, gasping as she surfaced, and clutched the combing of the cockpit. It took her half a dozen tries to heave herself out of the numbingly cold water and onto the top of the boat, but she managed at last and threw herself into the rear cockpit. Without Vicky's weight in the other one, the bow of the kayak bobbled out of the water, making steering difficult. But she paddled as if her life depended on it, which it did.

Once she felt reasonably certain the security guards weren't going to shoot her, she laid the paddle across the deck and rested. Annie's orange had rolled to the back of the kayak interior and it took enormous effort to retrieve it, but she did, as much for the comfort of having Annie's gift as for the sustenance of the fruit.

She bit into the first section, and the bright sweet citrus juice spilled across her tongue. The taste matched the color of the sky reflected on the bay. Lily finished the orange, secured the paddle by sliding it inside the kayak, and then closed her eyes to nap.

40

LILY GUESSED IT TO be at least six o'clock in the evening when she awoke. It would be dark in a couple of hours. The tide must have turned because she was drifting north. Lily withdrew the paddle from the cockpit and began paddling.

She paddled and paddled, resting when she could no longer pull another load of water. By now, the tide ripped out the gate at maximum ebb. This helped for as long as the San Francisco peninsula blocked her to the west, but when she reached the broken expanse of the Bay Bridge, the tide wanted to suck her west and out the gate. Her arms were jelly. Even the ache was gone. They were just numb and limp. But with the strength of the current, she couldn't afford to rest for even a second. Rather than angling for Berkeley, she headed directly across the bay, going for the Oakland harbor, where she hoped she could ride a countercurrent close to shore.

In the middle of this most strenuous paddling of the entire day, someone finally spotted her. The man piloting a Chris-Craft motored over and drew up alongside.

"Come on board," he called out. "Grab the ladder."

People packed the deck of the small boat, their faces gyrating with panic. Lily didn't know a lot about boats, but even she could see that the Chris-Craft was too small to safely navigate out the Golden Gate and into the open ocean, especially with this heavy of a load. They were probably headed south, from where she'd just come, to disembark in Newark or Redwood City.

Lily shook her head.

The man ignored her refusal and tossed a white lifebuoy, holding onto his end of the rope. Lily didn't have the words, hardly even the voice, to say that she wasn't climbing on board the Chris-Craft, motoring south with this group of strangers, stepping on land too many miles away from anything she cared about.

She let the lifebuoy flop into the water. She dug in her paddle and propelled herself away from the boat.

"It'll be dark momentarily!" the captain yelled to her retreating back. "You can't just float out here in a kayak all night!" With that, he pulled up alongside her a second time.

"I need to get back to Berkeley," she told him, her tongue so dry and her thirst so great that she could hardly understand her own words. "Can you drop me there?"

"Honey, Berkeley is ruined. The lucky ones are *leaving* Berkeley."

"She isn't making sense," a woman on board said. "We need to just haul her up and get going."

"You can't haul someone onto a boat who doesn't want to get on it," the captain said. Then back to Lily, "Come on, honey. Grab the ladder."

"The tide's gonna take her out the gate," another passenger observed.

"Berkeley," Lily said to the boatload of refugees, jutting her chin toward the east. Then she paddled away in earnest, not looking back. The motorboat didn't pull up alongside her a third time, and she didn't watch its retreat, but she heard its engine fading to the south.

Though the smoke had thinned, what remained saturated the colors of dusk. The sun sank into the sea, the struts of the Golden Gate Bridge a blurry purple against the creamed crimson sky. Lily tried to imagine what Suzette would look like flying over the bridge.

For the longest while, Lily paddled in place, moving neither forward nor backward, the current equal to her effort. For five minutes? For an hour? She didn't know. She maintained a stasis of survival: here, now, alive. Behind her, the wide Pacific Ocean, miles deep, deathly cold, raucous with waves. Ahead of her, the possibility of drinking water and companionship. Overhead, the sky cradled a half-moon, rocking, humming, glowing, as if reminding Lily of her promise.

Then, as the last bit of day blackened into night, a breeze blew in off the ocean. It squeezed between the peninsulas and shoved Lily's kayak toward the eastern shore of the bay. If she were ever to believe in God, this would be the moment to do so. It was as if *someone's* will moved her.

She knew that this new wind could also fuel the fires. But for now, the shocked geometry of the city looked quiet, deserted, near dead. Nothing moved. In the stillness, she could practically see night fall. Having made it to the far side, Lily hugged the shoreline and paddled toward Berkeley.

The breeze quickened and cooled. She thought she imagined the first sign of dampness, just a cool softness in her nostrils, but soon tiny droplets wetted her forearm hairs. She licked them. Now a mist moistened her face, too.

Lily paddled in front of the Berkeley Marina breakwater and into the harbor mouth. The moonlight made a path of sparkles and she followed it to the black shapes of the docks and the wide opening where she found a paved boat launch. As the bottom of the kayak scraped against the floor of the inclined ramp, Lily laughed out loud at Vicky's invention. Her land-worthy boat was like the technological equivalent of the first sea creatures who grew legs and crawled onto land. Lily felt like one of those original creatures herself. Her legs buckled as she took her first steps.

Lily rolled the kayak to the top of the ramp so that it wouldn't get washed away with the next tide. Someone else might be able to use it. The water fountain at the edge of the marina parking lot worked!

Lily drank. Then she said goodbye to her most worthy vessel and began to walk.

The cool drizzle bathed the smoky air. Lily walked up the middle of the dark and deserted streets, navigating around rubble, tripping on debris. She passed piles of embers from fires that had burned earlier in the day. These, along with the moonlight, helped light her way. She stopped when she got to what remained of City Hall, afraid to go the rest of the way. Maybe this was what madness felt like: forward motion directed by the finest filament of hope, surrounded by a firestorm of fear and doubt; action based on a wild departure from the odds. She was at least three hours late.

As the marine layer, a thick bank of fog, rolled eastward, the air got cooler and wetter. Lily wanted another nap. Why not? Why not lie down right here in the field where she and Travis had made love and sleep a bit? She could put off finding out what remained for her.

Sleep or run, that was the choice. Lily ran. She turned right on Milvia Street and then left on Kittredge, her eyes well adjusted to the urban night. The library hulked grandly as ever, housing all the wisdom people had amassed over the centuries. Parked in front, at the top of the stairs leading down to the front door, was the dark shape of a motorcycle, and next to it, on the ground, the lean skeleton of a bicycle. Sitting on the stairs in front of the library were the dark silhouettes of Wesley and Annie.

41

No one hugged or even spoke for several long moments. Wesley stared, that gaze of his simultaneously hesitant and intense, as if he wanted the relief of looking away but couldn't do so. He wore his usual white T-shirt, black jeans, and worn-out dress shoes, all damp from the drizzling rain. His black leather jacket lay on the cement next to the bike.

"He said three can fit on the motorcycle," Annie announced loudly, as if Lily and Wesley might otherwise jump on the Harley and leave her alone in the dark on the library steps. She still wore the Air Jordans and her madras shorts, and sometime during the day she'd acquired a zippered warm-up jacket with dark stripes down the arms.

"You're here," Lily said.

"Duh," Annie said.

"We should go," Wesley said.

Lily hugged Annie and then put a hand on Wesley's arm. He started to step back, as if bearing touch was difficult, but stopped himself. She wanted to tell him how thinking about Suzette had helped.

"We saved this for you." Annie produced a hunk of cheese and a box of crackers. They had water, too, and a bag of raisins. Lily stared at the food, evidence of their trust, afraid that if she reached for it, the mirage would evaporate.

"Did you get Vicky on a plane?" Annie asked.

Lily wanted to eat, not talk, and anyway, that was a story, not an answer, and so she merely nodded. She bit into the cheese hunk. The sharp, creamy moldiness punched her taste buds.

"Hurry up and eat," Annie said. "We need to get out of here. Here's your backpack."

Lily sat on the step and ate her supper. The food strengthened everything. She thought she could feel the calories course down her arms and legs, motivate her fingers and toes. "Okay. Let's go."

"Up and over the hills?" Wesley asked.

"Can we do one thing first? I need to swing by the church. It's just a few blocks away."

"Hello?" Annie said. "Ex*cuse* me? We've been like waiting here for *hours*, literally."

"I know," Lily said. "It'll just take a minute."

"We have to go," Wesley said, climbing on the bike and starting the engine. Soft, fine raindrops glistened in the headlight's yellow beam. He opened the throttle and motioned for Annie to get on, which she did, scooting to the very back of the white leather seat. Both of them looked at Lily. Annie patted the thin space between their two bodies where they expected her to squeeze in. But Lily picked the bicycle up off the cement. "Please," she said, even though she knew they couldn't hear her over the motorcycle's engine. She took off pedaling toward Trinity Church.

Lily dropped the bike in the church parking lot. The community room door was locked, and so she ran around the block, trying all the other doors to the church. She found a corner entrance completely blackened by fire. The charred stench let her know the fire hadn't been out for long. Lily approached slowly, holding her hands out to feel for hot spots. She heard the rumbling purr of the Harley rolling slowly up the street behind her, and she glanced back at the pair of them, her follow team.

Afraid to touch the brass doorknob, Lily kicked at the burnt door and it crumbled.

"Be careful," Wesley shouted.

"Kalisha!" Lily hollered into the hole she'd made.

She kicked out an opening big enough to step through and went in. She moved slowly, checking the walls for heat, but luckily the fire hadn't penetrated past this corner entrance. She heard Wesley and Annie at the door behind her, and then a moment later felt the child's hand on her back.

She had so little to go on. The way, when she'd asked, Kalisha had looked briefly over her shoulder toward the interior of the church. The way Lily had never seen her leave the building after work. The place was a maze of hallways and classrooms, all dark.

"You have a flashlight in your pack," Annie said. "Or do you enjoy running into walls?"

"Food. Light. You're a miracle-worker, Annie."

Lily switched on the flashlight. The dim beam lit the hallways and at last Lily found the sanctuary at the heart of the church. A cluster of candle stubs burned on the altar, and the flickering light made the place feel primitive. Bats whooshed like tiny black phantoms.

The three of them walked up the aisle between the pews like a devastated bridal party, slowly and reverently. Lily hesitated at the steps to the altar, but then climbed them.

Behind the big wooden pulpit she found a little camp. Blankets had been hastily stuffed into the pulpit's cavity, along with a half-eaten sandwich on a plate.

"Please," Lily said to Wesley and Annie. "Could you please wait for me outside?"

Annie scowled. "I know what you're doing."

Lily held a finger to her lips and shook her head hard, managing to silence Annie.

Wesley still wore an expression of shock, a look that said, *This is a dream, right?*

She wanted to reassure him. He had come to the library. He had waited for her. He had accepted Annie.

"Thank you," she whispered. "I'll just be five minutes."

Annie grabbed a fistful of Wesley's T-shirt and tugged. "She's stubborn as a cow. She won't take no. Come on. I'll come get her if she's not out in five." Halfway down the aisle, he turned and Lily tossed him the flashlight.

She waited, her eyes adjusting to the candlelit cavern. The round stained glass window above the apse brooded wine-red and blood-blue and mustard-ochre, the gloomy colors nearly indecipherable at night, and yet concentrated, like a serum.

"Kalisha! Where are you? I want to see you."

She sat down in a front pew. People came here to talk to God, to bridge their biology to the unknown. Who could blame them for trying? That bridge was so very long.

Lily considered saying a prayer. After all, when in Rome. It surely couldn't hurt.

Maybe just the idea of saying a prayer delivered an answer. Sal's matching Electra-Glide! It was even on their route out of town. Lily didn't know if God had spoken to her, but just in case, while the channels remained open, she quickly put in a word for Vicky, too. That's when she saw movement in the corner of her eye, a figure approaching from behind.

"It's you," Kalisha said.

Lily jumped to her feet. "Kalisha! I'm so glad to see you. Are you okay?"

"Where have you been?"

"I'm so sorry I disappeared!"

"I guess I knew you'd never stick it out."

"That's not fair. You know me. You know—"

"What I know is that the day you didn't show up, we were raided. Now a whole lot of people don't eat."

Lily's mind staggered. "You couldn't possibly think—"

"What was your relationship with Travis Grayson?"

"Travis? Are you saying *he* raided the church?"

"His goons."

Lily dropped back onto the pew. "Oh, Jesus. I'm sorry. I'm *sorry.*"

"So. You and Travis."

"No! I mean, I did sleep with him, sort of. Just once." As if the number of times helped ameliorate anything.

"Sort of."

"I know that's something you wouldn't understand," Lily said. "You with your philosophy PhD and your work ethic. But yes, I made a big mistake."

Kalisha's expression shifted, maybe eased, in the candlelight. "I do understand mistakes."

"Well, that surprises me."

"And I don't have a PhD."

"You lied?"

"Of course not."

"Look, I don't know anything about the raid. His goons beat up my sister, too. I can't believe you'd think that of me."

"I don't know what to think anymore."

"After everything we've been through together."

"Trust is hard for me sometimes." A palpable tenderness roughened her voice. She sat down on the pew beside Lily. "But you're right: I do know you. I'm sorry."

"Thank you." Then, still reeling, "I don't understand why he'd raid the church. He had a thriving Cluster at the reservoir. Tons of resources."

"What I heard on the street? Pretty much everyone in the Cluster had moved on to other camps. It was just him and a couple of boy scouts gone round the bend. I doubt he even knew what his henchmen were up to anymore. Anyway, he's gone."

"Gone?"

"You didn't hear?"

Lily managed to shake her head.

"Travis shot himself."

Lily pressed her fingertips to her temples and closed her eyes. The cheese and crackers and raisins churned in her stomach. She felt the blast, a sharp pain in her own skull; saw the side of his head explode, the flying chunks of flesh, spraying blood. It was as though having slept with him forced her to fully imagine his last corporal act.

"When?"

"A couple days ago."

"Where?"

"Over at the reservoir."

She pictured the place where he'd painted her face and breasts with mud. She remembered the emptiness of the camp, his claim that everyone had been "deployed" for the day. Early this morning, when the goons beat up Vicky, Travis was already two days dead.

The candles sputtered. Their dimming light splotched across the dark wood of the pulpit and altar. Above their heads, the flap of bat wings displaced air, making tiny puffing gusts. Lily thought of Suzette, imagined her posed, wings folded, up on the rafters. Wesley and Annie were waiting.

"It's time to leave," Lily said, squelching back her monstrous and inappropriate grief. She had loved Travis, or at the very least, she'd loved the idea of him. "Come on."

Kalisha ran a hand, fingers spread, over the top of her head. She looked around her sanctuary.

"I think I can get us out of here," Lily said.

"How'd you know where to find me?"

"I didn't know for sure. I hoped."

"Hello? Lily! Come *on*." Annie barreled down the aisle of the sanctuary, swinging the dull beam of the flashlight around like a sword.

"Jesus," Kalisha said. "You have that kid with you."

"Fuck you," Annie said.

"I'm not going anywhere with her," Kalisha countered.

"Annie," Lily said. "Light the way out for us."

42

THE MOON BACKLIT THE fog, making it glow, as their caravan inched up Grizzly Peak. The tiny droplets in the foggy wrap soothed. Wesley drove as slowly as he could while keeping the motorcycle, with its three passengers, upright. He pulled to the side of the road and stopped every few minutes so that Lily, riding the bicycle, could catch up.

When at last they pulled onto the fire trail next to the Space Sciences Lab, Kalisha asked, "What makes you think she hasn't already left with her bike?" It was a good question, but how could Lily explain Sal's love for a pair of escaped hyenas? The others waited at the trailhead while she rode the bicycle out to the compound. She climbed the fence, dropped to the other side, ran up the hill, and pounded on the shed door. It had been nearly eighteen hours since she'd talked to Sal this morning. Any reasonable person would have left. She pounded again and heard a loud thud, like a big piece of furniture being shoved against the inside of the door.

"Sal! It's me, Lily!"

A rough scraping sound was followed by the door opening. "I thought you left."

"Get the bike. We're all leaving together."

"Do you have Vicky?"

"Come on. Hurry up. This is it."

Her face convulsed and she raised her voice. "Do you have Vicky?"

"I'll tell you everything later. Get the Harley."

"Just tell me if she's safe."

Lily nodded, unwilling to take time for the more elaborate truth.

Sal's slow gait as she walked to the Harley told Lily that she wasn't coming with her. "Move aside," Sal said. She nudged up the kickstand and pushed the bike out the door. "Take it." She wiggled the handlebars.

"They're wild, Sal. They can look after themselves."

"If the public finds out..."

"There no longer *is* a public."

"I'm responsible."

"Vicky is waiting." It might not be a lie. "You need to..." Lily almost said, choose people, not hyenas, but realized that might backfire.

Sal looked up the hillside and then down the fire trail, as if looking for them one last time, as if they lurked in the woods, watching, and might emerge and beg her to stay, declare their reciprocal love. Like a fairy-tale gone awry: Sal's unleashed beauty, her excessive devotion for the perverse beasts.

A few minutes later, the five of them—Sal and Annie on one Harley, and Lily, Kalisha, and Wesley on the other—crested the summit of Grizzly Peak, heading out the same route Lily had ridden with Wesley last month. It was after midnight and the fog had rolled back. The stars were dim but visible, the half-moon a bright beacon. They had a grand view of the brooding cities hundreds of feet below.

Sandwiched between two new friends, Lily felt like she was migrating, moving on to new, more habitable locations. Hadn't people been doing that for all their years on earth? She pictured the world map, with the arching arrows, showing how people left Africa first, pushed north into Asia and west into Europe. Hunger, cold, fire, drought—all manner of calamities—had been driving people to new places for millennia. She liked to think of herself riding one of those arrows, part of a migration, the new exodus.

Somewhere on the mountain below, the two hyenas, continents away from their homeland, were also on the move.

43

FIRST, THEY SLEPT.

Sal had thought of Whiskeytown Lake, west of Redding, and sometime in the morning they found a trail leading to a private stretch of the red-soil shore. It was hot, well over ninety degrees. They all said they were going to splash into the lake. But when Annie lay on the ground under a pine, the rest flopped nearby, on their backs, splayed.

Lily hadn't lain down since the earthquake more than twenty-four hours earlier. Then too she'd made the soil her bed, pressing her breasts against earth's naked skin. The ground had begun shuddering, then rocking hard. She had liked it, had felt pleasure in the rumbling interface. Now, with every muscle in her body aching, the memory of that pleasure was surreal.

Travis was dead. She tried to admit that information, but it too felt surreal, as if it belonged to another life entirely.

Lily rolled onto her side and found Wesley a few feet away, also on his side, looking at her. She scooted over, the pine needles and dry dirt clods scratching her arms, and touched his hip bone. It jutted out between the top of his black jeans and the bottom of his white T-shirt like a fossil, a clue to the history of humankind. She left her hand there as waves of sleep washed her away.

Lily awoke at dusk. The air was a bit cooler, but not much. She sat up and looked west, across the huge lake, at the snow-dusted peaks of the mountains called Trinity Alps. She tried to get up, but everything hurt. She took off her shoes and examined the raw patches and bubbled skin. She could barely move her arms; every muscle seized with pain from the hours of paddling the kayak. Her hip joints, too, ached from the long cramped hours on the motorcycle. She wanted the cool water of the lake, but she'd have to stand and walk to get there.

Sal was collecting firewood, wandering slowly into the forest and returning, just as slowly, bringing one stick at a time to the shore camp. Kalisha paced the beach, as if she were planning her future. Wesley and Annie were both gone. Lily forced herself to stand and staggered over to Sal.

"Where's Annie?"

She shook her head.

"Wesley?"

"We pooled our money. He went to town for food and gas."

The faraway ping of a stone hitting the lake water drew Lily's attention, and there she was, down the beach, throwing rocks. Lily hobbled toward her, wincing with every step.

Annie pretended she didn't notice her approach, kept bending to pick up stones and tossing them into the lake. Her tan plaid madras shorts stuck to her thighs. Pine needles and dirt plastered her bare back. She scowled.

"I was thinking of taking a swim," Lily said nodding at the lake.

"Go ahead. Why are you telling me?" Annie fired another rock.

Lily walked back to the edge of the trees and shed her T-shirt and jeans, panties and bra, leaving them in a pile on top of her sneakers. She walked, naked as the day she was born, right by Annie and waded into the cool water. It hurt, same time as it soothed, the cold on her hot raw skin. She dove in and flipped onto her back, closed her eyes, and floated face to the twilit sky. Water and air. Safe, she thought, and alive. She righted herself and, standing on the lake bottom pebbles, flicked the droplets from her hair.

Annie sat on a big stone at the water's edge, watching. Lily swam out to a deeper part of the lake and scrubbed her hair. With her legs dangling in the depths of the lake, she washed the rest of herself. Then, dog-paddling back toward shore, she shouted for Annie to come in.

The furrows on Annie's brow deepened.

Lily waded in and pulled on her clothes. As she sat dripping next to her, Annie stood up and walked away, in the opposite direction of camp.

"Annie!"

"You don't know what you're talking about!" she shouted. "Leave me alone."

She looked like a big bear charging down the beach, away from Lily, a bundle of fury and wildness. Lily remembered the leggings she liked to wear in Berkeley, the rhinestone bobby pins and gardenia lotion. She must be uncomfortable covered with dirt, pine needles, sweat, and road grime, with nothing to wear but boys' shorts. She must want to feel the relief of the lake water.

Lily pushed herself up and made her way down the beach after her. They walked like this, with Annie several yards ahead, for at least five minutes. Finally, she wheeled around and opened her mouth for another verbal attack. Lily guessed she'd silently rehearsed something much worse, but all she said was, "You don't have any idea!"

Then the tears came, fat rolling ones. Her lips trembled and her cheeks shook, but she didn't break eye contact. In that moment, in the periwinkle light of dusk, Lily saw all the babies she and Tom thought they'd made, and the shattered hope each time she got her period. She saw the three babies from that first day at the church, especially Herbert, whose mother had been crushed by a support beam. She saw the baby who flew from the window of Travis's apartment building and got caught. She even saw Angelina's baby.

Here, Lily realized, is mine: a big thirteen-year-old.

"You…" Annie spat. "You…you think it's just *easy*. To take off your clothes. To go in the water. *I told you:* I CAN'T SWIM." She wrapped her arms around herself, covering her chest.

Annie had been so brave yesterday, but now, with some sleep, with the prospect of safety, maybe her courage was imploding. Maybe the wilderness, night falling on this massive lake and the surrounding mountains, scared her.

"I'M NOT PRETTY LIKE YOU," she shouted. "I'M FAT. I HAVE UGLY SKIN."

Annie was right: Lily didn't have any idea. She'd have to make it up. She put her hands on her hips and said, "Annie, you're a big strong girl with a beautiful body. Your skin is the color of autumn sunlight."

Annie stood perfectly still. She looked as though she were memorizing Lily's words. Then she disassembled again. "I HAVE HAMBURGER FACE!"

"Yeah. You have bad acne. That'll go away eventually. And right now you have those gorgeous glossy black curls."

That was maybe the wrong thing to say. She, or someone, had sheered them short and boyish. Annie resumed rock-throwing.

"They'll grow out, too," Lily said, as though that had been where she was going all along. "We'll get you some pretty barrettes."

"Boys don't wear barrettes."

"But you do."

Annie dropped the rock in her hand and stood facing Lily, her arms dangling at her sides, her eyes wide, as if she were waiting for a full, plausible, and acceptable explanation for everything.

Lily scrambled for something to say and came out with, "I learned a new word not so long ago. Philtrum. It's the groove in your upper lip. It's from the Greek, meaning "to kiss" or "to love." I'm thinking of that word now because your philtrum is one of the prettiest ones I've ever seen."

Annie whispered, "I've never kissed anyone."

"You will. Some day."

"Nobody kisses fat people."

"Not true. People kiss fat people all the time. Take Sal, for example. She's kinda fat. My sister kisses her a lot."

"Vicky?"

"Yeah. Vicky."

Annie's eyes blinked in rapid comprehension, the kind of understanding that only young people have, where the truth isn't stopped by multiple filters. She appeared to accept everything Lily said about kissing.

"Where is Vicky?"

"I don't really know." Lily held out her hand. "Come on." The sun was long gone. Darkness hovered over the lake, swirled around the mountains. "We're safe. No one can see us."

Annie took her hand, and they walked to the water's edge. Fully dressed in her sneakers, jeans, and T-shirt, Lily started wading in.

"Wait," Annie said. She sat down and pulled off Binky's Air Jordans. She arranged them neatly, side by side, on the shore. Then, leaving her shorts on, she took Lily's hand again. She was shaking.

When they got knee-deep, Lily stopped. She cupped water from the still-sun-warmed top layer of the lake and doused Annie's legs. Next she washed the pine needles off her back. Annie wouldn't let Lily touch her belly or her chest, but she splashed these herself and then she did her face. Lily bent over and stuck her own head back in the water and scrubbed her scalp again. She righted herself and shook like a dog.

"I might fall in, though."

"Here." Lily got behind her and put her arms around her middle. "I got you. You can bend down now and you won't fall."

Annie washed her hair and then surprised Lily by dunking her entire head. When she came up, she was scowling, but probably felt better.

By the time they got back to camp in their wet clothes, Wesley had returned and Sal had a nice fire going. She and Kalisha had placed logs in a circle around the blaze. Wesley unpacked cans of baked beans, a loaf of bread, and a jar of peanut butter. They all drank lots of fresh water with their supper. The stars came out bright and plentiful, a million sparkles on the lake.

Sal said, "I just hope Vicky keeps her mouth shut, wherever she is."

"That would be a miracle, if she did," Lily said.

"I can see her telling some prison guard to fuck off. That, or that she liked her ass." Sal thought for a minute and then added, "It's hard to say what the worst outcome of *that* would be."

"She has my driver's license. If they arrested her, they'll think they've arrested me."

Sal laughed. "You'll have to go into hiding. We'll have to construct a new identity for you."

Lily didn't think that was so funny.

Kalisha poked the fire with a long stick, sending a flurry of sparks into the air.

"Both my mom and dad were killed in the war," Annie announced. "My best friend Binky was murdered on Telegraph Avenue. Plus, I'm a girl."

Wesley reached into the backpack behind his place on the log and brought out a chocolate bar. He held it out to Annie, but she got up off the log and walked away from the fire, into the darkness.

"So, like, there's this huge bottomless depth," Wesley said. "It's impossible to navigate. It's like an endless swim to the surface. But then, after what feels like an eternity, you do surface, for bits of time anyway, and you start seeing, in the distance, other people's stories. They're like islands. Landmarks that help you navigate. Something to swim toward, a place to rest."

A muffled sob came from Annie's dark pocket outside the firelight's reach.

"Annie," Lily said. "Come back."

Kalisha poked, causing another miniature explosion of sparks.

"Anyone else want chocolate?" Wesley broke up the bar and handed out pieces.

"What if we were the start of a new tribe?" Lily said. "We could be the turning point in human evolution. A whole new species branching off. Right here, right now. *Homo sapiens* becoming *Homo compati*."

"What's *compati*?" asked a sniffling voice from the dark.

"I like that," Kalisha said, poking the fire again. "From a species of know-it-alls to a species of care-it-alls. Except I'd want to keep in the knowing part. They aren't mutually exclusive."

"What's mutually exclusive?" Annie called out.

"If you come sit down, I'll tell you."

"To start a tribe, someone would have to reproduce," Sal said, and then she hooted.

"It's not crazy," Lily said. "Imagine people getting love right."

"*Lubh*," Kalisha said.

"I'm just saying."

"We need to find Vicky," Sal said.

"What we need," Kalisha said, "is money."

44

BY DAWN, ANNIE WAS gone.

Lily sat up from a deep sleep and counted only three other bodies under the pines: one sprawled, voluptuous, with a thick auburn mane tousled across her head and shoulders; another with black hair, skin the color of bleached bones, and a long, rail-thin body; the last curled into herself, protective, her also-skinny limbs held close, her dark scalp showing under sparse hair. There was no honey-colored fat child sleeping anywhere nearby.

Lily splashed lake water on her face, trying to clear her thinking. She was probably in the woods relieving herself. Lily waited. Annie didn't appear. So Lily walked south along the beach until a logjam blocked the way. She turned around and walked much farther in the other direction. When she returned to camp and Annie was still missing, Lily started shouting, which woke up everyone else.

For over an hour, all four adults scoured the shoreline and treed areas around Whiskeytown Lake. At nine o'clock, Wesley stripped off his clothes and dove into the lake. At first Lily thought he'd given up and was just going for a swim. But when she saw him dive and surface, dive and surface, she understood what he was doing.

In between dives, he did a gentle breaststroke, facedown, scanning the lake bottom.

Lily collapsed on a log next to the still-smoking fire pit and finally cried. Travis was dead. Vicky was missing in action. Annie was gone.

With lake water streaming down his face and chest, Wesley crouched in front of her and took her hands away from her face. His brown eyes were clear, his lashes dripping. "Hey," he said. "We'll find her."

"How?"

Wesley had a scar down the center of his chest. He'd swum in only his white Fruit of the Loom briefs. His skin, despite the heat, was covered with gooseflesh.

"If she drowned," Sal said, "she'd be on the surface. This water is too warm for a body to sink."

Wesley pulled on his jeans and T-shirt.

"Where?" Lily asked.

"Town, I'm thinking," Kalisha said.

They took both bikes. Lily and Wesley checked the café where the Greyhound bus stopped three times a week, but the waitress hadn't seen a chubby, biracial thirteen-year-old. They searched the library and grocery store while Sal and Kalisha asked at the motels.

At noon, the four met up on Main Street and decided that the most likely scenario was that she'd hitchhiked out of town. After all, she specialized in running away. Lily slid off the Harley and sat on the curb.

"The little shit," Kalisha said. "At least she didn't steal one of the bikes."

"Annie's not a thief," Lily said dully.

"You're forgetting the chocolate puddings."

"You're not serious, are you? You are! Jesus, Kalisha. That was *pudding*."

"Just saying."

"She's a kid. She was hungry. Her friend was hungry."

"I got a couple hundred hungry people in Berkeley who all wait their turn and take their share." Kalisha looked into the distant south, as if searching for her flock.

Lily sighed. "Well, she's gone. So you don't have to worry about her taking any more of your pudding."

Kalisha broke down, crumpled right on the hot sidewalk pavement, and freed two long shuddering sobs.

"Oh!" Lily cried. "Jeez. I'm sorry."

Kalisha wiped the tears from her face with her forearm and shook her head hard, already back in control. "I fought so hard for that program. And now it's gone. Completely, totally ransacked."

Lily felt foolish for thinking they'd been talking about puddings.

"That was my family," Kalisha said.

"I know."

They all waited in the hot sun for inspiration, their next move.

"Speaking of pudding," Sal finally said. "I'm hungry."

"You want to buy some food?" Wesley asked. "Go back to camp?"

"Yeah," Sal and Kalisha said at the same time.

"Okay," he said. "I'll meet you there by dusk."

"Where're you going?" Lily asked.

"Hop on, if you want."

She climbed on the bike and wrapped her arms around Wesley. He pulled away from the curb. Lily put her cheek against his back and tried to cry again, but she couldn't now. So instead she let the vibration of the bike's tires on the pavement stir her. At the end of Main Street, he turned onto a residential side street. When they reached the end of that, where the houses petered out into open fields, he turned and toured down the next parallel residential street.

This was definitely a needle-in-a-haystack strategy. What would Annie be doing on a sidewalk in a tree-filled Weaverville neighborhood?

Lily didn't stop him. She liked holding onto him, pushing her face against his damp white T-shirt. He smelled like the pine needles he'd slept in last night. They rode slowly, moving into pockets of cool shade and then back out into melting pools of hot sun, and back again into shade. Wesley swung his head, searching, while she buried her face in his ribs. She wondered how it would be with both of them so very skinny, their essences barely housed by bodies.

After they had covered all the streets they could find in Weaverville, Wesley began again. This time he drove randomly, riding up and down the paved roads, turning when he wanted, banking the bike more steeply than he needed for the turns. Sometimes he made figure eights in the middle of a quiet intersection for no reason at all other than the sumptuous feel of the movement. They used the tank of gas as if they weren't broke.

The sun hung low and golden, blinking through the leafy neighborhood trees, when Lily saw a round, bare-chested person in tan madras shorts pushing a lawn mower across a big green field of grass. The lawn belonged to a small red house. Wesley saw, too, and as he slowed the Harley to a putter, the person with the lawn mower disappeared into the parallelogram of shade on the right side of the house, next to a rotting wooden deck.

It couldn't be Annie. Why would she be mowing a lawn in Weaverville?

Wesley parked next to the curb. Lily climbed off the bike and together they crossed the expanse of green.

Annie stepped into the last of the sunlight to meet them and smiled a huge, delighted smile. "Hi!" she called out.

Lily detonated. "What the fuck do you think you're doing?"

Wesley took hold of Lily's elbow.

Annie looked shocked, and then angry. She scowled and reached into her pocket. She pulled out a roll of cash. "This is my third yard. We need money."

Wesley let go of Lily's elbow and grabbed Annie in a restraining hold.

No, Lily realized, it was a hug. A big, long hug.

Annie thrashed in Wesley's arms, throwing the beginning of a tantrum, furious at being unjustly accused. Annie sputtered the word "she" over and over.

Lily leaned against the rotting wooden deck and fought the urge to yell more, to cry, to explode. Trying to calm herself, she hefted her butt up on the deck and let her legs swing under the wood planking. Breathe, just breathe. Annie is safe. More than safe—taking action, figuring out the next steps before any of the adults had. Breathe, just breathe. As she swung her legs harder, dissipating the anger, taking in the relief, Lily's heel hit something soft and papery. She heard a muted *thunk* as the object fell to the dirt below.

Yellow jackets surged out from under the deck. A crazy silent pause, like a dream bubble, inflated the moment, as if she had hours for reflection rather than a moment. Lily thought: *Feral dogs, men with guns, dehydration and hunger, epic saltwater journeys—these I survive, only to face, in the end, tiny stinging insects.* She thought: *I don't want to die.* She thought: *Life isn't fair, not even close to fair.* She thought: *Wait! Where is Vicky?* She thought: *Not even bees, her sweet honey-making, pollinating coworkers; no, these were yellow jackets, paper-making menaces in striped uniforms, and yet every bit as lethal to her as bees.* She thought: *I want to live.* In that time warp, where a moment blossomed into a lifetime, an adrenaline-fueled fervor for more, more of everything—food and love and sex and beauty and stories and trees and soil and song—kicked in. As the army of stinging insects swarmed in confusion, a blur of yellow and black, she writhed, kicking and swinging, as if she could individually fight off each one.

They landed, all over her arms, throat, and face. Dozens if not hundreds of them buzzing onto her pale skin. The first sting zapped away her protracted bubble of reflection. Her mind went blank as the venom entered her arm. More yellow jackets stung her hands, neck, cheeks, eyelid, each invasion bringing acute pain. As the poison flowed into her bloodstream, Lily abandoned her body. She floated over the deck, the big grassy field, and watched herself succumb to the attack.

"Uh," Lily wheezed. The nausea swelled in her throat and she couldn't breathe. "Uh," she gurgled.

"Bees!" Annie shouted.

Lily funneled back down into her body, with its swollen throat and thick tongue and aching limbs. She felt her stomach heave, as if vomiting, as if expelling all her inner organs. Someone—she recognized Wesley's pine scent—lifted her off the deck. Annie screamed, as if yellow jackets could hear, as she flapped her shirt at the swarming hive, trying to protect Wesley as he carried Lily away. Lily felt grass against her back, heard Wesley ask her questions, though she couldn't understand the words.

What happened next felt exactly like an injection of epinephrine into her thigh. Lily returned to consciousness with a cold washcloth on her forehead. She opened her eyes to see Wesley and Annie kneeling beside her. A man with kinky gray hair tied in a ponytail, a handlebar mustache, and red-rimmed eyes stood behind them.

He said, "She don't look so good."

"Was that an EpiPen shot?" Lily wheezed.

"Yeah," Annie said, holding up the used auto-injector. "I saw it in your pack yesterday. My mom was allergic, too."

"Well," the man said, biting his mustache with his lower teeth. "Don't sue me. I don't have nothing but this house. I was just trying to do the kid a favor."

"Don't worry," Wesley said. "We're grateful to you."

"She still needs to go to the emergency room," Annie said.

"I guess I can take you," the man said.

A few hours later, though covered with hives, Lily walked out of the hospital breathing and talking. She'd given the hospital administrators her health insurance card, but without ID, they said they couldn't process the claim. The bill, surely for thousands of dollars—this was the emergency room, after all—would go to Tom. Lily was sorry. She didn't want him responsible for her anymore. But truly, the idea of thousands of dollars to save her life seemed ludicrous. Shouldn't people have their lives saved? She'd done nothing other than anger a swarm of yellow jackets. She shouldn't find it funny—Tom certainly wouldn't—but she did. Thousands of dollars for wasp stings and a saved life. Walking from the hospital to the parked truck, she had to stop, bend over, and grab her knees from laughing so hard at the absurdity and from the sheer joy of being alive. Her companions looked at her with sympathetic smiles. They didn't know the exact joke, but everyone was happy.

"He'll sort it out," Lily told them, told the universe at large. "That's what he's good at. I'm sure I'm still on his health plan. I mean, if he vouches for me, won't the insurance pay?" Then she doubled over all over again and laughed so hard it hurt.

The man drove them back to his house, parked the pickup in his driveway, and walked them to the Harley at the curb.

"Nice bike," he said. "That's the first year of the Shovelhead engine."

"Yeah," Wesley said. "She's a beaut, isn't she?"

"Hell, yeah."

"What's your name?" Lily asked.

"That don't matter," he said, maybe still afraid of getting sued, maybe just humble.

As Lily tried to thank him, he cleared his throat so loudly and continuously she couldn't make herself heard. Wesley straddled the bike, and Annie got on, followed by Lily. Wesley started up the engine and, with that roar obliterating the possibility of more conversation, the man reached into his back pocket and withdrew his wallet. He took out all the bills he had and handed them to Wesley.

Wesley shook his head, probably said something like, "We can't take this," but the man turned his back and walked toward his house. Lily, Annie, and Wesley watched him open the front door, go inside, and close it without ever looking back.

On their way back to camp, Lily asked Wesley to stop at the big box store. She took Annie to the girls' clothing department and told her to pick out whatever she wanted. Annie chose a lavender camisole, a sea-blue blouse, and a pair of white Capri pants.

"What about shoes?" Lily asked.

Annie shook her head vehemently and they both looked down at the Air Jordans with the sparkly red laces.

"Yeah," Lily said. "Those will look good with what you picked out."

Annie checked her face to see if she was making fun of her. She wasn't. So Annie nodded in agreement, and they carried the purchases to the checkout stand. There were three people ahead of them, and Lily used the wait time to be grateful for each breath.

She tried to not think about the hives that still ached and itched. Wesley milled just beyond the cash register, looking at some power saws on sale, and Lily wanted to know what he was thinking.

Annie nudged Lily out of her daze, pushing her forward when the line moved. Near the cash register, Lily picked up a copy of *The Trinity Journal* to look for news about the Bay Area. A front-page story covered the new earthquake, the fire at the Chevron refinery, and the new influx of National Guard troops to "secure the region." The soup kitchens and other community organizations that sprang up after the first earthquake had led, according to this story, to de facto governments that slowly overstepped their missions and eventually battled for control of the region's remaining resources. Lily huffed at this gross oversimplification, this media reach for drama. The reporter totally missed the vast numbers of people who selflessly helped others. But maybe every story lied by omission. Maybe every story had many true faces.

"Sometime," Lily said to Annie, "ask me to tell you about Travis."

"Okay." She saw Annie memorize the request.

Was it too harsh a story for a thirteen-year-old? She'd been exactly Annie's age when she began her correspondence with him.

As the man in front of them paid for his lighter fluid and bag of briquettes, Lily flipped the paper over and looked at the headline below the fold. *"Hyena" Virus Threatens Computers.* In smaller type, a subheading announced, *Hospital Worker Cracks Security Code.* The dateline: San Francisco, CA.

According to *The Trinity Journal*, the fast-spreading virus already had infected millions of computers. The purpose, severity, and malevolence of the infection had yet to be determined, but it was believed to be highly dangerous with possibly devastating effects. So far, however, the only consequence of the virus was that it placed a large-font message on people's desktops that read, "Long live hyenas!"

The article explained that the source of the virus had been traced to San Francisco General Hospital, and that employees there were being scrutinized for possible authorship. Someone, according to the article, had used the confusion resulting from an overpopulation of patients, due to the recent earthquakes across the bay, to take advantage. The hospital administration promised criminal prosecution.

Federal agents were already involved, and they asked for the public's help in deciphering the covert meaning of the word "hyenas." They advised people whose computers had contracted the virus to leave them powered down until more information became available.

Lily knew the virus would prove to be benign. She also knew that Vicky's delight in devising and implementing the project would be the drug that healed her.

45

KALISHA BUILT AN EVEN bigger campfire tonight. She and Sal had bought a large tin pot in town, and they simmered a stew of artichokes, Vidalia onions, tomatoes, and farro over a bed of coals. Sal carved sharp points on long sturdy sticks so they could roast chunks of pork. It was well past midnight when Lily, Wesley, and Annie arrived back at camp, but Kalisha and Sal had waited, worrying and now intensely relieved. As they took places around the campfire, they passed a flask of cold lake water.

Despite the late hour and wilderness darkness, Annie bathed and changed into her new outfit before joining the others at the fire. As soon as she sat down, even before eating, she told the whole story of how she'd hitched into town and knocked on doors in residential Weaverville asking for work, and then in great animated detail she told them about the yellow jacket attack and how she'd been the one to get the EpiPen from Lily's pack and administer the shot.

"You saved my life," Lily said.

"Duh."

"I don't ever want you hitchhiking again. Ever."

"You always got something to say." But Annie smiled, pleased at the maternal rebuke, noting the word "ever" used twice.

"Next time," Kalisha said, "give us a heads up when you decide to disappear."

"You know what?" Annie shot back at Kalisha.

"You look really pretty in your new clothes," Sal interrupted.

Annie squinted suspiciously and looked around the fire at everyone's faces. She bunched her mouth.

"Say 'thank you,'" Lily said.

Annie swatted the air in front of her face, even though the smoke swirled straight up into the sky.

"So listen," Kalisha said quietly. "I need to go back. I need to get the kitchen at Trinity going again. There're plenty of hungry people still there."

The fire popped. The stars shone steady. The black lake, just beyond, lapped.

"Ha!" Wesley held up his speared chunk of pork and turned it in the light. "Roasted perfection."

"I got us plums from a client's tree. For dessert." Annie reached for her knapsack and pulled out a fistful. "Ripe ones."

"'Client,'" Kalisha quoted, shaking her head.

"Yeah," Annie said. "*Client.*"

"I have a surprise." Lily retrieved her own backpack from behind her log and pulled out *The Trinity Journal*. She held up the paper and pointed at the headline below the fold. "Vicky," she said. "It's Vicky."

"Let me see!" Sal grabbed for the paper, but Lily held it out of reach.

"I'll read the article out loud."

Annie gasped at nearly every sentence, and Sal started laughing halfway through the report. When Lily finished reading, she and Sal entertained everyone with Vicky stories. Lily told about her doing square roots in her head, the *SCUM Manifesto* paper, her chair collection, the wheeled kayak that happened to save her life, and how that was always how things worked for Vicky.

"She has a quirky—" Lily started.

"Understatement," Sal said.

"—kind of prescience," Lily finished.

Sal told about other inventions and, with promptings from everyone, but mostly Annie, a full and detailed accounting of their love affair. They ate the plums and tossed the pits into the forest.

When the fire was just a bed of embers, Annie yawned and said, "I guess we better go get her."

46

ANNIE, SAL, AND KALISHA lay down in the usual spot under the pines. Wesley and Lily walked deeper into the woods. As they tripped on small logs and clumped undergrowth, Lily thought, *rash, impulsive.* She didn't know this man.

But this time she *knew* she didn't know him. Didn't that make it different?

They came to a flat bed of pine needles and lay down on their backs, looking up into the meshed ceiling of evergreen boughs. He hooked his ankle with hers. She found his hand.

"I want us to all stay together," she said.

"Kalisha wants to go back."

"We could go with her. We could help her get the kitchen going again."

"You think?"

"She can't do it alone. We'd need to scavenge equipment. Find food sources."

Wesley turned onto his side and propped his head in his hand, elbow in the duff. "We could fetch Vicky, too."

"Really? You want to do that?"

"Yes."

Lily laughed. "Really? That easy?"

"It won't be easy. But yes. *Yes*. Kalisha will need help."

"I want to feed people."

Wesley made a sound of assent.

"Food," Lily said. "Stories, too."

"You're right," he said. "Tribes need stories."

"What's our creation myth?"

The canopy of pines blocked out most of the starlight. She could hardly see his face. She reached carefully and found his chin, moved her fingers up to touch his philtrum. He seemed to stop breathing. She slid her fingertips to the right, following the contour of his mouth.

"I haven't in so long," he said.

Lily kissed his cheek, held his ear in her cupped hand. She waited a beat and, when he didn't speak again, kissed his mouth. He shifted, awkward. She reached her hand under his T-shirt and felt the hard ridge of that long scar. He put a hand on the side of her head and pulled her against him.

She didn't know this man. She was going on so little: a cowboy nose and skin like piano keys, a writer of stories, a broken heart and scarred chest, a tendency toward reticence and yet the ability to say yes. As for the future, if there were one, they would likely hurt each other, maybe even betray or enrage.

Her own body was a mess of bee sting welts and receding hives, lots of heat and itch, not to mention a very recent memory of death averted.

None of the above stopped them. Lily wanted everything now, and why not? They made love, and then told stories, and then made more love. At one point they laughed so loudly that someone—they couldn't tell if it was Annie, Kalisha, or Sal—shouted a response.

Sometime in the very early morning, rain began to fall, soon penetrating the forest canopy and dripping onto their two sleeping bodies. They were soaked by daybreak.

47

ANNIE AWOKE AT DAWN. As the rain wetted her face, she listened for the voices of Wesley and Lily somewhere back there in the trees.

I saved her life. Annie hugged herself hard to calm the crazy beating in her chest. *I saved her life.*

ACKNOWLEDGMENTS

Для especially helpful interviews about earthquakes, I thank Richard Allen, Director of the Berkeley Seismological Laboratory, and Professor and Chair of the Department of Earth and Planetary Science at the University of California at Berkeley, as well as Greg Fenves, former chair of the Department of Civil and Environmental Engineering at the University of California, Berkeley, international expert in structural engineering, and currently president of the University of Texas at Austin.

A lengthy and detailed report, "Scenario for a Magnitude 7.0 Earthquake on the Hayward Fault," produced by the Earthquake Engineering Research Institute with support from the Federal Emergency Management Agency, and published in Oakland, California, by the Earthquake Engineering Research Institute in September 1996, was very useful.

A clan of hyenas did truly live on university land in the Berkeley hills as part of the Berkeley Field Station for the Study of Behavior, Ecology, and Reproduction, from 1985 until 2014. Their calls could be heard on quiet mornings and evenings. When the researchers lost their funding, the hyenas were relocated.

I thank Trinity Church of downtown Berkeley, where I volunteered for two years serving dinners in their free meals program, for their continued service. I've fictionalized the church and the program in this novel. Thank you to Curtiss Mays who provided me with all of my motorcycle expertise, and to Debra Slone for her insightful paper on post-disaster library services. Phillipa Caldeira, another extraordinary research librarian, found answers to several questions and offered important reading suggestions.

The smart and hardworking people at Rare Bird Books have been a joy to work with, and I am grateful to them for finding merit in my story. Special thank yous to Julia Callahan, Tyson Cornell, Gregory Henry, Hailie Johnson, Jake Levens, and Guy Intoci. My agent, Reiko Davis, connected me to Rare Bird Books, and in other ways too many to count has greatly enhanced my writing life. Thank you, Reiko.

For reading drafts, research, discussion, and offering ideas, I also want to thank Sherman Alexie, Alison Bechdel, Dorothy Hearst, Barb Johnson, Frans de Waal, Martha Garcia, Jane McDermott, Patricia Mullan, Kim Stanley Robinson, Carol Seajay, and Elizabeth Stark.

I am particularly indebted to Frans de Waal and Adrienne Zihlman, whose work in understanding the roots of compassion and altruism, as well as women's roles in human evolution, inspire me. They and other scientists are working long and hard to present the fullest possible picture of our capabilities, countering the long-held models of our forbears as "man the hunter" and the "killer ape."

I also want to acknowledge the group of scientists who in 1986 met and wrote the Seville Statement on Violence. The statement begins:

> Believing that it is our responsibility to address from our particular disciplines the most dangerous and destructive activities of our species, violence and war; recognizing that science is a human cultural product which cannot be definitive or all-encompassing; and gratefully acknowledging the support of the authorities of Seville and representatives of the Spanish UNESCO;

We, the undersigned scholars from around the world and from relevant sciences, have met and arrived at the following Statement on Violence. In it, we challenge a number of alleged biological findings that have been used, even by some in our disciplines, to justify violence and war. Because the alleged findings have contributed to an atmosphere of pessimism in our time, we submit that the open, considered rejection of these mis-statements can contribute significantly to the International Year of Peace.

Misuse of scientific theories and data to justify violence and war is not new but has been made since the advent of modern science. For example, the theory of evolution has been used to justify not only war, but also genocide, colonialism, and suppression of the weak.

While no one disputes the human propensity toward violence, too little attention is given to our equal (perhaps greater?) cooperative and compassionate abilities. Thank you to the small group of researchers in many fields of study who are asking the question, *Why is there peace?* rather than, *Why is there war?*

✤ ✤ ✤

For further information about what it means to be human, I offer the following bibliography:

Dahlberg, Frances, ed. *Woman the Gatherer*. New Haven: Yale University Press, 1981.

De Waal, Frans. *Good Natured: The Origins of Right and Wrong in Humans and Other Animals*. Cambridge: Harvard University Press, 1996.

De Waal, Frans. *My Family Album*. Berkeley: University of California Press, 2003.

De Waal, Frans. *Peacemaking Among Primates*. Cambridge: Harvard University Press, 1989.

De Waal, Frans. *Primates and Philosophers: How Morality Evolved*. Princeton, NJ: Princeton University Press, 2006.

De Waal, Frans. *The Ape and the Sushi Master: Cultural Reflections of a Primatologist.* New York: Basic Books, 2001.

De Waal, Frans. *Our Inner Ape: A Leading Primatologist Explains Why We Are Who We Are.* New York: Riverhead Books, 2005.

De Waal, Frans and Lanting, Frans (photographs). *Bonobo: The Forgotten Ape.* Berkeley: University of California Press, 1997.

De Waal, Frans and Tyack, Peter L. *Animal Social Complexity: Intelligence, Culture, and Individualized Societies.* Cambridge, MA: Harvard University Press, 2003.

Drea, C.M. and Frank, L.G. *The Social Complexity of Spotted Hyenas.* Boston: Harvard University Press, 2003.

Hager, Lori D., ed. *Women in Human Evolution.* London and New York: Routledge, 1997.

Hart, Donna and Sussman, Robert W. *Man the Hunted: Primates, Predators, and Human Evolution.* Cambridge, MA: Westview Press (Persea), 2005.

Keltner, Dacher, Marsh, Jason, and Smith, Jeremy Adam, eds. *The Compassionate Instinct: The Science of Human Goodness.* New York: W.W. Norton, 2010.

Klein, Richard G. and Edgar, Blake. *The Dawn of Human Culture: A Bold New Theory on What Sparked the 'Big Bang' of Human Consciousness.* New York: John Wiley & Sons, 2002.

Kruuk, Hans. *The Spotted Hyena: A Study of Predation and Social Behavior.* Chicago: University of Chicago Press, 1972.

Leakey, Richard and Lewin, Roger. *Origins Reconsidered: In Search of What Makes Us Human.* New York: Little, Brown, 1992.

Leakey, Richard. *The Origin of Humankind.* New York: Basic Books, 1994.

Marks, Jonathan. *What It Means to Be 98% Chimpanzee: Apes, People, and Their Genes.* Berkeley: University of California Press, 2002.

Rice, Stanley. *Encyclopedia of Evolution.* New York: Checkmark Books, 2007.

Savage-Rumbaugh, Sue and Lewin, Roger. *Kanzi: The Ape at the Brink of the Human Mind.* New York: John Wiley & Sons, 1994.

Sawyer, G.J. and Deak, Viktor. *The Last Human: A Guide to Twenty-Two Species of Extinct Humans.* New Haven: Yale University Press, 2007.

Scott, Eugenie C. *Evolution Vs. Creationism.* Berkeley: University of California Press, 2009.

Solnit, Rebecca. *A Paradise Built in Hell: The Extraordinary Communities That Arise in Disaster.* New York: Penguin, 2009.

Stringer, Chris and Andrews, Peter. *The Complete World of Human Evolution.* New York: The Natural History Museum, 2005.

Watson, Peter. *Ideas: A History of Thought and Invention, from Fire to Freud.* New York: Harper Perennial, 2005.

Winston, Robert and Wilson, Dr. Don. *Human: The Definitive Visual Guide.* New York: Smithsonian, 2004.

Wood, Bernard. *Human Evolution: A Very Short Introduction.* Oxford: Oxford University Press, 2005.

Woods, Vanessa. *Bonobo Handshake: A Memoir of Love and Adventure in the Congo.* New York: Gotham Books, 2010.

Wrangham, Richard and Peterson, Dale. *Demonic Males: Apes and the Origins of Human Violence.* New York: Houghton Mifflin, 1996.

Zihlman, Adrienne L. *The Human Evolution Coloring Book.* New York: HarperCollins, 1982.

Zihlman, Adrienne L. and Tanner, Nancy. "Women in Evolution. Part I: Innovation and Selection in Human Origins." *Signs: Journal of Women in Culture and Society*: Vol. 1, No. 3, 1976.

Zihlman, Adrienne L. "Women in Evolution, Part II: Subsistence and Social Organization Among Early Hominids." *Signs: Journal of Women in Culture and Society*: Vol. 4, No. 1, 1978.

Zimmer, Carl. *Smithsonian Intimate Guide to Human Origins.* Toronto: Madison Press Books, 2005.